William Evans, Rhys Prichard

The Welshman's Candle

The Divine Poems of Mister Rees Prichard

William Evans, Rhys Prichard

The Welshman's Candle
The Divine Poems of Mister Rees Prichard

ISBN/EAN: 9783337407766

Printed in Europe, USA, Canada, Australia, Japan

Cover: Foto ©Andreas Hilbeck / pixelio.de

More available books at **www.hansebooks.com**

THE

WELSHMAN's CANDLE:

OR THE

DIVINE POEMS

OF

Mr. *REES PRICHARD,*

SOMETIME

Vicar of LANDOVERY, in *Carmarthenſhire,*

Now *firſt* TRANSLATED into *Engliſh* Verſe
By the Rev.

CARMARTHEN,
PRINTED·FOR THE TRANSLATOR BY J. ROSS.

M,DCC,LXXI.

the learned, the gay, or the great, but were profeſſed-
ly compoſed for the Edification of the Vulgar; not
but that the former may chance to find ſeveral things
among them worthy of their Notice and Attention.

As the Work contains about 480 Pages, and an almoſt countleſs Number of Verſes, the Tranſlator once
thought of contracting ſeveral of the Poems, by prun-
ing away a great many Tautologies, wherein the Author very much abounds; owing, it may be preſumed,
to his great Deſire of inculcating a valuable Sentiment,
or important Precept,—ſo as to impreſs it more for-
cibly, and more durably on the Minds of his Readers,
that it might be, at all Events, retain'd by them in one
form or another. —— He likewiſe deſigned to have
omitted ſome Thoughts and Expreſſions evidently cal-
culated for the conception and taſte of the lower Claſſes
of Mankind only; which would undoubtedly have
added Strength and Beauty to the Work, as the Rays
of the Sun operate more powerfully, when concent'red
in a Focus :——But he thought himſelf obliged to drop
that Deſign, as ſoon as he conſidered that the far greater
Part of the *Welſh* would have deem'd it a high Piece of
Preſumption, at leaſt, in him, if not a Sacrilege, to
have either alter'd or diminiſh'd any Part of their beloved Author's Work ;—and perhaps it might not then
have been ſo extenſively uſeful among them. He has
however taken the Liberty of changing the Metre in
many of the Poems at his Pleaſure, in order to make
them more agreeable to the *Engliſh* Reader, and to avoid
too great a Monotony, which is generally diſguſtful
and fatiguing to a nice poetical Ear. The fair Ma-
nuſcript of this Work, prepared for the Preſs by the
Author, was unfortunately loſt in the Time of the Ci-
vil Wars ; ſo that many of the Poems are now appa-
rently imperfect and defective,——being only (as his
firſt Editor Mr. *Stephen Hughes* confeſſes) Fragments
pick'd out of his rough Draughts and foul Papers. It
is clear, from his Epiſtle Dedicatory in Verſe, that he
in-

intended to have had this Work printed, had he lived;
—which wou'd have been a very defirable Circum-
ftance, as every Poem wou'd then have been thoroughly finifh'd, and receiv'd it's laft Polifh from his own
Hand.

As the. Tranflator affumes no more Merit to
himfelf from this Performance than that it is the only
Tranflation of Mr. *Prichard*'s Poems, hitherto publifh'd,
fo he thinks himfelf accountable for the Errors of *that*
alone. As to the original Faults and Imperfections of
the Work itfelf, or the erroneous Doctrines it may
contain, if any, he does not think himfelf refponfible
for them;—but fhall leave the Author (as Mr. *Pope*
fays) to anfwer for them himfelf;—and that he may
very well do, — fince, like *Abel*, tho' dead, " He yet
" fpeaketh," in this his Work which he has left behind
him. I wou'd therefore advife the minor Critics, both in
Poetry and Divinity, to take heed how they attack him,
—at leaft, 'till they fhall have, firft of all, frequently
and carefully read over their Bibles; for I can affure
them that they will find him, like *Apollos*, ftrong and
" mighty in the Scriptures;"——and, indeed, if I may
be allow'd to fpeak, I look upon this whole Work of
our Author's, to be an Affemblage of many of the
moft inftructive and didactic Parts of Scripture.

As the few authentic Memoirs, now to be found,
of the venerable Author's Life, follow this Preface, the
Tranflator will not attempt to fay any thing farther of
him here; he fhall only add fome Obfervations, rela
tive to the Method Mr. *Prickard* has taken of convey-
ing Inftruction to his Countrymen: A Perfon, that was
to take but a little Pains, might eafily trace it down
from the earlieft Antiquity, even to our own Nation,
and to our own Times; witnefs the Song of *Mofes*, of
Deborah and *Barak*, and the Divine Compofitions of
the Royal Pfalmift, which, together with many other
of the moft fublime Parts of the facred Pages, were, it
feems, wrote in *Hebrew* Verfe:———That it has prov-
ed

ed effectual in our own Country, the Story of *Adelmus* sufficiently evinces,—who a little before *Edward* the Confessor's Time, by his excellent Faculty in Poetry, and Singing, (we may presume his own Compositions) wrought such wonderful Effects upon the People, for the civilizing their Manners, and for their Instruction in the Duties of their Religion, that *Lanfrank*, by his own Authority, thought good to make him a Saint.

Even the rigid *Calvin* tells us, " That remarkable " and illustrious Transactions used to be described in " Verse, so that they might be in the Mouths of all ; " and that a perpetual Memorial of them might be " established ; for, by these Means, *says he*, a Point of " Doctrine becomes better known, than if it was to be " delivered in a more simple Manner." ———— " *Res* " *insignes & præclaræ carmine describi solebant, ut omnium* " *ore circumferentur,* ——— *sic enim celebrior fit doctrina,* " *quam si simplicius traderetur.*" Calvin in Isai. v. 1.

I am farther informed, that in the Protestant Countries in *Germany*, instead of loose Ballads, as in other Countries, they recreate their Minds, at their Work, on the Road, in the Fields, and in the Gardens, with the Divine Carols or Hymns, composed by *Luther*, or other good Authors, for that Purpose. See Jenkin Thomas Philips's *Life of* Ernestus *the Pious*, p. 46.

But the best Example which I can possibly adduce in Favour of our worthy Author's Mode of Instruction, is that of *Grotius*, who, as Dr. *Patrick* tells us in his Preface to his Translation of the most excellent Treatise *De Veritate Christianæ Religionis*, wrote it in his own Language, and in Verse ;——— which Way, I suppose he chose, continues the Doctor, because it was the ancient Manner of delivering the most useful Things, as he himself observes in his Prolegomena to Stobæus's *Florilegium*, where, as a Proof of it, he alleges that of *Homer*, who says *Clitemnestra* did not incline to Vice, 'till she had lost him, who was wont to sing to her. For Precepts of Wisdom, so taught, are exceeding charming

_ ing to the Minds of Youth, —— being not only more
eafily imprinted on the Memory, but touching the Affections more powerfully, and more to the quick, than
when otherwife more fpoken at large; —— and therefore the public Laws were in the more ancient Times
thus written, as *Ariſtotle* informs us ; ——and that true
Religion might be more eafily convey'd into People's
Minds, and fix'd there, *Apollinarius* tranflated all the
Works of *Mofes* (as *Sozomen* tells us) and the reft of the
Holy Bible as far as the Reign of *Saul* into heroic
Verfe, in Imitation of *Homer*'s Poems. *Suidas* fays, He
put the whole Old Teftament into fuch Verfe ;——and
it is not improbable, as what he did on the Pfalms is
ftill remaining. Doctor *Watts* will be for ever remember'd for his ufeful Compofitions of this Nature. But
I fhall fay no more upon the Advantages of this Mode
of propagating Chriftian Knowledge, ufed by our Author, and many other eminent Writers, than juft to
remark that, as many more read for Amufement than
Inftruction, they will frequently take a Book of Poems
into their Hands, who wou'd be quite terrify'd at the
Sight of a large Syftem of Divinity, or a long Treatife
in Profe on any religious Subject; fo juft and true are
thofe often quoted Lines :

" *A Verfe may find him, who a Sermon flies,*
" *And turn a Pleafure to a Sacrifice.*"

A N

THE

L I F E

O F

Mr. REES PRICHARD,

O U T   O F

W O O D's *Athenæ Oxonienses.*

REES PRICHARD was born, as it feems, at *Llanymddyfri*, in *Caermarthenfhire*, and being educated in thofe Parts, he was fent to *Jefus'* College, in 1597, aged 18 Years, or thereabouts, ordained Prieft at *Witkam* or *Whytham*, in *Effex*, by *John*, Suffragan Bifhop of *Colchefter*, on *Sunday*, 25th *April*, 1602, took the Degree of Bachelor of Arts in *June* following; and on the 6th of *Auguft*, the fame Year, had the Vicarage of *Llanymddyfri*, before mentioned, commonly called *Landovery*, collated on him by *Anthony*, Bifhop of *St. David*. On the 19th of *November* 1613, he was inftituted Rector of *Llanedy*, in the Diocefe of *St. David*, (prefented thereunto by the King) which he held with the other Living by Difpenfation from the Archbifhop, 28th of *October*, 1613, confirmed by the Great Seal on the 29th of the fame Month, and qualified by being Chaplain to *Robert* Earl of *Effex*. In 1614, *May* 17th, he was made Prebendary of the Collegiate Church of *Brecknock*, by the aforefaid *Anthony*, Bifhop of *St. David*; and by the Title of Mafter of Arts, (which Degree he was perfuaded to take by Dr. *Laud* his Diocefan) he was made Chancellor of *St. David* (to which the Prebend of *Llowhadden* is annexed) on the 14th of *September*, 1626, upon the Refignation of *Richard Baylie*, Bachelor of Divinity

vinity of *St. John*'s College. — In *Wales* is a Book o
his Compofition that is common among the People
there, and bears this Title,

    Gwaith Mr. RLES PRICHARD, *gynt Ficcer,* &c.

The Works of Mr. *Rees Prichard,* fometime Vicar
of *Landovery* in *Carmarthenfhire,* printed before in three
Books, but now printed together in one Book, *&c.* with
an Addition in many things out of MSS. not feen before
by the Publifher; befides a fourth Part now the firft
Time imprinted, *Lond.* 1627*; in a thick 8vo.

It contains four Parts, and the Whole confifts of fe-
· veral Poems and pious Carols in WELSH, which fome
of the Author's Countrymen commit to Mem˜ry, and
are wont to fing. He alfo tranflated divers Books into
WELSH, and wrote fomething upon the thirty-nine Articles, which, whether printed I know not; fome of it
I have feen in MSS. He died at *Llanymddyfri,* about the
Month of *November,* in fixteen hundred and forty-four;
and was, as I prefume, buried in the Church there. In
his Life-time he gave Lands worth 20 l. *per Ann.* for the
fettling a free School at *Llanymddyfri,* together with an
Houfe to keep it in: Afterwards the Houfe was poffeft
by four School-mafters fuccefively, and the Money paid
to them. At length *Thomas Manwaring* (Son of *Roger,*
fometime Bifhop of *St. David*) who married *Elizabeth,*
only Daughter of *Samuel,* Son of the faid *Rees Prichard,*
did retain (as I have been informed by Letters from
thence) and feize upon the faid Land, under Pretence
of paying the School-mafter in Money, which was ac-
cordingly done for an Year or two. But not long after
(as my Informer tells me) the River *Towy* breaking
into the Houfe, carried it away, and the Lands belonging thereunto, are occupied at this Time, 1682, by
Roger Manwaring, Son and Heir of *Thomas* before mentioned; fo that the School is in a manner quite for-
gotten.

THE

---

* *Qu.* Whether *Wood* did not write 1672, as the Author died in
1644, and his Work was not printed in his Life-time?

SUBSCRIBERS NAMES.

A.

JOhn Adams, Whitland.

Countefs of Albemarle, Spring-Gardens, London, 2.

John Bartlet Allen, Creffelly, 4. — David Allen, ditto.

Mrs. Mary Allen, Fobfton.

George Andrew, Narberth, 2.

Thomas Archard, Carmarthen.

B.

Thomas Baldwin, No. 10. Bow-church-yard, London.

Rev. William Higgs Barker, Carmarthen, 2.

Rev. Miles Baffet, Swanfea, 2.

Rev. Thomas Baffet, Lanelay.

John Bateman, Surgeon, Narberth

Rev. R. Beadon, St. John's Coll. Camb. 4.

Thomas Bennet, Lalefton, 4.

William Bennet, ditto, 6.

Mrs. Elifabeth Bennet, Swanfea.

Mrs. B. Bevan, Laugharne, 4.

Mrs. Eliz. Bevan, Swanfea, 2.

George Bowen, Llwyngwair, 4.

James Bowen, Attorney at Law, Cardigan, 4.

Rev. James Bowen, Rofecrowther.

Rev. James Bowen, Meline.

Rev. Hugh Bowen, D.D. Camrofe.

William Bowen, Troed-yr-aur.

William Bowen, Jordanfton.

William Bowen, Haverfordweft.

Jonathan Brigges, Lawrenny, 4.

O. Brigftocke, Blaen-y-pant, 4.

Captain Robert Brigftocke, St. Ifmael's.

Mrs. Lettice Brigftocke, Llwyn-pinnar.

Richard Bevan, Surgeon and Man-midwife, Swanfea.

C.

Jo. Chapman, St. Clears.

James Child, Begelly, 4.

Rev. Mr. Cleaveland.

Rev. Thomas Clement, Lanon.

Abraham Clibbourn, Haverfordweft.

Sociable Club.

Thomas Colby, Rhofygilwen.

Captain Stephen Colby, Fynnoneu, 4.

Mifs Colby, Bletherfton.

Charles Colins, Swanfea, 2.

Eliz. Colfworthy, Haverfordwoft.

Thomas Cornock, ditto.

Peter Curgurven, Slebech.

D.

The Right Reverend the Lord Bishop of St. David's, 2.
Morgan David, Lanegwad.
Rev. Robert Davies, *Rector of* Newton Nottage, 4.
Rev. Thomas Davies, Langadock, 2.
Rev. John Davies, *Rector of* Ilton
Rev. Edward Davies, *Rector of* Portfcewet, Monmouthfh.
Rev. Theo. Davies, Lanelly.
Rev. Morgan Davies, Langunnor.
Evan Davies, Penlan, 2.
James Davies, Landaff.
Thomas Davies, Blyne.
Mifs C. Davies, ditto.
Wyrewood Davies, Glantowy.
Edward Davies, Brecon.
John Davies, Henllan.
Arthur Davies, Landovery.
Philip Davies, Cwmfidan.
Daniel Davies, Brodey.
Jofeph Davies, Narberth.
John Davies, Lampeter Velfrey.
Benjamin Davies, Carmarthen.
Ben. Davies, Neath, Pembr.
Edward Davies, Minware.

E.

William Edwards, Johnfton, *M. P.* Haverfordweft, 4.
Rev. James Edwards, *Vicar of* Landeveilog.
Thomas Edwards, Cawfton.
John Edwards, ditto.
Thomas Evans, Newton.
Thomas Evans, Aberlafh, 4.
Iltid Evans, Kencoed, 4.
Herbert Evans, Dole.
Rev. Hugh Evans, Landow.
Rev. William Evans, *Vicar Choral of* St. David's.
Hugh Evans, Landilo.
Lewis Evans, Langwathan.
Benjamin Evans, Longridge.
William Evans, Caire.
Thomas Evans, Yftrad-tafodog.

F.

Benjamin Ferrier, *Queen's Coll.* Camb.
Mrs. B. Foley, Ridgeway.
William Ford, Stonehall.

G.

Thomas George, Molefton.
R. Gofnell, Haverfordweft.
Thomas Griffies, Coed.
Rev. Jonathan Griffies, Bettws, 2.
John Griffith, Clinderwen, 4.
Evan Griffith, Glanrŷd.
Rev. John Griffiths, Dorney, Bucks, 2.
Thomas Griffiths, Errhyd, 2.
Cornelius Griffiths, Cwmnewidion.
James Gwyn, Alderfgate Street, London.--Mrs. Gwyn. do. 6.
Rod. Gwynne, Glanbrane, 4.
Morgan Gwynne, *Surgeon*, Narberth, 4.
Rice Gwynne, Cardigan.—Griffith Gwynne, Plâs-y-meibion.

H.

Mrs. Halifax, Ewel, in Surry.
Edward Hancorne, Birry, 4.
Rev. William Harries, St. Dogwells.
Thomas Harries, Trefiffilt.
Rev. George Harries, Letherfton, 2.
John Harries, Priskelly, 2.
John Harries, Caftle-piggin.
Rev. John Harris, Moat.
    G. W. Hayard. Carmarthen, 2.
Mrs. Heberden, Pallmall, London.
John Henfleigh, Panteague, 4.
Rev. John Higgon, *Rector of* Landevallteg, 4.
William Higgon, Newhoufe.
Rev. John Holcombe, Tenby.
    George Holcombe, *Canon of* St. David's.
    William Holcombe, Pembroke.
John Hooper, Briftol.
W. R. Howell, Maefgwyn, 6.
Rev. Howell Howell, Lanboidy.
John Howell, Albemarle-ftreet, London, 2.
Thomas Howell, Fynnon-velen.
Edward Hughes, Aberllolwin.
John Hughes, Morva.—David Hughes, Laugharne.

I.

Gilbert James, Bletherfton, 4.
Doctor R. James, Carmarthen, 6.
Thomas James, Gelly-fawr.—John Jarrit, Black-pool.
Gabr. Jeffreys, Swanfea, 2.
Mrs. Jones. Sunny-hill, 4.
Mrs. Jones, Lanina.

SUBSCRIBERS NAMES.

Mifs Grace Jones, ditto.
Mrs. Jones, Trewern.
Thomas Jones, *Attorney at Law*, Carmarthen, 2.
David Jones, Derry, 6.
George Jones, London.
Richard Jones, ditto, 4.
Richard Jones, Swanfea.
Philip Jones, Llwyn.
Henry Jones, Brunant
Rev. John Jones, Lampeter Velfrey.
    John Jones, Lanon.
Owen Jones, *Officer of Excife*, at Haverfordweft.
John Jordan, Dumplefdale.

K.

Richard Knethel, Hook.
Rev. Watkin Knight, Highway.
Thomas Kymer, Robeftone-hall 4.
Rev. William Kymer, Stowey, Somerfet.

L.

Rev. Watkin Lewes, Newport, 2.
Rev. John Lewes, *D. D.* 4.
James Lewes, Gellydowill, 2.
William Lewis, Llanllear, 2.
Rev. Thomas Lewis, Gwinfe, 2.
Richard Lewis, Henllan.
John Lewis, Haverfordweft.
Evan Lewis, Pentlepoyer.
Stephen Lewis, Trevach, 2.
Thomas Lewis, *Landfurveyor*, Haverfordweft.
George Lock, Jordafton.
Thomas Lloyd, Cwmgloyn, 4.
John Lloyd, Cringa, 4.
Rev. Thomas Lloyd, Llandebye, 2.
John Lloyd, Penlan, 2.
Thomas Lloyd, Bronwydd.
Rev. John Lloyd, Lanarth.
Jer. Lloyd, Carmarthen.
John Lucas, Stouthall, 2.
David Llwyd, Berllandowill, 2.

M.

Sir William Manfel, *Bart.* Ifhcoed, 2.
Rawleigh Manfel, Swanfea.
S. Martin, Withy-bufh, 4.
John Matthews, Bridgend.
Rev. John Matthias, Caftle-bigh, 4.
    William Miles, Cowbridge,

Rev. Joſhua Morce, Begelly.
Robert Morgan, Carmarthen, 2.
Charles Morgan, Carmarthen.
David Lloyd Morgan, Cardigan, 2.
Thomas Morgan, Lanwinio.
Rev. Evan Morgan, Manerdeivy.
John Morgan, Swanſea.
Rev. Thomas Morris, Pembrey.
Thomas Morſe, Saundersfoot.

N.
Capt. William Needham, Haverfordweſt.
Robt. Nelſon, Swanſea, 2. — Miſs Nelſon, Do. 4.
David Newland, Blaencorſe.
Mrs. M. Nicholas, Do.

O.
David Ormond, Tre newydd.
Rev Walter Owen, Kilyrychen, 2.
Charles Owen, Landovery. — John Ochletree, Lanfernach.

P
Rev. Mr. Payne, Langadock, Crickhowel.
Edward Parry, Carmarthen.
Lewelin Parry, Cwmcunon, 2.
Col. Paterſon, 63d Regiment.
George Phelps, Lud-church.
Sir Richard Philipps, Bart. Picton-caſtle, 8.
I. Philipps, D. D. Langoedmore, 4.
Rev. Jeremiah Philipps, Boſheſton, 4.
Philipps Philipps, Lampeter, 4.
Rev. Edward Philipps, Rector of Begelly, 4.
John Philipps, Lampeter, 2.
Mrs. Dorothy Philipps, Do.
Mrs. Grace Philipps, Do.
Miſs Cecilia Philipps, Do.
Charles Philipps, Landebye, 6.
George Philipps, Coedgain.
Richard Philipps, Kidwely.
Rev. John Philipps, Llwyncrwn.
S. L. Philips, Haverfordweſt.
Major Gen. Richard Pierſon of 36 Regiment of Foot.
William Plummer, Briſtol.
Thomas Popkin, Kettlehill, 4.
Capt. John Poyer, Grove, 16.
Mrs. Anne Poyer, Do.
Miſs Poyer, Merrixton.
William Powel, L.L.D. Nanteos, 4.
Rev. Joſhua Powell, Lantwit Major.

Mifs Price, Kilgwynne.
Thomas Price, Landovery.
Rev. Del. Prichett, *Subchantor of St. David's*, 2.
Rev. Richard Prichett, *Fellow of St. John's Coll. Camb.*
Rowland Prichard, Swanfea.
John Prichard, *Do.*
John Propert, St. David's.
John Protheroe, Egermont, 2.
Jofeph Protheroe, Newton.
Jof. Pryce, Gelly-hir, 4.
R. Prytherch, Nant y gollen, 3.
Charles Pugh, Hereford.

R.

John Ravenfcroft, Laugharne.
Owen Rees, Capel-dewy.
Rev. Oakley Rees, Carmarthen, 3.
    Tho'. Rees, Mydrim, 2.
    William Rees, Little-Newcaftle.
William Rees, Laugharne.
David Rees, Carmarthen.
Hon. George Rice, Newton, *M. P. Carmarthenfhire*, 8.
Walter Rice, Llwyn-y-brain.
David Rice, Carmarthen.
Mifs M. Richards, Narberth.
John Roberts, Swanfea.
Rev. William Rogers, *Rector of* Chumleigh, Devon, 4.
    John Rogers, Carmarthen, 2.
Lewis Rogers, Kidwelly.
George Roch, Clarefton.
John Roch, Haverfordweft.
Nich. Roch, Pafkefton.
Tho' Elbridge Rooke, Ivy-thorn, Somerfet, 2.
John Rowand, Briftol, 4.
Rev. Henry Rowe, St. Petrox.
    John Rowland, Llangeitho, 4.
John Runwa, Hook, *Lieu. in the Navy.*
James Ruffel, Carmarthen.

S.

Rev. E. Sandford, Laugharne.
Stephen Saunders, Perth-y-berllan, 4.
William Scourfield, Moat, 8. — Henry Scourfield, *Do.* 2.
Rev. David Scurlock, Blaencorfe
Rev. E. Seys, *Rector of* Yftradgynlais, 2.
Daniel Shewen, Swanfea, 2.
Francis Skyrme, Lawhaden, 4.
John Smith, Jeffreyfton.

James Smith, Bolſton, Court. Herefd.
David Stephens, Haverfordweſt.
Sir Thomas Stepney, *Bart.* Lanelly, 2.
James Stewart, Carmarthen.
Thomas Stokes, Haverfordweſt.
Hugh Stonehewer, Carmarthen.
Simon Surman, Scotch-well.
Rev. John Summons, *Vicar Choral* St. David's.
John Symmons, Lanſtinan, 4.

T.

Rev. Mr. Taſker.
Robert Taynton, Cowbridge.
Mrs. Jane Thomas, Manervabon, 4.
Iltid Thomas, Swanſea, 10.
Rev. John Thomas, Llandiſilio.
WilliamThomas, MathewThomas, PhilipThomas, Swanſea.
David Thomas, Lanboidy.
Roger Thomas, Landewy-velfrey.
Mrs. Trevannion, Slebech.
John Tucker, Sealiham.
Rev. Benjamin Twining, White-houſe.
  Joſeph Twining, Ampney-park, Gloc'.

V

Richard Vaughan, Golden Grove, 4.
John Vaughan, Dolegoome.
Gwynn Vaughan, Jordaſton.
E. Vaughan, Trecoon, 4.
Capt. J. Vaughan, *Do.* 2.

W.

Miſs Warren, Longridge, 2.
John Warren, Haverfordweſt.
Rev. Thomas Walters, Landough.
John Watts, Bletherſton.
Rev. Robert Wells, Penmain.
A. White, Swanſea.——Daniel Wier.
Rev. John Williams, *Canon of* St. David's. 2.
  Thomas Williams, Pilroath, 3.
  John Williams, Cheriton, 2.
  David Williams, Kidwely.
  John Williams, St Iſmael's.
  Edward Williams, St. Bride's major.
Thomas Williams, High-Street, Haverford, 4.
John Williams, Corngafr, 2.
John Williams, Kilſant, 2.
Henry Williams, Lanegwad,
John Wogan, Wiſton, 4.——Lewis Wogan, *Do.* 2.

Additional SUBSCRIBERS,

Since the former LIST was printed off.

C.

JOhn Campbell, Stackpool-Court, Pembrokeſhire, 4.
John Chambre, Lanfoiſt, Monmouthſhire, 2.

D.

Richard Davies, Court-y-gollen, Monmouthſhire, 4.
Edmund Davies, *Attorney at Law*, Pontipool, Monm. 30.

E.

David Edwards, *Surgeon*, Landilo, Carmarthenſhire, 2.

G.

D. J. Gwynne, Taliaris, Carmarthenſhire, 4.
Ho. Gwynne, Lanelweth-Hall, Radnorſhire, 6.
Marmaduke Gwynne, Brecon, 2.

H.

R. Banks Hodgkinſon, Edwin's-Ford, Carmarthenſh. 2.

J.

Rev. Rowland Jay, Rooſe, Glamorganſhire.
Robert Jones, Fonmon-Caſtle, Glamorganſhire, 4.
Thomas Jones, Pen-cerrig, Radnorſhire.
Mrs. Jones, Fonticary, Glamorganſhire, 6.

L.

Thomas Lewis, Laniſhen, Glamorganſhire, 4.
Rev. William Lewis, Newhouſe, Glamorganſhire, 2.
David Lewis, *Vicar of* Pentirch, Glamorganſhire.
William Llewelyn, Cardiff, Glamorganſhire, 2.
Charles Lloyd, Brecon.
Francis Lloyd, Trebarried, Breconſhire.

M.

Edward Mathew, Lanfoiſt, Monmouthſhire, 2.
Charles Morgan, *M. P*. Breconſhire, 4.
John Morgan, *M. P*. Monmouthſhire, 4.
J. Morgan, *Surgeon*, Builth, Breconſhire, 2.
Rev. William Morgan, Brecon.

Iltid

N.

Iltid Nichol, St. Athan, Glamorganfhire.

O.

Sir William Owen, *Bart.* Orielton, Pembrokefhire, 4.

P.

Charles Powell, Caftle-madoc, Breconfhire, 2.
William Powell, *Attorney at Law*, Brecon.
Rev. Ger. Powell, Lanharan, Glamorganfhire, 4.
Samuel Price, Park, Glamorganfhire.
Thomas Pryce, Dyffryn, Glamorganfhire, 4.
William Proger, Lanfoift, Monmouthfhire.

S.

Robert Savours, Glamorganfhire.

T.

William Thomas, Lanbradach, Glamorganfhire, 3.

W.

John Walton, *Surgeon*, Cowbridge, Glamorganfhire.
Walter Wilkins, Maeslough, Radnorfhire, 4.
Rev. John Wilkins, *M. A. Rector of* Differth, Breconfh. 2
Jeffry Wilkins, Brecon, 2.
Penry Williams, Penpont, Breconfhire, 4.
John Hanbury Williams, Colebrook.
Thomas Williams, *Attorney at Law*, Cowbridge, 1.
William Williams, *Mercer*, Brecon.

THE

T H E

Welſhman's Candle.

An EPISTLE from the AUTHOR to a certain noble LORD*, to whom, it is imagined, he intended to dedicate his Book.

1 Y gracious LORD!——
        Be not ſurpriz'd to ſee
        An humble Clergyman, of mean degree,
With ſuch a ſimple Book the Man accoſt,
Who is by all eſteem'd his country's boaſt!

2 The Zeal you for the Church of God have ſhown,
Your ſervice to your country and the crown,
The favour you've for *Welſhmen* ſtill exprefs'd,
Muſt fill with gratitude each *Welſhman*'s breaſt.

3 Though thouſands ſtrive your character to raiſe
With countlefs ſums of tributary praiſe ;
Permit e'en me, my Lord! however low,
Amongſt the reſt, my worthlefs mite to throw.

4 The LORD of Hoſts himſelf did meekly deign
To take the widow's mites, without diſdain ;
Nor proudly deem'd the well-meant gift, too ſmall,
Or of no worth ; becauſe ſhe gave——her all.

5 Do you, my deareſt Lord! the like receive
From One, who has no better thing to give ;

B   Yet

* Suppoſed to be Robert earl of Efſex, whoſe chaplain he was.

Yet with a better prefent would be glad
To honour You — if He a better had.

6 But You, our country's glory ! merit more,
And more fhou'd have—if more was in my pow'r;
Yet weigh'd according to it's kind intent,
This gift yields not to thofe by princes fent.

An EPISTLE to the READER.

1 THE glory of the Lord !—my country's gain,—
The fuit of friends,--the poor's affecting ftrain--
Caus'd me to print this little work of mine,
For my compatriots of the Cambrian line.

2 Becaufe they take in fermons no delight,
But idle fongs with eagernefs recite,
I, for their good, have thus employ'd my time,
And put the doctrines, that enfue, in rhyme.

3 For as I faw fame'd Sai'/b'ry's labour'd ftile
Neglected by the unlearned of our ifle,
I therefore took a metre fhort and plain,
Eafy to read, and eafy to retain.

4 And this my Book, The Welfhman's Candle, nam'd ;
' Becaufe therein I've moft fincerely aim'd
Each ignorant and darkling mind to light,
And taught him, how to ferve his God aright.

5 To give the unletter'd an affifting hand,
Who, at the beft, but little underftand,
Thefe Poems I compos'd with pleafing care :
The reft, I ween, have better Paftors far !

6 God grant the Welfh fufficient light to know,
And ferve him, whilft they fojourn here below—
God grant this Candle, as it was defign'd,
May give unerring light e'en to the blind !

ADVICE

ADVICE to hear, and to read, the Word of God.

1 WHoe'er, of any fex or age,
   To heav'n above wou'd learn the way,
His guide muft be the facred Page—
Or elfe he needs muft go aftray.

2 The way is difficult and long,
And few the tedious journey go,
Vaft croffes round each trav'ler throng,
And ftrait the gate he muft pafs thro'.

3 Above the fun and moon heav'n lies,
And ftrange and arduous is the road—
Thy ladder's Chrift, to fcale the fkies---
His word, thy lamp, to fhew thee God.

4 Of fenfual joys full many a rock,
And many a fea of worldly woe,
The paffage with obftructions block,
E'er one can to thefe regions go.

5 Full many a winding thou may'ft count,
Or be in floughs and deferts loft,
E'er unto heaven thou canft mount,
Without God's word, they can't be crofs'd.

6 Unto the dreary realms of woe,
A man may fink, without a guide,
But none to heaven e'er did go,
Without the Gofpel, to refide.

7 'Tis not the fun's, or moon's, fo bright,
'Tis not the ftars' that gleam on high,
But the fweet Word and Gofpel's light,
That can direct thee to the fky.

8 Take thou the lantern of thy God,
To light thy falt'ring fteps along,---
Tread the ftrait path thy Saviour trod,
Thou foon fhalt be, the faints among.

9 The Word's a candle, to give light,
 The Word will ſhew thee, where to tread,
 The Word will guide thy airy flight,
 The Word to heaven will thee lead.

10 The Word's far beaming light purſue——
 Whate'er thou'rt bid by Jeſus, do——
 Whatever He forbade, eſchew——
 And thou ſhalt ſtrait to heaven go.

11 The Goſpel is the lucid ſtar——
 That darts it's cheerful gleam abroad,
 He, who purſues it's rays——tho' far,
 Needs never fear to miſs his road.

12 The Bread of Life, each there may meet,
 To feed the body and the mind——
 A lamp, to light his ſtumbling feet——
 A bridle, his looſe tongue to bind.

13 Thence milk, to nurſe the weakling, flows——
 Thence manna, hungry ſouls to feed——
 Thence wine, to ſoften human woes,
 And comfort give, to all that need!

14 An oil that can the pangs aſſuage
 Of conſcience, and o'er ſin prevail——
 A balſam is the ſacred page——
 An antidote, ne'er known to fail!

15 A maul, to beat each knob full low——
 A rule, the erroneous to conduct——
 An ax, to lop each ſtraggling bough——
 A maſter, children to inſtruct.

16 The Word's a trump, that ſummons all
 To judgement——and a bell's the ſame,
 That men does to repentance call——
 A herald 'tis, peace to proclaim——

17 The Word's a mirror, that diſplays
 Our vices and our latent ſtains,
 And bids us all amend our ways,
 Whilſt the clear light of day remains.

18 The

18 The Word's the Seed divine, whence fome
Poffeffors of heaven's happy coaft,
Chrift's brethren and God's fons, become————
And temples of the Holy Gholt.

19 Without the Word, there's no relief,
None can be refcu'd from the grave——
For of all means it is the chief,
That Chrift ordain'd, our fouls to fave.

20 Without the Word, no mortals can
About God's attributes agree,
Nor well the aweful myft'ry fcan
Of Three-in-one, and One-in-three.

21 Without the Gofpel, none God's Will
Can know, or worfhip him aright——
None can his facred laws fulfil,
Until the gofpel gives him light.

22 None e'er can learn, without the Word,
The fall of man,—or e'er explain,
How he, thro' Jefus was reftor'd
To his loft righteoufnefs again.

23 Without the Word, none can believe——
None can believe, unlefs they hear,
Or unto Chrift due homage give,
For Faith gains entrance through the ear.

24 God ne'er was known without the Word,
To turn a fingle foul from fin:
But, through the Gofpel of our Lord,
To fave th' elect he oft is feen.

25 The Apoftles, in the days of yore,
And Gentiles were converted——none,
Without it's efficacious pow'r,
Cou'd e'er approach God's facred throne.

26 St. Peter, by the Gofpel's aid,
At once among the Jewifh train,
Above three thoufand converts made,
After that they had JESUS flain.

B 3   26 'Tis

27 'Tis by the fowing of the Word,
And thro' the holy Spirit's aid,
The worft of finners are reftor'd,
God's fons and Chrift's own brethren made!

28 Whate'er man wants, God's Word fupplies;
Then fearch it with a critic's care——
'Twill make thee to falvation wife——
For, lo! eternal life is theré!

29 Chrift for the gofpel bids thee ftrive,
With all thy might and all thy main,
More than for all this world can give——
If thou wou'dft endlefs life attain.

30 As for the breaft, a child implores—
As the' hart lows for the fprings, when dry——
As fun-bake'd lands call out for fhow'rs——
So for the Gofpel doctrines cry.

31 Sell all thy goods——fell all thy land ——
Sell e'en the fhirt upon thy back——
Sell all thou haft at thy command——
Rather than thou God's Word fhou'dft lack.

32 Much better 'tis, that thou fhou'dft roam,
Without the cheerful light of day,
Without meat, drink, fire, bed, or home,
Than that God's Word fhould be away.

33 'Tis fad to live in fuch a place,
Where the fun fhines not all the year——
But much more difmal is their cafe,
To whom God's light does ne'er appear.

34 Ne'er in a clime, where there's no day——
Nor in a land, where there's no rain——
Nor fhip, without a compafs, ftay——
Ne'er, where there is no prieft, remain.

35 Quit thou the parifh, town, and ground ——
Quit father, mother, friends, and kin ——
Quit houfe and home—if the fweet found
Of God's word can't be heard therein.

36 'Tis better in some cave to hide,
  And sometimes hear the gospel there—
  Than in the richest vale reside,
  Where one can ne'er the Gospel hear.

37 'Tis hard in darkness to remain
  Where comfort never yet appear'd—
  But harder 'tis to stay in vain,
  Where the bless'd Word was never heard.

38 To Turkey, 'tis not worse to go,
  Where none our God, or know or fear,
  Than 'tis to dwell, where thou canst no
  Instruction have, no Gospel hear.

39 To London go, o'er Britain roam,
  The ocean cross, the globe surround—
  But never think of coming home,
  Until thou hast the Gospel found.

40 'Tis hard to see the sun and rain,
  In all the hamlets 'round appear,
  Whilst that wherein thou dost remain,
  Has neither of them all the year.

41 If there's no sermon to be found,
  Which thou in thine own church mayst hear,
  Go to the churches all around,
  And hear one ev'ry Sabbath there.

42 Whene'er thy stomach meat requires,
  Thou to the pantry wilt repair,——
  But when thy soul it's food desires,
  Thou for it's cravings dost not care.

43 What boots the body's full repast,
  If thy poor soul for hunger dies?
  Can One the least enjoyment taste,
  If in distress the Other lies?

44 'Tis bad, quite bad, upon the whole,
  When these our bodies are not fed:
  But worse by much to starve the soul,
  For want of it's celestial bread.

45 Then

45 Then to the clergy cry amain,
   Due food unto thy foul to give:
   Since thou doft them with tithes maintain,
   Bid them thy famifh'd foul relieve.

46 From the prieft's lips receive the word,
   As if from Chrift's own mouth it came—
   He was commiffion'd by the Lord
   To warn thee, and from fin reclaim.

47 Shou'd fome poor curate, mean in drefs,
   As Chrift commands, reprove thy ways,
   Though he his thoughts fhou'd ill exprefs,
   Thou'rt bound to do, whate'er he fays.

48 Although the gofpel of our Lord
   Judas himfelf fhou'd come to preach,
   Yet it may fave thee, tho' the Word
   He might, involv'd in error, teach.

49 To vices, fhou'd thy Paftor run,
   Yet if his doctrine fhou'd be true,
   His leffons learn, his manners fhun——
   E'en Paul and Peter's faults efchew.

50 Mind not his perfon, or addrefs—
   If well, or meanly clad, ne'er note—
   The gofpel's merit is not lefs,
   Shou'd he be cloth'd in homefpun coat.

51 Take pearls from toads, with venom fill'd—
   Take gold from hands, that are not clean——
   Take wine from cafks, with duft defil'd----
   Take knowledge e'en from lips obfcene.

52 The gofpel of thy faviour hear,
   However poor the preacher be----
   The Word, if not the perfon, bear,
   'Twas Chrift himfelf that fent it thee.

53 Deep in thy mind his dictates fow,
   Nor let the fiends fteal thence a part----
   The Word's a feed, that there will grow,
   If thou wilt plant it in thy heart.

54 Search

54 Search then the Scripture, night and day,
  And read it with obſerving eyes,
  It's dictates punctua'lly obey,----
  So ſhalt thou prove extremely wiſe.

55 Keep it at all times next thy heart---
  At work, at play, at home, abroad,
  Unto thy ſons it's ſenſe impart-----
  And ground them in the Word of God.

56 Still let that chain adorn thy neck----
  Still let that frontlet grace thy brow---
  Still let that ring thy finger deck----
  And ne'er a ſtep without it go.

57 Make it thy comrade on the way----
  Make it thy bedfellow by night----
  Make it thy ſtudy all the day----
  Do all it bids thee, with delight.

58 Make it thy councillor and friend,
  And more thou'lt learn from ev'ry page,
  (So it thy footſteps ſhall attend)
  Than from the moſt enlight'ned ſage.

59 Leave it not, in the church, behind
  With him, who did the ſubject treat---
  But bear it homewards in thy mind,
  And to thy family repeat.

60 Make thou God's word thy higheſt treat---
  Be it the prime of food to thee-----
  And, when thou'rt cloy'd with other meat,
  Thy choice deſert then let it be.

61 This wholeſome Food, each morning, taſte---
  Be it, each noon, thy conſtant fare----
  And, ev'ry night, a ſweet repaſt
  Of this celeſtial Bread, prepare.

62 As thou thy body doſt preſerve
  With meat---thy ſoul with manna feed---
  Let not the One, with hunger ſtarve,
  Whilſt thou ſupplieſt t' Other's need.

63 The

63 The Bible, in thy native tongue,
 May now e'en for a crown be got,
 Sell then thy all, and be not long,
 E'er thou the precious book haft bought.

64 No chattels with it equal are---
 No goods are of fuch real ufe---
 No treafures can with it compare---
 Nor any thing thou canft produce---

65 'Twill comfort give, and 'twill advife---
 'Twill give thee pleafure, and fuccefs----
 'Twill make thee to Salvation wife----
 'Twill give thee endlefs happinefs----

66 'Twill give thee bread, to fate thy foul---
 'Twill give thee milk, to feed the poor---
 'Twill give thee wine, to fill thy bowl---
 'Twill give a falve for ev'ry fore------

67 Who wou'd not then the bible buy,
 Which does all other goods excel?
 To purchafe it, who wou'd not try?
 His houfe, his all, who wou'd not fell?

68 This is the pearl, which Jefus told
 All them, that heeded his advice,
 To buy---like him, who wifely fold
 His all, that he might reach it's price.

69 Since God has deign'd to give each page,
 That does his holy word contain,
 To *Wales*---let's join, at ev'ry age,
 To ftudy it with might and main.

70 O let us then be all agreed,
 Women and men, with one accord,
 To buy a book,---that each may read
 In his own tongue, the bleffed word!

71 Since God has now vouchfafe'd the fame
 In our own tongue---O let's not wafte
 Our time, but all attempt, for fhame,
 To read it, with the utmoft hafte.

72 Let not the labour fruitlefs prove,
Which coft in England fuch a fum—
Left we fhou'd not account above
For fuch a crime, the day of doom.

73 O let's, of ev'ry fex and age,
In our good neighbours footfteps tread,
Who can with eafe the facred page
In their own native language read.

74 'Twill be for us a burning fhame,
If we do not attempt, e'er long,
To mafter and to learn the fame,
Since now 'tis in our mother's tongue.

75 More than a crown, now 'twill not coft,
The value of a fingle fheep,
Which in fome ditch may foon be loft,
Whilft nightly ftorms the mountains fweep.

76 If, in a family, but one
Is with the ufeful talent bleft,
To read the fcriptures—he alone
May eafily inftruct the reft.

77 Each *Welfhman* in a month, or fo,
May learn, if he'll the ftudy mind,
To read all that he needs to know:
What's that?——if One be well-inclin'd.

78 Ah me! that Chriftians cannot give
One crown, of all that they poffefs,
Or one month's time, whilft here they live,
To learn the doctrines they profefs!

79 Women and men of low degree,
The very abjects of the land,
You always may in England fee,
Each with his Bible in his hand.

80 With us, ('mongft thofe, who moft abound,
And fumptuoufly their tables fpread)
Scarce can a prayer-book be found,
Or One, who can his bible read.

81 Alas'

81 Alas! that they, in wealth who roll,
Shou'd be, by coblers in their ftalls,
· Surpafs'd, in what concerns the foul,
And beft will decorate their halls !

82 Will they not, in the day of doom,
Againft the rich in judgement rife,
And to condemn their folly come,
Who their falvation thus defpife ?

83 They teach each tradefman's daughter, there,
To read the books that moft excel————
Whereas the Gentry's daughters, here,
Can fcarce the *Pater nofter* fpell.

84 'Tis to the *Welfh* a foul difgrace,
They're in religion ftill fo young,
That not the tithe of all the race
The fcriptures read, in their own tongue.

85 Let's then, for fhame, together join
To learn, from the heav'n-infpired code,
The ground-work of our Faith divine,
And ftrive to read the word of God.

86 So fhall we know, and truly fear
Our great Creator, whilft we live————
And if we know and fear him here,
We all fhall endlefs life receive.

87 God grant the *Welfh* fufficient grace,
Rightly to know and dread the Lord,
And God enable all the race,
In their own tongue, to read his word !

To the Sons of BRUTUS.

1 YE fons of Brute, of Trojan blood,
A lively, lovely, loving brood,
Attend in hafte, and to my ftrains draw nigh,
With an obedient heart appear,
And with a fix'd attention hear,
My doleful plaint, and heart-affecting cry.

2 Th'

2 Th' unceafing wheel of reftlefs fate,
  Early each morn, each ev'ning late,
'Till Death, ftill whirls about the fatal ball
  Of life ——— yet thoughtlefs on we run,
  Until the whole is fairly fpun,
And we to endlefs torments headlong fall.

3 For, like a fhip that proudly gay,
  Still glides along its wat'ry way,
Whilft on the deck the failors dance, or fleep,
  Our time here paffes fwift away,
  And will not for it's owner ftay,
Whatever coil or clutter he may keep.

4 Pale Death ftill follows at our heels,
  And like a filent felon fteals
Along, with trembling pace, and footfteps flow,
  Still ready, with unerring dart
  To pierce each unfufpecting heart,
And give, amidft our vain purfuits, his blow.

5 For, like a bubble on the ftream,
  E'er we of any danger dream,
The aerial particle of life is flown ;
  And yet, fo thoughtlefs ftill are we,
  We don't the gaping pit-fall fee,
'Till to perdition we all tumble down.

6 This world's a dotard, fick all o'er,
  E'en juft now knocking at Death's door,
And tending to the grave with th' utmoft hafte,
  His head turns round, he bows, he faints,
  His heart with apprehenfion pants,
His gall, and all his vitals ftrangely wafte.

7 Yet void of awe, or confcious fear,
  The thoughtlefs fons of men appear,
To conftitution they too much confide ;
  As feamen truft (when dangers prefs,
  And they are all in deep diftrefs)
The found'ring bark, 'till bury'd in the tide.

8 O! let not us, who are but duft,
 To a deceitful world ftill truft,
That breaks, like ice o'er the fallacious ftream,
 And drops us, at our fate unfcare'd,
 To the dread judgement unprepare'd,
E'er we can well of it's intention dream.

 9 But let us all with anxious care,
 For the great feftival prepare,
(The hour Chrift comes, no man on earth can fay)
 And to our Saviour's prefence prefs,
 In trim array and proper drefs,
And veftments fuited to that folemn day.

 10 And let us never be furpriz'd
 In fin, nor be in drink difguis'd
At our laft hour, (left we the feaft retard)
 Our lamps without or oil, or light——
 Our talents not employ'd aright;
But all our reck'ning juft, and well prepar'd.

 11 The ax (ye finners be afraid!)
 Has to the copfe long fince been laid—
Soon from the floor fhall the light chaff be blown——
 The angel threatens, even now,
 The brambles with his fithe to mow,
And then the trafh fhall to the flames be thrown.

 12 A dreadful doom hangs o'er our heads,
 And at our doors old Time now treads,
The trumpet longs the fhrilly blaft to found---
 The fea, the church-yard, and the field,
 And Hell itfelf, now yearn to yield -
The dead in their repofitories found.

 13 The Judge himfelf is quite prepar'd,
 Efcorted by a fainted guard——
The day is nigh, this globe fhall be deftroy'd—
 When God fhall all the fons of men,
 Before his righteous throne convene,
There to account for all they've here enjoy'd.

14 Yet

14 Yet ftill we madly venture in,
   To gorge ourfelves on filth and fin,
Not thinking of our reck'ning or our doom:
   We ftill our talents mifapply,
   And ev'ry paffion gratify;
Let death and vengeance come, when they will come.

15 Like the ancients e'er the deluge came,
   Like Sodom, e'er the o'erwhelming flame,
(Not worfe the cafe of Pharoah and his crew!)
   We fin with all our might and main,
   And ftill go on to fin again,
Nor the leaft fign of reformation fhew.

16 As filthy fwine can feaft on draff,
   As thirfty oxen water quaff,
We fwill and drench ourfelves with heady drink;
   We wallow in each foul defire,
   As hogs delight to roll in mire,
And never of the confequences think.

17 Prefumptuoufly we curfe and fwear,
   And Chrift himfelf in pieces tear,
And for a ftraw, or any trifle, fight;
   Without the leaft remorfe, or awe,
   ('Till beggar'd quite) we go to law,
But leave the poor in a moft piteous plight.

18 The fun and moon, with wat'ry eye,
   Our vicious converfations 'fpy,——
The earth too groans; becaufe fo ill we live——
   Angels are pain'd at heart the while;
   Becaufe we Chriftians are fo vile,
And for our manifold tranfgreffions grieve.

19 The prieft, the farmer, and the hind,——
   With artifans of ev'ry kind,
*The Bailiff, Judge, and Gentleman, each ftrives
   With moft amazing infolence,
   Which fhall the Godhead moft incenfe;
Nor can I fay, who worft, amongft them, lives.

20 In

---

* The chief magiftrate of a Corporation—I fuppofe the author
meant in this place.

20 In Indolence, the Clergy live,
   The venal Judges bribes receive,
The Gentry tipple in each paltry inn;
   The Farmer, but as yesterday
   Unufe'd to drink, now topes away,
And fmokes his tube, as if it were no fin.

21 The fins which Sodom overthrew,
   The vile exceffes Parthia knew,
The thefts, which erft difgrac'd the Cretian ftrand,
   The frauds, wherein the Greeks excell'd,
   The idolatries Samaria held,
Are rife in ev'ry diftrict of the land.

22 I blufh, the vices to difplay,
   We *Welfhmen* act in open day,
And grieve our immoralities to fhew:
   . Yet 'tis my duty to reflect,
   Shou'd I th' unwelcome tafk reject,
That God will bring them all to public view.

23 Befides it better is by far,
   That I fhou'd now thofe fins declare,
To make us now repent, whilft here below,
   E'er in the dungeon's difmal gloom,
   We all receive our joylefs doom,
Since here no marks of penitence we fhow.

24 Therefore, my countrymen, I wou'd
   Fully perfuade you, if I cou'd,
To pray for pardon, to avert your fate,
   And here on earth your morals mend,
   Before your lives draw to an end,
And you wou'd fain reform, when 'tis too late.

25 For 'tis in vain to fob and figh,————
   In vain to tremble and to cry,
When once we at the Judge's bar are caft:
   However loud we cry, there's nought
   But ftricteft Juftice to be got,
When once the time of reformation's paft.

26 Then

26 Then let us all refolve this hour
(E'er Jefus comes in all his pow'r
From heaven, to judge each good and evil foul!)
His favour to implore in hafte,
E'er we be into prifon caft,
And force'd in floods of flaming fire to roll.

The Second PART.

27 ENrage'd, with his angelic hoft,
He'll come—and come unto our coft,
Upon our heads his vengeance to begin,
And with his light'ning's dreadful blaze
He will the guilty fouls amaze
Of thofe, who now are fo alert to fin.

28 Then, all our terrors to complete,
Becaufe his anger is fo great,
His friends and fervants whom he lov'd fo dear,
(When he in all his wrath fhall come,
To execute his final doom)
Nay, e'en the angels too, fhall quake for fear.

29 The fun's bright rays fhall turn to night,
The moon fhall not give forth her light,
The heavens themfelves fhall tremble with difmay,
The ftouteft of the fons of men
Shall fhrink for fear and terror then,
And fhriek aloud through horror of that day.

30 Each flinty rock fhall rive in twain,
Each mountain fink into a plain,
The feas themfelves fhall, on that day, grow dry —
The worms that in the waters creep,
The fifh and monfters of the deep,
Shall in the bottom of the ocean die.

31 Each fort and ftrong-built caftle fhall,
To it's foundation, piece-meal fall,
And ev'ry building in the world be burn'd———

C   The

The firmament fhall melt on high,
The ftars fhall tumble from the fky,
And all this globe be to a cinder turn'd.

32 When Jefus Chrift, with glory great,
And ev'ry kind of pow'r replete,
To judge us fev'rally, fhall quit the fky———
What human face fhall not turn white?
What heart not fhudder with affright,
When he Chrift's fign in heav'n aloft fhall fpy?

33 What horror, and what deep diftrefs,
Muft ev'ry guilty mind opprefs?
What comfort can the creft-fall'n culprit know,
When he beholds fuch woe and dread,
The whole creation overfpread,
And thinks 'tis for his fins alone they flow?

34 Monarchs, and leaders of the fight,
And giants once of matchlefs might,
The proud, th' oppreffors, fhall bewail their fate,
And to the cloven mountains call,
That they upon their heads fhou'd fall,
And fcreen them from their righteous Judge's hate.

35 Then, after all this vaft ado,
The archangel fhall his trumpet blow.
How very loud, and very clear the blaft!———
So very loud, and very clear,
The dead the piercing found fhall hear,
That calls them to account for all that's paft.

36 The dead fhall then afcend the sky,
E'en in the twinkling of an eye,
From duft and rottennefs, where low they lay,———
The living too fhall then be change'd,
And ev'ry foul in order range'd
On high, where they fhall for their vices pay.

37 And there their Judge and fovereign Lord,
Unfheath'd his keen and glitt'ring fword,
Impartially their actions fhall obferve,

And

And, in his balance weigh'd with care,
To all he will affign their fhare
Of good and evil, juft as they deferve.

38 He will not look into the eyes
Of emperors, nor abbot's prize ·
For their gay robes, their ftate, or hoarded treafure;
But equal juftice he'll difpenfe,
Both to the peafant and the prince,
And neither dread their pow'r, nor their difpleafure.

39 When once he opes his books, he'll rive
The heart of ev'ry man alive;
And all their faults expofe to open view,
And for each deed deferving blame,
He will reproach them with the fame,
And make injuftice his vaft fortune rue.

40 He'll not with one loofe word difpenfe,
Nor with a farthing's vain expence,
Nor moment, fpent without due weight and heed—
No vanity, nor wafte of time,
Nor act obfcene, nor heinous crime;
But all muft then be anfwer'd for with fpeed.

41 The fornications of the great,
And gentlewomen of eftate,
Who ufe the fervant, when the hufband's gone——
The crimes, the murders now abroad,
Each daring theft and private fraud,
Shall then to ev'ry prying eye be fhown.

42 What afpects full of ghaftly woe?
What aching hearts fhall mortals know?
What gloom and grief fhall on each brow be feen,
And on thofe guilty bofoms prey?—
Who now, alas! this very day,
So forward are, fo very fond of fin!

43 But not a mouthful fhall be loft,
Nor bit nor drop of all the coft,
That to the poor, for Jefus' fake is given;

With

With int'reft it fhall be repaid——
While mifers rue the crumbs of bread
Refufe'd to fuch— by being banifh'd heaven.

44 Then fhall the' Almighty Shepherd keep
The goats divided from the fheep,
And each be try'd for his own fins alone ;
Thefe fhall in Paradife be place'd,
With ev'ry blifs and honour grace'd,
Whilft thofe fhall to th' abyfs of hell be thrown.

45 The righteous, at the pref'rence glad,
In robes of dazzling whitenefs clad,
Shall foar directly to the facred domes,
A firm poffeffion to fecure
Of realms, that ever fhall endure,
Affign'd by God for their eternal homes.

46 Then fhall the reprobated ftock,
And all the folks that make a mock
At prefent of their Judge, and that dread day,
In clufter'd heaps be hurried down
To hell, and into chains be thrown,
Where endlefs torments on their fouls fhall prey.

47 In hell, on Abraham, they fhall roar,
(So fierce the fire ! their pain fo fore !)
And for a drop of water fue in vain :
But though they fhou'd forever roar,
They ne'er fhall have one mouthful more,
Nor the leaft portion of relief obtain.

48 For falfhood ever fhall remain
In prifon there, and racking pain,
Nor even hope for refpite from his woe :
He there fhall gnafh his teeth for rage ;
But nothing fhall his pains affuage,
Nor fhall his fuff'rings e'er ceffation know.

49 And there fhall we affur'dly go,
Hanging our lips and foreheads low,
Becaufe our time we fo abfurdly fpend,

Becaufe

Becaufe we do not watch and pray,
And do not (e'er that awful day
Of vengeance comes) our vicious lives amend.

50 Let us unfeign'd repentance fhow, .
   Whilft Time does of the change allow:
To-morrow never was by any caught!
   Let us, this very Now, begin
   To quit all vanity and fin,
E'er we are to our final reck'ning brought.

51 Thou Saviour God, who of thy grace
   Haft brought falvation to our race,
And from infernal flames thy fervants freed,
   O, fave us, in the day of doom,
   When we to thy tribunal come,
And to the blifsful feats of Eden lead!

52 Shou'd any of the *Cambrian* land,
   In *South* or *North Wales*, here demand,
Who fung thofe ftrains, that warn them to furmount
   Their danger,——fay, 'twas one whofe aim
   Was to preferve them free from blame,
And to remind them of their dread account.

The wretched Condition of M A N by N A T U R E.

1 RASH Adam to the fiend of old,
   Mankind for one dear apple fold;
And none can from his fangs get free,
'Till Jefus gives him liberty.

2 The Devil in a dreary gloom
Keeps ev'ry foul, 'till Chrift fhall come,
To make him his condition fee,
To break his chains, and fet him free.

3 This dungeon is fo very dark,
That we can't fee a fingle fpark,

C 3

Nor

Nor ought of our own wretched plight;
'Till Jefus comes to give us light.

4 What days and nights pafs o'er our head,
With pitchy darknefs are o'erfpread,
And none his woeful ftate can view,
'Till Chrift does his condition fhew.

5 We in our fins unweeting die——
We think not our perdition nigh——
Our lives in difmal gloom we fpend—
Yet feek not our fad ftate to mend.

6 Thou to the Devil's camp doft go——
Thou art unto thyfelf a foe——
Thou more and more aftray doft roam ;
'Till Jefus come to fetch thee home.

7 Thou e'er thy birth was try'd and caft,
And thy tremendous doom is paft,
And, if Chrift's aid thou canft not gain,
Thou ever fhalt cond mn'd remain.

8 The ferpent's fting has pierc'd thy heart,
Thy very foul groans with the fmart ;
Then, for a cure, to Chrift apply,
Or elfe, without his aid, thou'lt die.

9 Thy foul by Satan was bereav'd
Of all the gifts from God receiv'd ;
Chrift only can reftore the fame,
And hide thy nakednefs and fhame.

10 Fell Satan with his fiery dart,
With poifon fraught, has pierc'd thy heart,
Intreat of Chrift to eafe thy pain,
Or thou with Satan muft remain.

11 Thy foul like a meek lamb appears,
Among fierce lions, wolves, and bears:
Then foon to Chrift for fuccour pray,
Or thou'lt become their certain prey.

12 The Devil has thy foul befet,
And hamper'd in his ftrong-mefh'd net,
And nought on earth can refcue thee,
'Till Jefus comes to fet thee free.

13 A faithful flave to vice thou'ft been,
And wallow'd ev'ry day in fin;
Then fue to Chrift, and he will give
Thee Grace, a righteous life to live.

14 Thou art by Nature born in fin,
The child of wrath, like all thy kin,
Ask Chrift then, to be born again,
Left thou fhou'dft ever fo remain.

15 Thou doft the Devil's laws obey——
Thou art quite fubject to his fway——-
Beg then of Chrift to refcue thee
Out of his paws, and fet thee free.

16 In thee the ftrong One keeps his court,
Like thofe, who garrifon a fort;
'Till Jefus comes his arms to feize,
Thy bofom ne'er will be at peace.

17 Thou waft an ufelefs branch before,
That nought but acid fruitage bore,
And, if Chrift alters not it's kind,
'Twill be to hell's fierce flames confign'd.

18 Satan, to God made thee a foe————
To make thy peace, to Jefus go,
By whom thou muft be reconcile'd,
E'er thou canft be, once more, his child.

18 Thou, like a little chick, doft play
Amongft the rav'nous birds of prey;
And, if Chrift fcreens thee not beneath
His wings—thou muft be torn to death.

20 Thou thro' a dreary vale doft go——
The paths of peace thou doft not know——
And if thy fteps Chrift fhou'd not light,
Thou'lt headlong feek the realms of night.

 21 Thou

21 Thou doſt deſerve all kinds of woe,
(Doom'd, e'er thy birth, to hell to go)
And, if his aid Chriſt does not deign,
For ever damn'd thou muſt remain.

22 Thou art a foe to thy beſt friend,
Thou art a ſlave unto the fiend,
Thou'rt ſhut up in his ſty obſcene,
'Till Jeſus comes, to waſh thee clean,

23 Thou doſt in ev'ry point tranſgreſs —
Thou'rt liable to each diſtreſs——
Thou'rt to each pain and woe a prey—
'Till Jeſus laves thy ſins away.

24 Thou'rt bad, without—and bad, within—
Thou'rt void of Grace, but full of ſin ---
Thou'rt foul, impure, and fooliſh quite,
'Till Chriſt the ſinner bleaches white.

25 Such is, 'tis plain, each perſon's caſe,
(If we the ſacred ſcriptures trace)
Until again the ſinner's born,
And Chriſt reforms his ſtate forlorn.

26 If not aſſiſted by the Lord,
And to his priſtine ſtate reſtor'd,
No man (no more than the foul fiend)
Can, of himſelf, his life amend.

27 Not Peter, Paul, nor any One,
(But Jeſus Chriſt our Lord alone)
Supernal, or infernal, can
Preſerve the ſin-polluted man.

28 Search heav'n, ſearch earth, and ſearch the air,
The ſea, and all therein, with care——
And thou ſhalt find it true, that none
Can ſave a ſoul, but Chriſt alone.

29 If thou doſt not his aid implore,
Thy fallen nature to-reſtore,
Thou ſhalt in hell's abyſs be laid,
Becauſe thou didſt not beg his aid.

30 No

30 No man on earth his foul fhall fave,
But he, who fhall that favour crave,
For Chrift, his blefs'd Redeemer's fake;
Whatever buftle he may make.

31 Nor will the Lord falvation give,
But to the man that fhall believe
In him (however loud his pray'r)
With a faith, lively and fincere.

32 Whoe'er in Chrift believeth well,
Shall furely fave his foul from hell ;
But he, who does not—ne'er fhall fave
His foul, nor any favour have.

The LIFE and DEATH of CHRIST.

1 LET ev'ry Chriftian who defires to know,
What to his Saviour happen'd here below,
Draw near——whilft I his Incarnation tell,
And what, 'till death, unto our Lord befel.

2 The word was God (e'er heav'n and earth were made,
Or the foundations of the world were laid.)
The Second Perfon of the facred Three,
And the Creator of all things that be.

3 He was the Lord, before he left the sky,
Coequal to his Sire in dignity,
And o'er the countlefs hoft of angels reign'd,
E'er he to vifit finful mortals deign'd.

4 He was a God---of matchlefs pow'r and might--
He was a Lord---of glory infinite---
He was a King---than ev'ry fov'reign highe'r—
He was in all things equal to his Sire.

5 When, to redeem us, he the skies forfook,
Our form and fafhion on himfelf he took,
Nay, e'en our flefh from Mary did affume——
A fpotlefs virgin trom her mother's womb !

6 Who by a wond'rous pow'r, yet well believ'd,
The holy Spirit's gracious pow'r! conceiv'd——
And, tho' betrothe'd, when marriageable grown,
She, 'till his birth, by man was never known.

7 Thus did the Son of God a man become,
By Grace divine, in Mary's virgin womb,
And, though her nature only form'd the child,
Yet it was ne'er by any sin defile'd.

8 Two natures in our blest Redeemer join,
That is to say—the human, and divine:
This does the mother, that the Sire, declare;
They're both distinct, and yet both perfect are.

9 The Son of God, and yet a mortal's son,
And though thus complex—yet he is, but One:
The Son of Man, without a father, made——
The Son of God, without a mother's aid!

10 As to his manhood, in his human state,
'Tis my design at present to relate
The form and manner of his wond'rous birth,
When, to redeem us, he came down on earth.

11 When to fair Bethl'em Mary had arriv'd,
(Where David and his anceftors erst liv'd)
To be enroll'd, and Cæsar's tax to pay,
Her reck'ning was fulfil'd that very day.

12 But as large companies had throng'd each inn,
There was no place for her to lodge within;
So in an out-house she, for want of room,
Was force'd to drop the burden of her womb.

13 There, without state or any vain parade,
The meek-eye'd virgin, on the litter laid,
Amongst the cattle, our Redeemer bore,
On Christmas-day—a day not fame'd before!

14 Thus born, without a single groan or throe,
(Which all her sex are doom'd to undergo)
In swaddling clothes, with a young mother's joy,
She bound, tho' heaven's King! the beauteous boy.

15 And

15 And, when with care fhe had the infant dreft,
  She in the manger laid him down to reft :
  Tho' in mean circumftances, yet content
  With whate'er Providence had kindly fent.

16 A train of guilelefs fhepherds God difpatch'd,
  Who in the field that night their flock had watch'd,
  To worfhip him before the break of day,
  As in the manger the fweet infant lay.

17 Warn'd by a band of angels from the skies,
  And fill d with heart-felt pleafure and furprize,
  To happy Bethle'm (with the fole intent
  Of feeing the Mefliah) glad they went.

18 They were commiffion'd, by divine command,
  To let th' expecting people underftand,
  That Chrift was come—the promis'd Seed, of old,
  From the beginning of the world foretold———

19 And tell to all—that with united voice
  They at the gladfome tidings fhou'd rejoice ;
  Becaufe that, on that fame aufpicious morn,
  The glorious Saviour of mankind was born.

20 The angels then their tuneful voices rais'd,
  And in fweet hymns their great Creator prais'd,
  Afcribing Glory unto God above,
  Who to mankind vouchfafe'd fuch wond'rous love!

21 Soon after this was feen a radiant ftar,
  Exceffive clear, and vifible afar,
  Whofe beamy luftre bright'ning all the air,
  Was thought the Birth of Jefus to declare.

22 Three hoary fages, from the diftant Eaft,
  Who had the meaning of the portent guefs'd,
  Led by the guidance of the friendly flame,
  In fearch of Jefus, to Judea came :

23 To Herod they apply'd, when there arriv'd,
  The greateft Tyrant that had ever liv'd !
  To know where Chrift, the Jew's expected King,
  Was to be born, and from what ftem to fpring.

24 The Rabbi all, with one accord agreed,
That Chrift was to be born of David's feed,
In Bethle'm-judah, as it was of old
By Micah in his facred page foretold.

25 Thus advertife'd, the fages took their way,
'Till guided by the ftar's refulgent ray,
They came to Bethle'm, where, tho' forely tire'd,
With earneft zeal for Jefus they enquire'd.

26 But when they juft had to the houfe arriv'd,
Where the bleft Infant with his parents liv'd,
The ftar, which led them from their native land,
Seem'd o'er the ftatelefs door to make a ftand.

27 They enter'd to the homely cot with joy,
And faw the Virgin with her lovely Boy,
Then on their bended knees upon the floor
They fell—the gracious Sov'reign to adore. .

28 There various gifts they offer'd at his feet——
Gifts that to Chrift, in all refpects, were meet—
Gold, the pure product of the wealthy Eaft——
With od'rous Myrrh—and incenfe, of the beft.

29 When Herod the unwelcome tidings heard,
That Chrift, the true Meffiah, had appear'd,
Whilft in his fwathes as yet the Babe was dreft,
He fought to flay Him at his mother's breaft.

30 A bloody, butchering, and murde'rous crew,
Whom void of all humanity he knew,
He fent the children all around to flay,
Rather than Chrift fhou'd not become his prey.

31 The cruel foldiers, to their orders true,
Inhumanly the hopes of Bethle'm flew:
All, about two years' old, alike did fare;
Even the Tyrant's fon they did not fpare.

32 But Mary, warn'd this maffacre to fhun,
At midnight rofe, and with her Infant Son
To Egypt travell'd, by divine command,
, Oblige'd to flee, and quit her native land.

33 There

33 There Chrift fome time among th'Egyptians paft,
Until his parents heard the news at laft,
That Herod, from whofe cruelty they fled,
· Who fought to' affaffinate the Child, was dead.

34 On Herod's death, who had the Infants flain,
Unto Judea Chrift return'd again,
Where to his mother due refpect He pay'd,
And even Jofeph cheerfully obey'd.

35 At twelve years old, a Wonder to relate!
He with the Rabbies enter'd to debate,
Until thofe fages wonder'd how a Child
Cou'd be with fuch prodigious Knowledge fill'd.

36 When He, at thirty, to the Baptift came,
And was baptis'd by him in Jordan's ftream,
The Holy Ghoft defcended from above,
And hov'ring, perch'd upon him, like a dove.

37 Meanwhile the Father from on high declar'd
His will aloud, whilft all the people heard——
" This is my only Son, my beft belov'd,
" Who is by me, in all refpects, approv'd."

38 And, after this miraculous defcent,
He to the defert, to be tempted, went;
Where, though he by the fiend was fore affail'd,
In each affault the baffled tempter fail'd.

39 This conflict o'er, He travell'd all around,
To fpread the glorious Gofpel's gladfome found,
And his ftupendous miracles to do,
In ev'ry place, where He thought fit to go.

40 He, firft of all, turn'd water into wine——
Then heal'd all, whom He faw with ficknefs pine
The blind, He caufe'd to fee—and the deaf ear
Diftinctly, ev'ry Word He fpoke, to hear.

41 He made the crippled Lazar nimbly go,
" And leap exulting, like the bounding roe,"
He made the woman, who had many days
Been bent, her back as ftrait as ever, raife.

42 Upon

42 Upon the boist'rous Billows, far from shore,
He walk'd erect, and still'd it's noisy roar,
And by a single Word, whene'er He pleas'd,
When most it rage'd, the tempest he appeas'd.

43 To prove, that He was God---three diff'rent men
He rais'd from death, and bade them live agen,
Laz'rus, tho' he'd been three days dead, was one---
Jairus's daughter—and the Widow's Son.

44 With five small loaves five thousand men He fed,
How great his pow'r !—how filling was the bread !
Two ships He freighted at one wond'rous draught,
Tho, they, who trie'd before, had nothing caught.

45 Many a furious fiend He dispossess'd,
And gave each miserable Maniac rest :
Malchus' ear, shorn off by Peter's sword,
Without a salve, He with a word restor'd.

46 Many a miracle besides He wrought,
To prove the sacred doctrines that He taught,
E'er Judas to destroy Him lent his aid,
And for a bribe his blessed Lord betray'd.

47 He ne'er was tax'd with guile at any time,
And none cou'd justly charge Him with a crime ;
He, like a lamb with innocence replete,
Was little honour'd, tho' his pains were great.

48 But when the hour, ordain'd by God, drew nigh,
When He, for our offences, was to die,
The traitor came, in seeming virtue bold,
And for a trivial sum his Master sold.

49 Scarce half a crown was to the villain paid,
When to the Jews his Saviour he betray'd,
Whom they to Caiaphas tight-pinion'd bore,
Although by Annas question'd much before.

50 When they to Caiaphas had led him bound,
False witnesses encompass'd Him around,
Who to his charge unnumber'd falsehoods laid,
And things, that He had never done, nor said.

51 The

51 The Pontiff then examin'd Him full hard,
About a thoufand ftories he had heard,
And bound Him by an Oath to let him know,
Whether he was the Son of God, or No.

52 And yet becaufe he publicly confefs'd
That he was Chrift the fon of God—the reft
Wou'd fain have murder'd him, altho' untrie'd,
Or ftone'd him on the fpot, until He die'd.

53 Some on his face their filthy fpittle threw——
Some o'er his eyes in fport a cov'ring drew——
Others with rods his facred Perfon bruife'd,
And with infulting buffetings abufe'd.

54 Next morn, the Chief of the affembled tribes,
The populace, the Levites, and the fcribes,
Brought Jefus bound, unto the Judgement-hall,
There to be trie'd, and judge'd before them all.

55 When Pilate had examin'd him a while,
And found in him no fault, nor any guile,
His hands he wafh'd before them—and, at laft,
Tho' with regret, the fatal fentence paft.

56 He firft of all condemn'd him to be ftripp'd,
And after that to be feverely whipp'd,
He then was fentence'd to be crucify'd,
Like a bafe flave or felon, 'till he die'd.

57 Thus Chrift was ufe'd by that inhuman throng,
And forely fcourge'd from ftreet to ftreet along,
Nor was there left an inch from head to heel,
Whereon the blood-ftain'd lafh he did not feel.

58 Then Pilate's foldiers, fierceft of his foes,
Advanc'd, and robb'd the fuff'rer of his clothes,
And in their ftead the vile infulting crew,
A robe of fcarlet o'er his fhoulders threw.

59 They platted next a new invented crown
Of thorns, and o'er his temples prefs'd it down,
Until the blood well'd from each fpouting wound,
And ftreaming down his cheeks, inrich'd the ground.

60 In

60 In his right hand an ample reed they place'd,
And with feign'd homage the proceffion grace'd,
Mocking Him with farcaftical abufe,
And crying, " Hail thou fov'reign of the Jews."

61 Robb'd of his clothes, which he was ufe'd to wear,
On his bare back, his crofs they made Him bear;
Tow'rds *Calvary* he dragg'd it on with pain,
Where, on its brow, the guiltlefs Lamb was flain.

62 But, as they went to crucify the Lord,
His hands and feet they barbaroufly bore'd,
And faften'd each (a fhocking fight to fee!)
With three ftrong nails of iron, to the tree.

63 Yet, though fo great his woes, fo fierce his pain,
His mouth he never op'ned to complain,
Nor fpoke a word unto the favage band,
More than a fheep beneath the fhearer's hand :

64 But, on the crofs, (when moft acute his pains)
His foul, and all the blood that fill'd his veins,
He offer'd as a facrifice for fin—
For all the fins of all the fons of men !

65 His foul he recommended to his Sire,
The Judge, whofe juftice all men muft admire,
Whom he befought, with his departing breath
To pardon the inhuman Jews his death.

66 Thus on the crofs the bleffed Jefus die'd—
Who, his heart's blood, forth gufhing from his fide,
With love unutterable, freely gave,
The fouls of his true votaries to fave !

67 And thus God gave his beft-beloved Son,
When he a thoufand woes had undergone,
To fuffer on the crofs, that we might live,
And from hell-torments our loft fouls reprieve !

68 Then let us praife Him, both by night and day,
And never fail our bounden thanks to pay,
For the vaft love and mercy He did fhow,
When to redeem us, He did ftoop fo low.

69 All thanks and laud unto the God of heaven,
To Father, Son, and Holy-Ghoſt, be given,
Who bought the ſouls of men, at ſuch a rate,
And led to bliſs from ſuch a wretched ſtate!

A Rehearſal of Christ's Love towards the World.

1 COme, hear me relate our Redeemer's vaſt love,
 When to purchaſe our ſouls he firſt came
 from above;
That love bear in mind, which then coſt him ſo dear,
And ſtill, whilſt you live, his bleſt memo'ry revere.

2 When Satan eſſay'd with ſuccefs to deceive
(Transform'd to a ſerpent) our Grandmother Eve;
We then for an apple were ſold ev'ry one,
And none cou'd redeem us, but Jeſus alone:

3 Who, when he our woeful condition did 'ſpy,
Expreſsly forſook the pure Regions on high,
Diſdain'd not to enter the pure Virgin's womb;
But, to ſave us from hell, did our nature aſſume.

4 So Mary grew pregnant of Him, we adore,
(How wond'rous a thing!) by the Spirit's great pow'r,
Though a maid ſcarce to years of maturity grown,
And tho', all her life, ſhe a man ne'er had known.

5 When her reck'ning was up, e'er the dawning of day,
Her Son ſhe brought forth on a bundle of hay,
In a ſtable at Bethl'em:-- in ſwaddling clothes dreſt,
In a manger ſhe afterwards laid him to reſt.

6 At his birth there were angels from heav'n employ'd;
(Who at their commiſſion were quite overjoy'd)
To proclaim to the world, that on that very morn,
Chriſt Jeſus, their bleſſed Redeemer, was born.

7 When the three Eaſtern Magi firſt lift up their eyes,
And ſaw the new ſtar, that illumin'd the ſkies,
They left their own country, and travell'd from thence
To worſhip the Babe, not regarding expence.

D   8 When

8 When Herod the birth of our Saviour firſt knew,
To ſlay him, he ſent out his butchering crew,
And, left Chriſt ſhou'd 'ſcape, he deſtroy'd ev'ry one
Of the Infants at Bethl'em, nor ſpar'd his own ſon.

9 But Mary, ſhe ſilently 'roſe in the night,
And to Egypt retire'd with her Child in a fright;—
And there ſhe reſided—how long can't be ſaid——
'Till Herod howe'er, and his butchers were dead.

10 Chriſt came back again on vile Herod's demiſe,
To a nation exceſſively dull and unwiſe,
Where the Goſpel He preach'd to a wrong-headed
throng,
Who lov'd not the truth, for--I can't tell how long!

11 He deign'd moſt extra'ordi'nary wonders to do,
That he was the promis'd Meſſiah, to ſhow:
Yet the Jews, nor the truth, nor his wonders, believ'd,
But ſought to deſtroy him, as long as he liv'd.

12 Mark'd out from the reſt by a trait'rous embrace,
He by Judas was ſold to that reprobate race,
Whoſe Avarice drove him (ſo wretched was he!)
To end by a halter his days on a tree.

13 The night Chriſt was ſeiz'd, an effuſion of blood
Sweated down from his head to his heels in a flood,
On thinking how bitter the pains! how ſevere!
Which he for the ſins of each age was to bear.

14 With torches and ſtaves, he a priſo'ner was made,
As late after ſupper devoutly he pray'd:——
With cords he was bound, and then hurry'd along
Before the high-prieſts by the loud-ſhouting throng,

15 Pilate queſtion'd him afterwards cloſely a while.
But cou'd not find in him tranſgreſſion, or guile;
Yet wrongfully ſentence'd the guiltleſs to die,
Though his hands he had waſh'd---and, he cou'd not
tell why.

16 He order'd him, firſt, to be whipp'd 'till the blood
From his head to his heels his bleſt body o'erflow'd,
Then

Then (that Chrift might be fix'd to the Crofs) he
     , commands
Strong nails to be drove thro' his feet and his hands.

17 A large crown of thorns on his head, next, was place'd,
And he with a robe of fine fcarlet was grace'd,
On the knee, with mock homage, he then was ador'd;
With blows and grimace they infulted the Lord.

18 With the crofs on his fhoulders they forc'd him to go
Tow'rds Golgotha, (never confid'ring his woe!)
To which they affix'd him alive, in great pain:
Thus Chrift on the crofs was moft cruelly flain!

19 And, yet though his grief and his pains were fo vaft,
When the nails, thro' his hands and his feet, they drove
    faft;
As fheep when they're fhorn feldom murmur or bleat,
His lips he ne'er ope'd, tho' his wrongs were fo great!

20 But with pitiful accent his Father befought,
To pardon the Jews this deteftable fault,
Becaufe that they were not then confcious of guilt,
Nor knew 'twas the blood of their Saviour they fpilt.

21 And thus from this life did our Saviour depart,
When he on the crofs had firft fuffer'd the fmart,
The Woes, and the Penance, and Vengeance entire,
Which God for the fins of the world did require.

22 At the price of his blood, by a death full of pain,
He reconcile'd man to his Father again,
And the favour of God to us finners reftor'd;
Then ftill, whilft we live, let us all praife the Lord!

23 On the crofs, he the fins of us all did fuftain,
And wafh'd in his blood, 'till not one did remain—
He made us all, kings, and all priefts unto God:
Then ftill, whilft we live, let us Jefus applaud!

24 The law he fulfill'd, and his Sire fully pleas'd,
Our pardon he bought with his blood, and releas'd
Our fouls from hell's dungeon---our fentence he tore:
Then little, and great, let us Jefus adore!

 26 The

25 Like Samſon, he conquer'd the powers beneath,
　　And our brethren's accuſer, the old Dragon, by death!
　　By bruiſing his head, he the victory gain'd:
　　Then let us praiſe Chriſt, who the palm has obtain'd!

26 The wrath of his Sire he did fully efface—
　　He made us his ſons by adoption and grace—
　　He gave us a ſhare in the kingdom of God—
　　Then ſtill, whilſt we live, let us Jeſus applaud!

27 For us crowns of gold, (to encircle each brow)
　　And elegant robes of the whiteneſs of ſnow,
　　He purchaſe'd—and alſo the kingdom of God:
　　Then ſtill, whilſt we breathe, let us Jeſus applaud!

28 All poſſible glory, thankſgiving, and pow'r,
　　Be 'aſcribe'd to the Trinity now, and each hour—
　　All praiſe and applauſe, to our Saviour, and Head:
　　And, to this, let *Amen* by each Chriſtian be ſaid!

Let us go to BETHLEHEM.

1 LET's to Bethle'hem all advance,
　　With ſong, with merriment, and dance,
　　And ſee the bleſt Redeemer, born
　　To us, on this auſpicious morn.

2 In Bethle'hem He is to be ſeen,
　　In the ſtable of an inn;
　　Let us there our gifts beſtow———
　　Let us all to ſee him go.

3 This is the Saviour God above
　　Sent, out of his paternal love,
　　To ſave us from Death, griſly king!
　　And with him our ſalvation bring.

4 Let us go there to ſee, this morn,
　　How, when, and where, the babe was born;
　　That we may view his bleſſed face,
　　And worſhip Him upon the place.

5 A

5 A radiant ftar our way will light,
   And ferve to guide our footfteps right,
   'Till to the happy fpot we come,
   Which He has chofen for his home.

6 The fhepherd-train is gone before
   With joy, their Saviour to adore;
   Let us with hafte thofe fwains purfue,
   And pay our homage to Him too.

7 The child is in the ftable laid,
   And in his fwaddling clothes array'd;
   Where in a manger He, between
   An ox and Jofeph may be feen.

8 The Magi now are on their way,
   Their off'rings at his feet to lay-----
   Gold, myrrh, and frankincenfe, the beft
   Of all the produce of the Eaft.

9 Let us thefe fages overtake,
   And hear the fpeeches that they make,
   And learn from them what gifts to bring,
   And how we beft his praife may fing.

10 For gold ---- let us aright believe----
   For myrrh--- let's true repentance give ----
   For frankincenfe --- let's praifes leave,
   And Chrift our prefents will receive.

11 The angels all rejoice on high,
   And pleafure brightens all the sky,
   The hofts of heav'n hymn their King;
   Why fhou'd not men his praifes fing?

12 Let's to Bethle'hem all repair,
   To fee the prime of wonders there,
   The Godhead human nature take,
   And fuffer for his people's fake!

13 Let's th' Eternal, go and fee,
   Who made the skies, the earth, the fea,
   The ancient Alpha, fource of light,
   Become an Infant in our fight!

14 Let's go vifit God the Word
On Mary's lap————the heaven's Lord
In human flefh and nature dreft,
And hanging at his mother's breaft!

15 A babe, above his mother's years,
And fully equal to his Sire's!————
His mother's father;————daughter's child!------
Though fpeechlefs, amiable and mild!

16 Let's to Bethle'm go, and fee
The Son of God on Mary's knee,
Or Mary dandling in her hands
The babe, who all the world commands!

17 Let's go fee, Death's Victor, bound
In folds of fwaddling-clothes around,
And Him, who'll pull down Satan's throne,
Quite helplefs to a manger thrown!

18 Let's, the Meffiah, go and fee,
The Founder of Chriftianity,
Our Saviour, glory, grace, and reft,
Now fucking at his mother's breaft!

19 Let's go fee the woman's Seed,
Ordain'd to make the ferpent bleed,
And bruife his baneful head, who firft
Taught man to eat the fruit accurft.

20 Let's go fee the wond'rous Son,
Form'd of his mother's flefh alone————
A mother, fcarce yet fully grown!
A mother, yet by man not known!

21 Let's this mother go to fee————
This mother, from pollution free!————
The daughter, lull her Sire to reft!————
The Father at his daughter's breaft!

22 Let's fee the architect divine,
Who made the fun and planets fhine,
And form'd the firmament's vaft plain,
Let's fee him in a ftable lain!

23 Let's

23 Let's fee the God, in glory great,
Wont with his fpan the skies to mete,
Now bedlefs in a manger laid,
And in a forry drefs array'd!

24 Let's go fee the bleffed Lamb,
(Such ne'er before a fhepherd came)
The Lamb of God, fent down in time,
To free the world of ev'ry crime!

25 Let's go fee our Saviour dread,
Ordain'd to judge the quick and dead,
Who will convey us all on high,
On angels pinions to the sky.

26 See, ftruck with aweful rev'rence dumb,
Omnipotence, now weak become!
The God, man---and the man, God, fee!
Who fees Him fo---thrice blefs'd is He.

CHRIST is All in All.

1 'TIS Chrift, 'tis Chrift himfelf, that's all in all;
Without Him, man muft to perdition fall:
No thing, no perfon, befides Chrift alone,
Can for the fins of human kind atone.

2 The ferpent with an apple man deceiv'd ----
The ferpent man of Paradife bereav'd ----
The ferpent poifon'd all the race with fin ---
The ferpent to hell's horrors hurl'd them in.

3 Each man on earth as certainly muft go
Into the dungeon of infernal woe,
As if he there had been already got;
If Chrift from that fad doom preferves him not.

4 Chrift left (to buy us) the angelic hoft ---
Chrift fave'd us, when we ev'ry one were loft ----
Chrift from all kind of woes our bofoms free'd----
Chrift to celeftial blifs our fouls will lead.

D 4
5 From

5 From the fell dragon's mouth---the lion's paws----
The toils of Satan,----and the tiger's claws---
Chrift fnatch'd us ev'ry one---and what is more,
From hell's deep dungeon, and the Devil's pow'r.

6 Satan can not deftroy and murder more,
Than Jefus can with eafe to life reftore :
All that the ferpent's pois'nous fting has flain,
Shall by the Lamb's own blood be heal'd again.

7 Chrift is the woman's Seed, ordain'd of yore
By God, to trample on the ferpent's pow'r,
To crufh his fkull, to overturn his fway,
And from his fangs to fnatch the deftin'd prey.

8 To conquer Satan, none can e'er fucceed,
Unlefs affifted by the woman's Seed :
None can efcape from his tyrannic fway,
Unlefs by Jefus he be fetch'd away.

9 Chrift only, is the Seed, the' Almighty pow'r
Promis'd to Abraham in the days of yore,
To free us from the curfe, wherein we live,
And give us all the Bleffings, heav'n can give.

10 Chrift, is the Shiloh fent us from above,
Our Slavery and Bondage to remove,
From vice our erring footfteps to reclaim,
And teach us to adore the facred Name.

11 Chrift is the Tree, whence ev'ry one that lives
On earth, his food, and nourifhment receives :
No one fhall death's eternal forrows meet,
Who fhall of it's immortal fruitage eat.

12 Chrift is the Ark, which from th'o'erwhelming deep,
Did Noah erft, and all his houfehold, keep :
Chrift likewife is the only Ark can fave
The prefent age, from fin's all-cov'ring wave.

13 Chrift is the Ladder, Jacob did behold,
Which reach'd from heaven down to earth, of old :
Up this, all muft afcend, who fain wou'd rife,
And fcale the fteepy fummit of the skies.

14 Chriſt is the mighty Seer, ſent from the sky,
  And his own boſom, by the Lord moſt high,
  His ſacred will and pleaſure to declare :
  Let us, on pain of death, his mandates hear.

15 Chriſt is the brazen Serpent, who is found
  Alone to cure the fie'ry ſerpent's wound :
  Let us to Him our ev'ry ail make known,
  And He will heal us with a look alone.

16 Chriſt's the high-prieſt, who offer'd up his blood,
  His heart's warm treaſure, for his church's good,
  Upon the croſs to his eternal Sire,
  To ſave the world from everlaſting fire.

17 Chriſt is a King, endue'd with might and grace,
  Who wiſely governs his elected race,
  Who plucks their haughty adverſaries down,
  That each may win and wear a glorious crown.

18 Chriſt is the watchful Shepherd, who does keep
  From ev'ry ill his ne'er-neglected ſheep ;
  So that no lion, wolf, or beaſt of prey,
  Can from his flock one lambkin ſteal away.

19 Chriſt, and Chriſt only, is the Prince of Peace,
  Who cauſed his Father's furious wrath to ceaſe,
  And by his blood, ſhed on the curſed tree,
  Made God and man, before at odds, agree.

20 Chriſt is the Roſe, in Sharon's wilds that blooms,
  And fills the deſert with it's ſweet perfumes,
  That by it's colour elevates our hearts,
  And to our fainty ſpirits life imparts.

21 Chriſt is the Balm of Gilead, only found
  Of force to cloſe each widely-gaping wound,
  Which Satan gives, with his ſin-pointed dart,
  To each bad conſcience, and polluted heart.

22 Chriſt is the Manna, ſent us from above
  By God himſelf, out of his wond'rous love :
  Whoe'er, with faith, ſhall on this banquet feaſt,
  Shall never more by hunger be diſtreſt.

23 Chriſt

23 Chrift is the Pafchal Lamb, that erft was flain
For fin, when on the crofs He fuffer'd pain;
Who, by his blood, each foul fo well does keep,
That Satan from his fold can't fteal a fheep.

24 Chrift is the Altar, whereon, night and day,
Prayer and praife, fweet incenfe! all fhou'd lay—
Sweet incenfe, lighted by devotion's fire,
For their Creator, light's immortal Sire.

25 Chrift's the Phyfician, whofe moft precious blood
Alone, can do the finful Chriftian good,
And heal thofe Pains which vile tranfgreffors feel—
Thofe rankling pains which nothing elfe can heal.

26 'Tis Chrift, and Chrift alone can intercede
For us with God, and with our Maker plead :
'Tis Chrift, and Chrift himfelf alone, that can
Make up the deadly breach, 'twixt God and man.

27 Chrift is our Advocate,—'tis he alone
Can plead our caufe, before th' Almighty's throne,
When Satan, ever our accufing foe,
Wou'd fain obtain our final overthrow.

28 Chrift is our fov'reign Lord—Chrift is our Prieft—
Chrift is our Prophet——our Protector's Chrift—
Chrift is our Shepherd---Chrift's our Judge, fo dread,
Chrift is our Saviour---Chrift's our chief and Head.

29 Chrift is the Alpha, e'er the ages paft——
Chrift is the' Omega, which muft always laft——
Chrift is falvation's fource, as well as end——
Chrift is our patron, and ne'er-failing friend !

30 Chrift has th' ufurping tyrant Death o'erthrown---
Chrift's death has fpoil'd, and made his arms his own--
Chrift has devour'd the ghaftly-vifage'd king—
Chrift has bereav'd Him of his pointed fting.

31 Chrift all the keys of Death does clofely keep,
As well as thofe of Hell's tremendous deep ;
So that no Fiend or Angel e'er can hope
Without his leave, their clofe-barr'd valves to ope.

32 Chrift

32 Chrift is the Pelican, fo kindly good,
   That heals his young-ones with his flowing blood,
   And brings them back to light and life again,
   When they were by the wily ferpent flain.

33 Chrift is the Pelican, fo kindly good,
   That heals his brethren with his heart's dear blood,
   And brings them fafely back to life again,
   When they, thro' fin, had been by Satan flain.

34 There is no falve, that ever yet was found,
   Nor medicine, can heal fin's deadly wound,
   Befides our bleffed Saviour's precious blood,
   The fole fpecific, that can do us good!

35 Chrift is the Pearl, which we fhou'd all explore,
   The man, who has it, never can be poor!
   To find it, over lands and oceans hafte——
   To purchafe it, when found, fell all thou haft.

36 Chrift is himfelf the whole that's requifite,
   (To fave our fouls) in the Almighty's fight:
   For nought can to the Deity atone
   For the loft fouls of men, but Chrift alone.

37 'Tis Chrift himfelf, and it is Chrift alone,
   Chrift unaffifted, and Chrift league'd with none—
   Chrift, without ought but Chrift himfelf, can keep
   The fouls of men from Hell's unfathom'd deep.

38 Chrift is the ranfom, for tranfgreffion paid——
   Chrift is our off'ring, facrifice, and aid——
   Chrift is our treafure——Chrift's our only gain—
   Chrift is the Saviour of the faithful train.

39 Chrift is with ev'ry ufeful gift replete,
   Which for the fouls of finful men is meet——
   In Chrift alone is found each faving grace,
   Expedient to preferve a wretched race.

40 Chrift is himfelf our perfect Righteoufnefs——
   Chrift is our Wifdom, and our Holinefs——
   Chrift fave'd us, and Chrift bought us with a price
   Chrift is our comfort—Chrift our Saviour is.

41 Chrift

41 'Tis Chrift, and Chrift alone, that can affuage,
And totally remove his Father's rage————
'Tis Chrift himfelf, and none, but Chrift, that can
Reftore, and juftify, corrupted man.

42 Chrift, without help from either man, or maid—
Chrift, without any faint's, or faintefs' aid——
Chrift, and nought elfe but Chrift alone, can keep
The fouls of men from the wide-yawning deep.

43 Chrift, and Chrift only, felt the racking pain,
Whilft on the Crofs He did for us remain;
And none affifted Him, to fave us, then——
Not even one of all the fons of men.

44 Peter, thro' fear, his fuff'ring Lord deny'd,
The' Apoftles either fled, or turn'd afide,
And timid Mary nothing did but weep:
Whilft Jefus only die'd to fave the fheep.

45 No one but Chrift himfelf has ever been
Beneath the cumbrous weight of all our fin:
None ever fweated drops of Blood before,
But Chrift, when He our foul tranfgreffions bore.

46 None for our fins, but Chrift, was crucify'd,
Nor to redeem his chofen poeple die'd:
No one, but Chrift, his father fully pleas'd——
No one, but Chrift, our wounds' vaft anguifh eas'd.

47 No one, but Chrift, cou'd pluck our fouls away,
When they were otherwife the Devil's prey:
No one, but Chrift, the tyrant Death o'er pow'r'd,
And the Devourer, none but he, devour'd.

48 Chrift only has Death, grimface'd monarch! foil'd
Chrift only has all pow'rs that are, defpoil'd——
Chrift has the bond, that tie'd us down, repeal'd--
Chrift paid our ranfom, Chrift our pardon feal'd.

49 'Twas Chrift, our peace with the Almighty wrought,
'Twas Chrift, our blifs and our Salvation bought,
'Twas Chrift, that all of us God's children made--
'Twas Chrift, that fave'd us by his potent aid.

50 'Twas Chrift, and Chrift alone, that did the whole,
And from diftrefs drew each devoted foul:
Nothing but Chrift alone, thro' God, can fave
Our fouls from hell, our bodies from the grave.

51 Ne'er was there Angel, Prophet, Saint of yore,
Nor any man, that woman ever bore,
Nor any one but Chrift himfelf, who e'er
Did as the Saviour of mankind appear.

52 Our God, to fave a Race forlorn, thinks fit
No angel's mediation to admit,
No mortal's merits, or no martyr's blood,
Nought but Chrift's own, can do a Chriftian good.

53 Chrift is for fin the prop'reft recompence,
There can't a better be for man's offence,
A fmaller recompence can't be allow'd,
(So vile is fin!) than the Beloved's blood.

54 Put no man's blood with Chrift's upon a par,
And no one's merit's e'er with Chrift's compare:
The blood of finful wretches, fuch as we,
Can never with our Saviour's blood agree.

55 The blood of Chrift, his covenanted blood
Alone, can cleanfe tranfgreffion's fetid flood:
For not the blood of all the martyrs flain
Can wafh away thy very flighteft ftain.

56 'Tis not a work by faints, or angels, done,
But 'tis the Work of Jefus Chrift alone,
The' endanger'd fouls of finful men to fave
From Satan's wiles, from hell, and from the grave.

57 Two fev'ral natures muft in one unite,
E'er man can fhun the gloomy realms of night;
Before our ever-bleft Redeemer can
Preferve one foul, he muft be God and man.

58 The Work of God or man alone, can't keep
A fingle finner from hell's hideous deep:
But God and Man, united both in one,
Can for the fins of all the World atone.

59 Mankind's

59 Mankind's Redeemer muſt be God and man,
   E'er He (conſider well the wond'rous plan!)
   Can ſave thy ſoul, and ſet it wholly free
   From penal fire, and endleſs miſery.

60 He muſt be God, and for his might ador'd,
   E'er He can ſtay the fury of the Lord,
   And reſcue thee from Satan, and the foes
   Of ev'ry ſort, that wou'd thy bliſs oppoſe.

61 E'er He for man can ſuffer,—He muſt be
   A Man, from ev'ry vice and error free,
   Whoſe death muſt be equivalent to all
   The deaths of thoſe on this terreſtrial ball.

62 In all the earth beneath, or ſkies above,
   There's not a Saviour ſo replete with love,
   As the incarnate Word—nor ſuch another
   As Jeſus Chriſt, our God, and yet our brother.

63 There's not a creature of all thoſe that dwell
   On earth, can ſave a ſingle ſoul from hell;
   That is a taſk, no other power can
   Perform, but our Redeemer, God and Man.

64 There is no ſure Salvation to be found,
   Tho' you ſhou'd ſearch the univerſe around,
   But that which is thro' Jeſus Chriſt attain'd,
   Whom God, to reſcue us from death, ordain'd.

65 There is no name beneath the copes of heaven,
   No other name to ſinful mortals given,
   Whereby they may be ſav'd from death, but One;
   And that's the name of Jeſus Chriſt alone.

66 God will of none, but Jeſus Chriſt admit,
   To be his partner—none beſides is fit
   To be with Him in the great Work conjoin'd,
   Which is to ſave the ſouls of all mankind.

67 The Son of God himſelf is not inclin'd,
   That any creature ſhou'd with Him be join'd,
   The world's Salvation fully to ſecure!
   For who like Him, is perfect? who is pure?

68 He, of Himſelf, will ſave his choſen race,
Or elſe He never will in any caſe,
(So inconſiſtent's the conjunction!) deign
With any creature in the Work to join.

69 Chriſt will not give (how good ſoe'er they are)
To ſaint or angel, any part or ſhare,
To man, or idol form'd of gold or ſtone,
Of th' adoration due to Him alone.

70 Shou'd any be of ſo inſane a mind,
As to attempt another guard to find,
Let Him, who liſts, the pow'rleſs guard purſue;
But let him nothing have, with Chriſt, to do.

71 To Saints, or Images,———let ſome apply,
And on their impotent ſupport rely;
But my poor ſoul will never ſeek for one
To give it aid, but Jeſus Chriſt alone.

72 Give me, O God! thy well-beloved Son,
'Tis Chriſt, 'tis Jeſus Chriſt, I beg alone,
Whate'er, beſides, thou addeſt to my ſtore,
Give me but Chriſt, and I ſhall aſk no more.

73 Give me, O God! for my Protector, Chriſt——
Give me Chriſt for my King, and for my Prieſt,
My Prophet, my Redeemer, and Support,
To whom I may in each Diſtreſs reſort!

74 Tho' nought but Chriſt ſhou'd to my ſhare be given
By our immortal Sire, that dwells in heaven,
I have enough———I have the whole I crave,
If I have Chriſt———though nothing elſe I have.

75 If I have Chriſt, He'll change my nature quite,
And make the child of hell, a child of light—
From Satan's ſlave, and from a man undone,
I then ſhall be Chriſt's member, and God's ſon.

76 Though I ſhou'd gold and ſilver have in ſtore,
With houſes, and wide manors in my pow'r,
What boots it, ev'ry thing I want, to have,
Unleſs I've Chriſt, my ſinful ſoul to ſave?

77 Take

77 Take out my heart—take out my precious eyes--
Take all my wealth, my friends, whom most I prize;
Take all, in short, I have:——but don't, I pray,
Take my Redeemer, Jesus Christ away.

78 Let Soldiers talk of wars, and battles fought——
Let Sailors talk of wealth from India brought—
Let Misers talk of chests with gold well stor'd—--
But let the Christian's talk be of the Lord.

ADAM'S RACE.

1 ADAM and Eve's, unhappy, sinful, Race,
Late heirs apparent of the fiery lake,
To you, great joy is come——your sorrows chase,
And from your stupid lethargy awake!

2 To-day (says th' angel Gabriel, ever-true,
The faithful bearer of Jehovah's will)
Was Jesus Christ, the Saviour, born to you,
Your chief support in each incumbent ill,

3 Then let us shout aloud, rejoice, and sing,
And with Hosannahs make the skies resound;
For now, to earth, the' Almighty peace did bring,
And his Good-will did tow'rds mankind abound.

4 This is the prop, the branch, the woman's Seed,
For Adam's comfort, by God's promise, given,
To crush beneath his heel the serpent's head,
When he from Eden's blissful groves was driven.

5 This is old Sarah's Seed, Jehovah deign'd
To promise Abraham, all his race to bless,
From Age to Age, 'till royal David reign'd,
The noblest branch sprung from the root of Jesse'!

6 This is the Shiloh, Jacob erst foretold,
To be the solace of the mournful Jews,
When they the crown, their monarchs wore of old,
Shou'd to an Idumean stranger lose!

7 This

7 This is the Prince, the' Emmanuel benign,
  The virgin-mother's long-expected boy,
  Promis'd to Ahaz by the Word divine,
  To lead us to the realms of endlefs joy!

8 This is the Judge, foretold in Micah's page,
  From Bethle'hems little city to arife!——
  This is the eternal Chief, from age to age
  Ordain'd to lead his vot'ries to the fkies!

9 This is the Prophet and the promis'd King!
  This is the Prieft, decreed to quell the foe!
  This·is the Victim, offer'd for our fin,
  And doom'd the works of Satan to o'erthrow!

10 You've heard how Satan erft, with wiles replete,
  Old mother Eve in Paradife deceiv'd,
  Rafhly of the forbidden fruit to eat,
  And how her hufband part from her receiv'd!

11 When thus the Fiend our Parents overcame,
  And taught them God's commandment to tranfgrefs;
  Subject to death, both they and we, became,
  And to each form and fpecies of diftrefs.

12 From Death and Hell no perfon cou'd be found
  Our fouls, by his own fuff'rings, to relieve,
  But God's own Son, for Juftice moft renown'd---
  That God, whom by our fins fo oft we grieve!

13 This very Son of God moft high was doom'd
  The worft of deaths to fuffer on the tree;
  When He our flefh had readily affum'd,
  To fet us from his Sire's difpleafure free:

14 And had not God out of his mercy deign'd
  This Son to give—to fave us all from Hell:
  All there, without exception, had remain'd,
  For ever force'd in endlefs pains to dwell.

15 God, foon did at our wretched ftate relent,
  With tender pity and compaffion move'd;
  And, as he promis'd, to redeem us fent
  His only Son, whom more than all He love'd.

E.   16 To

16 To earth, from the delightful realms above,
    When he perceiv'd the proper time was come,
    God fent the object of his deareft love,
    Our flefh and human nature to affume.

17 A human body, in a happy hour,
    Our Saviour took from Mary, ftill a maid,
    Who, by a marvelous and facred pow'r
    Conceiv'd—without a thought of flefhly aid.

18 Wonder of wonders!——without fin, or blame,
    Our Lord was born, from one to man unknown--
    A perfect man, whom the' Holy Ghoft did frame
    Without man's help, by pow'r divine alone!

19 Mary, when fhe conceiv'd our Saviour firft,
    Was ftill a maid—a maid e'en at his birth——
    When marry'd, ftill a maid---and when fhe nurft--
    And ftill a maid, e'en when fhe left the earth.

20 But as our guilt Chrift undertook to bear,
    His very birth was fubject to diftrefs ;
    A wretched ftable was his palace, here——
    A fwathe, and fome poor clothes, his richeft drefs.

21 Yet, howe'er humble his appearance here,
    That all to Him might proper homage fhow,
    God caufe'd a ftar in heaven to appear,
    Bright as the fun, to wait on Him below.

22 Three royal Sages, from the diftant Eaft,
    E'en from Chaldea, came to feek the Lord,
    Who, on their knees, the fwaddled Babe addrefs'd,
    And as their Sov'reign King and God ador'd.

23 With three rich prefents, they the Babe did greet,
    Which to Chrift's offices did all belong,
    And humbly laid them at his facred feet——
    Gold, myrrh, and frankincenfe, of fragrance ftrong.

24 Defcending angels alfo came, and told
    That He was the Meffiah, promis'd man
    To be his Saviour from the days of old,
    By God himfelf, juft as the world began.

25 Heav'n

25 Heav'n ope'd, earth fhone, at this ftupendous birth,
  And the' angel cry'd, on that aufpicious morn,
  " Glory to God above, and peace on earth,
  " This Day the Saviour of the World is born."

26 Whate'er, thro' her negle&t, old Eve once loft,
  When fhe at firft the law divine tranfgrefs'd,
  We now (as we moft happily may boaft)
  By the Mefliah's birth, have repoffefs'd.

27 Our Saviour left the glorious realms of blifs,
  On purpofe to defeat our wily foe,
  To thwart his views, to fave us from the' abyfs,
  And to preferve us from all pain and woe.

28 So great was the Almighty Father's love
  For us, old Eve's vile, fin-polluted race,
  That He difpatch'd our Saviour from above,
  Out of mere pity to our woeful cafe.

29 So anxious too was Chrift our fouls to fave,
  Which now obnoxious to damnation lie,
  That his own life and foul He freely gave,
  And for his flock the fhepherd deign'd to die.

30 The Death, which we deferv'd, for us He bore,
  And clear'd our debts, which unaccounted ftood,
  He paid the forfeit, and the writing tore,
  And dearly bought our pardon with his Blood----

31 His heart's beft Blood He for an off'ring laid,
  And for our fake reproach and fhame endure'd :
  So God was reconcile'd, our ranfom paid,
  And our Salvation perfectly fecure'd----

32 That pardon, which with his own Life He bought,
  When to releafe loft finners from their chains,
  He laid it down, tho' void of any fault,
  And fave'd the world from everlafting pains.

33 If then on Him our confidence be laid,
  Certain remiffion fhall for us be found,
  Nor need we of thofe torments be afraid,
  With which the yelling vaults of hell refound.

34 For

34 For Satan is deftroy'd, and Death fubdu'd,
And Hell of it's affured prey defpoil'd;
The fouls of men by mercy are renew'd,
And all the fiends by the Meffiah foil'd.

35 Old Adam hurl'd us to the deep abyfs,
From Paradife with ev'ry pleafure bleft;
But Chrift reftore'd us to the feats of blifs,
Where we fhall ever with th' Almighty reft.

36 He is the guiltlefs Lamb, which in their ire
The Jews erft flew, Jehovah's gracious Heir!
The wifh of nations, and the world's defire!
Our only joy and folace in defpair!

37 He is the reprobated Corner-ftone,
The Rock, ordain'd to give the Jews offence;
But precious as a pearl, to us that own
Him, for our true Meffiah and our Prince.

38 Though, beyond meafure, our foul fins extend,
And, like Gomorrah's citizens, we live;
If we believe, and our bad lives amend,
He'll get us all a free and full reprieve.

39 One facred drop, of the bleft Blood He fhed,
Can wafh away our vile offences quite,
Tho' as the purple, deep—as fcarlet, red——
And make them than the drifted fnow more white.

40 If then we place our truft in Chrift alone,
And humbly ferve Him—He our fouls will bring
To Heav'n's bleft manfions, near his facred throne,
To chant the praifes of th' eternal King——

41 Thofe manfions, where fweet pleafure and delight,
Where peace and joy in fuch excefs abound,
As ear ne'er heard of—nor e'er blefs'd the fight—
Nor e'er in thought in any heart were found.

42 Then let us laud, with all our might and main,
Our Saviour Chrift, to us for ever dear,
Who, thro' Death's bitter pangs, our fouls from pain
Reliev'd, and from Hell's dungeons dark and drear.

34 O

43 O let us ftill each bleffed Perfon praife,
Which in the facred Trinity is found,
So ready, ever fince old Adam's days,
To bring men's fouls to heav'n from hell profound.

Advice to a Sinner, to come to CHRIST.

1 COme, thou vile wretch, thou veteran in fin,
    With faith and tears, come to the Son of God!
'Tis He, the Son of God, that calls thee in,
If thou art weary of thy cumbrous load.

2 'Tis Chrift himfelf, that calls thee from above,
'Tis Chrift commands, and who can difobey?
'Tis Chrift, that deigns thy troubles to remove,
If thou to Him, thro' faith, wilt come away!

3 Come thou to Chrift, however great thy crimes,
Come thou, thy life however vile and ill,
Come thou, and beg his needful aid betimes;
For he can fave thee, whenfoe'er he will.

4 Though thou in Adam once were ruin'd quite,
Though thou wert fnare'd by the infidious Fiend,
Though thou haft fo incens'd the God of might,
Believe in Chrift, He'll fave thee in the end.

5 Though thou wert in Iniquity conceiv'd,
Though thou fo very lewd a life haft led,
When thou haft once Chrift's covenant receiv'd,
He'll cleanfe thy filth, and raife thee from the dead.

6 Though thou by nature art to God a foe,
Though thou wert born of a corrupted line,
Believe in Chrift——thou fhalt no more be fo----
But a great fav'rite of thy Sire divine.

7 Though thou to Satan art become a flave,
Though to his wiles thou haft been made a prey,
Believe in Chrift---from Satan's den He'll fave
Thy foul, and bring thee up to perfect day.

E 3   S Though

8 Though thou Damnation doft deferve in hell,
And all the tortures that the Devils bear;
Believe in Chrift—in heaven thou fhalt dwell,
And thy Creator laud for ever there.

9 Though thou art now a headftrong rebel grown,
And turn'd a fiend, who waft a faint before;
Believe in Chrift—he'll take thee for his own,
And make thee, from a fiend, a faint once more.

10 Tho' thou'rt condemn'd, thro' ancient Adam's fault
Who poifon'd and infected all his race;
Believe in Chrift—and thou fhalt yet be brought
To heav'n, in fpite of Adam's foul difgrace.

11 Though Satan feiz'd thy bofom, as his prey,
And took poffeffion of the fencelefs feat;
Believe in Chrift—he'll take his arms away,
And out of doors the fell intruder beat.

12 Though thieves, of ev'ry virtue robb'd thy foul,
And wounded thee with a felonious rage;
The true Samaritan will make thee whole,
And thy deep wound's exceffive pain affuage.

13 Altho' the fie'ry Serpent ftung thy heart,
And fhot his venom thro' each rankling pore;
Believe in Chrift—and he'll allay the fmart,
And bathe thy wounds in his all-cleanfing gore.

14 Though thou haft often wander'd far from home,
Like a ftray'd fheep, juft perifh'd with the cold;
Believe in Chrift, He fpeedily will come,
And from the defert drive thee to his fold.

15 Tho' thou more than a thoufand times haft finn'd,
And tho' thofe fins as many ftripes require,
Believe in Chrift—thou fhalt remiffion find
For ev'ry crime, and ev'ry loofe defire.

16 Altho' thy fins are, as the fcarlet, red,
Or, like the deeper crimfon, though they glow;
Believe in Chrift—and with the blood he fhed,
He'll bleach thee white as any driven fnow.

17 Altho'

17 Altho' thy vices, than thy hairs were more,
   And did unto a countlefs fum amount;
   Thy bleft Redeemer, God and man, adore,
   And he'll forgive thee the immenfe account.

18 Take comfort, thy defponding fpirits raife,
   Believe in Jefus, thy Redeemer dear,
   Amend thy morals, quit thy wicked ways,
   And he from ev'ry ill will keep thee clear.

19 Chrift calls—Chrift fummons thee above the fky,
   Nay, Chrift invites thee to a blifsful home;
   Why wilt thou therefore obftinately die,
   Becaufe thou wilt not to thy Saviour come?

20 Chrift to the world, from the bright realms of joy,
   Exprefsly came, tranfgreffors vile to keep;
   His care, his bufinefs, and his fole employ,
   To gather, and to fold his ftraggling fheep.

21 Thou long, as all have done, haft gone aftray,
   Thou art, like us, without his aid undone:
   Why wilt thou not the gracious Call obey,
   And for protection to thy Saviour run?

22 The fins, which now o'erwhelm thy foul with fhame,
   Are not than Saul's, or any other's, more;
   Yet Saul receiv'd remiffion for the fame;
   And fo fhalt thou——if thou wilt Chrift adore.

23 Thy fins do not above his mercies foar,
   Nor are they fuch as Chrift can not efface,
   Nor can the errors of thy life be more,
   Than he can wafh away by his free grace.

24 Satan can ne'er contaminate thee fo,
   That Jefus cannot his affiftance lend,
   Nor fo pollute, tho' he his worft fhould do,
   But Jefus can thy wicked ways amend.

25 Chrift, man's perverfenefs can with eafe fubdue,
   And to a lamb the wolf, a faint the fiend,
   Convert——the veteran in vice, renew,
   And caufe God's foe, to be again his friend.

E 4   26 Chrift

26 Chrift only call'd Zaccheus from the tree,
    And alter'd by the Call his nature quite :
    So, at his pleafure, he can alter thee,
    And change thy colour foon from black to white.

27 Chrift is a Deity of wond'rous might,
    Who pardon's ev'ry contrite finner's vice,
    Who our degenerate nature fets to right,
    Who ruins Satan's labour in a trice.

28 Omnipotent he is, who bought thy foul,
    He can the breaches, Satan made, repair,
    And from thy breaft, with his corruptions foul,
    Eject the pow'rful fovereign of the air.

29 Though feven Devils revell'd in thy heart,
    Nay, though a Legion that retreat poffefs'd,
    Chrift, with a word, can make them all depart,
    Like flies before a tempeft, from thy breaft.

30 No creature has the power to deface
    The work, by his divine Creator done :
    Nor man, nor fiend, can rob thee of his grace;
    If thou wilt put thy truft in him alone.

31 There's not a foul, who does in Chrift believe,
    That to amend his life and errors paft,
    Does not fufficient grace from him receive;
    'Till he becomes another man at laft.

32 No one for grace to Jefus ever came,
    No one for help to Jefus ever cry'd,
    Who did not fpeedily receive the fame,
    And was not both with grace and help fupply'd.

33 Come then, and earneftly his favour crave,
    Nor let thy weighty fins retard thy foul:
    Chrift never came the finlefs folks to fave,
    But fuch as are contaminate and foul.

34 Chrift ne'er on purpofe left the realms of joy,
    But to preferve the fheep that went aftray ;
    It is his bus'nefs and his chief employ,
    To bring the ftragglers back to the right way.

35 Come

35 Come therefore, come to him with th' utmoſt ſpeed;
He ſpurs, he goads thee on, to mend thy pace :
Believe in Chriſt——be that thy conſtant creed,
And he'll preſerve thee by his ſaving grace.

36 God give thee grace this ſummons to attend ;
O may the gracious Call not prove in vain !
God give thee faith, thy morals to amend :
So thou from Chriſt ſhall grace and peace obtain!

Another Piece of ADVICE to Sinners to come to CHRIST.

1 COME all that are laden with vice, and with ſin,
  Come to your Redeemer, who bids you all in,
Come all to be eas'd of your fears, and your crimes,
He'll give you all reſt, if you'll come but betimes.

2 Come all to your Keeper, Redeemer, and Chief,
Your King, Prieſt and Prophet, he'll bring you relief,
Your Doctor, your Paſtor, your Rock and your Tow'r,
Your Saviour, who conquer'd the dragon of yore !

3 Come all unto Chriſt, without any reſtraint,
Who kindly invites each to make his complaint:
Be it great, be it ſmall, do but ſhow him your grief,
And aſk his aſſiſtance, he'll give you relief.

4 He'll make you all free, and your ſorrows allay,
He'll lend you his aid, and your debts he will pay,
He'll lighten your burdens, your tears he will dry,
He'll heal all your wounds, and you never ſhall die.

5 He'll peace from your Judge and your Father obtain;
By means of his Blood, he your pardon will gain ;
He'll bring you in favour with God, that's above,
And, long as you live, he'll preſerve you his love.

6 Your ſins, in his Blood, he will waſh all away,
His Spirit in each of your hearts he will lay,
He'll make you God's daughters and ſons, of mere love,
And co-heirs with him of his kingdom above.

7 He'll

7 He'll tread down the fiend, and his efforts defeat,
He'll rifle his arms, and his conqueft complete,
His ftrength he will blaft, and his forts overthrow,
And make you fubdue this inveterate foe.

8 Did you mortals but know, how tremendous your
cafe,   [grace,
How defperate your ftate, when depriv'd of God's
'Till to Jefus you came (you'd not eat, nor yet reft)
To better your ftate, and to cheer your fad breaft!

9 What are we by nature, and kind--e'en the beft---
But the children of wrath, if by Jefus not bleft,
But fervants of fin, and the flaves of the fiend,
And the victims of hell, and of death without end?

10 All, alas! by their fins are defile'd, every foul!
Like Negroes we're black and like hogs we are foul,
To Chrift we muft haften, to alter our grain,
And fcour all our filth, e'er we whitenefs can gain.

11 With our Maker, old Adam at odds did us fet,
Entirely unable to pay our vaft debt;
E'er we can be friends, we to Chrift muft repair,
Who, through grace and adoption will make each
his heir.

12 The Foe in his net ev'ry mortal has caught,
Decoy'd by the fruit, thro' our Grandmother's fault;
The fnare can't be broke, nor releas'd can we be,
'Till Chrift by his might and his grace fets us free.

13 The wolf holds our fouls, like a fheep, in his jaws,
Nor can we, nor dare we, get loofe from his paws:
Our Shepherd muft refcue us out of the fcrape,
Or elfe not a foul from his fangs can efcape.

14 The angel hangs over each houfe on the wing,
(So enormous our fins!)prompt deftruction to bring:
With the blood of the Lamb, we our lintels muft
fmear,
That the fiend may pafs on, and our families fpare.

15 All

15 All mortals are under the power of the Fiend,
   In a dark dreary comfortlefs dungeon confin'd,
   Chain'd down by their vices, 'till Jefus fhall come,
   To refcue them out of their horrible gloom.

16 From the pow'r of the Fiend, none can refcue a man,
   Or the bondage of fin, let them do what they can,
   'Till Chrift by main force the Deftroyer has bound,
   And place'd us all, out of the flough, on dry ground.

17 By nature we lie, ev'ry man that has breath,
   Without knowledge of God, in the fhadow of death:
   Chrift Jefus our hearts by his grace muft illume,
   E'er we can be drawn from that comfortlefs gloom.

18 All fin is fo odious, fo fetid, fo foul,
   It fpoils, it defiles, it infects ev'ry foul ;
   Nor can it's deep ftains be difcharge'd by'any means,
   'Till Chrift with his blood fhall our filthinefs cleanfe.

19 Like a mountain of lead, on our necks, fin depends,
   It ftrains all our finews, our backs down it bends,
   Our fouls, thro' the centre, to hell'twou'd deprefs,
   Did n't we fly to Chrift, for to make our loads lefs.

20 The Fiend, like a man in ftrong panoply bold,
   Of the hearts of each mortal has taken faft hold,
   Nor can the whole world thence the' invader expel,
   'Till Chrift comes, and hurls him down headlong
      to hell.

21 We all have been grievoufly ftung by the foe,
   Our fores, without ceafing, eternally flow,
   Nor can any leach upon earth do us good,
   'Till Chrift comes, and cleanfes our wounds with
      his blood.

22 The foe, of our ornaments, has us bereft,
   And of ev'ry virtue quite naked has left ;
   To Jefus, our brother, then let us all go,
   And He his own garments will over us throw.

23 We all have been dead in iniquity quite,
   Nor have we the pow'r to do any thing right,
                                        'Till

'Till Jefus, the giver of life, does arrive
To raife us from fin, and our fpirits revive.

24 When the ferpent has ftung you with luft through
      and through,
To the brazen One come, and your malady fhow :
Look intent upon Chrift, and you foon fhall have eafe,
The venom will drop, and the anguifh will ceafe.

25 Show. void of all dread, to your Saviour your fore ;
For fuch a Phyfician was ne'er feen before !
Each wound and complaint, ev'ry fin and each wheal,
With his Heart's precious blood He will tho-
      roughly heal.

26 No med'cine, no plafter, no phyfic, no falve,
No herbs, no emollients, you ever can have,
No noftrum, but Jefus's blood, can be found
To heal fin's wide-gaping, and anguifhous wound.

27 Full many there are, who all tumours can cure,
With moft of the ails, which poor mortals endure ;
But there's no phyfician on earth can be found
But Jefus alone, that can cure fin's deep wound.

28 No angel above, though their number's fo great,
. Though with ftrength and honour fo very replete,
Can fave one poor foul, that from virtue has ftray'd,
'Till our Saviour himfelf comes to give us his aid.

29 Tho' the faints of each fex were to join all their pow'r,
Since Adam was form'd, till the world be no more,
They cannot preferve, though fo much they excel,
Without Jefu's aid, one poor mortal from Hell.

30 Though thou all the beafts in the forefts that live,
And thy fubftance entire for an off'ring fhou'dft give,
Whole rivers of oil, thy fon, life, and blood——
Without Chrift's affiftance, they'd do thee no good.

31 Tho' the air's vaft expanfe, and the regions of day,
The earth, and the ocean, thou all fhou'dft furvey,
Thou no other perfon but Jefus could'ft find,
Who is able to fave; and what's more, well-inclin'd.

32 No

32 No Saviour but Jefus endeavour to have ;
As God, and as man, he's Almighty to fave :
There is not a name, befides his, under heaven,
Thro' which any help to our fouls can be given.

33 No fouls can be fave'd in the days, that now laft,
In thofe yet to come, or in thofe that are paft,
But they that are kept by Chrift Jefus alone ;
The reprobate crew fhall be damn'd ev'ry one.

34 With the ftrong arm of faith, thy Redeemer arreft,
Lay hold of him firmly, if thou wou'dft be bleft,
Nor quit the clofe gripe, 'till at laft thou haft gain'd
The grace to be fave'd, and his favour obtain'd.

35 Truft not to thy works, learning, wealth, or thy race,
Thy foul can't be refcue'd, unlefs thou doft place
In Chrift thy belief; and if e'er thou fhou'dft truft
Unto any befides, thou art utterly loft.

36 For all Adam's fons, fince the world firft was fram'd
By fin are polluted, and needs muft be damn'd :
To death and to hell, let them do what they can,
If by Chrift not preferv'd, they muft go ev'ry man.

37 Then all to your Saviour together repair,
To fave your loft fouls from the pit of defpair;
Whoe'er will come freely in heaven fhall dwell :
But all, who refufe, fhall be tumbled to hell.

38 Let none be fo ftupid, fo dull, and unwife,
As to turn from their Saviour and guide to the fkies,
None from death can efcape, or to heaven afcend,
Not a man can be fave'd, unlefs Chrift be his friend.

39 Not Noah, Job, Abraha'm, not Daniel, nor Paul,
Not Mary, nor Anne, nor the beft of them all,
Not the babe newly born, unlefs Chrift be his friend,
Cou'd, by worth of his own, be preferv'd from the
fiend.

40 Not a man (fuch a price our redemption did coft!)
Shall be fave'd, but thro' Chrift : all the reft muft
be loft.

Nought

Nought lefs, for the fins of mankind can atone
Than the blood and the death of our Saviour alone.

41 Of angels and faints, then, affiftance to crave
Is in vain: neither Pope, Mafs, or Friar, can fave,
Nor ought you can mention, whatever it be,
But the death of our Saviour: fo finful are we!

42 Nought lefs for the fins of mankind cou'd atone
· Than their utter extinction; unlefs there were one
Whofe death for the death of them all might fuffice:
And who, but our Saviour, cou'd pay fuch a price?

43 None therefore to God fatisfaction can make,
· But through Jefus' death, and for Jefus's fake:
Who feeks not his aid, (let him e'er fo well live)
He, for one of a thoufand no anfwer can give.

44 Some think, that by merits and works of their own,
By fafting and alms they for fin can atone,
To heaven afcend, and from hell-torments flee,
Without their Redeemer: fo ufelefs is He!———

45 But whilft thus, in fancy, to heaven they foar,
They'll fink into hell, like the Devil of yore:
And then they fhall fee, that no man can afcend
To the fkies of himfelf, without Chrift for his friend.

46 The Lord is not bound any pity to fhew;
For none is to man, nor fhall ever be, due:
But all men are bound to adore him alone;
All to him are indebted, but he unto none.

47 No mortal by prayer and alms can appeafe,
Or his Maker, by fafting and penitence pleafe;
'Till man and his Maker, thro'Chrift, have agreed,
Who muft hallow and bleach in his blood ev'ry
deed.

48 Chrift Jefus each finner muft juftly arrange,
And to his Creator's fimilitude change,
His thoughts he muft alter, his temper improve,
E'er he can inherit the kingdom above.

49 Chrift

49 Chrift, man with his Maker muft bring into grace,
And with his own blood his offences efface,
With all his own virtues he muft him inveft,
And give him his Spirit, e'er he can be bleft.

50 Chrift muft refcue our fouls from the pow'r of the
    Fiend,
Who in a dark dungeon ftill keeps us confin'd,
Faft bound, hand and foot, with fin's cumberfome
    chain ;
Or we in the Valley of Death muft remain.

51 Chrift, the fiend muft difarm, that poffeffes each
    mind,
And in gyves the incroaching invader muft bind;
He thence muft ejedt him, tho' loth to depart,
And garrifon keep his ownfelf in each heart.

52 Chrift muft make us the fons of his heavenly Sire
(By adoption and grace,we that right may acquire)
And make us the heirs of the Godhead above.
E'er we, howe'er good, can to Eden remove.

53 Chrift from each difafter poor mortals muft draw,
From the toils of the Fiend,and Death's mercilefs jaw,
And make us partake of his favour and grace,
E'er we in the kingdom of God can have place.

54 No mortal to heaven can poffibly foar
By his own condudt, his merits, or pow'r ;
Nor can He from Death and the Devil e'er run,
Without Chrift's affiftance,or God's vengeance fhun.

55 How can one God's anger and fentence efchew,
The curfe by the law, to iniquity due,
Death's keen pointed fting,and the pow'r of the fiend,
By worth of his own—unlefs Chrift be his friend ?

56 We all muft repent, with a heart moft fincere,
Believe with true faith, in our Saviour fo dear,
By the pow'r of his fpirit, our lives we muft mend,
And be totally change'd, e'er the fkies we afcend.
      57 Then

57 Then all to your Saviour together repair
With tears, a true faith, and a penitent air:
Whoe'er will come freely, in heaven shall dwell,
But they that refuse shall be cast into hell.

An EXHORTATION to worship our LORD JESUS CHRIST.

1 COME simple, come gentle, your sing-song give
    o'er,
And let us for once be combine'd,
On this happy day, our dear Lord to adore,
    And bear our Redeemer in mind.

2 When first our Creator the protoplasts made,
    In Eden the couple he place'd,
Where o'er the whole garden at pleasure they stray'd
    And pluck'd ev'ry fruit to their taste.

3 The fiend, when their happy estate he perceiv'd,
    How loving they walk'd o'er the plain,
Whilst all that they wanted or wish'd, they receiv'd,
    Without any labour, or pain——

4 To Eden soon came with the cursed design
    Poor Eve, as the weaker, to hook,
And thus he began her obedience to mine,
    But of Adam no notice then took.

5 Did you taste but a bit of the fruit of the tree,
    " Which now you're forbidden to eat,
Your eyes wou'd be ope'd, and like gods you wou'd be
    It's pow'rs and effects are so great!"

6 The apple she pluck'd, and a morsel she bit,
    Nor did Adam, to taste it, refrain:
When, alas! (for us all, how unhappy was it?)
    Their pleasure was soon turn'd to pain.

7 Thus they, thro' their pride, both obnoxious became
    To the pains to such crimes justly due,
And we, their descendents, all merit the same,
    So close we their footsteps pursue.

8 When

8 When our righteous Judge faw that fo hard was our fate
   And that we, thro' mere weaknefs, were fpent ;
  He gave us, in pity to our fad eftate,
   Chrift—to aid us where ever we went.

9 Our Saviour was born, as on this bleffed morn,
   And low in a manger was laid————
  A morn, that in mind fhou'd for ever be borne,
   Which brought us fo needful an aid !

10 Two natures in him, without mixture, are join'd,
   (A truth, we fhou'd always profefs !)
  The Godhead and manhood in him are combin'd,
   As we by our creed do confefs.

11 His Godhead is equal to that of his Sire,
   As we from his pow'r may perceive ;
  His manhood does not fo fublimely afpire,
   As we from the fcriptures believe.

12 Then was not God's love, all expreffion above,
   To us fuch a Saviour who gave,
  As like us was man (as the fcriptures all prove)
   In all things, if fin you do fave.

13 When ready to fink, and juft on the brink
   Of the pit, where the damn'd ever mourn,
  In unfpeakable pains, faft bound in fin's chains,
   Without any hopes of return,

14 He us freely bail'd, and our covenants feal'd,
   He only, his Sire cou'd appeafe,
  From woe he us brought, and our freedom he bought,
   He health gave, which never fhall ceafe.

15 Not gold of the beft, nor the wealth of the Eaft,
   The Deity's pardon cou'd buy :
  But the Son he love'd beft, the God-and-Man bleft:
   Let's all to this advocate fly.

16 By him God was pleas'd, and by him was appeas'd,
   And, without him, no pleafure cou'd take;
  Thro' him, in each grief, he will grant us relief,
   And hear each petition we make.

F   17 Himfelf,

17 Himself, man to fave, a pure victim he'gave,
    Left to Satan a prey we fhou'd fall,
Whofe head he made feel the full weight of his heel;
    But fave'd his own followers all.

18 Tho' our good works were more than the fand on the
    And Arithmetic's pow'rs did exceed,   [fhore,
For want of true faith (as our article faith)   Art. xiii.
    There's the nature of fin in each deed.

19 We comfort receive through faith, and believe,
    That, through faith, we are fave'd from our foes:
By grace, and thro' faith, as St. Paul himfelf faith,
    'Tis that God for his friends has us chofe.

20 No victim he fought from man for each fault,
    (Although he was treated fo ill)
But a fpirit contrite, and a heart pure and right:
    To hear him, then come with good will!

21 By faith we fhall have, whatever we crave,
    Nor is there a thing that we want,
But we fhall receive, if in Chrift we believe;
    Since he what he pleafes, can grant.

22 Thro' faith in the Blood of our Saviour, thus good,
    Our crimes fhall be wafh'd quite away,
When we muft give in an account of each fin,
    Before our Creator, one day.

23 Then put on your beft, and be decently dreft,
    In clothes fit for bride-folks to wear,
E'er to heaven you go, where there is no woe,
    When there you're oblig'd to appear.

24 Like faints be prepar'd, and be ftill on your guard,
    With oil in your lamps in good ftore;
Left the bridegroom fhou'd come unexpectedly home,
    And fuddenly knock at the door.

25 With alacrity ftill, as you're bound, do God's will,
    E'er the day of Salvation is o'er,
E'er a wide-fpreading gloom fhall the fun overcome,
    And you cannot work any more.

26 Then

26 Then watch night and day, and moſt earneſtly pray,
    That God may be ſtill your defence:
  For the time is now near, as the ſcriptures declare,
    When we muſt depart all from hence.

27 Be in charity ſtill, 'tis your Maker's dread will,
    And you ſhall a kingdom receive,
  Where you ſhall have eaſe, mirth, pleaſure, and peace,
    And joys, that no heart can conceive.

28 No ſickneſs ſhall there, nor yet ſorrow, appear,
    No poverty, care, nor diſtreſs;
  But the ſound of the lyre, with the heavenly quire,
    And bliſs, which no tongue can expreſs.

29 I warn you then all, be you great, be you ſmall,
    To pray from the ground of your heart,
  That God, in pow'r great, and with mercies replete,
    May bring you there, when you depart.

Another Invitation, or Exhortation to worſhip CHRIST JESUS.

1 COME all freſh and gay, let us keep Holiday,
    With hymns let us Jeſus adore;
  Let us him celebrate, both early and late,
    Who ſave'd us from death by his pow'r.

2 Aloud let us ſing, 'till the whole world does ring,
    And our notes to the heavens aſpire,
  That the angels above with our ſongs we may move,
    And teach them to join in the quire.

3 When nor men cou'd befriend, nor ſaints their aid lend,
    Nor angels, nor ought that's below,
  Any good cou'd have done, God ſent us his Son,
    To ſave us from ſorrow and woe.

4 What ſire with a ſcore of children, or more,
    The worſt unto death would expoſe,
  Or conſent to the loſs of one on the croſs,
    Or force him to fight for his foes?

F 2   5 Yet

5 Yet, with pity God mov'd, gave the Son whom he
    And esteem'd far above all the rest,   [lov'd,
For mortals to die, suspended on high,
    Although we were rebels profest.

6 Our Father let's praise then, on these holidays,
    With hearts full of ardor and love,
Who gave us his heir, distress and despair
    Far out of our sight to remove.

7 Next, let us applaud the Son of our God,
    Who health to the universe gave,
Who quitted the sky, and the glories on high,
    His servants from sorrow to save.

8 From heaven above, and God's bosom of love,
    For our great advantage, he came—
He came, for our sake, his manhood to take;
    And so we his brethren became!

9 The meek harmless Lamb to this nether world came,
    To a crib, from the regions above
And the heavenly host—to save us, when lost:
    So great his compassion and love!

10 Our ever bless'd Lord, I will call him the Word,
    Himself the great God, and God's heir,
Of Mary was born, as on this blessed morn,
    To save us from woe and despair.

11 The Godhead on high, who fram'd earth, sun, and sky,
    With the waters, that make up the main,
Our flesh did assume, and an Infant become,
    And then by base soldiers was slain.

12 Come then let us raise our voices, to praise
    Christ Jesus our Saviour and King;
With harp and with tongue, let us join all day long,
    And hymns to his honour let's sing.

13 All creatures that move, in the heavens above,
    'On earth, or in the' ocean below,
Let's freely invite in his praise to unite,
    And our Saviour's great goodness to show.

14 Like

14 Like Shadrach in fire, or the Baptiſt's old Sire,
    Like Miriam and Moſes, let's praiſe
  Our Saviour (who came from Hell's raging flame,
    To ſave us) the reſt of our days.

15 Then ſtill bear in mind our Saviour ſo kind,
    This ſeaſon devote to his praiſe,
  In gladneſs and joy, let us always employ,
    And grateful thankſgivings, thoſe days.

16 Heav'n bids us rejoice with heart and with voice,
    At church, or where'er we reſort,
  In the Giver of Peace, and of joys that ne'er ceaſe;
    So with wiſdom we ſeaſon our ſport.

17 Then let us this day with hearts blithe and gay,
    And faces that gliſten and ſhine,
  In Jeſus rejoice, with ear-thrilling voice,
    And ev'ry dull ſorrow reſign.

18 On this ſacred morn your houſes adorn,
    Your boards ſpread with cheer of the beſt;
  Of which,for Chriſt's ſake, let poor neighbours partake,
    And baniſh all grief from the feaſt.

19 Quite elated appear, take *enough* of good cheer,
    But *more*, like a peſtilence, ſhun :
  True bliſs never think in meat, or in drink,
    To find—but in Jeſus alone.

20 All the holidays long chant ſome heavenly ſong,
    Mere ſing-ſong, or ſatire, ne'er mind ;
  But truſt in the Lord, and in his holy word,
    From whom you ſure pardon ſhall find.

21 To taverns ne'er enter—to brothels ne'er venture—
    To ſpend ſo your time, is a ſhame !
  With nonſenſe and noiſe, you the fiend thus rejoice,
    And foully diſhonour Chriſt's name.

22 Quit your cards in a trice, and your rattling of dice,
    Your riots, which mankind debaſe——
  Your oaths loud and foul, which muſt ſhock each
      good ſoul,
  And Chriſt's ſolemn birth-day diſgrace.

23

23 In David's fweet page, or the Gofpels, engage,
  Inftead of your cards and your dice :
More proper by far, thofe holy books are,
  Than them fpotted panders to vice.

24 Exult then, and God your Redeemer applaud,
  His glories with tranfport recite ;
Your hands clap, and fing to the praife of heav'n's king,
  And take in the tafk true delight.

25 Let's laud to the fkies the Spirit fo wife,
  Who fhows from the gofpel's pure lore,
That pardon and peace, with joys that ne'er ceafe,
  Through Chrift, are ftill for us in ftore.

26 To the Father above—to the Son of his love—
  To the Spirit, that fanctifies all——
Be now, and each hour, all glory and pow'r,
  From each on this well-people'd ball.

An Exhortation to give God Thanks for our Redemption through Chrift.

1 O Let's applaud with one accord,
    And blefs, from day to day, the Lord,
  Who gave for us his only Son,
  When we before were quite undone!

2 Fall on your knees, both morn and night,
  Let adoration, pow'r, and might,
  Be unto Him afcribe'd alone,
  Who gave for us his only Son.

3 How vaft the debt, did we but know,
  Which we to our Redeemer owe,
  Nought wou'd we do, by night or day,
  But, on our knees, unto him pray.

4 When we to fuch a pafs were brought,
  By Satan's artifice, that nought
  Befides cou'd fave ; God deign'd to give
  His Son, loft mortals to reprieve.

5 By

5 By Satan's puiffance fubdue'd,
  We ftill with groans our fins had rue'd,
  Had we not been by Jefus bought,
  Who our Redemption freely wrought.

6 There was no method to affuage
  The God of juftice in his rage,
  But that his beft belov'd fhou'd deign
  For our Redemption to be flain.

7 There was no poffibility,
  A fingle foul from Hell to free,
  Did not the Juft-One for it's fake,
  An off'ring of his heart's blood make.

8 Chrift gave his blood, of worth immenfe!
  Unto his Sire a recompence
  For us—his life He did beftow,
  To free us from our mortal foe.

9 We were, like birds, caught in the net,
  Which Satan for our fouls had fet——
  The net, wherein inclos'd we lay,
  Chrift broke——and we flew far away.

10 We were, like fheep that go aftray,
  To wolves and rav'nous beafts a prey,
  When from Chrift's fold we dare'd to go,
  And follow'd our fallacious foe.

11 Chrift is the fhepherd, that, among
  The favage crew and hellifh throng
  To find us, ventur'd firft to come,
  And brought us on his fhoulders home.

12 We are, like him, who on the way
  To Jericho, was robb'd, and lay
  O'erwhelm'd with wounds upon the ground,
  Whilft none to lift us up was found.

23 Chrift's the Samaritan, fo kind,
  Who on the road our wounds did bind,
  And to the inn benignly led,
  Where we were comforted, and fed.

15 The

14 The ferpent (paradife within)
  Tranfpierc'd us with the dart of fin,
  But Chrift the wound, made by its dart,
  Heal'd with the blood, warm from his heart.

15 There was no med'cine to be found
  To cure the fie'ry ferpent's wound,
  But that of brafs intent to eye:
  There was no other remedy !

16 So nothing cou'd allay the fmart
  We felt, when pierc'd by fin's keen dart,
  Befides Chrift Jefus crucify'd,
  By the brafs ferpent typify'd.

17 In fuch a piteous cafe we ftood,
  As does the Pelican's young brood,
  When by fome pois'nous ferpent gore'd,
  E'er by their dam's own blood reftore'd.

18 Chrift faw us with his eye divine ;
  And, like the Pelican benign,
  He gave the blood, warm from his heart,
  To mitigate our wounds dire fmart.

19 Let us confider then our cafe,
  The vaft advantage, and the grace,
  That came unto a world undone,
  From Jefus' fufferings alone.

20 The fon of fin, the Devil's flave,
  The child of wrath, and of the grave,
  Each mortal was---and vermin's food---
  'Till Chrift redeem'd us with his blood.

21 What's man, without Chrift's fuccour, fay !
  But the Fiend's vaffal and his prey,
  Already doom'd by God to go
  From Eden to the realms of woe !

22 There's not a man, upon the whole,
  Who can from Death defend his foul,
  'Till he can Jefus' blood obtain
  To cleanfe him from each finful ftain.

23 Throughout

23 Throughout the world, there is not one
That can for his own sins atone,
'Till the Lamb's blood he shall obtain,
To pay his price, and ease his pain.

24 Christ is the spotless Lamb, ordain'd
The crimes, wherewith the world is stain'd,
To take away—and to assuage,
With his heart's blood, his Father's rage.

25 Christ is the priest, who now on high
Resides, and with incessant cry
A constant intercession makes,
And sheds his heart's-blood for our sakes.

26 Christ light to ev'ry mortal gives ——
Christ is the life of each that lives——
Christ is our comfort, and our guard —
Christ from the first, his aid prepar'd!

27 Without Christ's help, we're quite undone;
But we are save'd, through Christ alone:
Without Him, we can't God perceive;
But through Him, we with God shall live.

28 All to the dismal realms of woe,
But they who trust in Christ, shall go:
Without Him, none shall scale the sky,
How much soe'er they toil and try.

29 Let us in Christ then learn to trust,
The great Redeemer of the just,
And mind his precepts to obey,
If we in heaven e'er think to stay.

30 With his heart's-blood, the world Christ bought,
And from fierce flames our freedom wrought;
Yet thousands in the world shall go,
For want of Faith, to Hell below.

31 Though Christ was slain, our souls to save—
Though a full price for us He gave——
Yet none salvation shall receive,
But who alone in Him believe.

32 We fhall be faved, if we believe
   In Chrift ———if not———we fhall not live:
   He lives, who does on Chrift rely———
   Who does not truft in Him fhall die.

33 Not one, of any age, fhall go
   To the infernal realms below,
   But he who fhall refufe to truft
   In the Redeemer of the juft.

34 Heav'n's gate is open night and day,
   (None fuch from it are turn'd away)
   To ev'ry Chriftian, that's fincere,
   Of what degree, or rank foe'er.

35 No more they of their faults fhall hear,
   No more their vices fhall appear,
   Which thro' Chrift's Blood are all forgiven,
   And blotted from the rolls of heaven.

36 Chrift wafh'd our fins and filth away,
   Chrift will to blifs our fouls convey,
   Chrift bought thofe fouls, when loft and gone,
   And what he bought, fhall be our own.

37 Let's ne'er forget, 'till turn'd to clay,
   To praife our Saviour, night and day,
   Who has our fouls from ruin bought!
   For us, what wonders has he wrought?

38 Let's to our Chief, our Saviour, fhew
   All praife, and ev'ry honour due,
   All true refpect, and worfhip fit—
   Let heav'n and earth fay———So be it!

ADVICE to thofe who are defirous of obtaining God's Favour, and Forgivenefs of their Sins.

1 WHoe'er would have the fins forgiven,
     Whereby he has offended heaven,
   He muft with diligence purfue
   Thofe ufeful Precepts, that enfue.

Thou

2 Thou, firft of all, muft humbly own
  Thy fins, before the' Almighty's throne;
  Nought from thy God fhou'd be conceal'd:
  Since all things are to Him unveil'd!

3 And then endeavour to obferve,
  What punifhment thou doft deferve——
  Eternal death! — it is no lefs;
  Becaufe thou doft God's laws tranfgrefs.

4 For furely thou canft not but know
  Thy vices merit endlefs woe;
  Then meekly beg, for Jefus' fake,
  That he wou'd mercy on thee take——

5 And know that nothing can atone
  For fin, before the Godhead's throne,
  Befides Chrift's death, and precious blood,
  And the obedience which he fhow'd——

6 That Jefus, (thou muft too believe!)
  For fin did a full ranfom give,
  When on the crofs He bore difgrace,
  For all the fins of all our race——

7 And know too, that the God of heaven
  Accepts the fatisfaction given,
  And for Chrift's fake, does ftill remit
  Thofe fins the faithful may commit——

8 Believe too, that He'll pardon thee
  Thy errors and iniquity,
  If thou, with contrite heart fhalt make
  Thy fuit to God for Jefus' fake.

9 Conceal not then the fins, but own,
  To which thou'rt principally prone;
  For 'tis a folly to deny
  What's plain to God's all-feeing eye.

10 Freely condemn thyfelf, before
   The Deity's tremendous pow'r!
   Left thou fhou'dft on the day of doom,
   To open fhame and cenfure come.

11 Be-

11 Bewail each vile, and hateful fin,
As foon as thou the fame haft feen—
And ftrive againft it, night and day,
'Till thou haft caft it quite away.

12 Make thou thy heart profoundly figh,
Make briny tears ftream from each eye,
Make thy fad fpirit inly mourn,
And from it's vicious habits turn.

13 Then beg of God, that he'd impart
To thee a foft and tender heart,
And often grieve, when thou'rt alone,
For all the crimes, that thou haft done.

14 Ne'er ceafe to pray, and never reft,
'Till God has granted thy requeft——
Namely—a heart, that can relent,
Can grieve for fin, and can repent——

15 And when thou a good while haft griev'd
For the bad life, which thou haft liv'd,
The promifes divine hold faft,
As long as e'er thy life fhall laft.

16 God promifes to give relief,
And comfort thofe that are in grief,
And to forgive all, does confent,
Who from their very heart repent.

17 For all thy vicious courfes grieve,
And in thy Saviour, Chrift, believe,
Forfake them, whilft thou yet haft breath,
And thou fhalt never fuffer death.

18 For God has promis'd to provide
A Helper, Comforter, and Guide,
(In his own Son) to all that mourn,
And from their fins repentant turn.

19 His Word, befides, the Lord does give,
That he will all thy faults forgive,
And cleanfe thee from thy deep-grain'd crimes;
If thou wilt but repent betimes.

20 And

20 And if a penitent thou'lt prove,
    He'll grant to thee his grace and love———
    Mild, gentle, merciful, he'll be,
    And ever live at peace with thee.

21 He'll wash thee in the cleansing flood
    Of his dear Son's most precious blood,
    And scour away thy vices quite,
    'Till he has made thee lily-white.

22 Hold fast (and he will thee applaud)
    The sacred promises of God:
    The heav'n and earth shall both decay,
    E'er one of them shall pass away.

23 Then, as a snake, thy sins detest—
    A snake, that rears it's bloated crest,
    And, hid some mofs-grown brake beneath,
    Wou'd sting thee by surprize to death:

24 Approach not near the place, where sin
    May by her wiles allure thee in———
    Pass by with speed, her offers shun,
    Nor headlong to temptation run.

25 If thou wilt step too near the ground,
    Where basks the snake—thy heel 'twill wound—
    Or if thou'lt come too near the fire,
    'Twill burn, if thou wilt not retire.

26 Take therefore of thy self good heed,
    Nor near temptation's purlieus tread;
    'Tis better make a good retreat,
    Than meet with shame, and a defeat.

27 Do not unto thy sins incline
    Again, like dogs or filthy swine,
    Which, though they lately were wash'd clean,
    Return unto the nauseous scene.

28 Keep not bad company, whose lore
    Will make thee sin still more and more:
    It nought avails to God to pray,
    'Till thou from such hast turn'd away:

29 But

29 But cleave unto the godly race,
And note their converfe, full of grace:
For each good man's a ready guide
To lead thee, where the juft refide.

30 Unto the Godhead humbly pray——
To turn thee from each wicked way,
And to direct thee, whilft thou'rt here,
Truly to love him, and to fear.

31 Let not the fiend thy reafon blind,
Nor move again, to fin, thy mind;
But, through the Blood, which Jefus fhed,
Beneath thy feet the tempter tread.

32 Confort not thou with drunkards vile,
Left they thy morals fhou'd defile,
As the falt water of the tide
Corrupts the rills, that to it glide.

33 Quit then immediately thofe friends,
Whofe converfe, to debauch thee, tends:
Shun them, and their bad ways deteft,
As thou wou'dft pitch avoid, when dreft.

Advice to believe in CHRIST, and an Exhibition or difplay of the wonderful change that is wrought in the man that believes.

1 BELIEVE in Chrift, for thy Protector cry,
God offers him to all, both far and nigh,
Receive the gracious offer, and don't fail;
Or elfe, thou fhalt the lofs of him bewail.

2 The man, who Chrift with heart fincere receives,
And with a lively faith in him believes,
Chrift will on him his faving grace beftow,
To live like the bleft faints, whilft here below.

3 Chrift fhall to him his holy Spirit give,
That he, new-born, may a new creature live;
Chrift fhall quite change, and mould the man anew,
From a rafh rebel to a fubject true.

4 He

4 He gives his grace, our gloomy minds to light——
He gives his Word, to make us walk aright——
To rule us, he his holy Spirit grants——
He gives himſelf, to make up all our wants——

5 So that no ſoul in Chriſt can well believe,
Who ſhall not grace and ſtrength from him receive,
To emulate the conduct of the juſt;
If right his faith, and confident his truſt.

6 The grace of God, and a ſupernal pow'r,
Faith plucks from heav'n--to make a man give o'er,
And thoroughly abhor, his evil ways,
And lead a life of virtue all his days.

7 Unleſs thy faith extorts this grace divine,
And makes the renovated creature ſhine,
It is in vain;—it anſwers to no end,
Unleſs it ſerves thy errors to amend.

8 A lively faith does grace from Chriſt attract,
And ſtrength to put thy theory in act:
All it's old ſins it utterly forſakes,
And of the' whole man a renovation makes.

9 Howe'er corrupt the nature that's in thee——
However weak thy intellects may be——
Believe in Chriſt, invoke his holy name,
And, when he pleaſes, he can change the ſame.

10 Although the Jailer was a ſinful ſoul——
Though Paul was, once, as ſinful, on the whole—
And though Manaſſes was ſtill worſe agen——
Yet they, thro' Chriſt, were made quite diff'rent men.

11 So can he make of thee, thou ſinful ſoul!
Although by nature reprobate and foul,
A perfect ſaint—if thou in him wilt place
Thy truſt—thereby to get his aid and grace.

12 Chriſt, that great perſecutor Paul, reform'd,
And to a glorious preacher ſoon tran-form'd;
The woman too, of bad report and fame,
From a mere raven, a white dove became.

13 Believe

13 Believe in Chrift with heart fincerely true,
    And he'll thy mind and manners form anew————
    Chriftians he'll make out of a fiend-like race,
    And of the foe of God, a child of grace.

14 Prefume not, then, that thy belief is right,
    If Chrift thy nature has not alter'd quite:
    For Chrift a total change of manners gives
    To each, that faithfully in him believes.

15 Behold Zaccheus, Magdalene, and Paul!
    You foon fhall fee that Chrift will change them all:
    Their morals all at once are ftrictly juft,
    As foon as they in Jefus place their truft.

16 Tho', in the morning, Saul did all he cou'd,
    Like a fierce wolf, to fhed the Chriftian's blood;
    Yet, foon as he believ'd, this wolf became,
    By noon that very day, a perfect lamb.

17 Before Zaccheus was a Chriftian made,
    To rob the needy, was his daily trade;
    But, when he once believ'd, he gave the poor
    The greateft part of what he gain'd before.

18 Though Magdalene was once a reprobate,
    And finn'd, e'er fhe believ'd at any rate,
    Yet afterwards a virtuous life fhe led,
    And was declared a faint, when fhe was dead.

19 So fhalt thou ev'ry vicious habit leave,
    When thou fhalt once unto thy Saviour cleave:
    For, 'till there is this reformation wrought,
    Thy faith can only a mere whim be thought.

20 Faith, unaccompany'd by works, is dead————
    A formlefs faith—a trunk without a head————
    A faith, that blinds— a falfe, fallacious faith————
    A faith, that leads the ready way to death!

21 There is no fire, without attending heat—
    There is no water—but it muft be wet————
    There's no good vine—but is with clufters crown'd;
    No lively faith, without it's fruits is found!

22 Shou'd

22 Shou'd any one affirm, that he believes,
And yet repents not—he himself deceives:
His faith is nought, but froth—or, at the moft,
All his belief is but an idle boaft.

23 There is no true believer can do lefs
Than mend his morals, and his lufts fupprefs;
Becaufe that Chrift to all believers gives
His holy Spirit, to amend their lives.

24 Be not deceiv'd, thou finner moft obfcene,
Where there is faith, there holy lives are feen:
For if thy faith is worthy to be known,
By it's good works let it be plainly fhown.

25 If in thy faith there does no life appear,
If it no grace, in word and work, does bear,
'Tis but the name of faith upon the whole——
A faith, that never can preferve thy foul!

Advice to avoid bad Company.

1 WHoever a religious life wou'd live,
Submiffive to the will of his dread Sire,
He firft of all moft earneftly muft ftrive
From all bad converfation to retire.

2 He muft no more with debauchees confort,
But quit them all without regret or pain;
As Mofes quitted the Egyptian court,
And Lot and Abraham the Chaldean plain.

3 As weeds are known to choke the rifing grain——
As vinegar the fweeteft milk will fpoil——
As pitch, if touch'd, is apt thy clothes to ftain——
So vicious converfe will thy morals foil.

4 Beware the ferpent's fting—or thou fhalt fmart—
And from the plague, left it fhou'd kill thee, run——
And if Salvation thou haft much at heart,
With equal care all wicked converfe fhun.

G

5 From

5 From Sodom, like another Patriarch, fly——
Hafte from the idle and the vile away——
All faunt'rers quit—preferve thy foul, and try
To leave the faithlefs folk without delay.

6 Whilft Mofes ftay'd amongft the' Egyptian race,
Whilft Abraham fojourn'd with the Syrian crew,
The Lord ne'er deign'd to manifeft his grace,
'Till they aloof from fuch vile men withdrew.

7 The fons of Satan, and their friendfhips, flee,
Soon as thou canft, if thou art truly wife:
For there can never any concord be,
Between the fons of hell, and of the fkies.

8 The converfation therefore of the wife,
The good, and blamelefs, eagerly purfue:
For they will teach thee how to mount the fkies,
To know thy God, and pay him rev'rence due.

9 Whilft Saul the fteps of Samuel purfue'd,
A faint he grew, who was a fiend before;
But when his vile acquaintance he renew'd,
The faint became a very fiend once more.

10 Follow a Prophet——he'll enlighten thee——
Follow a Rabbi——thou fhalt walk by rule——
Follow a Saint——and thou a Saint fhall be——
Follow a Fool——and thou'lt be ftill a Fool.

11 Upon thy knees without ceffation pray,
That God to thee his fecret paths wou'd fhow,
And turn thee from each crofs and dang'rous way,
Into the road, wherein he'd have thee go.

12 Until the Sire of Light fhall clear thine eye——
Until thy Saviour fhall thy foul renew——
The path of Life thou never canft efpy;
No more than blind-men can the fun-fhine view.

13 Take thou the' Almighty's lantern in thy hand,
That it may always light thee on the road:
None fhall attain unto the promis'd land,
Unlefs illumine'd by the Word of God.

14 Whate'er

14 Whate'er is by the Word enjoin'd thee, do;
    And from whatever it forbids, refrain,
    And it will clearly teach thee how to go,
    Where thou fhalt favour, life, and mercy gain.

15 Take heed, take fpecial heed I thee require,
    That thou doft not thy carnal will obey,
    Nor live a flave unto thy heart's defire;
    But as the Gofpel's light fhall point the way.

16 But, if thou art upon improvement bent,
    Doft grace, and virtue, and falvation chufe—
    Follow the way thy bleffed Saviour went,
    Nor the fafe track, by him mark'd out, e'er lofe:

17 At firft it is with difficulty paft,
    And by the carnal with reluctance trod;
    But 'twill be fmooth and eafy at the laft,
    And lead thee foon and fafely to thy God.

18 The road to ruin, at the firft, is plain,
    And by all trav'lers eafy to be found;
    But when the fartheft end of it they gain,
    There lies a gulph, moft hideous and profound!

19 When virtue's path thou for a while haft try'd,
    Do all thou canft to keep it ftill in fight,
    Nor from it ever dare to turn afide,
    'Till it has brought thee to the realms of light.

20 It nought avails thy journey to begin,
    If thou returneft to thy fins again;
    No one the promis'd Crown fhall ever win,
    Who does not faithful, unto death, remain.

21 Judas and † Saul their courfe in hafte begun,
    As Demas did, who chofe this prefent world;
    Yet, as they fail'd, before the race was run,
    They three were to th' infernal prifon hurl'd.

22 Follow thy Saviour, both in deed and word,
    And tread the path, which he himfelf once trode,
    Perform with zeal the mandates of the Lord,
    And never deviate from the facred road.

† King Saul.   G 2   The

The LAMENTATION of a Sinner.

1 O God of Mercy, deign to hear
    My plaint, and lend a gracious ear!
A finner, in a piteous cafe,
Implores thy pardon and thy grace.

2 Although, I fear I've anger'd thee,
My gracious Sire! to that degree,
That, ftung by confcience, to the fkies
I dare not lift my downcaft eyes:

3 But, like the Publican, I bow
My head, in penitence, full low,
And, though chief of the finful crew,
Moft humbly for thy favour fue—

4 And I prefume this fuit to make,
Not for my own, but for Chrift's fake,
Who fuffer'd, on the' accurfed tree,
Unutterable pain for me——

5 And if I can no pardon gain
By virtue of His woes and pain,
I muft to hell directly go,
That region of eternal woe!

6 E'en from my infancy I've been
The child of wrath, and plunge'd in fin;
And to thy law no heed I gave,
But liv'd to ev'ry vice a flave.

7 Thy name, O Lord, I oft blafpheme'd,
And oft the fcriptures madly blame'd,
I ne'er the glorious Gofpel prize'd,
But as an old wife's tale defpife'd.

8 By the moft precious Blood that ftream'd
From Chrift, whereby I was redeem'd,
By day and night I often fwore,
Regardlefs of the pains he bore.

9 Thy Sabbaths I profanely fpent
In riot and vain merriment,
Or, which is worfe, in drunkennefs,
And ev'ry blameable excefs.

10 When other folks, of all degrees,
Were night and morning on their knees---
I, woe is me! in idle play,
In fome by-corner, pafs'd the day.

11 Though fweet, as honey, is thy word
To ev'ry pious foul, O Lord!
Yet, to my tafte, 'twas bitt'rer far
Than naufeous draughts of wormwood are.

12 Lewdnefs and luft I follow'd long,
Like one of that polluted throng,
Which in Gomorrah liv'd of yore,
'Till I was even at death's door.

13 I drank my glafs, caroufe'd, and joke'd,
And all day long tobacco fmoke'd,
As if for that alone I liv'd;
For which I now am fadly griev'd.

14 My youth in vanity and pride,
And in a thoufand fins befide,
I totally contrive'd to fpend,
Regardlefs of my latter end——

15 And now that folemn fcene draws nigh,
Not one jot better yet am I,
Than (if I muft avow the truth)
I was e'en in the heat of youth.

16 I've therefore often wonder'd, how
Thou fo much lenity didft fhow,
And how her jaws the' earth did not ope,
To fwallow me, like Dathan, up.

17 There's fcarce a fingle act of wrong,
Or crime, the lift of crimes among,
Which I, alas! did not plunge in,
Immers'd up to the very chin.

G 3

18 Had ſt.

18 Hadſt thou not been by nature kind,
   And to compaſſion much inclin'd,
   To Hell I had e'er this been thrown,
   There in fierce flames to make my moan.

19 O Lord, I frankly own to thee,
   That I have long deſerve'd to be
   Deprive'd quite of the vital air :
   So num'rous my tranſgreſſions are !

20 And waſt thou not, O God moſt high !
   So wond'rous good and gracious, I
   Had thought my load too great to bear,
   And been, like Cain, urge'd to deſpair.

21 Yet hence I comfort do receive,
   When nothing elſe can comfort give,
   That greater is thy mercy, far,
   Than all my foul offences are.

22 For though they be in number more
   Than are the ſands upon the ſhore,
   Yet is thy mercy much more wide,
   Than is the earth-ſurrounding tide.

23 I, therefore, truſt that where ſin reign'd,
   And over me a conqueſt gain'd,
   E'en there thy free celeſtial grace,
   Shall conquer all that's in me baſe.

24 O God, thou haſt moſt gracious been,
   And pardon'd many a heinous ſin ;
   Then be not more ſevere to me,
   Though ſinful to the laſt degree !

25 For when the Ninevites erſt quitted
   The countleſs ſins they had committed,
   Although their vices were ſo great,
   Yet they with grace became replete.

26 Although Manaſſes was of yore
   So vile—his like was not before ——
   Yet he thy gracious pardon gain'd,
   When from his vices he refrain'd.

27 The

27 The royal prophet David too,
Although his sins were not a few,
Yet when he humbly cry'd to thee,
Was, by thy grace, from sin set free.

28 And likewise Mary Magdalene,
Though long a most notorious quean,
Was, for the copious tears she shed,
By thy all-gracious favour free'd.

29 And the young prodigal of old,
(When he had all his substance sold)
Thro' grace obtain'd, thy will obey'd ;
Tho' he so long the fool had play'd.

30 I therefore hopes have entertain'd,
Though I have thy displeasure gain'd,
That I thy favour shall again,
For my Redeemer's sake, obtain.

31 With earnest, mournful, piteous cries,
With bleeding heart and streaming eyes,
For Jesus' sake, both night and day,
I humbly for forgiveness pray.

32 Remember, Lord! and bear in mind,
That Jesus, my Redeemer kind,
His heart's blood offer'd up for me,
As an atonement unto thee.

33 Remember too, that then He bore
Fierce pains for me, and anguish sore,
Nay, death, and all the pangs severe,
Which I myself deserv'd to bear.

34 Then, for His passion's sake, forgive,
And to thy mercy me receive——
And for his Sweat and Suff'ring's sake,
No other satisfaction take.

35 But freely now, whilst yet I live,
Forgive my sins, O God! forgive——
And head and heels, O plunge me, o'er,
In Christ's all-cleansing precious gore !

G 4

36 Although

36 Although my fins are deeply grain'd,
 As if they were with fcarlet ftain'd,
 One drop of that, thofe ftains will clear,
 And make them white as lawn appear.

37 I therefore place my confidence
 In Chrift's blood and benevolence ;
 In hopes that I, without annoy,
 May be receiv'd to endlefs joy—

38 And led to Chrift in paradife,
 Above the earth and nether fkies,
 To have my fhare of all the good,
 Which He has purchafe'd with His blood—

39 Into which ever-blifsful place,
 May God, of his abundant grace,
 Conduct us all : there to adore
 Him, for His mercy, evermore!

Godly Exhortations to a CHILD.

1 MY deareft child, to me draw near,
 Unto my precepts lend an ear,
 And, all thy life, to them attend,
 If thou wou'dft unto God afcend.

2 Thy God, whilft thou haft being, fear,
 Ever his aweful name revere,
 With all thy heart obey his will,
 His gofpel hear, his laws fulfil.

3 Still let the word of God prefide,
 Both as thy councillor and guide,
 Let it thy conduct wholly fway,
 Whatever thou doft do, or fay.

4 Be it a lamp—thy path to light—
 Thy tutor—to direct thee right,
 To take thee from all ill away,
 And lead thee to the fource of day.

5 Do nothing, be it small, or great,
   According to thy own conceit:
   For sin thy nature has deprave'd,
   'Till thou, thro' grace, again art save'd.

6 Strive then thy wayward will to rein,
   Since virtue is to it a pain,
   And, 'till by God's word, thou'rt set right,
   It still in evil takes delight.

7 Of sin, however small, take heed;
   Beneath her robe a sting is hid:
   Short pleasures bring a long regret,
   Sin owes to Death a certain debt.

8 If Adam did endure so much,
   Who only did one apple touch:
   What punishment must they sustain,
   Who all their lives in sin remain?

9 If thou, to err, dost once begin,
   Beware, lest thou again shou'dst sin:
   No price for the least sin is known,
   Besides the Blood of Christ alone.

10 Once free from sin, pollution shun,
   Nor dog-like, to thy vomit run,
   Or like to hogs, which tho' wash'd clean,
   To their lov'd mire return agen.

11 If Moses, from the promis'd land,
   Was for a single sin restrain'd;
   They sure, who've sinn'd a thousand times,
   Must forfeit heaven for their crimes.

12 Worse than a serpent, pride detest;
   Who soars too high, shall be deprest:
   Disgrace attends the haughty stride,
   And sudden slips the foot of pride.

13 If for his pride th' archangel fell
   From Heaven, to the' abyss of Hell;
   Where shall we, dust and dirt, be tost,
   If we our self-importance boast?

14 Never

14 Never defile thy Neighbour's bed,
　　To such crimes, fools alone are led :
　　For he that treads on glowing coals,
　　Must needs expect to burn his soles.

15 If Pharaoh, for that sin did smart,
　　Who only lusted in his heart
　　For Abraham's wife—what grievous pain
　　Must they, who've done the deed, sustain ?

16 Swear not by God's tremendous name,
　　All causeless oaths from Satan came :
　　The curse of God, like smoke, will fill
　　The house, wherein men God revile.

17 If king Senacherib was slain,
　　Because he took God's name in vain :
　　How can the Christian 'scape from ill,
　　Who shall Christ, and his blood revile ?

18 Observe with awe, the Seventh day,
　　Attend the church--hear, watch and pray--
　　Thy God invoke—thy pot forsake---
　　Nor the fiend's feast, the Sabbath make.

19 For if our God the man did slay,
　　Who gather'd wood upon that day,
　　Their bones shall He not rather break,
　　Who spend it worse than all the week ?

20 No portion of thy tithes detain,
　　Nor from thy offerings refrain ;
　　Thou robbest an avenging God,
　　If thou committest any fraud.

21 Who robs his God, shall feel his curse ;
　　For he, who tithes by fraud or force
　　With-holds, does heaven's blessings stop,
　　And hinders the' earth to yield it's crop.

22 Think drunkenness thy greatest foe ;
　　No drunkard shall to Heaven go :
　　Hell opes her jaws, and yawns amain,
　　The bloated brute to entertain,

23 If Efau was reproach'd of old,
   Who for a mefs his birthright fold:
   What keen reproaches fhall he hear,
   Who fells his foul, and heave'n, for beer?

24 Nor churl, nor ufurer, e'er be;
   Churls are the ftewards of the free:
   What fathers hoard thro' avarice,
   Their lavifh heirs fpend in a trice.

25 Sooner a camel, to and fro,
   May through a fmall-eye'd needle go,
   Than mifers cruel, and unkind,
   To heaven can an entrance find.

26 To grind the poor, be thou afraid;
   Chrift is a juftice can't be fway'd:
   To rob them, whofoever tries,
   Flies in his Saviour's face and eyes.

27 Ahab, becaufe (altho' in vain)
   He Naboth's vineyard fought to gain,
   Soon found his error to his coft,
   His children flain, his kingdom loft!

28 If Dives fell to Satan's pow'r,
   Who his own goods deny'd the poor;
   Where fhall the wealthy churls be thrown
   Who ftrip the poor, of all they own?

29 Take heed of theft, of fraud take heed;
   No real gains can thence proceed:
   Where-e'er they are, there's always lofs,
   The curfe of God, and ev'ry crofs.

30 If none of Achan's race were left,
   Who only hid a trivial theft;
   W'o'nt God his wrath on them pour down,
   Who rob the poor, of all they own?

31 Keep not (or thou fhalt fuffer for't)
   Unequal weights, or meafures fhort:
   For odious, in the' Almighty's fight,
   Is the falfe fcale, and fcanty weight.

32 Whate'ei

32 Whate'er a man thro' fraud obtains,
   Or by an unjuſt balance gains,
   Into a ragged bag is place'd,
   And, through the bottom, runs to waſte.

33 Touch not, whate'er thou doſt, a bribe;
   'Twill eat thee up, with all thy tribe,
   And will not leave a mite, among
   Thy race, that did to thee belong.

34 The leproſy Gehazi caught,
   Amongſt the clothes he ſo much ſought:
   So bribes will, 'tis as plain a caſe!
   Undo a man, and all his race.

35 Beware of lying, whilſt on earth;
   The ſerpent gave to lying birth:
   The truth, and nought but truth, ſtill tell;
   Lies owe their origin to hell!

36 If Ananias quickly die'd,
   Becauſe he to the Spirit lie'd,
   And, with his wife, met a ſwift fate:
   Still, whilſt we live, let's lying hate.

37 For his defeĉts, no one miſcall
   (God is the Maker of us all!)
   Or fool, or blind, or hunch'd, or lame:
   Who man reviles, reviles God's name.

38 If Chriſt will doom him to hell's pool,
   Who only calls his brother, fool:
   The man, who calls his parents names,
   Muſt ſure be doom'd to fiercer flames!

39 Wou'dſt thou the Son of God be ſtile'd?
   Ne'er ill for ill return, my child!
   Aid, and aſſiſt thy greateſt foe,
   Nor harm to any mortal do.

40 For, pray, what diff'rence canſt thou ſhew,
   Betwixt the Chriſtian, and the Jew,
   If 'tis allow'd thee to requite
   Evil for evil, ſpite for ſpite?

41 Ne

41 No mifchief do, in hopes to find
   Thy Judge compaffionate and kind;
   Or thou no favour fhalt obtain,
   But be confign'd to endlefs pain.

42 If in the prefence of the Lord,
   We muft account for each vain word:
   How fhall we anfwer, O my foul!
   For each bad deed, and bargain foul?

43 None of the goodly gifts abufe,
   Which God has given to thy ufe,
   The day will come, when thou muft give
   Account, for all thou didft receive.

44 If Chrift caft him to gloom profound,
   Who hid his talent under ground:
   Where fhall each fimple fot be fent,
   Who principal, and all, has fpent?

45 Be ftill prepare'd—to-day!—to-night!—
   Thy lamp well fill'd—thy garments white—
   Come to thy Judge in trim array;
   To-morrow next may be the day!

46 If Chrift, the gate fo quickly barr'd
   'Gainft thofe, who were almoft prepar'd;
   How can they hope for entrance there,
   Who ne'er, fince they were born, took care?

47 Lay ev'ry idle fport afide,
   And think what may thy foul betide:
   We all from hence in hafte muft go——
   Or to the realms of blifs, or woe.

48 If no one fhall to heaven go,
   Who ftrives not, all he can, to do:
   How fhall the man, who wou'd go there,
   Whilft he's afleep, or playing—fare?

49 None, e'er they've run, the prize obtain---
   None, e'er they've ferv'd, their wages gain--
   None, heav'n can earn, e'er they fulfil,
   Firft here on earth, their Maker's will!

50 Chrift

50 Chriſt, will on none the crown beſtow,
Who has not fought, and foil'd his foe;
Nor will He ever give to any,
Who have not labour'd here, a penny.

51 It nought avails to cry, Lord! Lord!
Heave'n is not got by one vague word:
But men muſt like true Chriſtians live,
E'er they to Heaven can arrive.

52 I therefore, ev'ry ſoul adviſe,
That wou'd aſcend the diſtant ſkies,
To live a life that's good and pure,
His own ſalvation to ſecure!

53 Shou'd any ask, Who wrote this ſong?
Say, 'Twas a ſwain, who much did long
(By ſuch advice as this) to keep
From Hell's abyſs his heedleſs ſheep.

ADVICE to a YOUTH.

1 DEAR child! thy letter came to me,
Replete with ſenſe and piety,
Which begs that my Advice I'd give,
How thou may'ſt as a Chriſtian live.

2 It is a ſign of grace to find
A lad ſo young, ſo well inclin'd
To know God's word——to learn the ſame——
The fleſh, and all it's luſts to tame.

3 Theſe good deſires to gratify,
Take this ſincere Advice from me,
And let it all thy ſteps attend
From childhood to thy latter end.

4 Remember, in the bloom of youth,
To ſerve the Lord thy God in Truth,
And thy Creator to adore,
E'er age ſhall have impair'd thy pow'r.

5 Begin

5 Begin, e'er thou doft older grow,
 Thy Saviour and thy God to know,
 His Statutes keep, his Word defire;
 So fhall thy age Refpect acquire.

6 Thy veffel, whilft it yet is new,
 In the pure wine of faith imbue:
 So fhall a fweet perfume attend
 Thy virtuous life unto it's end.

7 Deep in thy youthful bofom place
 The feeds of ev'ry Chriftian grace;
 Left the fiend's tares therein fhou'd breed,
 As 'twas not fown with virtue's feed.

8 Endeavour foon a bloom to fhow;
 As forward almonds early blow:
 The tree, that flow'rs not in the fpring,
 Will never fruit in autumn bring.

9 God does from all his fons demand
 The earlieft produce of the land,
 But, with abhorrence and diftafte,
 Rejects the fecond, and the laft.

10 To thy Creator therefore ftrive
 The firft-fruits of thy ftrength to give,
 And ne'er thy time abfurdly fpend
 To pleafure the infernal fiend.

11 Give not to him the wine's firft run,
 The dregs to Chrift, when that is done,
 Nor with thy ftrength the tempter pleafe,
 Whilft nought remains for God, but lees.

12 Curs'd is the fool, that gives the foe
 The prime of all his life below,
 And his Redeemer fain wou'd pleafe
 With feeble age, and wan difeafe.

13 Beware of fin, whilft yet a child;
 Whoe'er admits it, is defil'd,
 'Twill to a fecond nature go,
 And worfe and worfe thou'lt daily grow.

14 If thou art use'd, whilst young, to vice,
And early dost thy God despise;
When old, to leave it, will be quite
As hard, as 'tis to make black, white.

15 Give then, whilst young, thy very soul
And body too, without controul,
To serve thy Maker, and to fight
Against the foe with all thy might.

16 Like Daniel, whilst thou yet art young,
Avoid all liquors that are strong:
To dainty food be not inclin'd,
But fix on God alone thy mind.

17 Like Samuel learn, whilst but a boy,
To stand before thy God with joy,
And list to what thy gracious Lord
Shall tell thee in his written word.

18 Like young Josiah tread aright,
Tho' thou shou'dst be no more than ‡ eight,
Unto the law, attention give,
Fear God, and as his servant, live.

19 Like Timothy, the scriptures learn,
E'en from thy youth, and thou'lt discern
That they will make thee wondrous wise,
And to the height of virtue rise.

20 Like Christ, to church each Sabbath go
With them, to whom thou life dost owe,
And, when as yet scarce twelve years old,
Debates with learned Doctors hold.

21 Hear thou the law---the Gospel hear——
And well in mind both of them bear——
Then strive to live exceeding close
Unto the rules, prescrib'd by those.

22 Thou dost in a drear gloom reside;
Take then God's Word thy feet to guide:
Without the Gospel's Light none yet
Did ever into heaven get.

‡ Eight Years old.

23 Though

23 Though God above thou canſt not ſee,
Yet in his Word he talks with thee,
And ſhews thee, thence, his ſacred will,
Which he enjoins thee to fulfil.

24 Conſult the ſacred page, and ſee,
What is therein commanded thee,
And do, whate'er God wou'd have done;
What he forbids thee, let alone.

25 Take heed, by thee, that e'en the leaſt
Of God's commands be not tranſgreſs'd:
Death for the leaſt offence is due,
God's curſe, and endleſs woe enſue.

26 For ev'ry crime by mortals done,
Our righteous Judge inſiſts upon
The death of him, who did the deed——
Or Chriſt muſt ſuffer in his ſtead.

27 Where thou a thouſand times haſt ſwerv'd
From God, and death as oft deſerv'd——
Repent as oft, and ſin no more,
And pardon from thy God implore.

28 Confeſs thy ſins, both great and ſmall——
Unto thy God confeſs them all——
And thy paſt vanities bemoan,
And God will pardon ev'ry one.

29 Of all thy former ſins repent,
And of thy youth in error ſpent:
If tears thou doſt not for them ſhed,
They'll pull God's judgement on thy head.

30 Ephraim, 'till of his ſins aſhame'd,   *Jer.*xxxi. 19, 2c.
And David, 'till he ſore exclaim'd
Againſt them, cou'd no pardon gain:
Neither ſhalt thou, 'till then, obtain.

31 Until to-morrow ne'er delay,
Leſt Death ſhou'd drag thee hence away
This night, aſleep, unto thy doom,
When there's for penitence no room.

H   32 Myriads

32 Myriads of heedlefs ftriplings lie
In hell, who were refolve'd to try
Repentance, when old age once came,
But ne'er found leifure to reclaim.

33 Now, of thy fins repent with forrow,
We know not who may live to-morrow:
A gift, when offer'd, don't difdain,
Left thou fhou'dft ne'er be afk'd again:

34 And as thou doft tranfgrefs each day,
Each evening for remiffion pray:
Left, making water very faft,
The unpump'd fhip fhou'd fink at laft.

35 When once thou'rt from pollution clean,
Let not thy feet be foul'd agen,
Nor to the mire run with the hog,
Nor to his vomit with the dog:

36 But ftrive a different life to lead,
And in the paths of virtue tread,
And wifely aim thy fpan to fpend
In holy fear, unto it's end.

37 Be it thy tafk, both night and day,
Upon thy knees, to God to pray ;
Nor let one fun thy head pafs o'er,
Wherein thou doft not God adore :

38 And thy devotion to affift,
Whereby thou may'ft the flefh refift,
The law of God take, for thy guide
His holy Spirit, for thy aid.

39 The Word of God is mighty ftrong,
To bring thofe back, that have gone wrong,
And fenfe and wifdom to impart
Unto the young and fimple heart.

40 Whate'er the law enjoins thee, do——
Whate'er advice it gives, purfue :——
For if thou fhalt the law fulfil,
Thou fhalt furpafs thy Teacher's fkill.

41 Hold

41 Hold faft, with all thy force, in it,
And to it's yoke thy neck fubmit——
'Twill bring thee honour, grace, regard——
"In keeping it there's great reward."

42 If 'tis thy cuftom, in thy prime,
To pafs, in pious fort, thy time,
'Twill be thy pleafure and thy joy,
Thy days thus ever to employ.

43 Honour thy father's God, and he
In kind return will honour thee:
But if thou fhou'dft his law neglect,
He with contempt will thee reject.

44 Refpect him in thy younger years,
And he'll refpect thy hoary hairs,
And bid the birds thy victuals bear,
E'er thou fhou'dft want them, thro' the air.

45 Thou never to this world was fent,
Thy carnal fenfes to content;
But to adore the Lord moft high,
As angels do above the fky.

46 When from thy bed thou firft doft rife
Remember him, who rules the fkies,
Nor from thy chamber ftir abroad
'Till thou haft firft adore'd thy God.

47 However great thy tafk may be,
Thy bufinefs, or neceffity,
To neither of them all attend,
E'er thou haft made thy God thy friend.

48 No peace, no comfort, no fuccefs,
Shall e'er be there, nor happinefs,
Where various toils and cares abound,
But no regard for God is found.

49 Though Daniel highly was employ'd,
And a great monarch's fmiles enjoy'd,
Yet in his clofet, thrice a day,
He fell upon his knees to pray.

H 2

50 When

50 When to thy bufinefs thou doft fall,
    Let it be great, let it be fmall,
    Entreat of God thy work to blefs,
    And crown thy labours with fuccefs.

51 As God, of old, his bleffings fhed
    On youthful Jofeph's favour'd head;
    So will he profper thee, and thine,
    If thou'lt implore his aid divine.

52 Whate'er thou doft, or good or ill,
    Where-e'er thou art, He fees thee ftill;
    God ev'ry act of thine doft 'fpy:
    Sin not before his piercing eye!

53 To others, let each good be done,
    Which thou wou'dft to thyfelf have fhown
    To others, no worfe meafure ufe,
    Than thou thyfelf from them wou'dft chufe.

54 Do nothing, howfoever move'd,
    That is not by thy God approve'd:
    Do nought, for which thou fhame muft fear,
    When forc'd in judgement to appear.

55 No God, befides the true God, own,
    Serve him with care, and him alone,
    Invoke him, magnify him ftill,
    And he'll protect thee from each ill.

56 Ne'er take thy Maker's name in vain,
    But from that fatal fin refrain:
    For he fhall ne'er be guiltlefs thought,
    Who is addicted to that fault.

57 In holinefs each Sabbath fpend,
    From the beginning to the end,
    And do not the leaft part allow
    Of the Lord's day, to ferve the foe.

58 Be, to thy parents, honour paid,
    Give them refpect, and ev'ry aid;
    So fhall thy days be here increas'd,
    And thou be in thy children blefs'd.

59 Take

59 Take heed, left thou fhou'dft difrefpect,
   Or caft them down—for all expect,
   To fee the daughter, or the fon,
   That difobeys their will, undone.

60 Of foul adultery, beware————
   To keep thy veffel pure, take care————
   And let not (for the wealth of Rome)
   Chrift's members a vile whore's become.

61 Be to thy lawful confort true,
   With no one elfe have ought to do,
   Nor of the Spirit's temple dare
   To make the fiend's unhallow'd lair.

62 For heaven's fake, avoid excefs,
   And the vile fin of drunkennefs,
   Which to a fiend does man tranfmute,
   Or worfe, much worfe, than any brute.

63 Each fellow-creature ftill, no lefs
   Than thy ownfelf, love and carefs,
   And let no harm by thee be done
   In thought, word, deed, to any one.

64 To all the world be ftrictly juft,
   And be fincere in all thou doft:
   For no man's fake be thou fo mad
   To do the thing which God forbad.

65 Still by the laws directions go,
   In ev'ry thing thou haft to do:
   No work can ever perfect be,
   That does not with the law agree.

66 Reflect, my dear, thou art not fure
   Thy life fhall, through this day, endure:
   As guiltlefs let it then be paft,
   As if it were to be thy laft.

1 ALL, who wou'd eafe and happinefs obtain,
    And wifh in health and wealth and peace to live,
Muft, whilft they in this vale of tears remain,
To ferve their God with all their fpirit ftrive.

2 Whoe'er befides wou'd covet to efcape
Loffes, calamity, and urgent woe,
Danger, difeafe, adverfity, mifhap;
Let them to ferve their God devoutly go.

3 Each man alive fhou'd his Creator ferve———
And ferve him faithfully—with all his heart;
From his commandments he fhou'd never fwerve,
Nor ever from his facred will depart.

4 Of all the works we do—to ferve the Lord,
Is the moft needful, and by much the beft———
It always does the fureft gains afford,
And brings in greater int'reft than the reft.

5 That's the fole work, which was ordain'd for men,
E'er God firft form'd them in their mother's womb--
That is the work, they muft account for, when
They ftand before him on the day of doom.

6 To hear the word—to keep the law aright———
The Gofpel-doctrine fully to believe———
To live according to it's glorious light———
Is all the fervice God wou'd fain receive.

7 To do, whatever is by God enjoin'd———
Whatever he forbids thee, to efchew———
His Word to ftudy with an humble mind———
Is the true fervice God wou'd have thee do.

8 Two forts of fervices the Lord demands
From ev'ry one, that bears a Chriftian name:
A right belief he claims at all their hands———
With morals free from all offence and blame.

9 With

9 With true devotion, we muſt ſerve the Lord,
 Whether in public to his courts we come———
 Or whether he be privately ador'd
 By us, in a domeſtic way, at home.

10 When in the temple openly we pray,
 We muſt with reverence perform our parts,
 And join our brethren, on each ſabbath day,
 With notes united, and united hearts :

11 But when at other times, throughout the week,
 You pray with your own family at home,
 Or hear his Word, or call upon him, ſeek
 Some ſequeſt'red retreat, or private room.

12 God with a moral mind muſt be ador'd,
 And with a truly Chriſtian awe obey'd :
 Where'er you are, you ſtill muſt ſerve the Lord;
 Whilſt life yet laſts, this homage muſt be paid.

13 With wary circumſpection we muſt tread,
 According as his holy law directs———
 Not as our own imaginations lead;
 If we wou'd worſhip God, as he expects.

14 Our lives in virtuous actions we muſt ſpend,
 And do whate'er is pleaſing in his ſight,
 E'er we unto the dreary grave deſcend;
 If we wou'd ſerve our heavenly Sire aright.

15 Who ſerves not God with all the zeal he can,
 And with a faith, conſiſtent with his word———
 Let him e'en do his beſt—yet ſtill that man
 Can never by his actions pleaſe the Lord.

16 God from each Chriſtian all his heart expects,
 And what demeanour he wou'd have, directs :
 He muſt be ſerve'd with all the ſoul and mind,
 And with the ſtrength of all his limbs combin'd.

17 Make an oblation of thyſelf entire
 To God—thy body, as a victim meet———
 Then offer up thy ſoul unto thy Sire,
 To make the ſacrifice ſtill more complete.

       18 Chriſt

18 Chriſt purchaſe'd (when he hung upon the tree)
   Both ſoul and body with his precious gore;
   And that's the reaſon he expects, that we
   With both united ſhou'd his name adore.

19 Our gracious Father, and Almighty Lord,
   No partial, half-face'd, worſhip will allow;
   But muſt by all his ſervants be ador'd
   With all their pow'rs of mind, and body too.

20 The Sire of mercy is a Spirit bleſs'd,
   Therefore with ſpirit and with mind ſincere,
   And inward truth, he ſtill muſt be addreſs'd,
   And with a heart from all pollution clear.

21 In vain, are Pater-noſters hurry'd o'er——
   In vain, the outward man his prayers ſays——
   In vain, the lips their well-form'd accents pour,
   Unleſs the inward heart in ſpirit prays.

22 In any one, whom we a Chriſtian call,
   There's not (without, within,) a ſingle part,
   But God expects, he ſhou'd devote it all
   Unto his ſervice—e'en his very heart !

23 Although the Devil ſometimes is content
   To take a portion of the heart or ſoul;
   Yet Chriſt, our Saviour, never will conſent
   To take a part, unleſs he has the whole.

24 Devote thy ſoul, his holy name to bleſs,
   Let it exult, and joy in him alone——
   Devote thy ſpirit, freely to confeſs,
   What mighty things he for thy ſake has done.

25 Set thy affections on the things above,
   And let thy thoughts ſtill in thoſe realms abide,
   Where nought terreſtrial can divert thy love,
   And thou muſt to eternity reſide.

26 Devote thy body and it's members all
   To thy Creator's ſervice, and adore
   With all united, whether great or ſmall,
   And with due rites the everlaſting pow'r.

27 Devote

27 Devote thy heart, to worſhip and to love
  The Lord---let it invariably adhere
  Unto the great and glorious God above
  With perfect truſt, and confidence ſincere.

28 Devote thy tongue, to praiſe his holy name
  With all it's might, either by night or day,
  And his unbounded goodneſs to proclaim:
  In ev'ry place, whereto thou goeſt, pray.

29 Devote thine eyes to look upon him ſtill—
  Let them, unweary'd, on the Lord attend,
  And lift them up unto the ſacred hill,
  Whence all thy comfort, all thy joys deſcend.

30 Devote with reverence thy ready ear,
  His word, his will, and his commands to take—
  And with attention unremitted hear
  The promiſes, the ſacred pages make.

31 Devote thy hands, with commendable zeal,
  To ev'ry work that's excellent and good—
  And to thy needy neighbours freely deal
  A ſhare, of what thy God on thee beſtow'd.

32 Devote thy knees, their Maker to adore,
  And with unfeign'd reſpect before him bend—
  Aſcribing, when thou doſt his aid implore,
  To him all might, and glory without end.

33 Devote thy feet, his bleſſed paths to trace,
  And walk with wary ſteps in his wiſe law;
  Enter with reverence his holy place,
  And come unto his courts with pious awe.

34 Devote thy ſoul—devote thy utmoſt might------
  Devote thy body, and thy heart devote--------
  And all that is within thee, day and night,
  To praiſe the Deity with cheerful note.

35 Honour and glory, never-failing wealth,
  Peace, and proſperity of ev'ry kind,
  Juſt exaltation, length of days, and health,
  All men, who ſerve their God aright, ſhall find.

36 It

36 If thou, to worſhip God, ſhall never ceaſe,
   Come, what will come, and go, where thou wilt go,
   Yet ſhalt thou live in plenty, and in peace,
   In ſpite of all that's done by ev'ry foe.

37 Whate'er thou doſt, in country, or in town,
   The Lord himſelf will all thy labours bleſs,
   And, if thou payeſt him due homage, crown
   All thou haſt on earth with great ſucceſs.

38 Full ſhall thy houſe be—fertile ev'ry field——
   Grief and misfortune thou ſhalt never know——
   And much increaſe thy flocks and vines ſhall yield;
   If thou to God ſhalt due ſubmiſſion ſhow.

39 God gave thee Reaſon, and with wond'rous pow'r
   In his own likeneſs form'd with plaſtic hand:
   Thou'rt therefore bound his wiſdom to adore,
   Who ſo ſurprizingly thy members plann'd!

40 Chriſt bought thee with his blood from Satan's pow'r,
   It was not gold, which thy ſalvation wrought:
   Thou therefore muſt with zeal the Lord adore,
   Becauſe thou at ſo great a price wert bought.

41 God ſatisfy'd thy craving ſoul with bread,
   From thy formation to the preſent hour:
   Thou'rt therefore bound, becauſe thou thus wert fed,
   Thy benefactor ever to adore.

42 Thou, at the Font, didſt promiſe to obey,
   And ſerve with readineſs and truth, the Lord:
   If then thou from the Chriſtian faith ſhou'dſt ſtray,
   Thou'rt perjur'd, having broke thy plighted word.

43 God, ev'ry creature in the earth and ſeas
   Created for thy uſe—thou'rt therefore bound
   To worſhip him upon thy bended knees,
   From whom ſo many favours thou haſt found.

44 God cauſe'd the viſible creation here
   A prompt obedience unto man to ſhow;
   That man, in turn, as ready might appear
   To worſhip God, whilſt he reſides below.

45 He

45 He, that forgets to pay this bounden debt,
   In whatever ftation he is place'd below,
   Does the moft neceffary work forget,
   Which God appointed him, on earth, to do.

46 Heav'n, water, earth, and the angelic train,
   Birds, fifhes, beafts of ev'ry kind, agree,
   With ev'ry reptile crawling on the plain,
   To praife their Maker—each in it's degree.

47 Among the creatures, whether tame or wild,
   Gentle or ravenous, there is not one,
   That does not praife to it's Creator yield,
   Mankind excepted, and the fiend alone.

48 It is a fhame—it is a foul reproach,
   To fee each creature, howfoe'er defpife'd,
   With pure fincerity it's God approach,
   Whilft He's by man himfelf fo little prize'd !

49 O how fhall man lift up his guilty head,
   When Chrift declares—" I never worfe was ferv'd
   By any, than by man, for whom I fhed
   My precious blood, and by my death preferv'd !"

50 The obligation of each Chriftian's more,
   And ftronger is by far, on him, the tie,
   With proper faith his Maker to adore,
   Than on ought elfe God form'd beneath the fky.

51 Unto the gloomy realms of endlefs woe,
   None but the very worft of human-kind
   Shall ever with the wily tempter go,
   Who ferv'd not God with an obedient mind.

52 Left thou, with Satan in the realms beneath,
   Shou'dft broil in fulphur, and in quenchlefs flame,
   Negleft not, 'till the fearful hour of death,
   To ferve thy God, and glorify his name.

53 Enoch, becaufe he truly ferv'd the Lord,
   Never defcended to the pit beneath——
   But, in the flefh, to joys celeftial foar'd,
   Before he faw the dreary form of Death.

54 Noah

54 Noah, the' advantage of religion found,
　　When, in the ark, he and his houſe were kept
　　From danger ſafe—whilſt all the world was drown'd,
　　And by the all-deſtroying deluge ſwept.

55 Abraham, with honour and with wealth was bleſs'd--
　　The favour of his God——and with a ſon——
　　And all the lands the Canaanites poſſeſs'd————
　　Becauſe he ſerv'd the Lord, and him alone.

56 Iſaac, becauſe he worſhipp'd God of old,
　　Each eve'ning, as he muſe'd along the field,
　　Was bleſs'd with corn, above an hundred fold :
　　Such vaſt return did his devotion yeild !

57 Joſeph, becauſe the Deity he prais'd,
　　And wou'd not an adulte'rous wife embrace,
　　Was from a dark and diſmal dungeon rais'd,
　　And made chief ruler over Egypt's race.

58 Joſhua too, that chieftain bold and great !
　　Becauſe he cleav'd unto the Lord his God,
　　Did ev'ry army, he e'er fought with, beat————
　　And ev'ry land ſubdue, whereon he trod.

59 Of old, Elijah by the ravens care
　　Was in the deſert wond'rouſly preſerv'd—
　　Then in a fie'ry chariot through the air
　　To heaven rap't——becauſe his God he ſerv'd.

60 The three young captives, by their gracious Sire,
　　Were from the glowing furnace ſave'd of yore,
　　And walk'd unhurt, amidſt the raging fire——
　　Becauſe their God they in remembrance bore.

61 Daniel, who thrice a day his Maker ſerv'd,
　　Retiring to his room God's name to bleſs,
　　Was from the lions' den unharm'd preſerv'd,
　　And wonderfully ſave'd, in his diſtreſs.

62 Who, to the only God, due homage paid,
　　That did not retribution full receive ?
　　Who e'er his glory and his pow'r diſplay'd,
　　To whom he did not wealth and honour give ?

63 No

63 No one his temple door e'er enter'd yet,
   To whom fit fatisfaction was not made;
   No prieft, the fire e'er on his altar li't,'
   That was not for the fervice amply paid.

64 No one a cup of water e'er did give
   Unto the poor, for his Redeemer's fake,
   Who fhalt not for't an hundred-fold receive,
   And of the glories of his reign partake.

65 Chrift is the beft of Mafters, to obey,
   And therefore fhou'd the greateft reve'rence claim—
   Chrift does the moft, and fureft wages pay
   To all that faithfully invoke his name.

66 He is a Mafter, full of grace and might——
   A Mafter, glorious, and immenfely great——
   A mafter, that with mitres can requite
   And fceptres, all that on his altars wait !——

67 A Mafter, by whofe help they fhall be place'd
   On thrones above—where peace and joys abound----
   Where they fhall be with endlefs glories grace'd,
   And with felicity eternal crown'd !———

68 A Mafter, that will to each fervant give
   A glorious kingdom, and a golden crown,
   With fuch great things as heart can ne'er conceive,
   And fuch as never, here below, were known.

69 Who wou'd not, then, fo kind a Lord regard,
   And fall, upon his knees before him, down;
   That gives each vot'ry fuch a vaft reward,
   So rich a kingdom, and fo bright a crown !

70 Who wou'd not both the flefh and world defpife ?
   Who wou'd not Satan and his arts oppofe,
   That does reflect, how vaftly great the prize,
   Which God to all his fervants does propofe ?

71 Although no fervant, for his labour done,
   In ftrictnefs, ever yet, reward deferv'd,
   Yet God has promis'd—of his grace alone——
   A throne to each that has fincerely ferv'd.

72 A

72 A flave to Satan, and a flave to fin,
 A flave to death, and to the dreary grave,
 Is ev'ry foul, that has in fervice been,
 If he be not unto the Lord a flave.

73 When death fhall come, that irritated pow'r!
 To fummon ev'ry fervant to the grave————
 Which will fare beft, in that tremendous hour,
 The flave unto the flefh, or Jefus' flave?

74 When all the world, and all it's wealthy ftore,
 Shall in confuming flames pafs quite away————
 Which will fare beft, in that all dreaded hour,
 Who to the world, or Chrift, their homage pay?

75 When all God's Children fhall the fkies afcend,
 And all the flaves of fin be thruft below;
 What bitternefs of foul muft thofe attend,
 Who to their Lord did no obedience fhow?

76 Better a fingle hour entirely lent
 Unto the fervice of our bleffed Lord,
 Than a whole age in this world's fervice fpent,
 Which does no profit, or return afford.

77 In this world's fervice, we can nothing fave,
 But trouble, forrow, difcontent, and fhame————
 And muft through life be cheated to the grave,
 Leaving it naked, as we to it came.

78 How much foe'er we ftrive, the flefh to pleafe,
 We fhall at laft receive no greater gains
 From carnal pleafures, indolence, and eafe,
 Than a fhort life, and everlafting pains.

79 Whenever we have any fin obey'd,
 Though we fhou'd ferve it to our lateft breath;
 No other wages fhall to us be paid,
 For our long flavery, but fhame and death.

80 By ferving Satan, thou canft get no land,
 Though he might kingdoms, to feduce thee, fhow;
 For he has not a foot at his command,
 Befides the bottomlefs abyfs of woe:

81 But from Chrift's fervice, we fhall furely gain
   A glorious kingdom for our place of reft———
   Where, through his favour, we fhall ever reign
   In endlefs joys and honour, with the bleft.

82 Then let our ardor, whilft we live, appear,
   And let us cheerfully, to ferve him, go:
   For He's the very beft of Mafters here,
   And that's the very beft of works below———

83 And let us ftrive to fight with ev'ry foe,
   That fights with us, and ftops us whilft we run
   Our heav'nly race———or hinders us to do
   The work, that's moft expedient to be done.

84 O let us all, like workmen truly-wife,
   Juft, faithful, vigilant, and ftrictly-fair,
   (Whilft yet the time of grace before us lies)
   With readinefs to ferve the Lord repair!

85 For if we ferve him not on earth, whilft yet
   It is the time of grace—whilft yet 'tis day———
   We fhall be headlong hurl'd into the pit,
   Our homage to the devil, there, to pay.

86 Then, as in hell each wretched finner lies,
   The folly he fhall there too late repent,
   That he fo madly did his God defpife,
   Whilft fo much time in fin he idly fpent.

87 There fhall he fhed full many a bitter tear,
   And cry aloud, through mere excefs of pain;
   But fhou'd he cry his eyes out, he fhall ne'er
   From Satan's clutches make efcape again.

88 O, let us then, this very now, begin
   To ferve the Lord—whilft it to-day is call'd———
   And bid a laft adieu to ev'ry fin,
   By which we hitherto have been enthrall'd!

89 So fhall we (when our bufi'nefs here is o'er,
   And at the time we want affiftance moft)
   Adore for ever the Almighty pow'r
   In heav'n above, among the' angelic hoft:

90 Tó which bleft place, O my Creator dread!
For Jefus Chrift's fake, our Redeemer dear,
Do thou thy faithful fervants fafely lead,
That we may, with thy Saints, adore thee there.

Concerning PRAYER, and it's proper Requifites.

1 PUT off thy fhoes, e'er thou thy God doft greet,
 Thy afs, before thou facrificeft, bind——
Wafh, e'er the altar thou come'ft near, thy feet,
And weigh, what thou requefteft, well in mind.

2 Repent, e'er thou doft God by pray'r implore,
And thy devotions, let thy deeds attend——
Be thankful always, when thy pray'rs are o'er;
So fhall thy prayers up to heav'n afcend.

3 Satan will try to tempt thee, ev'ry day,
The flefh wou'd fain deceive thee, ev'ry hour,
The world, and it's delights, thy fall affay:
Seek thou, by pray'r, their efforts to o'erpow'r.

4 Prayer is good, in ev'ry land and clime——
Prayer is good, for men in ev'ry fphere——
Prayer is good, at ev'ry hour and time——
Prayer is good, on all accounts whate'er.

5 Pray'r is, a facrifice to God moft due——
A fure fupport, to guide the weak along——
A whip, to fcourge the fiend and all his crew---
A fanctuary, from ev'ry ill and wrong!

6 Nay, conftant prayer is a golden key,
Thy doors to open at the dawn of light——
A bolt, to fhut them at the clofe of day——
A fort, to guard from harm, both day and night.

7 Prayer, has foothe'd the moft obdurate breaft------
Prayer, has angels with fuccefs affail'd------
Prayer, the fierceft fiends has difpoffefs'd------
Prayer, has over God himfelf prevail'd!------

        S Then.

8 Then, with thy pray'r, let heav'n and earth refound--
Like incenfe, it perfumes the' etherial plains.----
On earth, it gives the fiend his deepeft wound------
And brings to thee thyfelf the greateft gains.

9 With faith--with rev'rence--with a foul ftrung high--
With ardent zeal, and minds that never ftray---
With knowledge---with a ftrong, inceffant cry-----
With clofe attention---'tis that men fhou'd pray.

10 Lift up thine eyes, thy knees devoutly bend,
Roufe up thy fpirit, and thy bofom fmite---
Open thy lips, thy hands abroad extend,
Pray with true fervor, and with all thy might.

11 Thou ne'er muft call on gods of gold, or ftone,
On faint or faintefs, thy requeft to grant;
But on the Lord, thro' Jefus Chrift alone,
If thou wou'dft have, whatever thou doft want.

12 No one, but God, can our condition know,
No one, but God, can give us any aid,
No one, but God, can hear our pray'rs, below---
To God alone then fhou'd our pray'rs be made.

13 God bids us call on him with fervent pray'r---
God promifes, if we'll but afk, to give---
God hears each wifh, and ev'ry good defire----
God can from trouble ev'ry foul relieve.

14 Not Abrah'am, nor St. James, can e'er pretend
The' internal feelings of our hearts to guefs————
No one, but God alone, can comprehend
Our wants, our woes, our forrows, and diftrefs.

15 To give to thoufands whatfoe'er they feek,
Only belongs unto the King of kings————
Although in various languages they fpeak,
And afk at once a thoufand diff'rent things.

16 The Virgin talks no Englifh, I fuppofe,
Neither does Martha, Irifh underftand,
No Welfh, as I prefume, St. Clement knows,
How can they then our mediators ftand?

I   17 Abraham

17 Abraham can ne'er our circumſtances know,
Neither can John afford us any aid,
Peter, in heav'n, can't hear us here below:
To God alone then ſhou'd our pray'rs be ſaid.

18 The Saints, of ev'ry ſex and rank, revere,
But thou may'ſt only God himſelf adore:
Give them the honour they deſerve—but ne'er,
On whatſoe'er pretence, their help implore.

19 There ne'er was Patriarch, or Apoſtle yet—
There ne'er was Prophet, as I've ever heard,
(For who cou'd ſuch a circumſtance forget?)
That e'er to any Saint his ſuit preferr'd.

20 There's not a promiſe in the Goſpel made,
That we ſhall, any thing we beg, obtain;
Unleſs, for it, we ſhall with zeal have pray'd,
And that, for Jeſus' ſake, the ſame we gain.

21 Chriſt, is the only Mediator known,
Chriſt, is our only Advocate above,
And there is none, but Jeſus Chriſt alone,
That can, for man, the dread Creator move.

22 Whate'er requeſts we ſhall to God addreſs,
They muſt be all preferr'd, for Jeſus' ſake,
Who ſits on God's right hand in perfect bliſs,
There to receive whatever pray'rs we make.

23 Let ſome to Cathe'rine, or St. David fly,
To Clement, Martha, Martin—any one:
But, for my part, I never will apply
To any—but to Jeſus Chriſt alone.

24 Seek then with earneſtneſs, whene'er you pray——
Seek the direction of the Holy Ghoſt:
For none can, with effect, their prayers ſay,
Unleſs they can of his ſure guidance boaſt.

25 Without the Spirit ſome may have eſſay'd
To talk with God, and ſtrove their pray'rs to ſay;
But no man can, without the Spirit's aid,
Converſe with God, or with attention pray.

26 Unleſs

26 Unlefs the confcience and the heart are join'd,
   The tongue-born prayer God will never prize;
   But that, which flows from an affected mind,
   Will always prove a pleafing facrifice.

27 Seek God, both with thy mouth, and with thy heart;
   For either of the two will not fuffice;
   But let thy fpirit with thy mouth take part,
   And then 'twill prove a harmony moft nice.

28 The pray'r, that iffues wholly from the heart,
   Is better much than thofe that only fpring
   From the bare lips, where t'other bears no part:
   For fuch a prayer is an odious thing.

29 Mofes more pleafingly his God addrefs'd,
   Upon his journey, tho' he nothing faid,   *Ex.xiv.*15.
   Than erft the Jews, when they their wants exprefs'd,
   And with the lips, without the Spirit, pray'd.

30 Whate'er thou afkeft, ask with faith fincere;
   Take no denial——ask with fervent mind——
   And what thou askeft, thou fhalt have--ne'er fear:
   Seek but with earneftnefs, thou'lt furely find.

31 The little birds their clamour never ceafe,
   Until their dams with food their noife have ftill'd:
   So man himfelf fhou'd never hold his peace,
   'Till God has ev'ry want and wifh fulfill'd.

32 How earneft fome will beg ('tis ftrange to fay!)
   For pence, or food their hunger to remove;
   And yet how fluggifhly the fame will pray
   For mercy, and the glorious joys above?

33 God is, to all that feek him, mighty kind——
   To all, that ask, he's ready ftill to grant——
   To grant to all, with an ungrudging mind——
   Largely to grant, whatever they may want.

34 As a fond mother ftill inclines her ears,
   When in the cradle her love'd infant cries:
   So God his creatures' fupplications hears,
   Removes their preffures, and their wants fupplies.

35 For how can God but hear each Chriſtian's pray'r,
   Since for the' elect his holy Spirit pleads,
   And, on the throne of his eternal Sire,
   For them their Saviour ever intercedes?

36 If thou ſhalt ask for ought, in Jeſus' name,
   Thou either, what thou askeſt, ſhalt obtain,
   (So thou doſt earneſtly entreat the ſame)
   Or, what is more expedient, thou ſhalt gain.

37 Shou'd God to grant thee thy deſire delay,
   Shou'd he not anſwer thy petition ſoon,
   'Tis that thou may'ſt with greater ardor pray,
   Or beg a larger, and a better boon.

38 Seek, firſt, the glory of thy gracious Sire---
   Seek, next, celeſtial happineſs to gain---
   God's kingdom and his righteouſneſs deſire---
   And all thy wants beſides thou ſhalt obtain.

39 Ask thou not ought, as long as thou doſt live,
   That is repugnant to God's holy Word:
   If thou ſhou'dſt ask, what he's not pleas'd to give,
   Thy prayer will but irritate the Lord.

40 To covet earthly things, is very wrong,
   When one may gain the wealth of Paradiſe---
   Or for ſome dirty acres here to long;
   But all the joys of heaven to deſpiſe.

41 As 'tis the nature of the ſwiniſh kind,
   To tear the turf, and nuzzle in the mire:
   So man by nature is to earth inclin'd,
   And does not to celeſtial bliſs aſpire.

42 Seek thou, whate'er the ſcripture does permit---
   Seek thou, whate'er's allow'd thee by the Lord;
   But ſeek it in the manner that's moſt fit,
   And moſt concordant with his written Word.

43 Whene'er to God thou prayeſt, be ſincere,
   And uſe no other language than thy own:
   Better a word or two, whoſe ſenſe is clear,
   Than thouſands mumbled in a tongue unknown.

44 He

44 He mocks his God, and does himſelf deceive,
　Whoe'er attempts to ask, he knows not what,
　And thinks to have, e'en what he can't conceive,
　By mere lip-labour, and unmeaning chat.

45 Ne'er let thy mouth thy lagging mind outſtrip,
　But tell thy heart to ponder well the whole :
　God ne'er regards the prayer of the lip,
　Without the full concurrence of the ſoul.

46 God, ev'ry thought and boſom ſecret knows,
　God, is himſelf the Sire and ſource of light,
　God, chuſes pray'r, as from the heart it flows ;
　But empty words are nothing in his ſight.

47 Caſt ev'ry ſin-polluted thought aſide,
　Whilſt thou to God thy prayer doſt prefer ;
　And let each worldly care, behind, be tie'd,
　Whilſt thou doſt with the Lord of hoſts confer.

48 Abra'ham let not his aſs approach the ſcene,
　Where he did erſt his ſacrifice prepare :
　Permit not thou a thought, that is unclean,
　To come---where thou doſt offer up thy pray'r.

49 Like Abra'ham, thou muſt drive away, whate'er
　Lights on thy ‖ ſacrifice---and boldly fight ‖*Gen.*xv.11
　With ev'ry thing that hinders thee to rear
　The walls of Sion to their proper height.

50 The greater earneſtneſs that Satan ſhows
　To turn thy thoughts aſide, when thou doſt pray :
　The more do thou his ſly attacks oppoſe,
　And fight againſt him, 'till he flees away.

51 As the fierce lion flees, and quits his prey,
　Soon as the crowing of a cock he hears :
　So does the fell deſtroyer skud away,
　Whene'er our faith-fraught prayers pierce his ears.

52 The buffalo cannot that place come near,
　Where young pigs ſqueak, or little chickens cry :
　Neither can Satan on the ſpot appear,
　Whence holy prayers are preferr'd on high.

53 Did not the wily fiend obferve with pain,
    That prayer leffen'd his extenfive fway,
    And feem'd moft likely to fubvert his reign,
    He ne'er wou'd hinder any one to pray.

54 If thou haft thy falvation, then, at heart,
    Thy Maker's glory, and thy own great need
    Of pardon—ne'er let Satan make thee ftart
    From hearing fermons—or thy pray'rs impede.

55 Whene'er thou prayeft unto God—ftill mind
    For ev'ry order in the church to pray————
    Nor let thy prayers ever be confin'd
    To thy ownfelf—like thofe the Pagans fay:

56 For none of them are of her holy race,
    Who pray not for her welfare and fuccefs,
    But mifcreant baftards, infamous, and bafe,
    And enemies to Sion's happinefs.

57 If Abra'ham kindly for Gomorrah pray'd,
    And for the other cities of the plain:
    Shou'd not we Chriftians beg our Maker's aid,
    And choiceft bleffings for his chofen train?

58 Chrift tells us all at any time to pray,   *Luke* xviii. 1.
    And ne'er the beneficial tafk give o'er:
    St. Paul, to Timothy does likewife fay,   *Eph.* ii. 8.
    That in all places we fhou'd God adore.

59 Thrice ev'ry day, for the Almighty's aid,
    The pious Daniel never fail'd to pray————
    The royal Prophet, ftill more pious, made
    His fupplications feven times a day.

60 Our bleffed Saviour pafs'd the live-long night
    In prayer—though nor fin, nor guilt he knew,
    And fpent each day, as long as it was light,
    In preaching to a dull and thanklefs crew.

61 Prayer is ever of the greateft weight,
    In ev'ry place—at any time, or hour;
    So that the heart is in a proper ftate,
    To beg a favour from the' Almighty pow'r.

62 Upon

62 Upon the boiſtrous ſea, or mountain's brow,
   At our own home, or any where abroad,
   Pray'r is a duty, which we always owe
   (Where-e'er we are) unto the' eternal God.

63 We all ſhou'd pray, like Peter in his room,
   Or elſe, like David, when a-bed he lay,
   Or elſe, like Daniel, in the dungeon's gloom:
   In ev'ry circumſtance we ſtill ſhou'd pray.

64 The ſacred fire upon the' altar li't,
   Never with-held from man it's radiance bright——
   To manifeſt that thou ſhou'dſt ne'er permit
   Thy zeal for pray'r to be extinguiſh'd quite.

65 Man is the temple, the Almighty loves——
   Man's heart the altar, gives him moſt delight——
   Pray'r is the ſacrifice, he moſt approves——
   Give him that ſacrifice, both morn and night.

66 Let not thy temple want this ſacrifice
   At early morn, or at the noon-tide hour,
   And don't forget at night, if thou art wiſe,
   To give due praiſe unto the' eternal Pow'r:

67 So ſhall thy God familiar be with thee,
   So ſhalt thou ever his aſſiſtance have,
   So ſhalt thou ever in his favour be,
   And thy dear ſoul from all it's dangers ſave.

68 There's nothing in the world that ſhou'd impede
   Good Chriſtians, their Creator to addreſs,
   And do the work they have to do beſide;
   Whatever trade, or calling they profeſs.

69 A man may do his uſu'al work, and yet
   With unremitted zeal and ardor pray;
   For mental pray'r will ne'er retard the feet,
   Nor any labour of the hands delay.

70 Moſes, the while he travell'd o'er the plain,
   Joſhua, whilſt amid the mortal fray,
   Chriſt, on the road, and Paul upon the main,
   Cou'd mind their buſ'neſs—and find time to pray.

        71 Although

71 Although excufes often are allow'd,
    In many a weighty and perplex'd affair;
    Yet no excufe fufficient can be fhow'd
    To fcreen, or palliate the neglect of pray'r.

72 Thou may'ft abfent thyfelf from church, when ill,
    And pardon for thy abfence may'ft implore:
    But, whatfoever thy complaint is, ftill
    Thou'rt bound to pray--until thou art no more.

73 Thou may'ft from act of charity forbear,
    When alms fufficient are not in thy pow'r:
    But yet thou never muft refrain from pray'r,
    However deftitute, however poor.

74 In ev'ry ftate, at ev'ry time and place,
    Prayer is feafonable and ufeful ftill;
    Let nothing hinder thee, in any cafe,
    With proper zeal this duty to fulfil.

75 Whether in deep diftrefs, or high in wealth,
    In ev'ry ftate of life, wherein we are,
    Or in difeafes, or in perfect health,
    A Chriftian may addrefs his God with pray'r.

76 No locks, no bolts, nor any human pow'r,
    Nor all the world, can ftop the rapid flight
    Of pray'r---or hinder it, at any hour,
    From pofting to the' immortal Sire of light.

77 Pluck from it's roots the quiv'ring tongue of man,
    Cut off his feet, or chain them---from his heart
    He ne'erthelefs, fpite of all hindrance, can
    His fervent pray'rs to his Creator, dart.

78 Whether on feaft or faft, by night or day,
    At morn or eve, or any time you will,
    Prayer to heav'n can wing it's airy way———
    Come when it will---it fhall be welcome ftill.

79 Efther, tho' queen, was not allow'd to fee
    (But at fome certain feafons of the year)
    Her royal lord---but prayer's always free
    To go to God, without reftraint or fear.

80 Get up, like Daniel, with the dawning light,
   And make thy fuit to God, at any hour,
   Or rife, like David, in the dead of night:
   For always ready is the' Almighty pow'r.

81 Tho' God to no man living does allow
   The honour, with his Saviour to confer----
   Yet ev'ry Chriftian's pray'r to heav'n may go,
   And, at all feafons, gain admittance, there.

82 Through ftorms and fhow'rs, thro' ocean and the fky,
   Through ev'ry fix'd or wand'ring ftar above,
   Prayer to God himfelf fhall mount on high,
   And with the rapid flight of lightning move.

83 Not heav'n or earth, or any human pow'r,
   Authority, or angel from the fky,
   Can hinder pray'r, at any time or hour,
   From holding conference with Chrift on high.

84 It needs not afk St. Peter for his key,
   But may through all the angels pafs alone,
   Without one obftacle to block it's way,
   Boldly unto our bleffed Saviour's throne.

85 Prayer will force the Deity, to hear
   Her plaints---and Chrift, her doleful caufe to plead--
   Prayer will make the Spirit interfere,
   With fighs and groans for her to intercede.

86 The Giver of each gift that's good, will ne'er
   Turn back the pray'r that's faithfully addrefs'd,
   But Chrift will blefs each heart that is fincere,
   Nor quit him, 'till he's of each wifh poffefs'd.

87 If prayer fhall not, what it afks, receive,
   It fome what, better yet than that, fhall gain---
   For Chrift an ardent pray'r will never leave
   To go for nought, or be preferr'd in vain.

88 What do we owe unto the gracious Pow'r,
   Who, to our praye'rs, does the permiffion grant
   To come unto his prefence, any hour,
   And to obtain from him whate'er we want?

89 Praye'r

89 Pray'r is an arm which reaches very far——
    E'en from the earth unto the etherial fky ——
    To her God's treafures never have a bar,
    But thence fhe takes, what may her wants fupply.

90 Prayer, of old, a mighty giant flew—   1 Sam. xvii. 45.
    Prayer, the lion's mouth fhut up of yore——
    Prayer, the gates of iron open threw——
    Prayer, can fave a man, at any hour.

91 Prayer, lock'd up the heavens long from rain——
    Prayer, the ocean turn'd to folid land——
    Prayer, rais'd up the dead to life again——
    There's nothing can the force of Prayer withftand!

92 What thanks fhou'd we, then, to the Godhead pay,
    Who to our Prayers a free admiffion grants,
    Whene'er we pleafe, without the leaft delay,
    And fatisfies with bounty all our wants?

93 All due refpect and rev'rence and renown,
    Be to the Donor of each bleffing given,
    To him be honour, pow'r, and homage, fhown,
    Who kindly hears us from the higheft heaven!

Advice, before PRAYER.

BEFORE thou doft attempt to pray,
    Of all thy vices paft repent,
And wafh the hateful filth away,
    That God may to thy pray'r affent.

2 God will no vile offenders hear,
    Nor thofe who finners are profefs'd—
    But they muft quit their vices, e'er
    The Lord will lift to their requeft.

3 If ftain'd with malice, rage, or pride,
    Or murder, thou fhou'dft there repair,
    Where God in glory does refide,
    He will reject thy finful pray'r.

4 The curfe of Moab they fhall gain,
  Who pray with a polluted foul :
  They ask, but they fhall not obtain,
  Becaufe their hands are ftain'd and foul.

5 Whoéver calls upon his God
  Muft lay all filthinefs afide ,
  And wafh his hands quite clean from blood,
  Or elfe his fuit will be deny'd.

6 God 's gracious to each penitent,
  Whofe reformation is fincere :
  Then of thy wicked ways repent,
  And God will thy petition hear.

7 If thou wilt leave thy vices quite,
  Although they were in crimfon dreft,
  Yet Chrift fhall make them lily-white,
  And lend an ear to thy requeft.

8 Whene'er to pray'r thou art inclin'd,
  Be to each idle thought averfe,
  And leave all worldly views behind,
  Whilft with thy God thou doft converfe.

9 'Tis bad, to fee fome fardel foul
  Brought on one's back to God's own dome,
  But worfe to fee a world-ftain'd foul
  Into God's aweful prefence come.

10 And when thou prayeft, pray for all
  True Chriftians, not excepting one ;
  Nor, like a felfifh heathen, call
  On God, to blefs thyfelf alone.

11 Firft, pray for kings, that they may grace
  Obtain, to rule their people well,
  In the true faith, in wealth and peace,
  And may in righteoufnefs excel.

12 Then for the clergy beg his grace,
  Clearly thofe myfteries to teach,
  Which in the gofpel they may trace,
  And fluently it's truths to preach.

13 For

13 For ev'ry magiftrate implore
His aid, the vicious to reftrain————
And that the Lord may grant him pow'r,
Juftice and virtue to maintain.

14 Then beg a blefling from thy God
On all that in the arts delight,
That they may fcatter all abroad
True faith, morality, and light.

15 For all the Commons of the land
Then pray unto the Lord above,
That each may in his calling ftand,
Replete with loyalty and light.

16 Pray, laftly, for the poor and low,
And all, who in oppreffion live,
That God to them may pity fhow,
And to each fuffe'rer comfort give.

A WARNING, or ADMONITION, to every
Man, to think on GOD in the Morning,
and to return him Thanks for preferving
him the preceding Night from all Evil.

1 WHEN firft thou wakeft, each fucceeding day,
Lift up to God above thy grateful eyes,
And due refpect to him be fure to pay,
Ee'r other thoughts within thy bofom rife.

2 'Twas He, that kept the prowling foe,
And watch'd thee carefully 'till break of day,
And fuffer'd not his eyes repofe to know,
Left in thy fleep thou fhou'dft become his prey.

3 For did not God and his celeftial train,
Around his fervants keep a conftant guard,
They all had by the foe, e'er this, been flain,
And fwallow'd up, afleep and unprepar'd.

4 By

4 By far more dange'rous is that mortal's ftate,
  Who lies a-bed without his Saviour's aid,
  Than that which did of old on Daniel wait,
  When he all night was with the lions laid.

5 The fcriptures tell us, that --by night and day----
  The Devil roams to feek the fall of man,
  Juft as a lion roves in fearch of prey,
  And tears and mangles ev'ry beaft he can.

6 Who can forbid the lion to devour?
  Who, but the fhepherd Chrift, his flock can keep,
  That without flumb'ring guards us ev'ry hour,
  And from the guileful fiend protects his fheep?

7 Think, then, how much thou art in duty bound
  To thank thy God, who has preferv'd thee ftill
  From Satan's machinations, fafe and found,
  And from the preffure of each other ill?

8 As God's demands, on thee, are vaftly large,
  Let thy returns of praife be likewife great:
  The grateful offe'ring on thy knees difcharge,
  And, night and morn, the' incumbent tafk repeat.

9 Think thou, how Satan flily might have ftole,
  And filently deftroy'd thee, in thy fleep,
  And into judgement haul'd thy heedlefs foul,
  If Chrift his watch around thee did not keep.

10 Think, that the foe thy children might have flain---
  Thy riches, as his legal prey convey'd-----
  Thy houfes burn'd, and martyr'd thee with pain,
  Had Chrift not lent thee his Almighty aid.

11 Think, that perhaps he might have touch'd thy brain,
  And that thou ever hadft diftracted rave'd,
  And neither reft, nor quiet known again,
  Waft thou, by Chrift, not from his malice fave'd.

12 Thy gratitude, on all occafions, fhow
  To thy true Shepherd, for his friendly aid,
  Who thee fo fafely guarded from the foe,
  That thou need'ft not be of his force afraid.

13 Suppofe

13 Suppose a Jew, the moft abhorr'd of men,
  Shou'd guard thee fleeping in the' inclement air,
  'Mongft rave'nous beafts, or near a lion's den:
  Wou'dft thou not thank him kindly for his care?

14 And yet, though Chrift protects thee ev'ry hour,
  Whilft thou amongft fierce lions fleepeft faft,
  Which are at all times ready to devour----
  Thou ne'erthelefs art thanklefs to the laft.

15 Open thine eyes--thy Saviour's goodnefs fee——
  Take warning—and his loving-kindnefs own——
  Return him thanks upon thy bended knee,
  For all the mercies he, to thee, has fhown:

16 So fhall he always keep thee fafe from ill,
  And under his extended pinions fcreen——
  And fo with eafe fhall he preferve thee ftill
  From ev'ry harm and peril unforefeen.

17 Take heed, thy heart does not indulge a thought,
  Take heed, left thou on ought fhou'dft fix thine eyes,
  Take heed, that with thy lips thou fpeakeft nought,
  'Till thou haft paid thy morning facrifice.

18 To God, the prime ideas of thy heart,
  To God, the prime of thy expreffions give,
  To God, the firft-fruits of thy foul impart;
  The fecond and the laft he'll not receive.

19 Juft at the dawn, before the rifing fun,
  The mounting lark his Maker's praifes fings:
  So man, e'er he has ought befides begun,
  Shou'd chant the praifes of the King of kings.

20 The little red-breaft, e'er he wets his bill,
  To his Creator chirps his morning pray'r,
  Who kept him the preceding night from ill,
  Though cold his lodging, and tho' coarfe his fare.

21 But many a man will from his bed arife,
  More heedlefs than the fongfters of the air,
  Or fwine, that grunting leave their odious ftyes,
  Nor thank him for his providential care.

22 O, 'tis

22 O, 'tis a fhame the fons of men fhou'd e'er
 Appear lefs grateful than the feather'd quire,
 Who, ev'ry night and morn, their voices rear
 To thank and laud their everlafting Sire !

A Morning THANKSGIVING
when we firft awake.

1 O God, my fafe-guard and defence,
   My fort, in ev'ry exigence,
 Receive my thanks—thou, who didft keep
 Me fafe, laft night, whilft I did fleep !

2 A watch, around my head, each night
 Thou placeft, when I'm conquer'd quite
 By fleep, and o'er me fpread'ft thy wing,
 When I've forgot each earthly thing.

3 Thou giveft me fweet eafe and reft,
 And ev'ry night with them I'm bleft,
 Whereby this feeble frame, O Lord!
 Is daily to it's ftrength reftor'd.

4 My gracious God does never clofe,
 Or wink his eyes, when I repofe,
 But whilft I fleep, within his arms,
 Secure he keeps me from all harms.

5 O, what a favour this !—that thou
 The King of kings, fhoud'ft ftoop fo low,
 As duft and afhes to regard,
 And unto man to be a guard!

6 The tithe can ne'er be paid by me
 Of all the thanks I owe to thee,
 Good God, the truth I freely own,
 Was it but for this gift alone !

7 All glory, pow'r, thankfgiving too,
 All praife, refpect, and honour due,
 Let us unto the Godhead pay
 For his protection, night and day.

Thanks

Thanks to Chriſt for Protection and Reſt.

1 MY Shepherd, who my ſoul didſt keep
   Laſt night, whilſt I was faſt aſleep,
From the grim wolf, beneath thy wing——
Thy praiſes, from my heart, I'll ſing!

2 Cloſe to thy breaſt, thou didſt me place,
   And in thine arms didſt me embrace,
Thou eaſe and reſt to me didſt give,
And I will thank thee, whilſt I live!

3 Thou hind'red'ſt Satan, to deſtroy——
   Thou hind'red'ſt villains, to annoy——
From fires and ſtorms thou didſt me keep,
And ſuff'red'ſt nought to break my ſleep.

4 Thy name, O Chriſt! be ever bleſt,
   Who doſt protect me, whilſt I reſt——
All glory be aſcribe'd to thee,
Who ſuch refreſhment giveſt me.

An ADMONITION to a MAN, when he dreſſes his Body, to pray for Clothes and Armour, for the Soul.

1 WHEN, in the morn, to dreſs thou doſt begin,
   Pray thou that God wou'd lend to thee his arms,
That, like a Chriſtian, thou may'ſt fight therein,
And boldly brave each enemy's alarms.

2 In vain doſt thou, from the inclement air,
   Thy body guard, and from the tempeſt keen,
If thou doſt not a proper garb prepare
Thy ſoul from ſin's deſtructive rage to ſcreen.

3 Seek, then, to ſave thee from each greedy foe,
   And ſin's aſſaults, the panoply of God——
Seek it, to ſhield thee from each preſſing woe,
And from the world, the fleſh, and Satan's fraud.

4 For

4 For we, without it, are defencelefs quite,
To ev'ry enemy an eafy prey——
And 'tis impoffible for human might,
Unarm'd with it, to conquer in the fray.

A PRAYER, whilft thou art dreffing, to beg the
Armour of God, to defend thee from the
affaults of Sin.

1   A R M me with all thy panoply divine,
    Thou Lord of hofts! thou God of matchlefs might!
That I may, like a Chriftian hero, fhine,
And overcome my enemies in fight!

2 From head to heel, let not a fingle part
Remain expofe'd, left I receive a wound,
(For great and dange'rous is the tempter's art)
In that fole fpot, where there's no armour found.

3 Let not the world, with all it's bawbles vile——
Let not the flefh, with ev'ry loofe defire——
Let not the devil, by fome curfed wile,
Caufe me to fin againft my gracious Sire.

4 Give me, O Lord! fufficient force and might,
That I may all my enemies o'ercome,
And under thy victorious banner fight,
'Till thou, in glorious peace, fhalt lead me home.

Another, on the fame Subject.

1   THOU Rock of my falvation, lend thy aid!
    Arm me in all thy panoply complete,
And leave no fingle member unarray'd,
Left the foul fiend thy warrior fhou'd defeat!

2 Upon my head let Hope's gay helm be place'd——
My breaft with Equity's bright corfelet grace——
The belt of Penitence gird round my waift——
And, on my feet, the Gofpel's fandals lace.

K   3 Give

3 Give me, thy word, for a two-edged fword—
  The fhield of faith, to ward off ev'ry dart,
  That Satan throws—and conftant pray'r, O Lord!
  To force the fell invader from my heart.

4 Give me affiftance bravely to engage
  With all the enemies that hem me in,
  With ev'ry carnal luft, and Satan's rage,
  The world's deceits, and ev'ry deadly fin—

5 Give me affiftance to attack them all,
  To break their ranks, and conquer them in fight—
  That on my knees I may right humbly fall
  To worfhip thee, like a true fon of light:

6 So fhall I march undaunted, ev'ry day,
  Beneath thy ftandard, through the field of death,
  And give thee praife, without the leaft difmay,
  O Lord, my God! whilft I have any breath.

An Admonition to a Perfon, whilft he wafhes himfelf.

1 WHene'er, to wafh thyfelf, thou doft begin,
    With earneftnefs to thy Creator pray,
  That he'll be pleas'd to cleanfe thy foul from fin,
  And wafh thy errors, in Chrift's blood, away.

2 To free thy flefh from outward filth—a flood,
  Nay, e'en a fea of water, wou'd be vain,
  Unlefs thy confcience in thy Saviour's blood
  Be cleans'd from vice and ev'ry inward ftain.

3 It nought avails thee, that thy face is clean,
  If thy corrupted mind be void of grace:
  God takes no pleafure in the man, I ween,
  Whofe heart is not as fpotlefs as his face.

A fhort

A short P R A Y E R, on the same Occasion.

1   O Wash me in the Blood, the Jews erst spilt!
      O wash me, Christ! from ev'ry conscious guilt!
  O wash my mind from ev'ry thought obscene!
  O wash me, from all foul pollutions, clean!

2 O wash my head and feet, and ev'ry part,
  As thou didst wash the Twelve, and cleanse my heart!
  Then wipe away my filth—and, to complete
  Thy work—bestow on me the Paraclete!

3 Wash me in penitential tears, my King!
  Wash me in Grace's and in Peace's spring!
  Than lilies whiter, wash me in thy gore,
  That I, in purity, may thee adore!——

A Morning PRAYER, to be use'd after a Person is up, wash'd, and dress'd.

1   O God of mercy, soft-eye'd Pity's Sire!
      For Jesus sake, my num'rous faults pass o'er;
  Which more Arithmetic, I own, require
  To count, than all the sands upon the shore.

2 There's not a law in all the sacred code,
  That I, woe's me! have not at times transgress'd—
  Nor hast thou any gift on me bestow'd,
  Which I have not to vicious ends address'd.

3 Bad are my thoughts, but worse my deeds by far—
  Foul is my tongue, and infinite my fraud———
  My temper's hot, but very cold my pray'r:
  Pardon me all, I've done amiss, O God!———

4 Pardon me all the crimes that I have done,
  E'en from my childhood to the present hour———
  Nor let the vengeance on my head come down,
  Which I've deserv'd from thy Almighty pow'r:

5 But give me grace and ſtrength for ever more
  To worſhip thee, with ſanctity of heart:
  Aid me, thy wond'rous goodneſs to adore
  In perfect honeſty, and void of art.

6 Remove each obſtacle, that's in the way,
  And interferes betwixt my God, and me——
  And give me pow'r, my due devoirs to pay,
  Still unfatigue'd, O Lord, my God! to thee!

7 From my vain heart each filthy vice eraze,
  Each habit I've been ill-accuſtom'd to-----
  And, whilſt I'm yet alive, the vacant place
  With ev'ry grace and virtue ſtock anew.

8 Teach me, to keep inviolate thy law-------
  Teach me, to love it from my very ſoul-----
  My rule of life thence let me ever draw,
  And always live according to that rule.

9 Direct me, by thy ſacred Spirit, ſtill
  To regulate each act, each word, each thought,
  According to the dictates of thy will,
  And thoſe commandments thou to us haſt taught.

10 My paſſions, and my appetites reſtrain,
  That I henceforth no wicked act may do;
  But may, o'er ſin, a perfect conqueſt gain,
  And that invete'rate enemy ſubdue.

11 Help me, O Lord, with thy celeſtial might,
  The world, the fleſh, the devil, to oppoſe----
  The victor's crown I then may claim of right,
  When I have conquer'd thoſe united foes.

12 Thy ſervant, Lord! beneath thy wings defend,
  And ſcreen me there from ev'ry rude alarm;
  Neither permit, by any means, the fiend
  To do my ſoul, or body, any harm.

13 Keep me, O Lord! from ev'ry ſlip, and all
  The trouble, ſhame, misfortune, loſs, and ill,
  Diſeaſe, or hurt, that may to me befal;
  So it be pleaſing to thy holy will.

14 Enable

14 Enable me, by thy bleſt Spirit's aid,
    In Chriſtian works to ſpend the preſent day,
    And, whilſt I in this vale of tears am ſtay'd,
    My bounden ſervice conſtantly to pay.

15 O, may this day, whereon I hail thee now,
    Be as diſcreetly and devoutly paſt,
    As if I, for a certainty, did know,
    That it *wou'd* be—what it *may* be—my laſt!

16 Let me not, Lord! the moral change delay,
    From morn to morn, unto my latter end;
    But, whilſt it hitherto is call'd to day,
    Let me begin my manners to amend.

17 Let not the fleſh, with daring inſolence,
    Cauſe thee to doom my precious ſoul to woe---
    Nor for ſome few precarious joys of ſenſe,
    Condemn it to eternal pains below.

18 Let not this world's delights and fleeting toys,
    Which vaniſh, like a morning miſt, away,
    Cauſe me to loſe the rights and real joys
    Of that bright world, which never ſhall decay.

19 Whilſt yet 'tis day, whilſt yet the ſun is ſtrong,
    Cauſe me to ſtrive and work with all my might,
    In thoſe concerns that to my peace belong;
    Leſt unawares I ſhou'd be caught by night.

20 Let me, O Chriſt! be always ready dreſt,
    (My lamp well trimm'd, and full of oil and light)
    And watch thy coming to the wedding-feaſt,
    Whilſt heaven's gate lies open to my ſight.

21 When moſt ſecure, when moſt in health I bloom,
    Let me not wholly unprepare'd be caught,
    But make me think ſtill of the day of doom,
    When all my faults muſt to account be brought.

22 Make me reflect, whene'er I am alone,
    On that exact account, which all that live,
    Muſt for each petty fault which they have done,
    Nay, e'en for ev'ry idle ſtory, give.

        23 Wipe,

23 Wipe, from thy well-kept regifter, away
  All my iniquities recorded there,
  And caft not in my teeth, on that dread day,
  The keen reproaches I deferve to hear.

24 Forgive me, now, the debt I ought to pay,
  The countlefs fums which by thy book I owe,
  And with the blood of Chrift blot quite away
  The utmoft farthing that to thee is due:

25 And when thou haft forgiven all that fum,
  Enable me to finifh my career;
  That my bleft foul to Paradife may come,
  And with my Saviour reft for ever there:

26 When I, with all the' angelic choir divine,
  And heav'nly hofts, fhall undifmay'd appear,
  And with extreme delight to praife him join,
  In endlefs joy, and happinefs fincere.

A Warning to guard, whilft it is yet Day, againft the Affaults of the World, the Flefh, and the Devil----and to put on, and to make ufe of, the Armour of God againft them.

1 A S foon as thou art wake'd from thy repofe,
    Refleсt---that thou haft three invete'rate foes,
  And each of them for thy deftruсtion waits,
  If thou doft not avoid his fraudful baits:

2 And yet, alas! the weakeft of the three,
  Is, e'en a thoufand times, too ftrong for thee,
  Unlefs thou weapons canft from Chrift obtain,
  And borrow'd might---the viсtory to gain.

3 Then of thy Saviour earneftly entreat,
  That he wou'd furnifh thee with arms complete,
  And fill thee with true fortitude of mind,
  To rout thofe enemies of humankind.

4 Upon

4 Upon thy head the Chriſtian's helmet bear,
  The ſtrongeſt hopes of heaven thou canſt wear,
  Through which the pow'rful ſove'reign of the air
  Can never hurt, or force thee to deſpair.

5 Place thou the ſhield of Juſtice at thy breaſt,
  Aſſur'd the Devil cannot e'er moleſt,
  Or with his dread artille'ry injure thoſe,
  Who with this ſhield his fierce attacks oppoſe.

6 With Righteouſneſs thy girded loins ſurround,
  Nor deign to uſe Hypocriſy unſound:
  For there's no neater, and no ſtronger wear,
  Than a true heart join'd to a mind ſincere.

7 Thy feet with ſandals from the Goſpel grace,
  Be patient in each circumſtance and place:
  Through many ſuff'rings and through many woes,
  The Chriſtian to his Sove'reign's palace goes.

8 Take Faith's ſtrong ſhield, the arrows to repel——
  The deadly ſhafts, ſhot by the prince of hell:
  A lively faith in Chriſt will always cool
  The fie'ry darts thrown from the flaming pool.

9 Take thou the ſcripture's keen, two-edged ſword---
  Take thou the mighty falchion of the Word————
  For that's the trenchant blade, which at a blow
  Can cut and cleave our fierce infernal foe.

10 About thee always keep the arms of God,
  Though they be many, and oft' deem'd a load;
  Leſt thou, without them ſhou'dſt perchance be found,
  And from the fiend receive a fatal wound————

11 And of th' all-glorious Trinity entreat
  That this alliance thou may'ſt ſtill defeat,
  And that he'd grace and ſtrength to thee afford,
  In thy profeſſion, well to ſerve the Lord.

12 Shou'd Satan ever find us off our guard,
  And without armour, his aſſaults to ward,
  We may be ſure he'll roughly-handle thoſe
  Who ſhall, unarm'd, his deadly force oppoſe.

K 4   13 For

13 For if this helmet's, on the head, not place'd——
The corfelet, on the breaft---and round the waift,
The belt---or if our feet are ever found
Unfhod---the fiend our fouls will furely wound.

14 Be therefore, like a foldier, ftill in arms,
Be ftrictly-watchful againft all alarms,
Left thou fhou'dft by the guileful foe be foil'd,
And of eternal happinefs defpoil'd.

15 Whene'er thou goeft from thy room, beware,
Left thou fhou'dft fall into fome latent fnare ;
For Satan ever feeks, to hook thee in,
And tempt thee to commit fome mortal fin.

16 Great is his rage, but greater his deceit-----
Greater his fraud than force, however great----
He, like a lion, prowls about each hour,
For ever feeking whom he may devour.

17 The ferpent's cunning, and the dragon's ire,
The lion's ftrength, the glaring tiger's fire,
The wolf's voracioufnefs, the fox's fraud,
Belong to Satan, when he roams abroad.

18 No fleep, nor reft he knows, by day or night,
E'er fince he fell from the empyrean height,
But always feeks, with all his might, to flay
Each heedlefs foul, he meets with in his way.

19 Therefore of all his ftratagems, take care,
Left thou fhou'dft fall unweeting to the fnare:
With ceafelefs praye'rs Chrift's matchlefs aid entreat;
And Chrift will help thee, Satan to defeat.

A Prayer againft the Temptations, and Affaults of the Devil.

1 O Thou, that keepeft hell's abyfs clofe-barr'd,
And o'er it's gates haft fet a conftant guard,
That Satan haft enchain'd, and death o'erthrown,
Hear my complaint from thy celeftial throne!

2 That

2 That bloody dragon, that malicious foe,
 Whom thou didſt bind, and gloriouſly o'erthrow,
 Still plots my ruin---if thou wilt not deign
 To grant thy help, his malice to reſtrain.

3 Both night and day, he roams with ſleepleſs eyes,
 And, like a lion, to deſtroy me tries;
 For ever prompt and ready to devour,
 Didſt thou not ſhield me from his deadly pow'r!

4 Each night that comes, and each returning day,
 He ſpreads his dang'rous toils a-croſs my way,
 And into them I tumble unawares,
 If thou doſt not preſerve me from his ſnares.

5 There's no forbidden fruit, of pleaſing hue,
 But he preſents it daily to my view————
 There is no ſin, but he wou'd tempt me to,
 That I may make my gracious God, my foe.

6 There's no good act, on which my ſoul's intent,
 Which the fell fiend attempts not to prevent————
 And oft, too oft! his curs'd attempt ſucceeds,
 And puts a ſtop to my beſt minded deeds.

7 I cannot eat a bit of bread in peace,
 I cannot take a wink of ſleep at eaſe,
 I cannot drink, or any work begin,
 But he aſſays to turn it all to ſin.

8 I cannot e'en a ſingle ſentence ſay,
 I cannot even bend my knees to pray,
 But Satan all his efforts ſtill applies,
 To make me ſin—e'en at my pray'rs he tries:

9 Nay, O my Saviour! when I'm moſt inclin'd
 To worſhip thee, with all my heart and mind,
 Then moſt he aims my purpoſe to prevent,
 By all the various wiles he can invent!

10 And ſhou'dſt thou let him looſe, without controul
 And due reſtraint, to over-pow'r my ſoul,
 Worſe then, I'm well-convince'd, wou'd be my caſe
 Than that of Job, and all his former race.

11 Obſerve,

11 Obſerve, O Lord! his bloody minded hate,
His roar ſuppreſs, his daring pride abate,
Fetter his feet, and bruiſe his baneful head,
Shorten his chain---let not his poiſon ſpread.

12 Thou haſt, O Chriſt! the dreadful dragon bound,
Thou both his thighs didſt with thy chain ſurround,
Thou didſt deſpoil him of his boaſted arms,
Thou haſt preſerv'd our ſouls from all alarms.

13 Let us in thy bright panoply be dreſt,
Infuſe thy mighty Spirit in each breaſt,
Teach thou our hands to war, with ſkill and might,
And let us not be vanquiſh'd in the fight.

14 Let not the ſerpent, our frail ſouls beguile,
Let not the dragon, thy weak ſervants foil,
Let not the lion, thy elect undo,
Let not the fiend, thy faithful ſons ſubdue.

15 Lo! we are weak, and he is form'd for war;
But thou, O Chriſt! art ſtronger yet by far:
On us, ſome portion of thy might beſtow,
And then, tho' weak, we ſhall o'ercome the foe.

16 Wiſe is the ſerpent, we, alas! but dull,
The dragon too, is of devices full:
If therefore thou ſhalt not thine aid afford,
The fiend will ſteal thy ranſom'd flock, O Lord!

17 Make us all wiſe, to ſee each wily ſnare,
Wary, that we may of his nets beware,
Strong, to reſiſt the efforts, he may uſe,
And cautious—all his offers to refuſe.

18 With favour on thy ſervants, Lord! look down,
Aſſiſt thy brethren to obtain the crown,
And all, who fight beneath thy banner, aid,
To bear their croſs, and cruſh the ſerpent's head.

Advice, to guard againſt the Temptations of the Devil.

1 SHOU'D Satan promiſe thee, or houſe or land,
  If thou wou'dſt kneel and worſhip at his feet :
  Tell him, he has not at his own command
  A foot of ground, beſides the' infernal pit.

2 Shou'd Satan ever tempt thy hands to touch
  Thy neighbour's wife, and to defile his bed :
  Tell him that vengeance ever waits on ſuch,
  And hovers dreadful o'er each guilty head.

3 Shou'd Satan tempt thee o'er thy bowl to ſtay,
  'Till drunkenneſs has overwhelm'd thy ſoul :
  Tell him that drunkards at the latter day,
  Shall in fierce floods of fire and ſulphur roll.

4 Shou'd Satan prompt thy tongue to ſwear and curſe,
  And make thy Saviour's blood and wounds it's theme,
  Tell him there can be no tranſgreſſion worſe,
  Than thy Redeemer's ſuffe'rings to blaſpheme.

5 Shou'd Satan ever tempt thee to oppreſs
  The Orphan—ſay, 'tis ſcarce a greater ſin
  To pull out Chriſt's own eyes—than to diſtreſs
  The helpleſs Orphan, that has loſt his kin.

6 Shou'd Satan prompt thee, to make uſe of fraud,
  Or make thee play the perjur'd liar's part———
  Tell him, the righteous Judge, the' eternal God,
  Has fix'd an hatred of them in thy heart.

7 Shou'd Satan tempt thee, in the gloom of night,
  The ſecret works of darkneſs to tranſact———
  Tell him, that God, who is the ſource of light,
  With his all-ſeeing eyes ſurveys each fact.

8 Whene'er he tempts thee foully to belie,
  Or ridicule a brother, maim'd or lame———
  He fain wou'd then perſuade thee to defie
  The living Lord, and curſe thy Maker's name.

9 Whene'er

9 Whene'er he prompts thee to repeat or make
  A lie—to flay thy precious foul he aims
  With shamelefs front, or plunge it in the lake,
  That ever rages with fulphureous flames.

10 Whene'er he feeks to drive thee to defpair,
   He thinks to force thee to the realms below,
   Where bloody Cain, and Saul, and Judas are,
   Though thou the trueft penitence fhou'dft fhow.

11 Whenever Satan by his efforts tries
   To turn thy footfteps from the temple-door———
   He flily feeks to keep thee from the fkies;
   Becaufe at church thou didft not Chrift adore.

12 Tho' he attempts to make thee turn away,
   Whilft God's own Minifters the Gofpel preach,
   He only aims to barricade the way,
   Left thou fhou'd chance the tree of life to reach.

13 If in the church he tries to make thee nod,
   (Where Chriftians fhou'd, to pray'r alone, refort)
   He only ftrives to make thee mock thy God,
   In his own temple, and his holy court.

14 Beware of fleeping, then, when thou fhou'dft pray:
   Worfe than a Devil is the man, that dares
   To mock his God, upon a Sabbath day,
   And on his knees, with hypocritic airs.

15 Shou'd Satan ever tempt thee to delay,
   At the communion-table to appear;
   Thy feal of pardon he'd fain fteal away,
   By hindring thee to pay thy homage there.

16 If from thy heart, the Gofpel of the Lord
   Which thou haft heard, he ftudies to efface———
   He tries to rob thee of the pow'rful word,
   By which alone thou canft improve in grace.

17 If he can once prevail on thee to bear
   A Chriftian name, yet no religion have———
   He'll make the fervant of the Lord appear
   The Devil's drudge, and moft devoted flave.

18 If he a fruitlefs faith wou'd have thee boaft,
   On which no works concomitant attend————
   Thou'lt find it, dead—and find it, to thy coft,
   A faith, that cannot fave thee, in the end.

19 Shou'd he from penitence thy foul reftrain,
   'Till death, and make thee each good work poftpone:
   He hinders thee God's mercy to obtain,
   Until perhaps the time of mercy's gone.

20 Satan will leave no fort of fcheme untry'd,
   By means whereof he may expect fuccefs,
   No ftone unturn'd, no meafure unapply'd————
   'Till, if he can, he brings thee to tranfgrefs.

21 The tempter roves about, both night and day————
   By night and day, then of his wiles beware:
   For there's no place, wherein he will not lay
   His toils, our heedlefs footfteps to enfnare.

22 At church, in thy own grounds, at home, abroad,
   Intent on work, or unreferv'd at play,
   At table, in thy bed, or on the road,
   Satan, where-e'er thou art, wou'd there betray.

23 Be therefore, like a warrior, ftill prepar'd,
   And never fail thy panoply to wear,
   And on thy actions keep a conftant guard————
   Left Satan fhou'd thy foul in pieces tear.

24 Woe unto him, who was in Childhood wild,
   In youth, a fpendthrift, and a churl, in age!
   Since he, thereby, has Satan's will fulfill'd,
   Throughout his life, in ev'ry diffe'rent ftage.

25 Take heed, my foul—of Satan's wiles beware:
   He always aims all ages to trepan————
   In all thy paths he'll lay a latent fnare,
   To catch thy carelefs feet, whene'er he can.

26 He'll ftrive to make thee pafs thy youthful days,
   Ever in fruitlefs, vain purfuits employ'd,
   In dancing, riot, and fuch idle ways————
   Ways of all virtue and all merit void.

27 In manhood, he will try to take thee in,
    With women and with wine thy time to waste,
    And thy pure veffel to defile with fin,
    With foul concupifcence, and deeds unchafte.

28 When age comes on, he'll labour to divert
    Thy thoughts from God, and penitence fincere,
    And ev'ry purpofe of thy foul pervert
    To muck-worm avarice and worldly care.

29 Endeavour then, whatever ftage thou'rt in,
    From Satan's fnares to extricate thy mind,
    Who'll feek thy utter ruin by the fin,
    To which he finds thy nature moft inclin'd.

ADVICE to pray earneftly, and on all Occafions, fuppofed to be addrefs'd to his own Son.

1 FORGET not, on my bleffing, thrice a-day,
    Thy bounden facrifice of praife to bring,
    And on thy bended knees devoutly pray
    Before thy God, thy Saviour, and thy King.

2 Before thy room thou quitteft, with the light——
    Before thou dineft, at the noon of day——
    Before thou fuppeft, at the' approach of night——
    On thefe three times, do not neglect to pray.

3 Lift up thy hands to pray for thy fuccefs,
    E'er they are put to any ufe befide,
    And beg of God thy ev'ry work to blefs,
    Before thou haft thyfelf to work apply'd.

4 Thou may'ft fome fhort ejaculation fay,
    Even when, on thy tafk, thou'rt moft intent,
    And fhou'dft with never-ceafing ardor pray;
    Though God has given thee thy heart's content.

5 Though thou with heavy labour art opprefs'd,
    And greatly hurry'd on a market-day——
    Yet even then, it is by all confefs'd,
    'Twill do thee much more good, than harm, to pray.

6 Though

6 Though David did in martial fkill excel,
  And troubles more than any mortal bore——
  Yet, feven times a-day, he always fell
  Upon his knees, the Godhead to adore.

7 Whilft with the kings of Canaan war he wage'd,
  Jofhua pray'd—yet fought with all his might ;
  His heart was in devotion then engage'd,
  E'en whilft his hands were bufy in the fight.

8 Their praye'rs ne'er ftopp'd whatever they began,
  Nor put their undertaking to a ftand ;
  But rather forwarded each happy plan,
  And fanctify'd whate'er they took in hand.

9 Accuftom thou thy felf to pray with zeal,
  In ev'ry work thou doft—and thou fhalt fee
  That pray'r can do more good than tongue can tell,
  And be a happy furtherance to thee.

10 The Hufbandman and Hind may full as well,
  E'en whilft at plough, to their Creator pray,
  As to their cattle fome dull jargon tell,
  Or filly fingfong, all the live-long day.

11 E'en Travellers may Pfalms devoutly fing,
  Or pray in fpirit, as they ride, or walk,
  As well as they may make the welkin ring
  With their loofe ballads, or their noify talk.

12 Nay, Shoe-makers and Tailors may enjoy
  Some time to pray, whilft they their trades purfue :
  For whilft their hands they at their craft employ,
  Their minds may be employ'd in prayer too.

13 Old women, whilft they turn the fpinning wheel,
  May each perform her tafk without delay,
  And maidens twirl about the rattling reel,
  And yet find time enough befides to pray.

14 Though thou fhou'dft be, with Mofes on the hill—
  Or elfe, with Ifaac, walking o'er thy ground——
  Or in the temple with St. John—yet ftill,
  Where-e'er thou art, to pray thou'rt always bound.

15 Before

15 Before thou goeſt from thy houſe, entreat
  Thy gracious God, to give thee good ſucceſs,
  And all thy labours, whether ſmall or great,
  With his accuſtom'd providence to bleſs.

16 'Tis God, that makes our undertakings ſpeed,
  'Tis God, that ev'ry bleſſing to us gives,
  When he is worſhipp'd, all our works ſucceed,
  But when neglected, then a curſe arrives.

17 His ſpirit beg, to guide thee on thy way,
  His grace too beg, to aid each faint effort,
  His bleſſing beg, on all thou doſt eſſay,
  And he himſelf will be thy ſtrong ſupport.

18 Let ev'ry act with Jeſus be begun------
  His help implore, to bring it to an end----
  To him aſcribe the glory, when 'tis done :
  So ſhall ſucceſs on ev'ry act attend.

19 As God made Joſeph's ev'ry work ſucceed,
  And all that faithful Daniel did of yore ;
  So will he forward, for thee, ev'ry deed,
  If thou ſincerely wilt his name adore.

20 For if thou doſt not pray aright to God,
  Like Jonah, thou a baſeleſs booth ſhalt make-----
  Or elſe, like Peter, thou ſhalt ſpread abroad
  Thy nets---and yet a ſingle fiſh not take.

21 Thou, night and day, in trouble and in pain
  Shalt fret and fume, and like a Miſer moil---
  Yet all thy labour ſhall be quite in vain,
  And thou nought better, after all thy toil.

22 In vain it is, to riſe up with the light,
  In vain it is, to eat the bread of care,
  In vain, to watch the tedious winter-night,
  If we without God's holy bleſſing are.

23 In vain it is new palaces to raiſe,
  In vain it is, to garriſon the fort,
  In vain it is, to toil throughout our days,
  If God does not our weak attempts ſupport.

24 Left

24 Left all thy labours, then, fhou'd fruitlefs prove,
Pray thou with fervor, if thou wou'dft fucceed——
Pray unto God to blefs thee from above:
So fhall he fully profper ev'ry deed.

ADVICE, to the FARMER.

1 E'ER thou thy hands upon the plough doft lay,
Firft lift them up, and to thy Maker pray,
Thou and thy hinds—that he thy work may blefs,
And crown thy labours with the wifh'd fuccefs.

2 In vain it is, a large domain to plow,
In vain it is, to harrow what you fow,
If God with-hold his blefling from the grain,
The feed will rot beneath the furrow'd plain.

3 'Tis God that fows—'tis God that makes the field
It's full increafe in time of harveft yield:
An hundred fold, or more, is fometimes given
To thofe, who place their confidence in heaven.

4 Whoe'er wou'd from the earth it's ftrength obtain,
And reap large crops of valuable grain,
Let him with fervent pray'r his God addrefs,
And he fhall meet with the defire'd fuccefs.

5 A fingle harrow, by the help of pray'r,
A greater produce fhall return by far
Than can be got by teams, perhaps a fcore,
Where none by pray'r invoke the' Almighty Pow'r.

6 Ifaac, by prayer's efficacious aid,
Was, in his corn, an hundred fold repay'd;
Whilft others, who neglected pray'r, fcarce found
Bare fix-for-one from their beft-culture'd ground.

7 The Lord, thy God, O hufbandman! adore——
With all thy heart his needful help implore,
That he the labours of thy hands may blefs,
And, to thy full content, thy ftore increafe.

L

The

The FARMER's PRAYER.

1 O Thou! by whom the univerſe was made,
   Mankind's ſupport, and never failing aid,
Who bidd'ſt the earth her various products bear,
  Who watereſt the ſoft'ned ſoil with rain,
  Who giveſt vegetation to the grain,
Unto a peaſant's ardent pray'r give ear!

2 I now intend, with care, my land to dreſs,
  And in it's fertile womb to ſow my grain;
  Which, if, O God! thou deigneſt not to bleſs,
  I never ſhall receive, or ſee, again.

3 In vain it is to plant, in vain it is to ſow,
  In vain to harrow well the levell'd plain,
  If thou wilt not command the ſeed to grow,
  And ſhed thy bleſſing on the bury'd grain.

4 For not a ſingle corn will ruſh to birth
  Of all that I've intruſted to the earth,
  If thou doſt not enjoin the blade to ſpring,
  And the young ſhoot to full perfection bring.

5 I therefore beg thy bleſſing on my lands,
  O Lord! and on the labour of my hands,
  That I thereby, may as a Chriſtian, live,
  And my ſupport, and maintenance receive!

6 Open the windows of the ſkies, and pour
  Thy bleſſings on them in a genial ſhow'r;
  My corn with earth's prolific fatneſs feed,
  And give increaſe to all my cover'd ſeed!

7 Let not the ſkies, like braſs in fuſion, glow,
  Nor the' earth, with heat, as hard as iron grow,
  Let not our paſtures and our meads of hay,
  For our ſupine neglect of Thee, decay!

8 But give us in good time and meaſure meet,
  A tempe'rate ſeaſon, and ſufficient heat,
  Give us the former and the latter rains,
  Give peace and plenty to the Britiſh ſwains.

9 The locuſt and the cankerworm reſtrain,
The dew, that blights and tarniſhes the grain,
The drought, the nipping winds,the lightning's glare,
Which to the growing corn pernicious are.

10 O, let the year be with thy goodneſs crown'd,
Let it with all thy choiceſt gifts abound,
Let bleating flocks each fertile valley fill,
And lowing herds adorn each riſing hill!

11 Give to the ſons of men their daily bread,
Give graſs to the mute beaſts, that crop the mead,
Give wine and oil, to thoſe that till the field,
And let thy heritage abundance yield.

12 Give us a harveſt with profuſion crown'd,
Let ev'ry field and yard with corn abound,
Let herbs each garden, fruit each orchard fill,
Let rocks their honey, kine their milk diſtill.

13 Proſper our handy-work, thou gracious God!
And further our endeavours with ſucceſs:
So, on our knees, ſhall we thy name applaud,
And night and morn our benefactor bleſs.

Advice, to the Traveller.

1 E'ER thou thy foot ſhalt in the ſtirrup place,
Beſeech thy God to bleſs thee with his grace,
And keep thee ſafe, 'till thy return again,
Whene'er thou travelleſt o'er hill or plain.

2 God's angel ſeek, thy footſteps to direct,
His wing from ev'ry danger to protect,
Upon thy journey for his bleſſing ſue,
And he will proſper all thou haſt to do.

3 As God an angel with Tobias ſent
For his attendant, whereſoe'er he went:
So ſhall he ſpeedy ſuccour ſend to all,
Who ſhall on him, e'en now, for ſuccour call.

 4 From

4. From the beſt Patriarch's ſervant learn to pray,
And call on God, whilſt thou art on thy way,
That he the purpoſe of thy ſoul may ſpeed:
So ſhalt thou to thy utmoſt wiſh ſucceed.

5 But if thou ſhou'dſt not, on thy bended knee,
Entreat the Son of God to ſpeed thee home:
Thou ſhalt oppreſſion on thy journey ſee,
And bootleſs back, without thy errand come.

6 To thoſe, that muſt a diſtant journey take,
Better is praye'r than wine, the thirſt to ſlake,
Better than forts, to ward the light'ning's glance,
Better than ought, to guard againſt miſchance.

7 Better is praye'r, to ſave thee from thy foe,
When on a dange'rous journey thou doſt go,
Than ſword or piſtol, or the fleeteſt horſe,
Than num'rous troops, or any human force.

8 The Deity with ceaſeleſs praye'r adore,
And on thy journey his ſtrong aid implore;
So ſhall he ſend his angels to fulfil
Thy heart's beſt wiſhes, and preſerve thee ſtill.

The Traveller's PRAYER.

1 THou guardian of the weak, thou poor man's friend!
Hear from thy glorious throne, Almighty God!
That doſt thine aid to fearful trav'lers lend,
The ſuit of one that journeys on the road!

2 I am oblig'd I know not where to go,
Nor know I whether I ſhall ever come,
Since 'tis a country I'm a ſtranger to,
If thou doſt not my journey proſper, home.

3 Lord, it is Thou, who governeſt this ball,
And all that is therein thou doſt direct;
So that no miſchief ever can befal
The men thou favoureſt, thy own elect!

4 I therefore

4 I therefore humbly make it my requeſt
  That thou in mercy wou'dſt my life ſuſtain,
  Where-e'er I go, and with thy favour bleſt,
  Bring me in joy and ſafety back again.

5 To lead the way, diſpatch an angel down,
  My ſolace, and protection to become,
  That he my buſ'neſs with ſucceſs may crown,
  And back again in health conduct me home.

6 Thy downy wings do thou expand abroad,
  Beneath their ample awning ſhade me ſtill,
  Suffer not any foe, upon the road,
  To do my ſoul or body any ill.

7 Send thou thy ſervant Raphael to direct
  My ſteps, as he did with Tobias go,
  The youth from ev'ry danger to protect,
  To guide his feet, and ſave him from the foe.

8 Be thou before me, like a cloud, by day,
  Like a bright blaze, by night, my God and King,
  To light, and bring me ſafely on my way,
  As thou didſt Iſrael erſt from Canaan bring.

9 The eaſtern ſages thou didſt erſt protect,
  And ſent'ſt a ſtar thoſe ſtrangers to attend,
  As thou didſt their's, do thou my ſteps direct,
  'Till thou haſt brought me to my journey's end.

10 As young Tobias thou didſt ſave of yore,
   Both from the river-monſter, and the fiend,
   So ſave me, Lord! by thy Almighty Pow'r,
   From all the perils, which may me attend.

11 Preſerve me, Lord! from Satan's ſweeping net,
   And his vile friends, who my beſt ſchemes ſtill croſs,
   Permit them not, by whom I'm thus beſet,
   To do me hurt, or bring me ſhame and loſs.

12 Let not loud thunder, or the light'ning's glare,
   Let not the ſtorm or tempeſt do me harm,
   Let not the wily fiend my ſoul enſnare,
   Nor any violence my heart alarm.

L 3   13 Preſerve

13 Preferve me from the fnares by robbers fpread,
   O'erflowing rivers, villains that beguile,
   A life corrupt, and an adult'rous bed,
   The dangers of the road, and comrades vile.

14 Rouze then my fainting heart within my breaft,
   Make thou my path, by thy kind furthe'rance, plain;
   Strengthen my fellow-trav'lers and my beaft,
   And bring us, to our wifhes, back again.

15 Succefs to all we undertake, impart,
   And expedite the bufinefs and defign
   Of ev'ry one that has an honeft heart,
   That all, to blefs thy holy name, may join.

16 Preferve us, Lord! from harm and ill fuccefs,
   Mifchance, mifcarriage, mifery, mifhap,
   Damage, difeafe, difafter, and diftrefs,
   Lofs of the road, or any dang'rous fcrape.

17 Conduct us back again in health, O God!
   Our dear relations and our friends among;
   That we thy name may, for thy aid, applaud,
   And fing thy praifes in fome facred fong:

ADVICE to a SOLDIER.

1 SOLDIER, before thou marcheft out to fight,
   To ferve the Crown, and in thy country's right,
   Pray to the Lord, and he'll to thee impart
   Strength, martial skill, and a courageous heart.

2 'Tis God, that gives the loyal foldier might,
   'Tis God, that gives him knowledge how to fight,
   'Tis by God's aid, his expert fingers know
   To tofs the Pike, or bend the ftubborn bow.

3 The God of armies is a warrior ftrong,
   A fafe retreat from injury and wrong;
   From him alone comes conqueft and fuccefs:
   Implore his aid, and He thy arms will blefs.

4 Prayer

4 Prayer is better and more ufeful far,
  To ev'ry Soldier in the time of war,
  Than any armour to fence off a blow,
  Or than a Sword is, to offend the foe.

5 The hands of Mofes, lifted up on high,
  To fupplicate affiftance from the sky,
  More than the fword of Jofhua deftroy'd,
  And all the troops that gallant chief employ'd.

6 Jonathan's prayer greater numbers flew,
  Among the Philiftine difheartned crew,
  Than were by Saul and all his army flain,
  In various conflicts on the' enfanguin'd plain.

7 More prevalent was David's praye'r by far,
  The' enormous giant to o'ercome in war,
  'Than thofe fmooth ftones which from his fcrip he took,
  Though thro' his forehead one of them he ftrook.

8 Elijah, though no weapons he employ'd,
  Befides his praye'rs, two captains erft deftroy'd
  With both the companies they brought along.
  What then, on Earth, than Prayer is more ftrong ?

9 The Praye'r of Judith of more ufe was found
  Than thofe ftrong walls, which did the town furround,
  To fave Bethulia's war-devoted tow'rs
  From Holofernes' defolating pow'rs.

10 Before thou entereft the mortal fray,
  Lift up thy hands immediately to pray,
  As valiant Jofhua was wont to do,
  So fhalt thou meet fuccefs againft the foe.

11 Thy hands for battle prudently prepare,
  And earneftly incline thy mind to pray'r,
  And thou fhalt find that Prayer can do more
  Than both thy hands againft an adverfe pow'r.

The

The Soldier's PRAYER.

1 THOU God of might, who doſt o'er hoſts preſide,
 Who doſt alone the doubtful battle guide,
Who doſt alone the joyful victo'ry gain,
O hear my prayer in this dread campaign !

2 Here in the crown's, our king and country's right,
We, for our lands, our goods, and nation, fight
With a perfidious and invete'rate foe,
That always ſeeks this kingdom's overthrow.

3 Confound, O Lord ! each miſchievous intent,
Each plot and ſtratagem our foes invent,
Their ſtrength diminiſh, and their pride abate,
Aſſuage their malice, blunt their keen-edge'd hate.

4 Be thou, O Lord ! thy feeble ſervants friend,
That we may manfully the crown defend ;
And give us ſtrength, however weak and few,
Thoſe pow'rful foes to conquer and ſubdue.

5 Do thou, O God ! our fainting hearts revive,
Do thou, our enemies before us drive,
With terror and diſmay their boſoms fill,
With ſhame and foul defeat purſue them ſtill.

6 Though we be but a ſmall and feeble band,
Compar'd to thoſe who in their army ſtand ;
Yet are we furniſh'd with ſufficient might,
If thou, O Lord, wilt for thy ſervants fight.

7 I know, O Lord ! thy power is not leſs
In few than many —thou canſt grant ſucceſs
E'en to the weakeſt—and doſt oft delight
Againſt the ſtrongeſt to exert thy might.

8 Thy ſervant Gideon thou didſt erſt employ,
The Midianites vaſt army to deſtroy,
Though but three hundred form'd his ſlender band,
And they, like locuſts, cumber'd all the land.

9 Jonathan

9 Jonathan and his armour-bearer, erſt,
  Unnumber'd foes ſuccefsfully diſpers'd:
  When thou their ſouls didſt with amazement fill,
  Who cou'd refiſt, or countermand thy will!

10 Thou gaveſt Shamgar ſuch refiſtlefs pow'r,
  Six hundred with a goad he ſlew of yore,
  And Samſon, with unequall'd ſtrength endue'd,
  A thouſand with an aſs's jaw ſubdue'd.

11 A woman's artlefs hand thou didſt employ,
  Jabin's head-captain Siſera, to deſtroy ·
  The ſtars themſelves, arrange'd in juſt array,
  For Iſrael fought, that memorable day!

12 So, if for us it be thy will to fight,
  Thou canſt ſupply us with ſufficient might,
  Our foes to conquer on the' embattled plain;
  Though we be but a ſmall and feeble train.

13 If thou, O Lord! appeareſt on our ſide.
  The heaven's, the earth, the ocean's furious tide,
  The ſun and moon, and ev'ry wind that blows,
  Will join with us to war againſt our foes.

14 If thou to favour us art well inclin'd,
  Nor Turk, nor Pope, nor Spaniard, need we mind:
  Nay, though againſt us hell itſelf ſhou'd puſh,
  We need not value hell itſelf a ruſh.

15 Thou haſt thyſelf, O Lord! a warrior ſhow'd,
  Thou only art with ſkill and ſtrength endow'd,
  Thou art the Giver of the laurel-wreath,
  Thou art our Shield againſt the pow'r of death.

16 'Tis thou, that ſtoppeſt war's rage, ev'ry where,
  'Tis thou, that ſnappeſt-ſhort the pointed ſpear,
  'Tis thou, that tie'ſt the war-horſe to his ſtall,
  'Tis thou, that art the conqueror of all!

17 Do thou give comfort to each drooping heart,
  Do thou unto our ſinews ſtrength impart,
  Do thou to us true martial ſkill afford,
  That we may fight the battles of the Lord.

18 Like

18 Like Joſhua, make thou our leaders ſtrong,
   That they like him, may chaſe the hoſtile throng,
   Their ſchemes and ſtratagems do thou attend,
   That they may bring them to a proſpe'rous end.

19 Strength, brave'ry, knowledge, puiſance, impart
   To all our ſoldier's, and a lion's heart:
   Might, will, and diligence on each beſtow,
   That he may fearleſsly confront his foe.

20 Around us let thy angels ſentry keep,
   And from our foes proteƈt us, whilſt we ſleep:
   A choſen troop of thy chief warriors ſend,
   From war's fierce rage thy ſervants to defend.

21 Do thou, O Lord! o'er all our hoſt preſide,
   And with thy wiſdom all our aƈtions guide:
   May all of us thy ſacred law fulfil,
   And nothing do repugnant to thy will.

22 Let us unto the King pay homage due,
   Let's to our fellow-citizens be true,
   Let us obedient to our leaders prove,
   And in our quarters live in peace and love.

23 Make each of us contented with his pay,
   Let us not take our neighbour's goods away,
   Let none of us oppreſs, or high or low,
   But aweful reve'rence to thy diƈtates ſhow.

24 Let us in no diſorders e'er engage,
   Nor any of our company enrage,
   Nor with our leaders mutinouſly ſtrive,
   Nor in vile courſes and debauche'ry live.

25 Let us no wife or maiden e'er oppreſs,
   Let us not any tender heart diſtreſs;
   Leſt thou thy wrath againſt ſuch deeds ſhou'dſt ſhow,
   And yield us up a prey unto the foe.

26 Make us all live, whilſt by the foe beſet,
   As if we all were in thy temple met,
   And make us call upon thee, ev'ry hour,
   To aid, and keep us by thy mighty pow'r.

27 As

27 As we are daily at the gates of death,
    Near the fpear's point and gun's deftroying breath,
    Let us each moment in thy fear abide,
    And caft our vile enormities afide.

28 Since none, O Lord! the hour or minute know,
    When they to thee a juft account muft fhow,
    O, may our lives be righteous and fincere,
    Before we at thy judgement feat appear!

29 Prepare us, Lord! that we to thee may come,
    And make us ready to receive our doom,
    Let us not live in fin a fingle hour,
    Left unawares it fhou'd our fouls o'erpow'r.

30 Permit us not in evil to proceed,
    Or the commiffion of a fingle deed,
    Which at thy dread tribunal muft be known,
    When we with fhame appear before thy throne.

31 Save us, O Lord! who call upon thy name,
    But overwhelm our enemies with fhame:
    Our gracious Sove'reign and his Kingdoms blefs,
    And crown our arms with conqueft and fuccefs!

ADVICE to the Dealer, or Drover.

1 IF thou'rt a Dealer, honeft be each act,
    And fairly pay for what to thee is fold;
    Be to thy promife and thy word exact:
    Credit is better oft than hoards of gold.

2 Of the neceffitous no vantage take,
    And be not ftudious of exceffive gain,
    With rogues no bargain or agreement make;
    Nothing will thrive that comes from fuch a train.

3 Buy not too much on tick, for all will fell,
    To fuch a purchafer, extremely dear,
    And fuch a trade will foon that wretch compel
    To quit the kingdom, or to difappear.

4 Take

4 Take heed that thou doft not thy chapmen cheat,
God will a fentence pafs on all deceit:
And tho' thou fhou'dft beyond the feas retreat,
Sure vengeance will on thy tranfgreffion wait.

5 They ne'er (the fcripture on that head is plain)
Shall roaft the prey, who ftudy to deceive :
For fraud to no one yet brought real gain,
It paffes off, like water through a fieve.

6 Of drunkennefs beware, whate'er thou doft ;
For drunkennefs will make the wealthieft poor,
And when a trader's oft in liquor loft,
In wine and ale he foon will fpend his ftore.

7 Take care of thy dear foul, to juftice cleave,
And do the poor no wrong, for confcience' fake :
For if a bankrupt thou the land fhou'dft leave,
Vengeance divine thy footfteps will o'ertake.

ADVICE to a young Man, before he goes a Courting.

1 WHEN firft thou goe'ft to court a maid,
If thou'dft fucceed, implore God's aid,
And take his Spirit for thy guide,
Or thou'lt ne'er get a worthy bride.

2 A wife with modefty endow'd
And grace, is the beft gift of God,
A gift, that none fhall e'er obtain,
But they that in his fear remain.

3 Then beg of God, this gift to have,
And his divine affiftance crave :
So fhalt thou meet with good fuccefs,
And all will favour thy addrefs.

4 Yet, e'er thou weddeft, as is fit,
Unto thy parent's will fubmit,
Afk their confent upon the knee :
So fhall thy nuptials happy be !

5 God

5 God unto them wou'd have thee bow,
   Beg their advice, their pleasure know,
   E'er thou presume'st a wife to take:
   So no improper match they make.

6 Yet he'd not have them force thy mind
   To marry, where thou'rt not inclin'd,
   One, whom thy heart cou'd never love,
   And ne'er cou'd thy affections move.

7 If full of Grace, if good in kind,
   In body perfect, and in mind,
   The maiden be——if bless'd with sense,
   With Virtue, Wisdom, Competence,——
   Follow where nature leads the way,
   And the divine command obey.

8 Thy parents must the choice approve,
   Or they'll resist the Lord above,
   And in thy bosom light a fire,
   To tempt inordinate desire.

9 Yet, if thou canst, ne'er fret thy sire,
   But him, in all he shall require,
   With filial duty seek to please,
   And he'll thy wishes grant with ease.

10 A Protestant, of blameless life,
   And truly pious, be thy wife:
   Scarce e'er agreed the spouse and dame,
   Whose principles were not the same!

11 Seek thou a maid, of honest kin,
   Oft constitution sways to sin,——
   And, if God does not guard her well,
   Young miss will fall, where madam fell.

12 Clean, neat and lovely let her be,
   From aukwardness and flutte'ry free:
   Cold, tasteless, joyless, faint, the love,
   (That's on a slattern plac'd) will prove.

13 Let her, whom thou'rt resolv'd to court,
   Be of good life and good report——

Her temper mild——her words be few :
Worfe than a fcorpion is a fhrew !

14 Let her be knowing, virtuous, wife,
And thou'lt above thine equals rife,
She'll fill thy houfe, thy fame advance,
And make thy heart with pleafure dance.

15 Courteous and clever, let her be,
And full of grace and charity :
Spare is his board, and hard his bed,
Who to unthriftinefs is wed.

16 Let her be pleafing to behold;
Neither too young, nor yet too old :
The old and cold will ftarve thy love,
The young thy jealoufy may move.

17 Like Sarah let her pleafe her fpoufe,
And liké Rebecca rule her houfe,
Like Rachel let the maid be fair,
And wife, like her, who Lemu'el bare.

18 Meek, mild, and gentle, let her be,
For manners, tempe'rance, piety,
Remark'd——obliging, nurture'd well :
Three kingdoms wealth fhe'll then excel.

19 Of worthlefs, vain, coquets beware,
And of the flawny trapes, take care,
Nor to the dow'r-proud flirt incline :
She'll prove a plague to thee and thine.

20 Shun one too fair, too warm, too free,
Or fhe'll a bofom-ferpent be :
For 'tis a chance that any find,
In a fame'd Toaft, a modeft mind.

21 Seek not the damfel to efpoufe,
Though rich, that cannot rule her houfe :
Like fmoke, mifts, floods, that fleet away,
Her wealth will leffen ev'ry day.

22 Shou'd two be plac'd before thy eyes,
One, merely rich——the other, wife——

Let

Let thou the worthlefs fortune go,
. And vig'roufly the wife-one woo.

23 The wife-one will increafe her ftore,
And daily raife her friends to pow'r,
'Till when her hand no refpite knows,
Her fleeplefs eyes feek no repofe.

24 The fool's the downfal of her race,
The wife-one e'en may cities raife,
The fool will make her hufband figh,
The wife will lift up her's on high.

25 The fool the ftouteft heart will vex,
And the moft wealthy fpoufe perplex;
She'll, to a little, much reduce,
'Till fhe has fhame'd her friends and houfe:

26 She's a dead weight, a bofom-pain,
A ceafelefs drop, a fhameful ftain,
A fnake that ftings, a yoke that galls:
Woe worth the Wight to whom fhe falls!

27 May heave'n direct thee to the beft,
And be thou in a Confort bleft,
With each good quality endow'd,
Belove'd by man, approve'd by God!.

The Praife and Commendation of a Good WoMAN.

1 AS a wife child excells the fcept'red fool,
Who of conceit and felfifhnefs is full—
As a good name exceeds the beft perfume,
And richeft Balms, that from the *Indies* come—

2 As Prudence and Difcretion, wealth furpafs,
As ftrength and courage are outdone by grace,
As a good man is of more worth by far
Than riches: (tho' nought can with God compare!)

3 So much the wife and pious maid, poffefs'd
Of a bare competence, is more carefs'd

Than

Than the dull Ideot, born to an eftate,
And lincally-defcended from the Great.

4 A virtuous, cheerful, and obliging wife
Is better far, than all the pomp of life,
Better than houfes, tenements and lands,
Than pearls and precious ftones, and golden fands.

5 She is a fhip with coftly wares well-ftow'd,
A pearl, with virtues infinite endow'd,
A gem, beyond all value and compare :
Happy the man, who has her to his fhare !

6 She is a pillar, with rich gildings grace'd,
And on a pedeftal of filver place'd,
She is a turret of defence, to fave
A weak and fickly hufband from the grave,
She is a gorgeous crown, a glorious prize,
And ev'ry grace, in her, concent'red lies !

Advice and Warning to the ADULTERER.

1 HEAR my advice, Adulterer obfcene !
And often in thy mind thefe precepts roll,
E'er thou doft hafte with appetite unclean,
And headlong paffion to deftroy thy foul.

2 Think what a fhameful bargain thou haft made,
E'er thou thy precious foul away doft throw :
Sum up the gains and loffes of thy trade,
And ponder well, where thou at laft muft go.

3 Thou goeft to a ftew or brothel vile,
To pleafe the body and the foul deceive,
To anger God, his temple to defile,
To part with Chrift, and to the Devil cleave.

4 Thou goeft, like a Fool, to fell thy foul,
(Thy foul, for which thy Saviour deign'd to die !)
The grace of God, and all the joys above,
Only that thou may'ft with a Strumpet lie.

5 O, Do

5 O, do not deal fo hardly with thy foul,
   Give it not to be tor'n by fiends in hell,
   Only that thou in thofe bafe joys may'ft roll,
   On which all carnal minds with tranfport dwell!

6 O, do not fell the' ecftatic joys above,
   The' angelic converfe, and the realms of light,
   The Godhead's favour, and thy Saviour's love,
   For the loofe pleafures of a guilty night.

7 Confider, paufe, thy roving hands reftrain ;
   That contract is a contract full of woe ;
   Don't for a tranfient pleafure, dafh'd with pain,
   The realms above and all their blifs forego.

8 Bite off thy tongue, pluck out thy wanton eyes,
   Avert thy face, and offer nothing rude,
   Take heed, left Satan conquer thee by lies—
   And dare not do an act fo vile and lewd.

9 Obferve, how Satan leads thee by a thread
   Into the ftews, where fin-ftain'd harlots dwell,
   (As to the flaughter-houfe an ox is led)
   And plunges by that crime thy foul to hell.

10 Hear thou the' Apoftles, and the Prophets hear,
   Hear what in fcripture 's ev'ry-where enjoin'd,
   " Of this deteftable offence beware,   Eph.v.5,6;
   " Left thou to hell's abyfs fhou'dft be confign'd."

11 Wilt thou be torture'd in the' infernal flame?
   Wilt thou in ever-burning fulphur fry?
   Only that thou may'ft clothe thyfelf with fhame,
   ·And in the' embraces of a harlot lie ?

12 Wilt thou remain in the drear gloom of hell?
   Wilt thou be' imprifon'd in that dark abyfs?
   Wilt thou with Satan's finful children dwell,
   Only that thou fome common punk may'ft kifs?

13 Wilt thou thy Saviour and the' angelic train
   Give up, with all the raptu'rous blifs above,
   And nothing by the filly bargain gain,
   But a vile Strumpet's proftituted love ?

14 For fhame return, the low purfuit give o'er,
   And home, with penitence, thyfelf betake;
   Part not with heaven to obtain a whore:
   Efau wou'd not fo bad a bargain make!

15 Be therefore well-advife'd, the Godhead fear,
   Regard thy foul, as long as thou doft live,
   Of fuch attachments cautioufly beware,
   Nor to a punk thy Saviour's members give.

16 But confecrate thy body unto God;
   For a pure body is the Godhead's fane,
   Chrift's member, and the Trinity's abode:
   Prefume not thou that temple to prophane.

17 There's not a fouler fiend can haunt thy breaft
   Than vile adultery, and loofe defire:
   'Twas that, which did deftroy both man and beaft,
   By water once, and will again by fire.

18 Adultery, that crime fo bafe and vile,
   Provokes our God, to pleafe the fiend and flefh,
   The Spirit grieves, his temple does defile,
   And crucifies the Lord of Life afrefh:

19 It damns the foul, whilft it the body rots,
   It foils the nuptial robe, and credit blafts,
   Pofterity with endlefs fhame it blots,
   The largeft fortunes and eftates it waftes!

20 With bafe-born brats it does the land o'erwhelm,
   (The wife have, oft before, obferv'd the fame)
   With wrongful heirs it does oe'r-run the realm,
   And crowds the church with women void of fhame.

21 The pleafures, the debauch'd and lewd enjoy,
   To beggary and want directly lead,
   And, like an overwhelming flame, deftroy
   The wealth of thofe, that ftain the marriage-bed.

22 Whatever fin, befides, the' offender does,
   It flays but one tranfgreffor at a time:
   But fornication two at once undoes,
   Whenever any do commit the crime.

23 Although

23 Although no other fin can break the band
Of thofe, that are by matrimony join'd;
.Yet foul adulte'ry lets no marriage ftand,
But by pollution does it's ties unbind.

24 Worfe than a thief, worfe than a murde'rer ftill,
Worfe is the' adulterer, than all the reft,
Who, by one act, two precious fouls does kill,
Even his miftrefs's, whom he carefs'd.

25 The hungry robber often fteals thro' need,
Only a wretched being to fupport:
But each adulte'rer does a needlefs deed,
And ftudies to deftroy his foul in fport.

26 The Pharifees, who gave not their affent,
That they fhou'd fuffer for the' unfeemly fault,
Who did revile their elders, did confent
To flay the woman in adulte'ry caught.

27 The law of God enjoin'd, in words exprefs,   Lev.xx.
To ftone the man and woman both, outright,   10.
Who fhou'd this pofitive command tranfgrefs:
So hateful is adulte'ry in his fight!

28 It is fo hateful to the Pow'r divine
And.all his angels, that he won't permit
The brethren with adulterers to dine,   1Cor.v.11.
And thofe who fuch impurities commit.

29 It is a crime fo foul, fo full of fhame!
That holy writ will by no means allow
The Saints, fo much as this vile fin to name, Eph.v.3.
Much lefs that act of wickednefs to do.

3Q Our Saviour in the Gofpel bids us try
To curb the eye from fo unchafte a fin:
For often, through the window of the eye,
The foul-corrupting mifchief enters in.

31 E'er thou fhou'dft luft for fome enchanting dame,
Pluck from it's focket thy lafcivious eye:
For he, that can't reftrain his luftful flame,
Shall in hell-fire to endlefs ages fry.

                    32 This

32 This vice, tho' yet 'tis but conceiv'd in thought,
  Is in the fight of God fo very foul,
  That though it fhou'd not be to Practice brought,
  The Theory indulge'd will damn the foul.

Advice to the DRUNKARD.

1 IF thou'rt a drunkard, fond of ale and wine,
  And fmokeft vile mundungus without end,
  Cry out with fpeed, unto the' Pow'r divine,
  To give thee grace, to conquer the foul fiend. -

2 If thou haft falle'n into Excefs's well,
  Quickly implore affiftance from above:
  For neither angel, man, or imp of hell,
  Can thence, without it, the drench'd brute remove.

3 The drunken fiend will never quit his home,
  (No more than Satan the dumb child of old)
  'Till Chrift fhall with his holy Spirit come,
  By fafts and pray'rs to force him from his hold. -

4 Pray, that thou always mayeft ftrength obtain,
  The monftrous fin of drunk'nefs to prevent;
  From all excefs, throughout thy life, refrain,
  And never go, where drunken folks frequent.

5 From the fot's pray'er no good can e'er enfue,
  Unlefs he fafts, and guards againft excefs:
  For praye'r and fafting only can fubdue
  The fiend, that takes delight in drunkennefs.

6 Though thou fhou'dft pray againft that odious fin,
  If thou doft not the dire temptation fhun;
  Thy praye'r to thee will not be worth a pin,
  Becaufe thou didft not from the tavern run.

7 The teeth of drunkennefs ne'er lofe their hold,
  But, like a lion's, ftrongly feize their prey,
  'Till Chrift fhall come, that Lion truly bold!
  To bruife his head, and fnatch thy foul away.

8 The

8 The horfe, that in a boggy flough has funk,
   Without much help, can never leave the pit:
   So neither can the man, that's ever drunk,
   Without Chrift's aid, his fwinifh habit quit.

9 Compel not any one to drink too-much,
   But let each drink, according to his mind :
   If fome drink deep, do thou not herd with fuch,
   Nor ever drink more than thou art inclin'd.

10 Refpect thy betters, when they are in place,
   But ftill refpect thyfelf, by drinking nought:
   If thou by bumpers think'ft to do them grace,
   By gracing them, thou'lt to difgrace be brought.

11 'Tis a fad health, a health replete with ill,
   To drink what neither gives thee health, nor joy :
   I ne'er fhall pledge the health (come, what come will)
   That fhall in any fhape my own deftroy.

12 Some fneer at me, becaufe I fober keep,
   And feldom feem to fmile at any one;
   Whilft many' a briny tear I kindly weep,
   To fee them all by fottifhnefs undone.

13 The fot, that fneer'd not many feafons fince,
   Becaufe my money in my purfe I kept,
   Has fince (becaufe I wou'd not lend my pence)
   Full many' a tear in fullen filence wept.

14 For Jefus' fake from drunkennefs defend
   Thyfelf, it is the very worft of crimes,
   It turns a man into a perfect fiend,
   Worfe than the brutes themfelves a hundred times.

15 Flee from the tavern, from excefs refrain,
   Seek not the champion, Liquor, to fubdue,
   For none e'er cou'd, o'er it, a conqueft gain,
   But they that timely from it's ftrength with-drew.

16 The famous Alexander erft fubdue'd,
   Where-e'er he march'd, the countries all around;
   But Liquor with fuperior might endue'd,
   O'ercame with eafe that conqueror renown'd.

M 3   17 'Tis

17 'Tis better run away, than brave the field——
    'Tis better flee, than fight a rabble rout——
    'Tis better far, than ftrive with drink, to yield;
    Or thou'lt be foil'd, if thou wilt fee it out.

18 An hundred times thou did'ft thy valour try,
    But ev'ry trial was as oft in vain:
    And if thou doft not from the victor fly,
    Thou certainly fhalt catch a fall again.

19 Many, o'er liquor, wou'd a conqueft boaft,
    And vaunt that they can full as firmly tread;
    Yet all, that ever try'd, the vict'ry loft,
    But they, that early from the conflict fled.

20 Approach the fire, thy fhins its heat fhall feel——
    Approach thou pitch, it will thy garments ftain——
    Approach a ferpent, it will fting thy heel——
    Approach ftrong liquor, it will turn thy brain.

21 Flee from a ferpent, left it fting thy heel——
    Flee from the plague, left it ftrike thee dead——
    Flee from the fire, left thou it's force fhou'dft feel—
    Flee from ftrong liquor, left it turn thy head.

22 Of all the flaves, wherewith this world is ftor'd,
    The worft is he, who is his belly's flave:
    For, whilft he lives, he'll feek no other Lord,
    Oe'r him fupreme authority to have.

23 The drunkard to the tavern goes, poffefs'd
    Of fenfe, of ftrength, and all his pow'rs of mind:
    He enters in a man, goes out a beaft,
    Spues like a dog, and grunts like any fiend.

24 The drunkard, God and all his gifts will leave,
    With his poffeffions he'll play faft and loofe,
    To the firft harlot he can find, he'll cleave,
    His memo'ry, money; nay, himfelf, he'll lofe.

25 None fcarce got drunk but vagabonds of yore,
    And the moft vile among the canting fort:
    But there's no room now vacant for the poor;
    So thick their Betters to the inns refort!

26 'Tis

26 'Tis bad to fee a judge difguis'd with beer,
    Or find a juftice fprawling in the ftreet——
    Tis bad, to fee a reeling, ftamme'ring peer——
    But 'tis far worfe, a drunken prieft to meet.

27 'Twere a good law, all drunkards to affign,
    Like tender infants, to a guardian's care:
    Since they, no more than infants, when in wine,
    Can rule themfelves, or mind the leaft affair.

28 The fot, no reafon has, himfelf to guide,
    Nor is of inftinct, for his ufe, poffefs'd:
    For want of either, o'er him to prefide,
    He's much worfe off than any other beaft:

29 He is, alas! fo very great a fool,
    He can't direct himfelf with any fkill,
    Nor fuffer others his concerns to rule;
    Though he himfelf directs them e'er fo ill.

30 Woe be to him that rifes with the light
    To drink, and ftill caroufes on, untire'd,
    Continuing his jollity, 'till night,
    And 'till he's by the long potation fire'd.

31 The flaming pit and Satan open wide
    Their jaws, to fwallow up all drunken men,
    E'er they can lay their beftial load afide——
    Or can find time to foberize agen.

32 Woe be thofe, that in their drink are ftrong,
    And able to contain the greateft load!
    Nor roots, nor branches fhall be left them long,
    But they fhall wholly be deftroy'd by God.

33 Woe be to him, who, only to difclofe
    His neighbour's weaknefs, puts about the bowl!
    The Lord, incens'd, will rank him with his foes,
    Becaufe he tries to flay his neighbour's foul.

34 From drunkennefs retire betimes away,
    Or thou'lt be bury'd in it's naufeous flough:
    When on a quickfand thou doft ufe delay,
    Thou'rt fwallow'd up, whilft thou'rt about to go.

     .   35 All

35 All other finners ftrive their faults to hide,
  Befides the leaden-headed fot alone:
  But he muft foolifhly difplay full wide
  Each odious·fin and crime that he has done.

36 Adam endeavour'd wifely to conceal,
  With fig-tree leaves his error and difgrace,
  But Noah, in his liquor, did reveal
  What Nature hid, before his children's face.

37 Our Saviour tells all Chriftians to beware,
  Left they with fots and Epicures fhou'd eat,
  And bids them fhun them with an equal care,
  As they wou'd from the plague itfelf retreat.

38 As fmoke will make the' half-ftifled bees depart,
  However loath, from their beloved hive :
  So drunkennefs will from the human heart,
  Each grace divine, and ev'ry virtue drive.

39 The king of Babylon, as Daniel fays,
  Was to a beaft transform'd for feven years :
  But, longer far than that, the drunkard ftays
  Difguis'd, and all his life a hog appears.

40 The drunkard's wages are—a fhort'ned life——
  An empty lodging——an uneafy bed——
  A ftomach foul——companions fond of ftrife——
  A tatter'd doublet——and an aching head——

41 His fire's inheritance, the fwinifh fot
  Sells, even all he has, as cheap as dirt :
  His Stock and Crop muft alfo go to pot :
  Nay, to buy liquor, he will fell his fhirt.

42 Bacchus is ftill the drunkard's real god;
  His church—a tavern, or a nafty inn;
  His landlady—the prieftefs of the' abode;
  His pot and pipe—his very next of kin.

43 Be fober, whilft thou art as yet but young,
  Let not thy belly ever rob thy back,
  Let not thy wafteful youth thy old age wrong,
  And make thee common neceffaries lack.

44 The

44 The law of God will have him ſtone'd outright,
　　Who ſpends in criminal exceſs his time,　*Deut.xxi.*
　　That the fell vice may be unrooted quite,
　　And others be deterr'd from ſuch a crime.

45 Chriſt unawares will to the drunkard come,
　　To puniſh him for his unſeemly crime,
　　And him to hell's infernal dungeon doom,
　　To gnaſh his teeth beyond the end of time.

46 May God then give to ev'ry Chriſtian grace,
　　To drink no more than nature does ſuffice——
　　Leſt he himſelf ſhou'd through exceſs debaſe,
　　And damn both ſoul and body by this vice.

A SONG concerning the Devil and the Drunkard.

1　FRom the fraudulent fiend, that ſtill without end
　　　　Moſt mortals trepans and beguiles,
　　Who wou'd hook us all in, to do ev'ry ſin——
　　God ſhield us, I pray, from his wiles!

2 As our ſhadows appear, when the weather is clear,
　　And follow where-ever we go:
　　Like a thief, ſo he ſteals, hanging cloſe at our heels,
　　And trying to bring us to woe.

3 May God keep us all, from Satan's ſad thrall,
　　(I pray from the depth of my ſoul!)
　　And Chriſtians ſecure, from vices impure,
　　And hell and the tempter controul.

4 Intempe'rance in drink, is the chief, as I think,
　　Of his wiles :——for it is from this vice,
　　Theft, gluttony, ſtrife, and uncleanneſs of life,
　　With ſwearing and curſing, take riſe.

5 Where ſots moſt abound, his trumpet he'll ſound—
　　" Come hither, my lads, to your beer,
　　We'll drink and we'll whore, throw the houſe out of
　　And I my own ſelf will be there."　　　　[door,
　　　　　　　　　　　　　　　　　　6 Like

6 Like a foldier, each fot, foon repairs to the fpot,
  Where by Satan he's fummon'd to meet,
And fwills off his bowl, not minding his foul,
  Whilft the poor are diftrefs'd in each ftreet.

7 Quite cool they begin, as the morn comes cool in,
  'Till the fun at mid-day gives it's heat :
There's a flufh in each cheek, and they lifp as they
  They faulter and fail in their feet.   [fpeak,

8 When they've drank each his quart, and are ready to
  " Come, landlady, fetch us fome more,   [part,
He cries, " Fill each pot, with the beft thou haft got,
  " We were not half jovial before.

9 " Come, bring us, with fpeed, a pound of the weed
  , " From India brought over the main,
  " With pipes long and white, a hot poker, or light ;
  " Nor let them be call'd for again.

10 " A rafher next bring, falt herring, or ling,
  " 'Twill give to our liquor a tafte :
  " Let's drink then away, 'till we're jolly and gay,
  " And the barrel has run out it's laft !"

11 The noife now grows great, and each flincher is beat
  That won't pufh the fuddle about.
  , " Come, lads ! let us drink, (he ftill roars) and ne'er
  " But fee all our liquor quite out."   [think,

12 Some fpue it again——fome keep it with pain,
  Whilft others juft fip, and no more :
Some, Englifh----fome, Welfh----fome, their French
  Whilft others in Erfe loudly roar.   [out will belch,

13 Some fwagger and fwear, like madmen fome tear,
  Whilft the fiend fpurs them on with a fneer——
  " Have at him, my boy !---thy good weapon employ,
  " For who would fuch injuries bear ?"

14 They're beat black and blue, perhaps murders enfue,
  Unhappy's the place where he goes,
The quarrelfome fiend, and the traite'rous friend,
  The monfter, that caufes our woes !

15 There's

15 There's none without fault. All with errors are fraught.
    The beſt is not free from his vice:
  But all are inclin'd unto ſins of ſome kind,
    And follow the' old Fox's advice.

16 O God, our beſt friend, give us grace to amend,
    And keep Adam's ſons from backſliding!
  Forgive us each ſin, and lead us all in
    To the kingdom, where thou art reſiding.

ADVICE, concerning the Government of our THOUGHTS.

1 THE mind of ev'ry man, alas!
    Is naturally vile and baſe,
  And thinks on nought, but what is bad,
    'Till it the ſecond birth has had.

2 There's no one can command his mind.
    To good, however well inclin'd,
  'Till God has give'n him grace and light,
    To guide his mental pow'rs aright.

3 Pray therefore hard, that He wou'd deign
    To change thy purpoſes again,
  And all thy reſolutions quite,
    'Till they be fix'd upon the right.

4 So God his Spirit ſhall impart,
    To turn the' intentions of thy heart,
  And all the counſels of thy breaſt,
    That thou may'ſt think on what is beſt.

5 Permit no ill to harbour there,
    Leſt it ſhou'd with it ruin bear :
  For evil Thoughts ſtill go before,
    To tell that Satan's at the door.

6 Place thou thy thoughts, and fix thy love,
    Upon the things that are above,
  (Where thy dear Saviour's even now!)
    And not upon the traſh below.

7 Let

7 Let themes celeftial crowd thy mind,
  Nought earthly there a place fhou'd find :
  Think on the place where thou muft dwell
  Forever—think on heave'n, and hell!

8 Reflect, what Chrift above the fkies
  Has bought for thee, his Blood, the price!
  " A crown of joy, the peace of God,
  " An endlefs life, a bleft abode!"

9 Reflect, that thou art ev'ry hour
  In fight of the Almighty Pow'r,
  Who thy whole conduct can efpy
  With the bare glancing of his Eye.

10 Reflect, that thy blood-thirfty foe,
   Roams, like a lion, to and fro,
   And prowls around thee ev'ry hour,
   Thy foul and body to devour.

11 Submit each thought, each work, each word,
   To the direction of the Lord,
   Left either fhou'd thy foul opprefs,
   And on the day of doom diftrefs.

12 O, think how thy dread Judge fhall come
   Upon the clouds, to feal thy doom!
   Prepare to meet him then, above,
   As a young bride to meet her love.

13 Remember thou, that ev'ry thought
   Muft on that aweful day be brought
   To ftrict account, before the Lord,
   As well as ev'ry work and word.

14 Reflect, that each of us muft go
   In turn, to his clay-cell below,
   Of one coarfe fhrowd alone poffefs'd,
   Though here with ample fortunes blefs'd.

15 Reflect, that death, with matchlefs force,
   Rides, Jehu-like, on his pale horfe :
   Nor old, nor young, can 'fcape his dart,
   Which rives impartially each heart.

16 Reflect,

16 Reflect, how, like a thief, death treads,
And hovers daily o'er our heads:
No trump proclaims him on the way,
'Till unawares he gripes his prey.

17 Reflect, that life is like a dream,
Or like a bubble on the ftream,
Or glafs, or china, by one ftroke,
Too eafily in pieces broke !

18 Think, how it fwiftly paffes by,
As fhips, thro' the' yielding billows, fly !
O think, how oft man's time is done,
Before he dream'd one half was gone !

19 Think, how this world lets all men go
Quite naked to the grave below,
And underneath their feet breaks fhort,
Like ice, when moft they want fupport !

20 Reflect, that ne'er fo great a fum,
Nor houfe nor lands, fhall ever come
For any man's offence to pay,
Upon the Lord's tremendous day !

21 Think, when death comes, that we muft quit
This world, and all that is in it ;
And be to Chrift's tribunal brought,
To anfwer there for ev'ry fault !

22 Think, how the riches thou hadft here,
And ev'ry office thou didft bear,
Shall quickly new poffeffors have,
E'er thou'rt fcarce ftiff'ned in thy grave !

23 O think, how fin, on that dread day,
Will on thy wounded confcience prey,
When all thy foul tranfgreffions paft
Shall in thy teeth be fully caft !

24 Think, how thou fhalt be force'd to give
A ftrict account, how thou didft live,
And anfwer make before the Lord
For ev'ry idle work and word !

25 Think,

25 Think, how the mighty then ſhall fear,
   (Who ne'er did God or man revere)
   And beg the Rocks, with piteous cry,
   To fall upon them from on high.

26 Think, how the righteous ſhall enjoy
   Eternal bliſs ! their ſole employ,
   Their great Creator's praiſe to tell;
   Whilſt all the wicked broil in hell!

27 Think, how the wicked toſs and turn,
   As in infernal flames they burn,
   And as the buſy worms, each hour,
   With ſateleſs teeth their fleſh devour !

28 O think on this ! and thou'lt deſpiſe
   The world, and all it's vanities,
   And on God's word, thro' faith, depend,
   With that bleſt world, that ne'er ſhall end.

29 The mind of man ſtill runs upon,
   The good or evil it has done:
   And if it be not fed with good,
   'Twill cram itſelf on filthy food !

30 Like mill-ſtones, is the human mind,
   It will itſelf to powder grind,
   Unleſs, as griſt, ſome virtue's thrown
   To it, to ſpend itſelf upon.

31 The taſk aſſign'd to thee, perform,
   When God gave thee a human form,
   And ſerve him, whereſoe'er thou art,
   Whilſt yet there's time, with all thy heart!

32 O think, that e'en a ſingle day,
   Whereon thou didſt the Lord obey,
   Is better than an age at laſt,
   In any other ſervice paſt !

33 O think, e'er thou doſt ſin commit,
   How thou muſt anſwer ſoon for it,
   And if thou, on that aweful day,
   Canſt run from endleſs death away !

34 Habi-

34 Habituate thy mind to good,
   Nor let it feed on chaffy food,
   It eafily may be reftrain'd,
   If it betimes be tightly rein'd.

35 'Tis eafy to put out a fire,
   E'er to the roof it's flames afpire:
   As eafy 'tis bad thoughts to quell,
   If you will them in time repel.

36 Then banifh ev'ry evil thought
   At firft, e'er it becomes a fault;
   Left Satan, full of craft and fraud,
   Bad thoughts fhou'd turn to deeds as bad.

37 Whilft young, the brood of Babel quell,
   Tread on the ferpent in the fhell.
   Cut out the cancer, e'er it fpread,
   Quafh bad thoughts, e'er they run a-head.

38 Let but one fpark thy thatch attain,
   The flames will o'er thy houfe foon reign:
   Let one bad thought poffefs thy foul,
   'Twill foon corrupt, and fpoil the whole.

39 Let no bad thought lodge in thy breaft,
   As foon therein let Satan reft:
   For, if thou giv'ft it lodging there,
   The foot-man fhews his lord is near.

40 To keep God's law, ufe all thy wit,
   And live fincerely up to it;
   Ne'er from thy mind his favours caft,
   But blefs him for whate'er thou haft.

41 No wicked ftratagem employ,
   Thy fellow-creature to deftroy;
   Murder is fuch a bloody deed,
   Of it, throughout thy life, take heed.

42 Do not thy neighbour's wife defire,
   Nor at her fparkling eyes take fire:
   Let not thy mind upon her run,
   The thought is fin—the danger fhun!

43 Let not a thought thy mind poſſeſs,
  How thou the orphan may'ſt oppreſs:
  Before the' Almighty ſuch a thought
  Is a foul wrong, and grievous fault.

44 Nor houſe, nor lands, nor gold, nor gain,
  Attempt by cheating to obtain:
  Such covetous deſires are quite
  A fraud in the Almighty's ſight.

45 Confine thy thoughts, nor let them go,
  In ſearch of trifles, to and fro,
  Or ought that muſt to reck'ning come,
  On the tremendous day of doom.

46 From evil thoughts thy mind command,
  As thou wou'dſt keep from theft thy hand:
  For ev'ry wicked work and thought,
✝ Muſt to a ſtrict account be brought!

ADVICE, how to govern our Thoughts, according to God's will.

1 LET all thy words a Chriſtian import bear,
   Let them, with grace, at all times ſeaſon'd be,
  That they may knowledge give to all that hear,
  And edify their ſouls in ſome degree.

2 Both life and death upon thy lips are hung;
  Guard thou them well from ſlanders vile and foul:
  Let no ſuch language e'er defile thy tongue;
  Keep well thy lips, and thou ſhalt keep thy ſoul.

3 In thy expreſſions, imitate the Lord,
  And ſpeak, as he was always wont, the truth:
  For no deceit, or no unſeemly word,
  Proceeded ever from his hallow'd mouth.

4 Be ſlow to ſpeak, but always ſwift to hear,
  Thy ears are twain, but ſingle is thy tongue:
  Loquaciouſneſs does nought but error bear:
  But none were hurt by being ſilent long.

5 Before

✝ I think this a valuable Poem
and inwardly inſtructive, in a very certain
fine Manner. JC—

5 Before thou fpeakeft, think a little fpace—
Think what the Lord himfelf wou'd have thee fay,
Then utter freely what is fraught with grace,
And tends to make, e'en Pagans, Chrift obey.

6 Let no foul language from thy heart arife,
No foolifh jefts, no drollery obfcene,
No taunts, no vaunts, no menaces, no lies:
Let decency in all thy fpeech be feen.

7 From flander, and from calumny refrain;
So fhalt thou fave thy precious foul alive :
But if thou doft not thy loofe tongue reftrain,
Thou fhalt correction for thy words receive.

8 Ufe thou the language of the holy land,
Of God, and of his Word, oft mention make:
For by thy language men will underftand
From what rich mine thou didft thy treafure take.

9 Let not tremendous oaths thy mouth defile,
Nor by the flefh and blood of Jefus fwear ;
Thou trampleft on thy Saviour's gore, the while
Thou doft proceed in fuch a vile career.

10 Ne'er of the Gofpel any mention make,
Without due fear, refpect, and rev'rence meet :
Whoe'er in vain God's holy name does take,
Shall be found guilty at his judgement feat.

11 Never fpeak more than what is requifite ;
But when thou fpeakeft, fpeak not what is wrong :
For if thou doft not fpeak the thing that's right,
'Tis better far that thou fhou'dft hold thy tongue.

12 Take heed thou art not of a double tongue ;
For God abhors all thofe, that falfehoods tell :
Lies from the father of all fiction fprung,
And ev'ry liar is the child of hell.

13 The truth with all thy faculties maintain ;
God, and good men do in the truth delight :
But liars never fhall belief obtain,
Although they fwear, and chance to fwear aright.

N   14 Ne'er

14 Ne'er let it be thy cuftom to traduce
 Thy abfent neighbour with an evil word:
 For flande'rous accufations and abufe,
 Cut deep—nay, deeper than a two-edge'd fword.

15 Bear not a tongue, that's bitter and perverfe,
 'Tis worfe than fhafts fhot from a giant's bow,
 Than poifon from an adder's tongue 'tis worfe,
 Worfe than the flames that in hell's dungeon glow.

16 If thou'dft be happy, mind this ufeful rule,
 " Call not another by opprobrious names :"
 For he, that calls his fellow-creature, fool,
 Deferves to feel Gehenna's fierceft flames.

17 Utter not thou, as much as thou doft hear,
 And ne'er, as much as thou doft know, reveal,
 But when thou'rt call'd to fpeak the truth, be clear ;
 Oft, 'till thou'rt call'd, 'tis beft the truth conceal.

18 Be cautious ever, whom thou doft commend,
 Be courteous, when thou wou'dft thy manners fhow,
 Be mild, whene'er thou doft reprove thy friend,
 Be libe'ral, when thou doft thine alms beftow.

A Prayer, concerning the Government of our Words and Lips, &c.

1 OPEN my filent lips, O Lord! full wide,
  To chant the goodnefs of my gracious God;
 My loit'ring tongue unto thy praifes guide,
 That I may boldly publifh them abroad.

2 With thy encomiums fill my mouth, O God!
 That I thy name with all my might may blefs,
 And 'mongft the countlefs multitude applaud
 The Sire of mercies for each good fuccefs.

3 Frame thou my words aright, my tongue reftrain,
 Direct thou all the' ideas of my heart,
 Clofe thou my lips, and open them again,
 That I may nought befide thy will impart.

4 Guard

4 Guard thou the portals of my mouth, O Lord!
 That I may no indecent language ufe,
 No bounce, no boaft, nor any filly word,
 No falfe report, nor any foul abufe.

5 Let ev'ry meditation of my foul,
 Let ev'ry deed, be innocent and right,
 Let ev'ry word be harmlefs, on the whole,
 O Lord! and truly-pleafing in thy fight!

ADVICE, to have One's Converfation and Demeanour always according to the Rules of the Gofpel.

1 BE thy demeanour of the Chriftian fort,
 Be it obliging, affable, and right,
 In ev'ry place to which thou may'ft refort,
 As is becoming in a child of light.

2 Be, like a ftar, that blazes forth by night,
 Be, like a candle, that illumes the room,
 Be, an example of the Chriftian light
 To all, that to thy company fhall come.

3 Be holy, in whate'er does God regard,
 Be juft, nor to thy neighbour ufe deceit,
 Be fober, and thyfelf with prudence guard,
 For thefe three points are of the greateft weight.

4 Be thou, as harmlefs as the gentle dove,
 Be, as the ferpent vigilant and wife,
 As patient as a lamb, in fuffe'ring, prove,
 And God will fuch a good behaviour prize,

5 Like Daniel with due moderation eat,
 And keep the flefh, by temp'rate diet, low,
 Beware of wine, and of high-feafon'd meat,
 Left thou fhou'dft wanton and rebellious grow,

6 Be chafte, be clear from ev'ry act unclean,
 Like Jofeph's, faultlefs let thy conduct be,
 Where-e'er thou art, thou ftill by God art feen:
 Be therefore pure, and from pollution free.

7 In all thy dealings be exactly fair,
   And in thy bargains ufe no fraud nor art;
   For God determines, with the niceft care,
   Between the guilty and the guiltlefs heart.

8 Let thy religion, and thy faith be right,
   And fear the Lord, thy God, with all thy heart:
   Do nothing that is evil in his fight;
   For he beholds thee, wherefoe'er thou art.

9 Unto thy Paftors due attention give,
   And ftrive thy Rulers in all things to pleafe,
   In love and friendfhip with thy neighbours live,
   And with all Chriftians in the bond of peace.

10 In thy expreffions always kind appear,
   Be, pertinently juft, when thou doft fpeak,
   Be, to thy promife, fteady and fincere,
   Be, in thy actions, and demeanour, meek.

11 In ev'ry company with prudence move,
   Amongft the worft, be thou a Saint in grace,
   And howe'er bad the multitude may prove,
   Be good, like Noah, 'mongft the giant-race.

12 Salute each perfon with a cheerful air,
   With courtefy to thy fuperiors bow,
   Authority, and hoary age revere,
   And due fubmiffion to thy betters fhow.

13 Be calm, and contumely fuffer long,
   And never give, to wrath and paffion, way,
   But bear, e'er thou art move'd to anger, wrong:
   For he that bears, will ever win the day.

14 Submit to thofe that are in higher place,
   For God is known the haughty to deteft;
   But freely to the humble gives his grace,
   And thofe that are of lowly minds poffeft.

15 Boaft not of any virtue thou haft got,
   Of wealth, or honours, that to thee may fall,
   But be extremely thankful for thy lot,
   Left God enrage'd fhou'd rob thee of them all.

16 Be in thy cloathing, always neat enough,
   And dres'd, according to thy calling, go:
   Cut out thy coat according to thy stuff;
   And neither be a sloven, nor a beau.

17 Transgress not thou, thy company to please.
   Death is the sentence that on sin is past.
   As often as thou dost thy sins increase,
   So many deaths thou dost deserve to taste.

18 E'er since the day transgression first began,
   Death and transgression have been firm allies:
   So that whoever dares transgress, that man
   Must fall to Death a certain sacrifice.

19 In thy expressions never be obscene,
   Nor in the closest solitude unchaste;
   But be thy conduct in each lonely scene
   The same, as if thou on the ‡ cross wert place'd.

20 Shou'd angel, man, or fiend, desire of thee
   To sin against thy God, when most apart,
   Remember thou, his *Seven Eyes* can see,   Zach.iv.10.
   And find thee out, however close thou art.

21 Though man, near-sighted reptile! cannot spy
   A thousand acts that are in private done;
   God sees them with his all-surveying eye,
   Though man imagines that he sees not one.

22 If thou dost think thy vices to conceal,
   God will the whole of thy design declare,
   And to the world, before the sun, reveal
   How bad thy thoughts and secret actions are!

23 Avoid conversing with the lewd and vile,
   To ev'ry Christian virtue dead and gone;
   For they'll thy morals fully and defile,
   As pitch will foil the clothes it drops upon.

24 As the fresh water, by the salt, is spoil'd,
   Soon as the river runs into the main:
   So the best morals always are defile'd
   By vicious converse, and imbibe a stain.

‡ Market-cross.   N 3   25 Beware

25 Beware the ferpent's fting, or thou fhalt fmart,
   And from the plague, left it fhou'd feize thee, run,
   And, if falvation thou haft much at heart,
   With equal care bad converfation fhun.

26 Love thou each godly perfon as thy eyes——
   Keep correfpondence with the juft and good——
   Follow the' examples of the learn'd and wife——
   But utterly abhor and fhun the lewd.

ADVICE concerning Eating and Drinking.

1 SEE, that thou fitteft not to eat,
   Before thou firft haft blefs'd thy meat!
   Nor rife from thence, 'till thou haft given
   Due thanks unto the Lord of heaven!

2 Chrift never touch'd e'en barley-bread,
   (Much lefs when He on better fed)
   'Till he had firft his victuals blefs'd,
   And for the fame his thanks exprefs'd.

3 For who wou'd eat the food, that's curft
   Since Adam's fall, e'er he had firft
   (By calling on God's holy name,
   And prayer) fanctify'd the fame?

4 'Tis terrible, and fad to fee,
   (And rude unto the laft degree,
   And full as impious as 'tis rude)
   Men rufh, like brutes, unto their food!

5 But 'tis as fad, when they are fed,
   To fee them rife from meat, to bed,
   Like hogs, that from their draff retire,
   To grunt and wallow in the mire.

6 No grace before their meat they fay,
   Nor for a bleffing on it pray,
   Nor when they breakfaft, fup, or dine,
   More thanks return than fatted fwine.

7 Although

7 Although it be the Lord's requeſt,
  When they their hunger have repreſt,
  That they to God due thanks ſhou'd give,
  Who fills with food all things that live.

8 Take heed, leſt thou ſhou'dſt eat too much,
  I wou'd not have thee dainties touch ;
  For dainties, eaten to exceſs,
  Will make the carnal part tranſgreſs.

9 If thou the fleſh, beyond it's need,
  Indulgeſt, thou a foe doſt feed
  Moſt fatal :——If thou giv'ſt it leſs,
  Thou doſt a truſty friend oppreſs.

10 Drink not too much, if thou art wiſe,
   A little, nature does ſuffice :
   Strong drink has oft been ſtronger found
   Than thoſe, that were for ſtrength renown'd.

11 'Twas wine, made Noah ſhew his ſhame,
   'Twas wine, did Lot with luſt inflame,
   'Twas wine, ſo many did undo,
   'Twas wine, did Philip's ſon ſubdue.

12 Of luxury and ſloth beware——
   Let not thy table be thy ſnare——
   Leſt Satan make thee go aſtray,
   When full, and againſt God inveigh.

13 The lark, whilſt at her meal, ſtill plies
   With ceaſeleſs diligence both eyes——
   One looks about for food, they ſay,
   The other marks the birds of prey.

14 So uſe thou, night and day, thy eyes ;
   Leſt Satan's wiles thy ſoul ſurprize——
   Who, whenſoever thou doſt eat,
   Wou'd fain enſnare thee by thy meat.

15 When-e'er the growſe-cock feeds, for fear,
   He turns his eyes ſtill here and there ;
   Leſt, whilſt he heedleſs fed at eaſe,
   The falcon ſhou'd his body ſeize.

16 So, whilſt at meat, let both thy eyes
 Be_ vigilant againſt ſurprize——
 Let one, thy Maker's works regard,
 T'other, againſt the fiend keep ward.

17 Eat thou no kind of meat at all,
 Shall make thy fellow Chriſtian fall :
 The ſcripture plainly does declare
 Thou no man ſhalt by meat enſnare.

18 Chuſe not alone to eat thy fare,
 But give the poor and ſick a ſhare :
 Call him that's weak to taſte thy feaſt,
 And let the foodleſs be thy gueſt.

19 Old Tobit never dine'd, before
 He call'd about him all the poor,
 Nor touch'd a bit of the repaſt,
 'Till he had given them a taſte.

20 Job, never thought his morſel ſweet,
 Unleſs the poor with him did eat,
 Nor ever felt true joy at heart,
 'Till he had given them a part.

21 Like him, thy gueſts, the needy make,
 And let them of thy meal partake,
 So ſhalt thou likewiſe, as his gueſt,
 Partake of Chriſt's celeſtial feaſt.

22 Repine not, but well-pleas'd receive,
 Whate'er the' Almighty deigns to give :
 The Patriarchs oft contented were
 With bread and water for their fare.

23 Beans, and a common ſort of Peaſe,
 Of old did holy Daniel pleaſe ;
 The prophets' ſons were likewiſe fed
 On homely fare, and barley bread.

24 Why then ſhou'd we not be content
 With whatſoe'er our God has ſent,
 So it ſuffices to aſſuage
 (Be' it more or leſs) keen hunger's rage ?

25 Our

25 Our bleffed Saviour was content
To feaft with Abra'ham, near his tent,
On common fare, though plain and good,
And never afk'd for dainty food.

26 But Now fcarce one is fatisfy'd
To have his table well fupply'd,
Unlefs on feve'ral cates he dines,
With paftry, and luxurious wines.

27 They muft have fauce with fifh and fowl,
As capers, famphire, rocombole,
E'er they can make a meal of meat :
Their luxury and pride's fo great !

28 For ufelefs fauces now coft more,
Than joints entire did heretofore
Of that fubftantial, wholefome meat,
Our good forefathers ufe'd to eat.

29 The fon of Philip, term'd the Great,
No fauce did with his victuals eat,
But what he in his ftomach brought,
When he had ftoutly march'd, or fought.

30 The elder Cyrus often took
His luncheon, near fome purling brook,
Whence he might water freely take,
And all his hoft their thirft might flake.

31 But now whene'er they fup or dine,
Our fqueamifh moderns muft have wine.
Claret, perhaps a pint, or fo,
E'er, down their throats, a bit can go.

32 God, give provifion to the poor——
God, make them bounteous, who have ftore,
God, pardon us, when we've trangrefs'd,
God, for our food be always blefs'd !

GRACE

GRACE before MEAT.

1 THou, by whom erſt five thouſand folks were fed
   With two ſmall fiſhes and five loaves of bread,
Fill us, thy humble ſervants, with ſuch food,
As ſhall to thy wiſe providence ſeem good!

2 Bleſs thou beſides the liquor and the meat,
Which thou haſt given us to drink and eat,
As thou didſt bleſs the paſchal lamb of yore,
And the two fiſhes, by thy wond'rous pow'r;

3 And give them ſtrength our beings to preſerve,
That we thy Godhead may adore and ſerve——
Such ſtrength, as of thy ſpecial favour, Lord!
Thou erſt didſt to Elijah's cake afford.

4 And cauſe them to refreſh this mortal frame,
To hearten, and to ſatisfy the ſame
With nouriſhment as good, as that low fare
Which thou for Daniel didſt of old prepare.

5 Permit us not, however rare or nice,
To take a morſel more than will ſuffice——
But juſt as much as may ſupport this frame,
And make us fit to glorify thy name.

6 But cauſe us to reſound thy praiſes ſtill,
Who with thy goodneſs doſt our bellies fill——
And make us own, that 'tis the God of might,
Who feeds us ev'ry morning, noon, and night!

GRACE after MEAT.

1 THOU, that feedeſt ev'ry creature,
   Whether tame, or wild by nature,
Receive our prayers, who humbly own
The plenteous goodneſs thou haſt ſhown!

2 'Twas thou, O Lord!—that fed'ſt us all,
E'er ſince our birth, both great and ſmall;
For which vaſt bounty to us ſhown,
We gratefully the favour own!

3 To

3 To quench our thirſt, no fountains flow————
No bread we have—no ſtrength to go————
No light to ſee—no pow'r to riſe————
But what thy bounty, Lord! ſupplies.

4 Therefore to thee, for food and health————
To thee, for plenty, peace, and wealth————
To thee, for bliſs and joys in ſtore————
To thee, be praiſe for ever more!

Another GRACE before MEAT.

1 THE eyes of ev'ry creature here below
Are fix'd on thee, whence all their bleſſings flow,
And earneſtly expect, O Lord! their food
From thee, the Donor of each gift that's good.

2 Thy libe'ral hand for their relief is ſpre'd
Full wide, and ev'ry living thing is fed
With food, that ſuits their ſeveral natures here,
Throughout the various ſeaſons of the year.

3 Then ſanctify, O Lord! thy ſervants meat,
And ev'ry meſs, and morſel, that we eat!
O ſanctify at ev'ry meal the fare,
Which Thou alone doſt for our uſe prepare!

4 And give us grace that we our notes may raiſe,
In ceaſeleſs hymns to chant thy deathleſs praiſe,
For all thy goodneſs and endearing care,
In giving us each day ſuch plenteous fare!

Another, before MEAT.

1 BLeſs thou the victuals which now deck this board,
Impart ſuch nutriment to them, O Lord!
That they our bodies may invigo'rate ſo,
That we may ſerve thee, as we ought to do.

2 Though many of our meats are mighty nice,
Yet in them all no innate virtue lies
To feed us, or our hunger to repreſs,
If thou thyſelf didſt not the creatures bleſs.

3 Pour

3 Pour then thy blessing on the gifts, **O Lord!**
Wherewith so freely thou hast crown'd this board;
Give them nutritious juices from above
To feed us, and our hunger to remove.

4 As the varieties, whereon we feed,
Oft indigestions in our stomachs breed,
And dangerous diseases oft arise,
Because we were intempe'rate and unwise:

5 Thy grace on us, most holy God! bestow
That we such tempe'rance at our meals may show,
That our provisions hunger may appease,
And neither cause distemper, or disease.

6 Infuse thro' them, to us such pow'r and might,
That each of us may worship thee aright,
And in his calling, thy bless'd name adore,
For Jesus' sake, who saves us by his pow'r.

Another GRACE, after MEAT.

1 THE labial sacrifice, O Lord! receive,
   Which now, to thee, we for thy mercies give;
Because so fully, whenso-e'er they need,
Thou, with thy creatures, dost thy servants feed!

2 So plentiful a meal at least demands
Some grateful retribution at our hands,
Though such a favour we deserve no more
Than many, who now beg from door to door.

3 Let all the mouths which thou with meat hast fed,
Now daily thank thee for their daily bread:
Let us at least for this repast, O God!
For ever thy benevolence applaud!

Another, before MEAT.

1 ALmighty God, in heav'n so high,
   Us, and these creatures sanctify—
These creatures, which thou, at our want,
To us, thy pasture'd sheep, dost grant!

2 And

2 And make us all confefs, and know,
That ev'ry perfect gift below
Proceeds from thee, (for thou art good)
Even our drink, and daily food.

3 And teach us all to blefs thy name,
And for thy gifts to laud the fame;
Becaufe thou doft thy fervants blefs,
More than they ever can exprefs:

4 And, for thy beft-beloved's fake,
We our petitions humbly make,
That thou to ev'ry wretch in want
At leaft wou'dft bread and water grant:

5 And wou'dft both day and night beftow
Thy grace, that we may here below
Serve thee, 'till to thy courts we come,
Thofe feats of blifs, our future home!

6 Where meat and drink of richeft tafte,
For ever undiminifh'd laft,
Where thy elected fons ne'er know
Hunger, or thirft, or any woe!

Another, after MEAT.

1 WHY doft thou with fuch dainty fare,
O Lord, thy humble fervants feed,
And take of us fuch ceafelefs care,
Whilft others are in woeful need?

2 Why unto us, lefs than the leaft
Of all thy fervants, fuch great ftore
Doft thou allow, yet leave the reft,
Our betters far, extremely poor?

3 For we ourfelves muft fairly own,
That we do not at all deferve,
That greater favour fhou'd be fhown
To us, than thofe who almoft ftarve.

4 But

4 But thou, O Lord! out of thy love
  And great benevolence, doſt give
  To us a portion, far above
  What they have; who much better live!

5 In hopes no doubt that we ſhou'd give
  Greater returns of praiſe to thee
  Than they, on ſuch mean fare who live,
  And worſhip thee with bended knee.

6 Then let our gratitude now raiſe
  (A tribute we ſhou'd ever pay!)
  Our voices to our Maker's praiſe,
  On ev'ry meal, and ev'ry day!

A GRACE, before SUPPER.

1 LET ev'ry man, his head and grateful eyes,
    To God, our gene'rous caterer, lift up,
  And beg of him with ſupplicating cries,
  To bleſs our victuals, whenſoe'er we ſup.

2 To ev'ry ſeve'ral animal that lives
  (Altho' their kinds and numbers be ſo great;)
  He at a proper time and ſeaſon gives
  It's due proportion of ſalubrious meat.

3 He is ſo gracious and ſo very good,
  There's not a bird that flutters in the air,
  But he provides it ev'ry day with food,
  Even with more than with a parent's care.

4 To man, he ſure will greater favour ſhow,
  Who with his own ſimilitude was grace'd,
  And freely, all he wants, on him beſtow;
  So that his truſt on him alone is place'd.

5 Herbs, corn, and beaſts, and what the ſeas produce,
  With all the diff'rent ſongſters of the wood,
  (Since they were made entirely for his uſe)
  God gave them wholly unto man for food.

6 Amongſt

6 Amongst the various fish that swim the sea,
Beasts of the wood, or reptiles of the earth,
God never made a single mouth, but He
Prepare'd it's aliment before it's birth :

7 But unto man, the creature of his love,
He gave whatever haunts the field, or wood,
Or cuts the waves, or wings the air above,
With liberty to use them for his food.

8 Why do not mortals well confider this?
Why do they not adore their God aright?
Were they thus wife, they then wou'd never mifs:
To praife their Maker, morning, noon, and night.

9 May God illuminate our blinded eyes,
That with our mouths we ever may adore
The goodnefs, that conducts us to the fkies,
And for his mercies praife him evermore !

10 Glory and honour to the' eternal Pow'r,
Who daily fills our bellies with his meat,
Be now afcribe'd, and at each future hour,
At ev'ry time, and ev'ry meal, we eat!

GRACE after DINNER.

1 THou haft, O Chrift ! our bellies fill'd,
And with thy choiceft dainties fed :
Fill too the mouth of man and child
With praifes for his daily bread.

2 Thou haft moft richly deck'd our board,
And crown'd us with thy plenteous ftore :
Give us then grace, henceforth, O Lord !
That we, for it, may thee adore.

3 Thy mercies our beft thanks require,
They very juftly are thy due :
Give us at leaft a ftrong defire
To pay thee all the debt we owe.

4 A

4 A dinner thou didſt now beſtow
  Our ſpirits to recruit and raiſe:
  We therefore ought to give thee, now,
  For theſe thy gifts our bounden praiſe.

5 Let all the creatures, thou doſt fill,
  For ever praiſe thee, whilſt they live,
  And bleſs thy loving-kindneſs ſtill
  For the proviſion thou doſt give.

Another after SUPPER.

1 FOR ev'ry meal's refreſhment we receive,
     Let us to God with due obeiſance bow,
  Who deigns ſo libe'rally our food to give,
  And never lets us want, or famine, know.

2 Let us return him thanks, with grateful hearts,
  For ev'ry gift we to his goodneſs owe,
  For ev'ry grace and comfort he imparts,
  For keeping us from poverty and woe.

3 Let us ſubmiſſively our God entreat,
  (All for the ſake of our moſt bleſſed Lord)
  In his due time our famiſh'd ſouls to treat
  With his celeſtial ſpirit, and his word.

4 Let us beſeech him plenteouſly to pour,
  On all our heads his bleſſings and his grace,
  That we may ev'ry day, and ev'ry hour,
  Unite with glowing hearts, to ſing his praiſe.

ANOTHER.

1 COme, women, children, come ye rural ſwains,
   Come praiſe the' Almighty for his gifts benign,
  Come praiſe our God, who ever kindly deigns
  To feed the hungry with a care divine.

2 Who with his goodneſs does each creature fill,
  At ev'ry ſeaſon of the rolling year,
  And gives us, of his own free gift and will,
  Sufficient maintenance, whilſt we are here.

3 He

3 He from the ground gives various sorts of grain,
   To make us bread—and creatures wild and tame—
   From the rock honey—fishes from the main,
   With many dainties, that I cannot name.

4 All flesh he feeds with the exacteft care,
   (As if oblige'd by the moft folemn ties)
   Forgetting not the fongfters of the air,
   The lion's roarings, or the raven's cries.

5 E'en man, in fecret, with the flow'r of wheat,
   And thofe rich liquors Epicures fo prize,
   With roaft and boil'd, and many kinds of meat,
   Our God, and none but God alone, fupplies.

A REBUKE, for neglecting to beg a Blefling on,
    and to return Thanks for, our Food.

1 OFT have I feen a blufh o'erfpread the face
     Of fome old finner, when he firft faid Grace,
   Though he long fince fhou'd have been whelm'd with
   Becaufe he ne'er before had faid the fame.   [fhame,

2 But fuch a fhame may no man ever fhew,
   The' example of his Saviour to purfue:
   But may each finner blufh, fhou'd he e'er dine,
   And eat his food unhallow'd, like a fwine.

3 The ox thofe hands, that give him fodder, knows,
   The ftupid afs, to whom his food he owes,
   And makes him all the poor returns he can;
   There's nought ungrateful in the world, but man!

4 But many men, more ftupid on the whole,
   Know not the gracious Shepherd of their foul,
   Who feeds them in his paftures green and gay,
   And loads them with his bleffings, ev'ry day.

5 Even the little birds their voices raife,
   And for their food their benefactor praife——
   With tuneful notes they laud him all day long;
   That 'tis a blifs to liften to their fong!

                    O   6 With

6 With emulation fire'd on ev'ry fpray,
   They feem to ftrive throughout the live-long day,
   Which beft fhall praife the bounteous God above,
   Who fills their bellies in the fecret grove.

7 But men are much more thanklefs and more dull,
   Who, when the Lord has fed them to the full,
   Yet in his praifes are, like fifhes, mute,
   And more ungrateful than the meaneft brute.

8 Do not fuch thanklefs folks as thefe deferve,
   That they fhou'd in the' infernal dungeons ftarve,
   Becaufe they will not their Preferver know,
   Nor any thanks for all his favours fhow ?

9 O, may no Chriftian ever ftudy then,
   To imitate fo vile a fet of men !
   But if he fhou'd——without the leaft difpute,
   I fhall pronounce him worfe than any brute.

A PRAYER on the fame Occafion.

1 PErmit us not, O God, thy gifts to wafte,
   Or eat our meat, as filthy hogs eat maft,
   Ne'er lifting up our heads, our hands, or eyes,
   To fee, from whence thofe benefits arife !

2 But make us lift our heads aloft, and know
   That all thofe mercies from thy goodnefs flow——
   From thee, the Donor of our daily food !——
   From thee, the fource of light, and all that's good !

3 Let us then with inceffant raptures laud
   The loving-kindnefs of our gracious God,
   And ever in his praife our fongs employ,
   For health, and ev'ry bleffing we enjoy.

ADVICE

ADVICE to diftribute to the Poor, according to every One's Circumftances and Abilities.

1 WOE to the rich, and mercilefsly-proud,
  Who ftops his ears againft the beggar's cry!
Unheard, unpity'd, he fhall cry aloud
From Hell's abyfs, where he fhall ever lie.

2 Whilft his relations and his children live
In luxury, and quaff the richeft wine,
He, in the' infernal prifons pent, fhall grieve,
And for a fingle drop of water pine.

3 In good St. James's holy page, 'tis faid,
That he's in faith and ev'ry virtue poor,
Who does not, in diftrefs, the widow aid,
And to the needy deal his hoarded ftore.

4 Saint John too tells us, that if any man
Beholds a brother troubled and diftreft,
And does not give him all the help he can,
The love of God dwells not in fuch a breaft.

5 Chrift faid, a camel, through a needle's eye,
Might with as little difficulty go,
As wealthy mifers up to heaven fly,
Who no compaffion to their brethren fhow.

6 Chrift made us ftewards of his treafures, here,
Which we are bound to deal among the poor;
Then let us freely, left we vex him, fhare
Among the weak and indigent our ftore.

7 Shou'd there but one of them thro' hunger fall,
His guiltlefs blood upon our heads fhall lie,
Not all the riches of this earthly ball,
Shall make atonement for him, fhou'd he die.

8 Without referve, be lib'ral to the poor,
If thou art rich, thy riches do not fpare——
A little give, if little is thy ftore——
Yet give it with a free and cheerful air.

O 2   9 Beftow

9 Beſtow thy bounty with a look ſerene,
    The willing giver 'tis that God does love:
Whate'er thou giveſt, give with placid mien—
Reluctant alms Chriſt never does approve.

10 Though to the poor thou but a part haſt ſhar'd
    (Although the whole was his) for Jeſu's ſake,
Yet has he promis'd thee a large reward,
Becauſe thou didſt on them compaſſion take.

11 Ne'er 'till to-morrow fooliſhly delay
    To do the good, which thou to-day canſt do—
Give freely—give with pleaſure, and ne'er ſtay:
Unpleaſing is the gift, that's grudge'd and ſlow.

12 Give alms, ſays holy Paul, whilſt yet you may,
And, whilſt you've time allotted you, do good:
For he that is a ſov'reign prince to-day,
To-morrow may be ſeen to beg his food.

13 Dives moſt ſumptuouſly at dinner fare'd,
On various meſſes, exquiſite in taſte:
But was of water, e'er 'twas night, debarr'd,
And force'd amidſt infernal flames to faſt.

14 That morn, of all the cates that deck'd his board,
The offals he to Lazarus deny'd——
That night, although for it he loudly roar'd,
He cou'd not, e'en with water, be ſupply'd.

15 The world, and all therein, he'd now give up
For one ſmall ſup, to cool his fev'riſh tongue ;
But he can not obtain a ſingle ſup,
Though he ſhou'd beg and pray for't, e'er ſo long.

16 He cannot boaſt, of all he once poſſeſs'd,
A ſingle drop of water now in ſtore:
(The miſer, who has now the fulleſt cheſt,
Perchance to-morrow may be quite as poor.)

17 He went from hence as bare and naked quite,
As when he firſt on this world's ſtage was ſet ;
And, if he heav'n cou'd purchaſe for a mite,
That ſingle mite he by no means cou'd get.

18 To day, the rich may have it in their pow'r
Much alms, upon the wretched, to beſtow :
To-morrow, they may thro' miſhap grow poor,
And be reduce'd to beggary and woe.

19 Let us then give, what we've to give, to-day,
(Perhaps to-morrow we of nought can boaſt)
To the diſtreſs'd, their hunger to allay,
And unto thoſe that want aſſiſtance moſt.

20 Give bread to ev'ry one that's in diſtreſs,
And God will with increaſe improve thy ſtore :
Thou ſhalt not find thy meat, or money, leſs,
For what thou kindly giveſt to the poor.

21 The Widow of Sarepta did not know,
For what ſhe ſpare'd Elijah, more diſtreſs ;
Though meal and oil ſhe did to him beſtow,
Yet ſtill her meal and oil were not the leſs.

22 I've ſeen the rich oft beg from door to door,
Becauſe they did the indigent aggrieve ;
But never did I ſee him truly poor,
Or much diſtreſs'd, who did the poor relieve.

23 Knave'ry, oppreſſion, vanity, exceſs,
The woeful want of ſeveral have wrought ;
But none to tribulation or diſtreſs,
Have by their charity been ever brought.

24 Happy the man (the royal Prophet ſays)
Who to the needy does aſſiſtance give !
The Lord himſelf ſhall (in his worſt of days)
That man from his adverſity relieve !

25 God, from all trouble will his ſervant take,
God, from his enemies his friend will keep,
God, will himſelf his bed vouchſafe to make,
When he through pain and ſickneſs cannot ſleep.

26 Whate'er they want unto the needy lend,
And God himſelf will deign to be their bail :
If thou ſhalt them in their diſtreſs befriend,
Chriſt will the debt repay thee, and ne'er fail.

27 Who, but a Jew, wou'd not his cafh lay out,
When he might have his inte'reft on the day?
Who, but a Jew, wou'd fuch a debtor doubt,
Who cent. per cent. can for his money pay?

28 You often truft to Chapmen that are worfe,
Tho' you have got a debtor to your mind :
Truft then your Saviour freely with your purfe
Better fecurity you ne'er can find !

29 An hundred fold is given by the Lord
To ev'ry Chriftian for his pounds and pence;
Dull is the ufurer, who won't afford
The poor fome cafh, on inte'reft fo immenfe!

30 No money e'er to better ufe is lent,
Than that which Charity can fairly boaft :
Since it returns the lender cent. per cent.
E'en at the moment that he wants it moft.

31 There are no treafures, all the world around,
That equal price with Charity can hold :
When troubles come, it will be better found
Than ready money, or than bullion gold.

32 Silver will ruft, and gold with ufe will wafte,
Rich lawns and filks to moths will prove a prey,
Our bread will mould, our liquors lofe their tafte;
But never will beneficence decay.

33 When houfes, lands, and ev'ry worldly ftore,
Shall in one common conflagration rife—
Then Charity above the flames fhall foar,
And, till thou comeft, wait above the fkies.

34 When pale-face'd death to fummon thee fhall come,
At Chrift's tribunal naked to appear,
Then Charity will, on the day of doom,
Be the beft ftore, thou canft bring with thee, there.

35 When houfes, lands, and ev'ry timid friend,
Shall leave thee in the fangs of Death alone—
Then Charity thy footfteps will attend,
And guide thee to thy great Creator's throne.

36 More

36 More gains shall to the charitable soul
  Accrue, who did the indigent relieve,
  Than to the needy, who receiv'd the dole:
  Since, for a *little*, he shall *much* receive.

37 Manna shall, there, for a few crumbs be had,
  And, for plain water, floods of joy be given!
  Each Christian, there, by Jesus shall be clad,
  For some few rags, in the gay robes of heaven.

38 Employ your riches properly and well;
  Secure their friendship, e'er the day of doom,
  That they may haul your happy souls from hell,
  And with you to the blissful regions come.

39 Thy treasures in the upper regions lay,
  Sell all thou hast, and give it to the poor,
  Nor, like an Idiot, foolishly delay
  To part with earth, that thou to heav'n may'st soar.

40 Before thee, by the poor, thy treasures send
  To that safe place, which robbers can't annoy;
  For whatsoever thou, to them, dost lend,
  Thou shalt from Christ receive again with joy.

41 Whate'er, unto thy children, thou may'st grant,
  Thy wife, or friends, belongs to them alone:
  But what thou givest Christ, and those that want,
  Is hoarded for thyself—'tis all thy own!

42 Before thee send thy wealth to Paradise,
  Then light thy lamp; for darksome is the way;
  And make thyself ('tis Jesus' own advice!)
  A purse that knows no bottom, nor decay.

43 Whilst time permits thee, freely sow thy grain,
  As God has bless'd thy labours with increase,
  And thou an hundred fold shalt reap again;
  Unless thy labours shall, e'er harvest, cease.

44 Among the poor and hungry share thy bread,
  And clothe the naked, shiv'ring with the cold;
  Give to the needy wanderer a bed:
  All this to thee by God himself is told ! Isi. lix. 7.

45 Be thou, inſtead of eyes, unto the blind,
    Let thou the lame ſtill find ſupport in thee,
    Aſſiſt the Widow, be to ſtrangers kind,
    And, to the fatherleſs, a father be.

ADVICE to ev'ry Maſter of a Family, to govern his Houſe in a religious Manner.

1 IF truly pious thou wou'dſt fain appear,
    And ſtrictly Chriſtian, whilſt thou liveſt here,
    To a ſmall church convert thy own abode,
    And make thy private houſe, the houſe of God.

2 Make thou a hallow'd church of thy abode,
    And let thy family, like angels, be,
    Where ev'ry one may duely ſerve his God,
    According to his calling and degree.

3 An holy temple make of thy abode,
    That all, within it's walls, may daily join,
    Without ceſſation, to adore their God,
    Early and late, with harmony divine.

4 Inſtead of ſtones, cut out and ſquare'd by art,
    Take thou good men, to rear the ſacred wall——
    Men, who have ever acted well their part——
    Religious men, to build thy church withal.

5 Let not an ill-hewn ſtone be found in it,
    Let not a reprobate the ſtructure raiſe ;
    God will no rough, unpoliſh'd, ſtone admit
    To rear a building, ſacred to his praiſe.

6 Then caſt aſide each rude, improper ſtone ;
    For God will not accept of ought prophane :
    Thy houſe muſt be the houſe of God alone,
    An hallow'd temple, not the Devil's fane.

7 For wicked folks, therein, the good excel,
    And are more proper Satan's fold to rear,
    And be the fuel of an endleſs hell,
    Than in the church of Jeſus to appear.

8 One rough, uneven ftone, one fhapelefs mafs,
Will all the beauty of the work deface :
One lawlefs man, that does in vice furpafs,
Will thee and all thy family difgrace.

9 Then place not in thy wall a lump unfit,
Odious to fee, improper for the end ;
Nor ever to thy houfe the vile admit,
Nor the unfaithful with the faithful blend.

10 Mis-fhapen ftones, that never felt the rule,
Will only undermine thy temple-wall :
So impious fervants, of all vices full,
Will foon fubvert, and caufe thy houfe to fall.

11 Drive the unclean far from thy houfe and home,
E'er thou canft think that Jefus there will ftay:
For Chrift will never to thy manfion come,
'Till the impure from thence are chafe'd away.

12 The fons of God, and children of the fiend,
In the fame church are not together feen :
No more than bees can ftay, where fteams offend,
Or a pure fpirit dwell with one unclean.

13 The Great will never amongft hogs refide,
Whofe ftench and hideous grunt they can't endure:
Chrift and his holy Spirit can't abide
In the fame houfe with thofe that are impure.

14 If, in thy houfe, a mifcreant, rebel rout,
A drunken, difobedient crew, be found,
Caft them, as fheep that are diforder'd, out;
Left they fhou'd ficken, and infect the found.

15 As Ifmael from Abraham's houfe was thrown,
Becaufe, againft his miftrefs, he rebell'd ;
So let the vile and finful, from thy own,
Without the leaft reluctance be expell'd.

16 The royal Prophet never wou'd permit
A wicked perfon in his houfe to be:
A vicious fervant do not thou admit
To live, for any ufe whate'er, with thee.

17 One wicked fervant fixes oft a ftain
On many, who deferve a good report:
Let not thou fuch, beneath thy roof, remain,
Nor tread the precincts of thy hallow'd court.

18 By men of virtue let thy work be done,
If thou wou'dft endlefs happinefs attain;
God, with fuccefs, will all the godly crown,
Whilft foul mifhap attends the finful train.

19 A fervant, that's like Jofeph truly good,
Will bring a blefling on his mafter's head,
Whilft, Achan-like, an irreligious brood,
On thee and thine, will num'rous evils fhed.

20 Shou'dft thou a pious fervant chance to have,
God, for his fake, will all thy fubftance blefs,
As he, in times of old, to Laban gave,
For Jacob's fake, unparallel'd fuccefs.

21 Better the fervant, that is good, and mild,
Who will with plenty, all thou owneft, blefs,
Than the vile mifcreant, that howe'er well-fkill'd,
Will bring a curfe on all thou doft poffefs.

22 Much better will the fervant's work fucceed,
That's harmlefs, quiet, and well-ftock'd with grace,
Than all the labours of an impious breed,
Though ftrong, and aptly fuited to the place.

23 A fervant that is wife, and well-inclin'd,
His mafter may convert and all the houfe;
As the good wife may turn her hufband's mind,
And make a Chriftian, of a heathen fpoufe.

24 If thou haft not a pious family,
To ferve thee truly in the fear of God,
Thy houfe will ne'er a facred temple be,
But Satan's den, or fome vile fiend's abode.

25 Servants of mighty ftrength will not avail,
The bufi'nefs of thy farm or fhop, to do,
If in their duty to their God they fail,
And are not ftrong to do His bufi'nefs too.

26 Unlefs

26 Unlefs he in the faith be found fincere,
   Receive not any one to thy abode ;
   And by no means admit a fervant there,
   Until he be the fervant too of God.

27 The Church of God does not a Turk admit,
   Nor any one, that of true faith is void,
   To her communion : Do not thou permit
   A reprobate to be by thee employ'd.

28 A fervant, without faith, can ne'er be true
   Unto his mafter, whether God, or man :
   For 'tis the cuftom of the faithlefs crew
   To fell them both, like Judas, if they can.

29 Get thee a fet of fervants to thy mind—
   Servants, that know their duty to their God—
   Servants, that are well-nurture'd, well-inclin'd ;
   If thou wou'dft make a church of thy abode.

30 Be thou to all thy family a light—
   A light, which fhall to their improvement fhine—
   Be thou to them a pattern fair and bright,
   In all that's honeft, moral, and divine.

31 Be thou a good example unto all,
   In word and deed, and in thy dealings juft,
   Within thy parlour, kitchen, or thy hall,
   Where-e'er thou art, and whatfoe'er thou doft.

32 Like Enoch, walk thou humbly with thy God,
   For ever vigilant, for ever wife :
   For ev'ry where, at church, at home, abroad,
   Thy Saviour fees thee with his feven eyes.

33 Ne'er fay, nor do, the thing that is not right,
   The thing that is not ftrictly juft and fit,
   Whether thou art in the Almighty's fight,
   At church, or in the market-place doft fit.

34 Be thou as pure and prudent in each act,
   Full as much care and vigilance exert,
   Full as religious be, and as exact,
   In thine own houfe, as if in church thou wert.

35 It is a debt, a debt all mafters owe,
  To teach their fervants the true Chriftian lore;
  That they may God and his commandments know,
  Believe in Chrift, and rightly him adore.

36 As Abra'ham all his family of yore
  The fear of God, and his true worfhip taught:
  So do thou teach thy houfehold to adore
  And know the Lord, and ferve him, as they ought.

37 Teach thou thy children, teach thy fervants, how
  Their heav'nly Sire they truly may obey,
  Teach them the Saviour, whom God fent, to know:
  For that to heaven is the certain way!

38 The law of God, in ev'ry fervant's breaft,
  Implant——of that, on all occafions talk,
  Whenever thou doft rife, or go to reft,
  At home, abroad, when thou doft fit, or walk.

39 'Tis God's command, that ev'ry fire fhou'd fhew
  His ftatutes foon unto his children dear——
  Or, like Phylact'ries, on their garment few,
  That they the fame, in mind, fhou'd always bear.

40 Each night and morn, unto thy menial train,
  A chapter from the holy Bible read;
  Make them repeat it, if they can, again——
  Make them fuch lives, as it has taught them, lead.

41 Be thou a councillor, prieft, judge, and king,
  Unto thy children, and domeftic train,
  That thou may'ft all beneath thy orders bring,
  And make them, in obedience meet, remain.

42 Be thou their Prieft, the Chriftian faith to teach,
  Be thou their Council, to advife them well,
  Do thou to them the Gofpel doctrines preach,
  And pray that they in virtue may excel.

43 Be thou their king, to force them to obey,
  And punifh thofe, who hurt the Chriftian caufe,
  And to confirm them in the proper way,
  By juft coercion, and by wholefome laws.

44 Over

44 Over thy houfehold, as a judge prefide,
And fentence pafs in an impartial way:
Unto the good and juft, rewards provide—
But punifhments to thofe, that difobey.

45 Make thou a fair and equitable law,
To bind thy congregation with it's bands,
And caufe thy people, through a pious awe,
To live exactly as that law commands.

46 Teach ev'ry one his duty to his God,
· And with thy finger point him out the way,
And, when he's perfect in it, let the rod
Oblige him, though reluctant, to obey.

47 Obferve their conduct with a father's care,
With hand and eye their fev'ral motions guide,
· Let no one by his words or actions dare,
Without due punifhment, to ftep afide.

48 Let all thy family, like ftars, appear—
Like ftars, that decorate the brow of night,
And yield to all the country, far and near,
Inftruction, honour, and celeftial light.

49 Make all, that under thy direction dwell,
In goodnefs and in piety exceed:
As Noah did the former world excel
In holinefs, and ev'ry virtuous deed.

50 Make thou thy bofom-wife to be a ftar,
Righteoufly-mild, and cheerfully-ferene,
Make her, to all her fex, a pattern rare,
In words and works, throughout life's various fcene.

51 Make thou thy children to thy rule fubmit,
Make them examples to a finful age,
Make them obey thy orders, as 'tis fit,
Like Rechab's offspring, in the facred page.

52 Make thou thy folk, to be the folk of God,
Like Philemon, in holy writ renown'd,
Who made a temple of his own abode;
So much in piety did it abound!

53 Such pious lives make thou thy fervants lead
In thine own houfe, as in the houfe of God,
Make them as cautioufly in private tread,
As if they in a facred temple trod.

54 Permit them not to dwell at large, at home,
Or do worfe things, than if in church they were,
Nor let them a lefs virtuous air affume;
But make them live as regularly, there.

55 Permit them not to violate the leaft
Of God's commands, e'er thou doft them reprove:
But foon as they fhall have in ought tranfgreft,
Do thou their fouls to true repentance move.

56 Permit not thou one fervant of them all,
To fwear by their Creator's holy name——
Or give that perfon, whether great or fmall,
Due and condign correction for the fame.

57 Permit them not to fpend their fabbath-days
In idlenefs, beneath the Chriftian name——
In revellings, or in unrighteous ways,
Without reproof immediate for the fame.

58 Let none amongft them hear the word in vain,
And never put in practice what they hear;
But let them talk, and talk it o'er again,
Until their progrefs in their lives appear.

59 Let none prefume to go to bed at night
'Till, on his knees, he has his homage paid——
His bounden homage——due to God of right,
E'er to repofe he has his body laid.

60 Let none amongft them, whether great or fmall,
Their wonted labours any day refume,
'Till freely on their bended knees they fall
To worfhip God each morning, in their room.

61 Let none their hands unto the plough-tail move,
Nor let them unto any work draw nigh,
'Till they have rais'd their minds to God above,
To beg his aid and bleffings from on high.

62 Let

62 Let no man whatfoe'er a journey take,
    Ride to a fair, or fail upon the main,
    'Till he his fervent pray'r to God fhall make,
    That he may homewards bring him fafe again.

63 Let no one his unhallow'd victu'als eat,
    Or ftuff his paunch, like a voracious fwine,
    'Till he has begg'd a blefling on his meat,
    And gratefully acknowledge'd aid divine.

64 Let no one quit, like a brute beaft, the board,
    Where he has his ungodly belly cramm'd;
    'Till he for his fupport, has thank'd the Lord,
    And with due gratitude his praife proclaim'd.

65 Whene'er thou worfhippeft the Pow'r divine,
    Let ev'ry one unto the room repair,
    And that none there's indiff'rent or fupine,
    Do thou thyfelf take a peculiar care.

66 Let them not ufe themfelves to vain difcourfe,
    To loofe expreffions, or unmanly taunts—
    Let them no fcandal vent, nor fwear and curfe—
    No boaftings ufe, or unbecoming vaunts.

67 Thy children and thy houfehold firmly bind,
    To ufe fuch words, as may their morals mend——
    Words, that will pleafe and edify the mind,
    And to each auditor's improvement tend.

68 Permit them not, unlucky tricks to ufe—
    Permit them not, the fimple to diftrefs——
    Permit them not, a cripple to abufe——
    Permit them not, the needy to opprefs.

69 Permit them not, to revel and caroufe—
    Permit them not, to fwill thy drink, like fwine——
    Permit them not to fmoke, within thy houfe,
    The weed—that makes their backs and bellies pine.

70 Permit them not in fafhions to delight——
    To curl their locks—or coftly garments wear;
    But let them ftill be creditably tight,
    And let them all with decency appear.

71 Ne'er

71 Ne'er let them faunter on a fabbath-day
To the green booths, where worldlings rendezvous,
Nor in the brutifh tippling-houfes ftay,
(Where Satan holds his revels) to caroufe.

72 Each Sunday to thy parifh-church repair,
There let thy family attend thee, all
There with the congregation join in pray'r——
There publickly on thy Creator call.

73 Let not thy family remain at home,
Nor during fervice-time behind thee ftay——
Let them not loiter, near the facred dome:
If they muft play, let them the morrow play.

74 Lay not too cumb'rous, nor too great a load
Upon thy fervants, on their working days;
But let fome hours of refpite be allow'd,
That they their backs,when tire'd with work,may raife.

75 Let them not, on the fabbaths, roam abroad,
But make them fearch with care the facred page,
And do with diligence the work of God,
E'er they in any other work engage.

76 Inftruct thy houfehold ev'ry fabbath-day,
In pfalms and hymns their Maker to applaud,
And argue with them, in a friendly way,
On their Belief, and on the word of God.

77 Whene'er they dine; nay, ev'ry time they eat,
By one of them be there a chapter read;
That the poor foul may have it's proper meat
And due repaft, when'er the body's fed.

78 Both morn and night, let fome one in thy houfe
The fervice read, and for the others pray;
For 'twou'd be better they their meal fhou'd lofe,
Than lofe the facred fervice of the day.

79 Let not thy family, on any day,
Without it's Mattins and it's Vefpers be;
Thy facrifice, both morn and ev'ning, pay,
For all the mercies God has fhewn to thee.

80 Let ev'ry corner of thy houfe be kept
  Quite clean (with nought impure let it be ftain'd !)
  And with the befom of repentance fwept,
  'Till thou the favour of thy God haft gain'd.

81 Wafh thou with briny tears the hallow'd ground—
  It's walls, inftead of ftones, with virtues raife—
  Let not thy altar without fire be found,
  Nor without incenfe—fuch as, " pray'r and praife."

82 Do thou thyfelf perform the parfon's part,
  Do thou thyfelf invoke the Pow'r divine,
  And make thy people, with a glowing heart,
  Along with thee in each petition join.

83 Each honeft mafter of a houfehold ought
  To act with care, and on a proper plan ;
  And, as a prieft, reprove them when in fault
  With the moft pow'rful language that he can.

84 The fame good order, which our church purfues,
  To keep her members all beneath her fway,
  Each private Chriftian in his houfe fhou'd ufe,
  To make his fervants his behefts obey.

85 Some one, or two, thy own affiftants make,
  Who, o'er the reft, as wardens may prefide,
  And thy affairs to their direction take,
  And, when thou'rt abfent, with difcretion guide.

86 Thou muft the morals of thy folks infpect,
  And their behaviour carefully obferve,
  That each delinquent may in time be check't,
  And duely cenfure'd, as his faults deferve.

87 Punifh the wicked, equal to his crime,
  Nor ever let him uncorrected go ;
  Left others fhou'd tranfgrefs another time,
  Becaufe thou mercy unto him didft fhow.

88 Let each offender of his faults be told,
  And be admonifh'd twice, or thrice, or more,
  E'er he's expell'd, and exile'd from the fold :
  But turn him out, if he'll not then give o'er.

P   89 If

89 If thou haft hire'd a maid that is a fhrew,
   And does not honour to her miftrefs pay,
   The door to her, as 'twas to Hagar, fhew,
   And let thy wife have, as fhe ought, her way.

90 To keep thy people idle, is not good,
   Give each his tafk, and make him do the fame:
   For idlenefs fupplies each vice with food,
   And is the parent, and the nurfe of fhame.

91 See, that thy family go ev'ry night
   Early to reft, and proper bed-time keep;
   For 'tis a cuftom, far from being right,
   That they fhou'd go, whene'er *they* pleafe, to fleep.

92 When it is time for them to go to fleep,
   Defire of Chrift on them his Grace to fhed,
   Defire of Chrift fecurely them to keep,
   Then take thy leave, and go thyfelf to bed:

93 But, firft, exhort them on their God to call,
   (With minds replete with a religious fire,
   Upon their bended knees) both great and fmall,
   Before they to their nightly reft retire:

94 And, left that God fhou'd take them unaware,
   And unprovided, to his judgement-feat,
   Conjure them all, each ev'ning to prepare,
   Before they fleep, their aweful Judge to meet.

95 If thus thou fhou'dft thy houfe and houfehold rule,
   Both thee and them, thy gracious God will blefs,
   With ev'ry Grace he'll crowd your bofoms full,
   And crown you all with ev'ry Happinefs.

96 Chrift in thy temple, then, will ftill remain,
   Chrift, when diftrefs'd, will hear thy plaintive cries,
   And, Chrift will take thee, and thy menial train,
   To all the' ecftatic joys of paradife.

The

The Duty of CHILDREN to their Parents.

1   ALL honour, reverence, and due regard,
      My fon! unto thy parents ever give:
  'Tis God's command!—and thou, for thy reward,
  Shalt, through his Grace, to length of days arrive.

2 Do thou whatever they wou'd have thee do,
  And act in ev'ry thing, as they defire,
  To all their orders strict obedience show;
  So they no fin, nor any crime, require.

3 Receive thy father's counfel and reproof—
  Receive the Precepts, which he deigns to give—
  Receive his difcipline, however rough,
  And thy inftruction at his hand receive.

4 If dull, if blind, if mad, if full of fire
  And fierce impatience—if to dotage gone,
  Pity thy aged mother and thy fire,
  And bear their frailties, as a duteous fon.

5 Shou'd they e'er fall to poverty and need,
  And not have means enough to find them bread,
  With kind indulgence the old couple feed ;
  As thee they, in thy helplefs childhood, fed.

6 Take thou example from the ftork, that feeds
  His fire, when old, and to him fuccour brings,
  Righting his neft, and fetching what he needs,
  Or foft'ring him, when weak, beneath his wings.

7 Do thou a leffon from the dolphins draw,
  Which help their parents, when by age o'erpow'r'd,
  And guard them, when they're weak, with filial awe,
  Left they by other fifh fhou'd be devour'd.

8 It is a fhame the fons of men fhou'd be
  Worfe than the rav'nous flutt'rers of the air ;
  Nay, worfe than e'en the fifhes of the fea,
  To thofe, to whom, for life, in debt they are.

9 If thou art, by thy rank or office, great—
However high thy calling, don't neglect,
(Though they be mean, and of a low eſtate)
To give thy parents honour and reſpect.

10 Though Joſeph, at his pleaſure, Egypt ſway'd,
And Jacob by the famine, then, was preſs'd,
Yet to his father he due honour paid,
Howe'er impov'riſh'd, and howe'er diſtreſs'd.

11 Though Solomon, then, wore the Jewiſh crown,
And ſat in ſtate above the vaſſal crowd,
Yet from his throne he oft deſcended down,
And to his mother in obeyſance bow'd.

12 Though Chriſt was God as well as man, and highe'r
Than all our race, and all in worth outweigh'd;
Yet, to his mother and reputed ſire,
He proper honour and obedience paid.

13 Though thou wert made a duke, thou ſtill art bound
To give thy parents, howe'er poor, reſpect ;
And though in wealth thou vaſtly ſhou'dſt abound,
Thou muſt not them, on that account, neglect.

14 Thy father is thy father ſtill, tho' poor,
And thou his ſon, although a lord or ſquire :
Whilſt thou'rt a ſon, and it is in thy pow'r,
God ties thee down to help thy humble ſire.

15 When in thy infancy thou ſcarce cou'dſt move,
And hadſt not meat nor drink, nor warm array ;
What then preſerv'd thee, but thy mother's love ?
Such obligations, how canſt thou repay ?

16 Long in her womb th' uneaſy load ſhe bore,
And with her blood nine months ſuſtain'd thee there,
Then calm'd thy hunger with her breaſts ſweet ſtore ;
Canſt thou enough reward her for ſuch care ?

17 Full many a night, when ſick, ſhe kindly trie'd
To eaſe thy pain, although her ſleep ſhe loſt,
And, when without that care thou muſt have die'd,
Still in her arms, 'till day-light, gently toſt.

18 Thy

18 Thy parents therefore filially revere,
  For the vaſt love they unto thee expreſs'd :
  The weight of penury ne'er let them bear,
  Whilſt thou'rt alive, and with a penny bleſs'd.

19 For the reſpect, the honour, clothes, and meat,
  Thou give'ſt thy hoary ſire in his diſtreſs,
  Thy ſon ſhall thee with equal juſtice treat,
  When palſie'd age thy powers ſhall oppreſs.

20 Shou'dſt thou e'er for thy father's bed preſume
  To lay a hair-cloth coverlet, thy ſon
  Shall keep the ſame in ſome cold outer-room
  For thee, before thy death, to lie upon.

21 The uſage thou doſt give thy ſire, when old,
  Shall be return'd to thee, if thou ſhalt live ;
  His grandſon ſhall requite, as I've been told,
  The ſcanty meaſure thou to him didſt give.

22 Be therefore to thy aged parents free,
  Be good, be kind, be dutiful, and give
  To them whate'er they can expect from thee,
  That in thy turn thou may'ſt the like receive.

23 Never clandeſtinely, like Eſau, wed,
  E'er their conſent thy parents freely give :
  God never bleſſes ſuch a marriage-bed ;
  Or 'tis a chance if it ſhou'd ever thrive.

24 With diſreſpect their counſels ne'er requite,
  Nor with irreverence their checks repay,
  Nor ever undervalue them, nor ſlight ;
  But earneſtly for their amendment pray.

25 Thy father's curſe, leſt thou incur, take heed,
  It ne'er departed from Cham's ſooty race :
  For Noah's curſe ſtill cleaves unto the breed ;
  You ſee it ſtill in ev'ry negro's face.

26 Becauſe his ſire he offer'd to deſpiſe,
  A grievous ſtain upon Cham's offspring came ;
  In their black ſkins it ſtill deep rooted lies,
  And nothing can eradicate the ſame.

P 3   27 Abſalom,

27 Abſalom, though moſt beautiful and young,
   Was, to his aged ſire, and king, unkind :
   God therefore in an oak the rebel hung,
   Whence by his hair he dangled in the wind.

28 Then to thy parents ſhew all due regard,
   Aſſiſt them both, when they aſſiſtance need;
   So God ſhall thee with length of days reward,
   Where-ever thou may'ſt chuſe thy life to lead !

Things, which a Perſon ought to meditate upon,
   on the LORD's-day, by going to Church—and
   how he ought to demean himſelf there.

1 REflect a while, whilſt yet upon the road,
     Where? before whom, thou go'ſt ! on what deſign!
   E'er thou arriveſt to the houſe of God :
   Then calmly enter to that place divine.

2 Thou goeſt to the' Almighty's own abode,
   Before the greateſt Sove'reign to appear,
   Thou goeſt with thy Maker and thy God,
   Upon thy knees, a conference to bear.'

3 Thou goeſt to Jehovah's ſacred place,
   To hear the language of thy gracious Lord,
   And commune with him, tho' not face to face,
   Yet through the medium of his bleſſed word.

4 Thou goeſt to confeſs thy ſins, before
   Thy God, who dwelleth in the realms above;
   Thou goeſt his forgiveneſs to implore,
   And grace and ſtrength, thy errors to remove.

5 Thou goeſt help and pardon to implore,
   With grace and abſolution from the Lord,
   By the Prieſt's lips, for all thou didſt before,
   In contradiction to his holy word.

6 Thou goeſt to addreſs thy heav'nly Sire,
   Who promiſes each needful boon to grant,
   Which thoſe corporeal frames of our's require,
   With ev'ry grace our ſinful ſouls may want.

                                    7 Thou

7 Thou goeſt to applaud th' Almighty's name,
For ev'ry gift which he vouchſafe'd to thee,
Thou goeſt his encomiums to proclaim,
Where his bleſt votaries aſſembled be.

8 Thou goeſt, with a pleaſure-blended awe,
Chriſt's Goſpel, and the word of life, to hear,
God's will reveal'd from heaven in the law !
Which only can direct a Chriſtian there.

9 Thou go'ſt the ſhare of that good gift to gain,
Which God does of his own free will beſtow,
To make the way wherein thou walkeſt plain,
And proſper ev'ry thing that thou ſhalt do.

10 Go therefore to the houſe of God with glee,
With ardent zeal unto his temple go,
And long within his ſacred courts to be,
As for the brook of Siloh, longs the roe.

11 Go cheerfully, go joyouſly to pray,
Go boldly, yet with aweful rev'rence go,
Go ſpeedily, go early in the day,
Go with ſubmiſſion and proſtration low.

12 Go to the temple with the firſt that come,
And be not idle, whilſt thou there doſt wait;
But be amongſt the laſt returning home,
And do the work of God without deceit.

13 Behave not there with liſtleſs indolence,
But do thy work, whilſt life endures, with care :
For curſed is the man, who void of ſenſe
Performs God's work without reſpect or fear.

14 Low, on thy bended knees, with rev'rence fall,
Upon heaven's King with eager accents cry,
With importunity unto him call,
Nor, if a Chriſtian, uſe hypocriſy.

15 Receive the Goſpel with a ready ear,
And in thy mind the precious treaſure ſtore,
Watch it, leſt ſable fiends the ſeed ſhou'd bear,
'Till 't has produce'd an hundred fold, or more.

16 Thine

16 Thine eyes from roving diligently keep,
   And hear the Gofpel, or devoutly pray,
   But neither idly chat, nor dully fleep,
   Or from the temple quickly hafte away.

17 The righteous Judge no hypocrite can bear,
   Who wou'd be thought the Godhead to adore;
   But with feign'd fervices and in fincere,
   Treats the Almighty and Omnifcient Pow'r.

18 The minifter through ev'ry pray'r attend,
   And be with him in each petition join'd:
   Repeat each word unto the very end,
   In perfect unifon of voice and mind.

19 Whene'er he preaches the celeftial word,
   Fix on the prieft attentively thine eye;
   Let all his words be in thy bofom ftor'd,
   And all his precepts zealoufly obey.

20 Whene'er he preaches the infpired word,
   See, that thou turneft not thy head away:
   The Gofpel is the power of the Lord,
   Which leads us fafe along falvation's way.

21 Return not thoughtlefsly, nor fimply, home,
   Before the fervice of the day be done;
   Nor e'er, for fear of fome great curfe, prefume
   To quit the church, until the prieft be gone.

22 Let thy demeanour in the church be right,
   Let it be Chriftian-like, fincere, and free,
   As if thou wert in the Almighty's fight,
   And ev'ry angel did thy actions fee.

Advice to prepare ourfelves, before we come to worfhip God in public.

1 PULL off thy fhoes, and make thy garments white,
   And fanctify thyfelf, e'er thou doft dare
Approach the throne of the dread Sire of light
In his own houfe, to offer up thy pray'r.

2 Goad

2 Goad up thy foul, to active life arife,
  Above terreftrial matters nobly foar,
  And view the' invifible with Faith's keen eyes,
  E'er thou addreffeft the Almighty Pow'r.

3 When thou, my foul! before thy God doft come,
  How vaft the diftance, think! 'twixt him and thee;
  And to approach thy Sove'reign ne'er prefume,
  But with fubmiffion, on thy bended knee.

4 The King of heav'n, who gave the angels birth,
  The God of vengeance, and the Source of day,
  The Judge of men, and Maker of the earth,
  Is he, to whom thou now woud'ft homage pay!

5 Come then with rev'rence, come with ardour, near,
  With holinefs and faith his prefence gain,
  Before the Deity with zeal appear,
  And thou thy bofom-wifhes fhalt obtain.

6 Lift up thine eyes, and fpread thy hands, betimes,
  And bend thy knees with fupplication meek,
  Beat, beat thy breaft, repent thee of thy crimes,
  Confefs thy fins, and for God's favour feek.

7 Invoke thy heav'nly Sire, each ftated hour,
  Seek thou his kingdom and his righteoufnefs,
  In his Son's name, with fpirit and with pow'r,
  And thou fhalt largely all the reft poffefs.

8 Seek thou God's glory, in the foremoft place,
  Seek, next, the things above this earthly ball,
  Seek then with zealous earneftnefs his grace,
  Seek all thou wanteft, thou fhalt have it all.

9 Before thou to the temple ent'reft in,
  Be fure that thou with upright fteps doft come,
  Difmifs each bad defign, each latent fin,
  And leave each worldly-minded thought at home.

10 As faithful Abraham, e'er he went to pray
  Upon the mount, did leave his afs behind;
  So ev'ry man fhou'd caft his fins away,
  And each prefumptuous thought fecurely bind.

11 Mofes

11 Moſes himſelf took off his ſhoes to pray,
  E'er he approach'd the radiant Source of light;
  Do thou, like him, throw ev'ry vice away,
  E'er thou appeareſt in the Godhead's ſight.

12 Joſeph array'd him in a decent dreſs,
  E'er he did to the Egyptian king appear:
  Do thou, like him, prepare thyſelf no leſs,
  E'er thou doſt to the King of kings draw near.

13 The pious Eſther waſh'd herſelf, before
  She by the Perſian monarch wou'd be ſeen:
  E'er thou approacheſt the Almighty Pow'r,
  Take heed, that thou'rt from all pollution clean.

14 Whenever thou doſt at the church appear,
  Obſerve, how pleaſant is the Lord's abode!
  When there thou comeſt, come with aweful fear,
  And due reſpect, before the Lord thy God.

15 Fall on thy bended knees, before the Lord,
  Before him in his courts ſubmiſſive bow,
  Nor let thy lips once drop a ſingle word,
  E'er thou haſt prais'd him with proſtration low.

16 None among all the glorious ſaints above
  Preſume to laud the Ruler of the ſkies,
  'Till they their crowns do from their heads remove,
  And fall upon their knees in humble wiſe.

17 How then can duſt and aſhes e'er preſume
  To tread his courts without ſubmiſſion due?
  Nay, even then, when they to worſhip come,
  And for forgiveneſs humbly ought to ſue?

18 Our Maſter Jeſus, when he pray'd, fell low
  Upon his face, before his glorious Sire:
  Yet ſcarce will any of his ſervants bow
  A knee, whatever they of God require.

19 The greater James ſo oft his God ador'd
  Upon his naked knees, that they at laſt
  (So very often he addreſs'd the Lord!)
  The camel's knees in callouſneſs ſurpaſt.

20 Moſes

20 Mofes and Aaron, Jofhua of old,
    With each good king, that rule'd the Jews of yore,
    And ev'ry prophet, that God's will foretold,
    Shew'd us, how we the Godhead fhou'd adore.

21 When thou haft fallen on the earth, before
    Thy Great Creator, with all due refpect,
    His gracious aid and favour to implore,
    E'er thou doft fpeak, on what thou fayft, reflect.

22 Daniel, before he fpake unto the king,
    Reflected long on what he had to fay:
    So ev'ry man fhou'd due reflexion bring,
    E'er he prefumes unto his God to pray.

23 When thou haft well confider'd what to fay,
    Thy bofom beat, before thou doft begin,
    Own thine unworthinefs, and humbly pray
    For pardon and remiffion of thy fin.

24 Cry out thus to him with a heart contrite,
    " Let me, O God! thy gracious favour gain,
    " Though I'm unworthy of thy favour quite,
    " Or that I fhou'd the leaft requeft obtain."

25 God is benign to all that beg his aid,
    To ev'ry one that afks, he freely grants,
    He gives to all, and never does upbraid,
    He gives abundantly, to each that wants.

26 Whate'er thou afkeft, that thou'lt have, believe,
    Take no denial, but with fervour crave,
    And what thou afkeft, doubt not to receive :
    Urgently afk, and thou the boon fhalt have.

27 Doubt not thy heavenly Father's pow'r, or will;
    Who gives to all, will freely give to thee :
    For he is well-inclne'd, and able ftill,
    A ready aid, and bountifully free !

A Prayer

A Prayer for them, who go to worship God in public.

1 THou God of mercy! Source of light and day!
    Giver of grace, and ev'ry useful boon!
For Jesus' sake, O, hear us, when we pray,
And grant thy people their petitions soon.

2 We now unto thy altar, Lord! draw near,
And are assembled in thy aweful sight:
O, may we there, just as we ought, appear!
O, give us pow'r to worship thee aright!

3 Our solemn meetings, my Creator, bless,
To ev'ry soul alacrity impart,
Our meditations prosper with success,
That we may worship thee with faithful heart.

4 O! place our souls in apt and proper frame,
Make us all ready and alert, O Lord!
To praise and glorify thy sacred name!
And hear with reverential awe thy Word!

5 Prepare our hearts, and sanctify each thought,
Quicken our zeal, O Lord! increase our love,
That we a due demeanour may be taught,
And worship with true faith the God above.

6 Up-lift our hearts, our sluggish minds up-lift,
Our cold affections with thy grace inflame,
Fix thou our thoughts, and for each gracious gift
Teach our mute lips to magnify thy name.

7 Tear from our hearts each vile and bad design,
And suffer not our thoughts to wander far,
Make us with profit hear thy word divine,
And with warm zeal to offer up each pray'r.

8 Let thy bless'd Spirit teach us all to pray
With ardent zeal, and vehement desire,
That thou may'st lend an ear to all we say,
And give us whatsoever we require.

9 Place thou thy fingers on our ears, O Lord!
That we may hear thy Gofpel, as we ought,
Enable us to underftand thy Word,
And to apply aright, what we are taught :

10 And when we've conn'd and underftood it well,
Empower us to do it, as we ought,
Empower us to practife it with zeal,
'Till it a large return of fruit has brought.

11 Do thou, O Lord! our parifh-paftor blefs,
That he, with knowledge grace and pow'r, may preach
The Word of Life, and with defire'd fuccefs,
Thy fervants from the facred Gofpel teach.

12 Enlighten thou his mind and thoughts, O Lord,
Inflame his heart, his tongue with knowledge fill,
That he may properly divide thy word
To all, according to thy holy will :

13 That we thereby may, from the fhades of death,
Be brought to light and comfort's fweet abode,
From the dark dungeons of the pow'rs beneath
Unto the fold, and kingdom of our God.

14 Make thou his fermons fruitful in each mind,
Make us digeft them with an ardent zeal,
Make us unto his perfon well-inclin'd,
If, as he ought, he labours for our weal.

15 Do thou, on him and us, thy bleffings fhow'r,
Do thou make pure, and fanctify each heart,
Do thou inftruct us by thy grace and pow'r,
That each may, as he fhou'd, perform his part!

A PREPARATION for the holy Communion.

1 LET ev'ry Chriftian, who wou'd chufe to know
How he fhou'd to God's bleffed table go,
Thefe precepts learn, and in his mem'ry bear,
E'er rafhly he prefumes to venture there.

2 E'er to the altar you abruptly go,
  Confider well, what you're about to do,
  And meditate on that myfterious cheer,
  Which you are foon to be refrefh'd with, there.

3 It is not at the feaft of fome great lord,
  Or at an emperor's tyrannic board,
  That you are fpeedily about to eat
  A food, which is than manna much more fweet.

4 More fweet than manna, if with faith fincere,
  You at Chrift's facred table fhall appear,
  But worfe than poifon far, if void of grace,
  You, Judas-like, approach that holy place.

5 Receive it then, as it deferves, be fure,
  With Chriftian decency and morals pure,
  With faith, with hope, with fanctity of mind,
  With perfect Charity for all mankind.

6 Take heed left, full of fin, you madly run
  To Chrift's blefs'd table—fuch a rafhnefs fhun ;
  Left you damnation for your pains obtain,
  Where others mercy and falvation gain.

7 Remember well, what purity of mind !
  What care ! what preparation ! God enjoin'd,
  E'er Ifrael was permitted erft to tafte
  The pafchal lamb, or touch that bleft repaft.

8 Remember too, how at that aweful fcene
  Our bleffed Saviour wafh'd his fervants clean,
  And wipe'd with his own hands each happy gueft,
  E'er he fhou'd tafte of that celeftial feaft.

9 O come not near the table of the Lord,
  Defile'd by luft, or any crime abhorr'd,
  E'er you are fully cleans'd from ev'ry fault
  And filthy ftain, wherewith your fouls were fraught!

10 Caft out all fin, and ev'ry foul deceit—
   Caft out wrath, envy, drunkennefs and hate—
   Caft pride, and each fallacious art, away ;
   For Chrift will never with fuch inmates ftay.

11 Remember how the Devil, fatal gueſt !
    Erſt enter'd Judas's unhallow'd breaſt,
    When he receiv'd the ſop, and raſhly eat,
    Though plunge'd in ſin, the conſecrated meat.

12 Do thou beware, leſt this befal to thee,
    (What once has been, thou know'ſt, again may be !)
    If, to the Euchariſt, thou ſhou'dſt preſume
    Laden with ſins, and unprepare'd, to come.

13 Keep the Corinthians ever in thy mind,
    Who erſt with ſeveral diſeaſes pine'd,
    Becauſe they unprepare'd and raſhly went,
    Without due thought, unto the ſacrament.

14 Take heed, leſt thou thyſelf ſhou'dſt e'er draw near
    To that bleſt board, without a pious fear:
    Reflect what aweful viands on it lie ;
    Leſt thou for thy temerity ſhou'dſt die.

15 Examine well thyſelf—be fully ſure
    Thy heart is perfectly ſincere, and pure—
    That thou haſt quite repented of each fault,
    And art with faith, hope, charity, well fraught.

16 Condemn thyſelf without the leaſt deceit,
    Leſt God thy condemnation ſhou'd complete,
    And, if thou doſt in ought deficient live,
    Beg thou of God to grant it, or forgive.

17 Four things are abſolutely requiſite,
    For ev'ry one that wou'd receive aright———
    True Chriſtian faith—Repentance unconfin'd———
    Love univerſal—and a thankful mind.

18 No one can ſafely be without the leaſt
    Of thoſe, who goes to that celeſtial feaſt :
    Whoe'er, without them, eats that hallow'd food,
    From his preſumption can expect no good.

19 A proper faith is neceſſary, firſt,
    To own that Chriſt, upon the croſs accurſt,
    Himſelf a ſacrifice for ſinners gave,
    That by his ſuff'rings he the world might ſave.

20 Faith does that pardon, with it's fruits, obtain,
Which Chrift for us did by his paffion gain ;
And, in the fupper he fo freely gives,
Faith, Chrift with all his righteoufnefs receives.

21 Chrift is not food, to glut the paunch defign'd,
Or for the ftomach and the teeth to grind,
But the foul's hunger fully to allay,
Thro' ardent faith, in a myfterious way.

22 None in the fpirit can enjoy the Lord,
Nor eat his body at the bleffed board,
Unlefs he's of that lively faith poffeft,
Which iffues from the contrite finner's breaft.

23 It, from the Gofpel, is exceeding plain,
That Chrift does in the realms above remain,
And that no mortal can his body eat,
But as a myftic, immaterial meat.

24 Faith therefore all, to gain their Saviour, need,
Faith all muft have, their famifh'd fouls to feed,
Faith all muft have, to elevate their heart;
If, in their Saviour, they wou'd have a part.

25 Chrift is a food, for hungry fouls defign'd,
Chrift is a food, to feed each faithful mind,
Chrift is a food, that muft thro' faith be eat,
Chrift is a fpiritual and mental treat !

26 Whene'er thou eateft this celeftial bread,
In fad remembrance of thy mafter dead,
Lift up, above this wicked world thy heart,
That thou, thro' faith, in Chrift may'ft have a part.

27 Repentance, next to faith, muft be obtain'd
From ev'ry fin wherewith thy foul is ftain'd,
With refolution to amend each day,
And from thy former faults to turn away.

28 Repent thou truly, with a heart fincere,
And for thy fins fhed many a briny tear,
Nor dare the table of the Lord attend,
E'er thou repenteft, left thou fhou'dft offend.

29 Caſt out the dregs, and keep thy body pure,
    Nor in a caſk unſweet thy wine ſecure,
    Leſt it ſhou'd fret, and force a paſſage out,
    And from the riven veſſel fly about.

30 Nor Father, Lamb, or Dove, will e'er remain,
    Where hate, and gloomy-minded malice reign:
    Then make thy veſſel clean, if thou wou'dſt taſte
    Thy Saviour's fleſh, and ſhare the ſweet repaſt.

31 Diſgorge thy fulſome load, conceal thy ſhame,
    All trifling talk, and vain purſuits diſclaim,
    Suppreſs thy wanton heat, thy temper rein,
    Amend thy life, from idleneſs refrain.

32 Waſh thou thy hands in innocence, thy ſoul
    In righteouſneſs, in charity, thy whole:
    So ſhall the man entire, from head to heel,
    Receive his Saviour, and his influence feel.

33 Love juſtice, and ſobriety purſue,
    Uſe purity and holineſs, indue
    The robe of perfect love, and let no ſtain,
    However ſlight, defile thy ſoul again.

34 Let not things holy e'er be hurl'd to dogs,
    Nor precious pearls be flung to filthy hogs,
    Nor manna to a dirty diſh conſign'd,
    Nor the communion to an impious mind:

35 But, in a golden pot, thy manna place,
    Chriſt's body with the fineſt linen grace,
    In a clean cask thy gen'rous wines ſecure,
    And the communion in a heart that's pure.

36 The third thing requiſite, which thou muſt get,
    E'er thou doſt eat, is charity complete:
    Ill-will, or ſpite, to no man thou may'ſt bear,
    Whether, thy friend or foe, from far, or near,

37 Love is the banner by Chriſt's ſervants ſhown,
    Whereby they are from any other's known;
    And 'tis by love (as men by liv'ry coats)
    That Chriſt diſtinguiſhes his ſheep, from goats:

Q   38 For

38 For Chrift will not permit that any gueft
Shou'd e'er partake of his celeftial feaft,
Who has not a fincere and guiltlefs mind,
That is in charity with all mankind.

39 Though of a thoufand gifts thou wert poffeft,
Thou fhalt not be to Chrift a welcome gueft;
But all thofe gifts will be of no avail,
If thou in perfeét charity fhou'dft fail.

40 In love unfeign'd with all thy neighbours live,
With all thy heart thine enemies forgive,
And if a wrong to any thou haft done,
Be reconcile'd, or let thy work alone.

41 Take heed, and come not to the feaft of Chrift,
Unlefs from fpite and malice you defift;
Left Satan with the bread fhou'd enter in,
And fill you full of ev'ry filthy fin.

42 Learn of the adder, though a worm, to caft
Each pois'nous paffion from thy breaft in hafte,
E'er to approach God's altar thou doft dare;
Left thofe fierce paffions fhou'd deftroy thee, there :

43 For as fome fay, who have the aétion feen,
The adder lays her poifon on the green,
Before fhe quenches at the ftream her thirft;
Left fhe fhou'd by th' envenom'd potion burft.

44 So caft all anger from thy bofom quite,
All envy, rage, malevolence, and fpite,
Or elfe, like wild and furious beafts, they will
Without diftinétion their own Keepers kill.

45 If thefe three virtues, " faith, repentance, love,"
Adorn thy foul, thou fhalt moft welcome prove;
Thou then may'ft go, and be thy mafter's gueft;
For Chrift himfelf invites thee to his feaft.

46 Think, when thou fee'ft the Prieft divide the bread,
And view'ft the wine into the chalice fhed,
Think, how the fpear transfix'd thy Saviour's fide,
And how his heart, pour'd out it's crimfon tide!

47 When

47 When bread and wine, juft hallow'd at the board,
   Thou doft receive, receive in thought the Lord,
   Receive him in thy heart with mind fincere,
   And fully feaft thy foul upon him, there.

48 We mafticate him not, (when Chrift we eat)
   Nor turn him down our throats, like common meat;
   But 'tis by faith, and by a thankful heart
   Alone, that we in Chrift can have a part.

49 Lift up thy mind, and foar above the skies,
   And look at Chrift with fupplicating eyes,
   Reflect what then he did and felt for thee,
   Whilft for thy fins he hung upon the tree.

50 Believe that Chrift, when nail'd unto the tree,
   For thee was facrifice'd, and die'd for thee!
   Believe that he, to buy thy foul, did bleed:
   'Tis then! 'tis thus, thou eateft Chrift indeed!

51 But fhou'dft thou ask, what good can thence arife,
   Or in the facrament, what profit lies,
   Shou'dft thou receive it with a Chriftian mind,
   True faith, and charity for all mankind?

52 Why! Chrift to thee, there, abfolution gives,
   And freely all thy fumlefs fins forgives,
   An abfolution, by thy God made good—
   An abfolution, feal'd with Chrift's beft blood!

53 Pardon and life, are thence, to thee fupply'd,
   With comfort, health, and ev'ry gift befide,
   He gives his fpirit, with each grace divine,
   And he himfelf, with all his gifts, is thine.

54 He makes thee all his mighty bleffings fhare,
   Such bleffings, as no language can declare!
   He will, in fpirit, in thy heart remain,
   And, if thou'rt grateful, there will ever reign.

55 He feeds thy fainty foul with fat'ning food,
   With his own body, and his precious blood,
   And gives thee his bleft Spirit from on high,
   As a fure pledge of immortality!

56 How art thou bound fuch goodnefs to applaud,
 And fing the praifes of thy Saviour-God,
 Who made thee of his glorious fupper eat,
 An entertainment with each good replete ?

57 O, what returns canft thou to Him e'er make,
 For all He did or fuffer'd for thy fake——
 To Him—who fed thy foul with heavenly food ——
 With His own body, and moft precious blood ?

58 Then be not fuch a brute, the church to leave,
 Where thou fo lately didft fuch food receive,
 E'er thou thy thanks haft to thy Saviour paid
 With grateful mind, for his celeftial aid.

59 Chrift, even barley bread wou'd never eat,
 Much lefs more delicate and fav'ry meat,
 Before He thank'd his Sire—nor wou'd forget,
 Where-e'er he was, to pay that bounden debt.

60 How can'ft thou then prefume the Lord to eat,
 And feed on Chrift, the very firft of meat !
 Yet never for the boon thy thanks impart,
 Thy bounden thanks——e'en from thy very heart ?

61 Nor yet invite heav'n, earth, and man to join
 The Seraphim, and all the hofts divine,
 To celebrate with thee the Lord above
 For his immenfe benevolence and love ?

A Prayer to be faid before receiving of the Sacrament.

1 O Lord ! who gracioufly waft mov'd
 To give us Chrift, thy beft-belov'd,
 To be for our tranfgreffions flain,
 And fouls defponding to fuftain !

2 O give me grace with pious care,
 Like a good Chriftian to prepare,
 That I, by faith, may eat Chrift's flefh,
 And on the Lord my foul refrefh !

3 O make my heart and confcience clear,
And make my veffel ftill appear
Quite pure, and purge'd from ev'ry fin,
That Chrift may freely enter in!

4 Strengthen my faith, my hopes improve,
Inflame my breaft with perfect love,
My body cleanfe, my fpirit guide,
That Chrift may in my heart refide!

5 Lift thou my thoughts up to the fkies,
Where my Redeemer Jefus lies,
My foul let him, thro' faith, fuftain,
That I may grace from Him obtain.

6 Perfuade me that there is from heaven
A pardon to all finners given,
And that I, for Chrift's fufferings fake,
Shall of his wond'rous works partake.

7 Make me believe, that he will reign,
And in my bofom ftill remain,
And that His fpirit from my heart
Will never, 'till my death, depart.

8 O let me not, like any brute,
The temple of my God pollute,
But ever keep the facred fcene,
Where he vouchfafes to fojourn, clean.

9 O make me chant, both day and night,
His praifes forth with all my might,
And may He ev'ry hour be bleft,
For the good cheer found at his feaft!

STANZA'S concerning fome PERSONS and
THINGS, that are mentioned in the Holy
Scriptures.

1 FROM Adam's lapfe, this ufeful leffon learn,
"As the leaft fin, there's nothing cofts fo much"
Thence, too, the danger thou may'ft well difcern,
" All things forbidden by the Lord, to touch."

 2 Old

2 Old Eve, by her offence and fatal crime,
   Has thrown a powerful warning in thy way ;
   That thou fhou'd'ft never dare at any time,
   Satan, before the' Almighty, to obey.

3 If Adam met with fo fevere a doom,
   Who only did a fingle apple eat ;
   Think thou, what they muft fuffer, who prefume
   To live entirely on fo. bidden meat !

4 How dange'rous is the fruit, whofe acid juice
   Corrodes the teeth of all the human race ?
   Be thou not one of thofe, my fon, who chufe
   To feed on fruits like them, in any cafe.

5 Had not our bleffed Saviour been fo kind,
   To fuffer death for us upon the crofs;
   The world had, for that fault, been all confin'd
   In Hell, and none cou'd have repair'd the lofs.

6 The dragon, though fo dange'rous, never dread,
   But in the woman's promis'd feed confide,
   Who has already bruis'd his baneful head,
   Pluck'd out his fting, and low'r'd his crefted pride.

7 If the old ferpent has transfix'd thy foul
   With fin's keen fting, thou'rt gone beyond refource,
   Or nothing in the world can make thee whole,
   'Till to the brazen One thou haft recourfe.

8 Old Adam for a fingle apple loft
   The blifsful fcenes of ancient paradife,
   Take heed, left thou the New One, to thy coft,
   Should'ft for fuch trifles lofe, if thou art wife.

9 Whoe'er, like Cain, with a felonious heart,
   Shall evil do : (for fo the fcriptures teach)
   Evil fhall never from his houfe depart,
   Until God's vengeance fhall the culprit reach.

10 Left thou, like Cain, that murderer of yore !
   Shou'dft fhed a guiltlefs perfon's blood, take heed :
   Whoever fheds his fellow creature's gore,
   Shall furely by his fellow creatures bleed.

11 Commit

11 Commit no murder in the gloom of night;
　　Juſt Abel's murder God himſelf reveal'd :
　　He will in public all thy crimes requite;
　　Though by the veil of ſolitude conceal'd.

12 Thy life with Abel's innocence adorn,
　　Fear God, and often to his courts repair,
　　And offer on thy knees, both night and morn,
　　To Him the conſtant ſacrifice of pray'r.

13 And when thy off'ring's to the altar brought,
　　Be it the beſt and choiceſt in it's kind :
　　The Godhead hates, or is not pleas'd with ought
　　That's wan and weak, or either halt or blind.

14 If thou an offering doſt freely make,
　　God will as readily the ſame receive :
　　But he will never that oblation take,
　　Which thou doſt not with real pleaſure give.

15 Though all the world were grown reluctant quite
　　To ſerve the Omnipotent, and ceas'd to pray :
　　Do thou, like *Enos*, all the World excite
　　To worſhip God without the leaſt delay.

16 Exhort them all to ſerve the Lord their God ;
　　'Tis each true Chriſtian's duty, to do ſo :
　　Proclaim his might, his praiſes ſpread abroad,
　　And thou to his eternal joys ſhalt go.

17 Walk thou, like Enoch, with the Lord moſt high,
　　His footſteps trace, and imitate his ways :
　　Remember too that his all-ſeeing eye
　　Thy ev'ry act, nay ev'ry thought, ſurveys.

18 To Enoch, what a recompence was given
　　For his devotion, piouſly obſerve !
　　E'er death he ſaw, he went direct to heaven :
　　Who wou'd not then ſo good a maſter ſerve ?

19 From Enoch's ſtory theſe three truths are plain——
　　Firſt, that thy precious ſoul ſhall never die——
　　Next, that thy body ſhall be rais'd again——
　　Laſt, that rewards await the juſt on high.

　　　　　　　20 Commit

20 Commit no fin, for though in private done,
    God will foon bring the fecret crime to light :
    But always live, as if each act was known
    To Him, and thou wert always in his fight.

21 Though thou wert with a giant's ftrength endue'd,
    God, when he pleafes, can thy pride fubdue,
    And make thee foon each creeping infect's food,
    If thou wilt ftill the paths of vice purfue.

22 If from the flood the giants cou'd not run,
    Nor from the wate'ry vengeance erft retire :
    How can the prefent pigmy race e'er fhun
    The inundation of o'erwhelming fire ?

23 However vile the world be all around,
    However numerous the finful crew,
    In thy Creator's fight be perfect found,
    And Noah's pattern all thy life purfue.

24 The cuftom of the vulgar crowd efchew,
    Who rufh to fin, as faft as e'er they can :
    Better *his* fteps, though fingle, to purfue,
    Who fears his God, and has refpect to man.

25 How odious all Adult'ry is, obferve !
    How hateful fin is in the fight of God !
    Since nothing lefs, to punifh it, wou'd ferve
    Than that wide deluge, which the world o'erflow'd.

26 If thou, like holy Noah, canft be pure,
    And canft perfection, like that patriarch's boaft :
    Like Noah, thou falvation fhalt fecure,
    While all the reft, beyond redrefs, are loft.

27 Better it is that patriarch's fteps to trace,
    With faith, perfection, and each virtue crown'd,
    Than 'tis the world's vile maxims to embrace,
    And with the vicious multitude be drown'd.

28 Whilft 'tis the time of grace, conftruct thine ark,
    E'er yet the deluge covers all the ftrand :
    It is by much too late to build a bark,
    When th' inundation overwhelms the land.

29 Better

29 Better by far it is, upon the whole,
    Safely with Noah in the ark to keep,
    Than in a fea of vices to plunge one's foul,
    Loft with the crowd in the unfathom'd deep.

30 Whene'er thou doft the rainbow's curve furvey,
    God's facred covenant recall to mind:
    His mighty deeds it's glorious beams difplay,
    For-ever merciful, for-ever kind!

31 Reflect with awe upon it's changeful hue!
    Azure and red, are it's prevailing dies:
    The watry deluge, was the azure-blue,
    In fie'ry-red, the future judgement lies.

32 When both the horns of this celeftial bow
    Are bent to earth, without a fhaft or ftring,
    It is defign'd that happy peace to fhow,   [King.
    Which reigns, thro' Chrift, 'twixt man and heav'n's

33 Beware of Satan, and his latent nets,
    When void of care, and moft at eafe, at home:
    Thy fteps, like Noah's, hourly he befets,
    And flily waits the moment to o'ercome.

34 Tho' Noah cou'd not, to adult'ry's net,
    By Satan in his youthful days be brought;
    Yet in a fatal hour fuccefs he met,
    And in his toils the hoary drunkard caught.

35 Shou'dft thou in fome Gomorrah chance to ftay,
    Where drunkennefs and fornication reign;
    Like Lot, from their vile converfe hafte away,
    Left their pollutions fhou'd thy morals ftain.

36 Shou'dft thou the town, where thou doft fojourn, fee,
    Sin againft God at an enormous rate:
    Like Lot from Sodom and it's confines flee,
    Before the ftorm defcends upon thy pate.

37 Better it is upon a defert plain
    To be with Lot, or in a cavern'd rock,
    Than in a finful Sodom to remain,
    Expofe'd, like it, to fuch a dreadful fhock.

38 Who

38 Who, whilst in Sodom, kept himself so well,
    So free from ev'ry fault, as holy Lot?
    Yet, in a cave, thro' drunkenness he fell,
    And there his former principles forgot.

39 Tho' thou hast 'scape'd from vice's dang'rous snare,
    And ne'er didst in Gomorrah's stews appear,
    Of sin's assaults in thy own house beware,
    When none besides thy bosom-friends are near.

40 If thou hast once the luck, the fire to shun,
    And art unhurt from flaming Sodom come:
    Take heed, lest thou a second time shou'dst run
    To equal danger for thy sins at home.

41 If thou from Sodom hast the luck to fly,
    Return not there by any means again:
    Lot's wife, because she backward glance'd her eye,
    Was turn'd to salt upon the' adjacent plain.

42 Open thine eyes, look round, and trembling own,
    That sin's severely punish'd by the Lord:
    Since he upon Gomorrah's lustful town
    A dreadful storm of fire and brimstone show'r'd.

43 Ah me!—how loud is vice's yelling noise,
    Dinning the Godheads ears both night and day!
    No respite knows her never-ceasing voice,
    'Till God with vengeance shall her crimes repay!

44 How foul, how fatal, were the monstrous crimes,
    Which brought perdition upon Sodom's race!
    The district stinks e'en to the present times,
    And smoke and sulph'rous steams still mark the place!

45 Never an angred father's curse deserve;
    Ham and his seed cou'd ne'er wipe out the stain;
    It's lasting marks the Negroes still preserve,
    And in their skins it ever will remain.

46 Like Shem, the foibles of thy Sire conceal,
    With filial piety his errors hide;
    Nor when his snowy locks his years reveal,
    Like Canaan the uncover'd sot deride.

47 With

47 With laudable refpect thy mother grace,
 And pay her all th' obedience that's her due;
 On thy right hand the honour'd matron place,
 As royal Solomon was wont to do.

48 Never in any work employ thy hand,
 To whate'er place thou travelleft abroad;
 Before, like Abraham, in the foreign land
 Thou rear'ft an altar, to adore thy God,

49 Believe each Word the Lord thy God has fpoke,
 For it is perfect, ftrictly true, and pure :
 The heav'ns and earth fhall pafs away, like fmoke;
 But that forever fhall, each jot, endure.

50 Where-e'er the Lord thy God commands thee, go,
 His dictates with alacrity obey,
 Whate'er thou doft, like Abraham, quickly do,
 And his beheft perform without delay.

51 Offer thy Son, fhou'd God that task require,
 And circumcifion with refpect receive,
 Abjure the idols of thy pagan fire,
 And at God s nod thy native country leave.

52 From Ifaac meeknefs and fubmiffion gain,
 From him, whatever happens, learn to bear:
 So fhalt thou favour from mankind obtain,
 And always live in thy Creator's fear.

53 Beware, left thou defile thy fpoufe's bed,
 Be pleas'd with her, that is already thine;
 As Ifaac erft was pleas'd with her, he wed;
 For that is pleafing to the Pow'r divine.

54 If thou with Jacob's gentle voice art bleft,
 Of Efau's rough and bloody hands beware:
 The Deity can ne'er enough deteft
 Foul deeds, tho' veil'd beneath expreffions fair.

55 When thou refolveft firft a maid to woo,
 To Jacob s conduct give efpecial heed :
 Like him, thy parents counfel ftill purfue;
 So fhall profperity attend thy feed.

56 Never

56 Never unto thy belly be a flave,
Efau was with the greateft fhame oppref's'd,
Who his own birthright unto Jacob gave
For one poor mefs of pottage ready drefs'd.

57 Fie on all wafte! on all exceffes fie!
Sell not heav'n's joys for either drink or meat:
Efau from Canaan was oblig'd to fly,
Who fold his birthright for a forry treat.

58 If with thy miftrefs thou art ask'd to lie,
However private, yet refufe the joy:
Like Jofeph from her hot embraces fly,
Nor for a kifs thy precious foul deftroy.

59 Go thou to prifon, ev'ry woe endure,
And lie in chains extended on the floor,
E'er thou with action luftful and impure,
Giveft Chrift's member to a filthy whore.

60 Love not a proftitute, nor e'er defile
The temple, where the Lord of hofts remains:
Jofeph wou'd ne'er have done a thing fo vile,
Though he was all his life to rot in chains.

61 Like Efau's, 'tis a bargain moft unwife,
A bargain, that will make thee wail and weep,
To fell thy bright reverfion in the skies,
A night perhaps with fome lewd punk to fleep!

62 Becaufe he wou'd not with his miftrefs lie,
Nor condefcend her wanton heat to cool,
Jofeph was rais'd by providence on high,
And Egypt rule'd, who did his paffions rule.

63 Better it is to be with Jofeph chafte,
Altho', in jail, you for your virtue be,
Than on a throne, like Herod, to be plac'd,
With an Herodias on your guilty knee.

64 Shou'dft thou thy father's bed with inceft ftain,
Though firft-begotten, thou his curfe fhou'dft get,
And Judah thy inheritance obtain;
Whilft thou haft nothing, but a long regret.

65 To fell thy brother, Simeon! is not wife ;
    Thou knoweft not what chance may yet prevail :
    Jofeph, when fold, to fuch a height fhall rife,
    That he fhall order Simeon to a jail.

66 Like Mofes, fweetnefs of behaviour fhew,
    Like him, be meek, and harmlefs as a child,
    Faithful, fubmiffive, affable, and true,
    Brave, without rafhnefs, without foftnefs, mild.

67 See !—what an army God of old employ'd,
    A mighty Monarch's ftubborn heart to bend !
    By lice and locufts, flies and frogs annoy'd,
    Pharaoh wou'd fain his wicked ways amend !

68 If thou a flave in Egypt wou'dft not be,
    But go, where milk and honey blefs the fhore,
    Thou muft pafs through the Erythre'an fea;
    Tho' ftrong it's furge, and terrible it's roar!

69 A man with too-much manna may be cloy'd;
    But who can't touch it, muft be nice indeed :
    Yet thou muft be of tafte and reafon void,
    If thou, before it, wou'dft on garlick feed.

70 E'er God will leave his faithful follo'wers need,
    He'll rain a fhow'r of manna from on high,
    Or elfe on quails his favourites fhall feed,
    At his command defcending from the sky.

71 Never refift the paftor of thy foul,
    Nor on the herald of the' Almighty jeft,
    Left the' earth fhou'd open and ingulph thee whole,
    If thou, like Korah, fhou'dft infult thy Prieft.

72 To thy vocation or profeffion cleave,
    And let the Clergy their own bus'nefs mind ;
    God to their care alone his ark will leave,
    Who to that facred office were defign'd.

73 From hence it may to all be clearly known,
    How ftrictly we fhou'd keep the fabbath day !
    Since God enjoin'd the Jewifh hoft to ftone
    The man, who broke it firft, without delay.

74 The

74 The fabbath in devotion fpend, and come
    Unto the temple, in thy beft array,
    Nor, whilft thou liveft here on earth, prefume
    To do the Devil's work on that bleft day.

75 The pow'r of God we hence may all behold,
    Who, at a man's entreaty, ftopp'd the fun: .
    For one whole day it's motion he control'd,
    And ftay'd it's courfe, until his people won.

76 How fhameful is it then, remember all,
    That that vaft orb fhou'd God's command obey ?
    Whilft we, vile worms! defpife his gracious call,
    And will not, at his mighty bidding, ftay.

77 Shou'dft thou e'er go, where idols are ador'd,
    Boldly, like Jofhua, this anfwer give,
    " I, and my family, will ferve the Lord,
    ' And will not own another, whilft I live."

78 The fhining fword, O Zimri, Zimri! fear,
    Hung by the God of vengeance o'er thy head!
    Behold, in Phineas' hand, the pointed fpear,
    Lifted, to ftrike thee, and thy ftrumpet, dead!

79 O Balaam! Balaam! ope thine eyes, and fee
    The angel juft defcended from above!
    Return, return, nor touch the venal fee,
    But hear the afs, thy avarice reprove.

80 A harlot love no better than the fiend,
    Thy bofom-fecrets ne'er to her impart—
    The ftiffeft neck fhe, like a twig, will bend,
    Though ftrong as Samfon, fhe will break thy heart.

81 Never encourage thofe that are to blame,
    But from their vices ftudioufly refrain ;
    Gibeah, with all her wealth, was fet on flame,
    Becaufe fhe did not her rude fons reftrain.

82 With heed, O Benjamin! my words attend:
    Why wilt thou ftrive to pull the wrath divine,
    (Becaufe thou wilt thy daring youths defend
    In all their vices) upon thee and thine ?

83 From

83 From Eli's fate, take warning, and beware !
   Thy children teach, and carefully correct :
   Whene'er the fire is ufe'd the rod to fpare,
   God with the fword will punifh the neglect.

84 Learn thou from Samuel, whilft yet a youth
   With ftrict fidelity to ferve thy God,
   And to the laft, unfhaken hold the truth,
   Unfhock'd by injuries, unftain'd by fraud.

85 From that juft judge thefe ufeful leffons draw,
   " All in their properties alike protect,————
   " Give fentence ftill, according unto law,
   " And as the rules of juftice fhall direct."

86 What gains cou'd Joel from injuftice boaft,
   From bribe'ry and corruption, void of fhame ?
   He loft his credit, and his office loft,
   But gain'd reproach, and a detefted name.'

87 Touch not the ark, like Uzzah—but beware——
   Leave to the prieft, what to the prieft is due——
   Be thy own calling and concerns thy care :
   For thou haft nothing with the ark to do.

88 When thou with pain and ficknefs art opprefs'd,
   Like Job thy patience filently difplay——
   Never blafpheme, however fore diftrefs'd :
   'Tis God that gives, and God that takes away!

89 Though God fhou'd take thy fubftance all away,
   Or by fome ficknefs feem to call thee hence—
   " Though God fhou'd kill me, yet (refignedly fay)
   " I ftill in him will place my confidence."

90 Like royal David from thy bed arife,
   And humbly on thy knees thy God adore—
   At midnight let thy pray'rs afcend the fkies,
   Whilft others on their downy pillows fnore.

91 It is a meet and mighty pleafant thing,
   Unto the Lord at dead of night to pray,
   And for his various gifts to thank heav'n's king,
   Soon as the dawn proclaims the new-born day.

92 Like

92 Like David, that renown'd feer! repent
Of all the crimes and evil thou haft done——
Like him, with ceafelefs tears thy fins lament,
'Till thou God's favour and his love haft won.

93 Weep, 'till thy couch with briny floods is drown'd——
'Till with thy bread thou haft thy tears devour'd——
Wear fackcloth——roll thyfelf along the ground——
'Till thou haft pardon for thy fins implor'd.

94 Although thy locks be of a lovely dye,
Yet from all pride, on that account forbear;
Left thou, like Abfalom, fhou'dft hang on high,
Caught, and entangled by thy flowing hair.

95 If David in the dark, and dead of night,
Shall with Uriah's charming confort fport;
Another, in the fun's meridian height,
Shall to his wives, without difguife, refort.

96 How fhort did that precarious pleafure laft,
For which his life inceftuous Ammon loft?
Ah me! how bitter was it, when 'twas paft?
How dear at length the tranfient rapture coft!

97 Thy precious foul in danger never leave,
Thy carnal lufts and pleafures to fulfil:
For thou, one day, moft bitterly fhalt grieve,
That thou, on Tamar, haft obtain'd thy will!

98 Thy houfe and thy concerns in order fet,
Like Hezekiah, with convenient care:
Thyfelf in readinefs this moment get,
And ftill for death, before death comes, prepare.

99 Thy neighbour's vineyard feek not to obtain:
Oppreffion daily pulls God's vengeance down:
For if thou thus fhou'dft Naboth's portion gain,
Thou for that fin fhalt forfeit Ifrael's crown.

100 O Ahab! Ahab! with ftrict juftice deal,
Nor luft thy neighbour's fortune to enjoy;
If thou, thro' perjury, his land fhalt fteal,
God will thy offspring to a man deftroy,

101 How

101 How great foe'er thy toil and trouble be,
    Thrice ev'ry day, like pious Daniel, fall
    Before thy Maker, on thy bended knee :
    For of all bufinefs that's the beft of all !

102 Shut to thy clofet door—kneel on the floor—
    Lift up thine eyes—unlock thy lips to pray——
    With humble attitude thy God adore
    And humble heart, at leaft three times a day.

103 Though thou fhou'dft to the lion's den be caft,
    Omit not, even there, thy wonted pray'r :
    The wildeft beafts will fhun their wifh'd repaft,
    And ev'ry true believer learn to fpare.

104 Thy knee before an image never bow,
    Tho' thou wert, therefore, force'd to quit the world,
    And tho', like Shadrach, thou wert doom'd to go
    Headlong, into a fi'ry furnace hurl'd.

105 Nought muft be worfhipp'd but our God alone :
    An idol is a triffle, nothing more ;
    Whether of gold, of filver, or of ftone,
    'Tis but a helplefs fcare-crow, void of pow'r.

106 When to thy lip thou lifteft up the bowl,
    Blafpheming God, but in the banquet bleft——
    Beware—left angry Death fhou'd feize thy foul,
    Like king Belfhazzar's at his impious feaft !

107 When, round the board, the goblet brifkly flies,
    Behold the hand, upon the ftucco'd wall,
    Writing thy dreadful doom before thy eyes,
    And thy intempe'rance's certain fall !

108 Thy charity, like Tobit, largely deal——
    To all that need, difpenfe around thy ftore,
    And never with contentment eat a meal,
    'Till thou fome part haft given to the poor.

109 Support the feeble—and interr the dead—
    The naked clothe—the friendlefs widow guide—
    The orphan's caufe with real ardor plead——
    Nor treat the ftranger with tyrannic pride.

R.   110 When-

110 Whene'er thou purpofeſt to take a bride,
 Beg thou of God his neceſſary aid:
 A Raphael then thy wandring ſteps ſhall guide,
 And lead thee to the moſt accompliſh'd maid.

111 Before thou goeſt with thy ſpouſe to reſt,
 Beſeech the Lord thy genial bed to bleſs,
 And hand in hand prefer your joint requeſt,
 That He may crown your nuptials with ſucceſs.

112 Thy parents, as Tobias did, revere,
 And, whilſt they live, ne'er their commands oppoſe;
 When dead, their bodies decently interr,
 For that's a duty ev'ry Chriſtian owes!

113 As ſtrictly juſt, throughout thy life, be found,
 As one who ne'er the goſpel's luſtre ſaw,
 And let thy death with as much faith be crown'd,
 As if thou nought hadſt heard e'er of the law!

114 Shou'dſt thou, O Chriſtian! aſk, who ſung theſe ſtrains,
 And ſtrove theſe truths in metre to comprize?
 It was a Chriſtian prieſt, who took the pains,
 In hopes thereby to help thee to the ſkies.

The AUTHOR's Letter to a Clergyman, who had
 deſired him to put the CATECHISM of the
 Church of England into Verſe.

1 I Know, my brother, 'twas thy fervent zeal
 For God, and for the Chriſtian commonweal,
 That made thee aſk me at the preſent time,
 To turn our church's doctrines into rhyme.

2 The Welſh, 'tis true, as thou may'ſt well diſcern,
 Are much more apt ſome idle ſong to learn,
 Than truths—that, far more worthy of their care,
 And of more value and importance, are.

3 Thou therefore didſt deſire me, as I gueſs,
 That I ſhou'd all thoſe points in verſe expreſs;
 That ſo the younglings of our flocks by rote
 Might learn to ſing with eaſe, what thus was wrote.

4 As foon as thou hadſt thy defign expreſt,
Immediately I granted thy requeſt,
And ſtrove thoſe ſacred precepts to reſtrain
In artleſs Stanza's, and in language plain.

5 I labour'd not at any thing exact,
But a ſhort meaſure, pleaſing, and compact,
Which the worſt memory might with eaſe retain,
That heard it only twice, or once again.

6 Receive with candor then this little taſk,
Which thou didſt lately with ſuch fervor aſk ;
And, though the work be not at all complete,
Yet it wou'd fain thy approbation meet.

7 If God ſome glory ſhall from hence obtain,
And our own flocks ſome ſmall improvement gain,
We both ſhall have, I fancy, what we want :
Succeſs to it may the Almighty grant !

8 May all thy wiſhes be by Him ſupply'd——
May He be thy inſeperable guide——
But, as my haſte is great, don't think me rude,
If I beg leave at preſent to conclude, &c. &c.

The CATECHISM.

Q. MY lively, lovely, little child ! declare,
What is thy Chriſtian name? and then in brief,
With ſerious heart, and an aſſured air,
Repeat aloud thy faith and thy belief.

A. The Chriſtian name I bear, is Conſtantine*;
And tho' in Adam I was loſt of old,
Yet now, at laſt, I'm ſave'd, thro' grace divine,
By Chriſt, the true Meſſiah, long foretold.

* A pupil, as 'tis ſuppoſed, of our Author, for whoſe inſtruction
this Catechiſm, perhaps, was at firſt verſify'd——and therefore thro'
overſight, his name was ſtill continu'd, as it anſwer'd to the rhyme in
the ſecond line, on which account I have likewiſe retain'd it.

R 2

Q. Who

Q. Who gave thee, fay, the name by which thou'rt call'd,
Tho' thou wert erſt with all the human race,
By Adam's ſhameful lapſe, to ſin enthrall'd,
The child of wrath, and in a wretched caſe?

A. My ſponſors at the font, with faith ſincere,
(As I have ſince been made to underſtand)
Gave me the name, which I am proud to bear,
According to our Saviour's own command.

Q. But what advantage thence to thee has flow'd,
When thou wert at the ſacred font baptiz'd
With water, by the miniſter of God:
Since ſo much woe is in thy life compriz'd?

A. A member I of Chriſt, am made thereby,
A child of the Almighty God above,
An heir apparent of the realms on high,
And happy in my bleſſed Saviour's love.

Q. What was the vow thy ſponſors then expreſt?
What was the ſolemn promiſe that they gave,
By which with equal tenure to the beſt,
Thou waſt entitled all thoſe rights to have?

A. Three ſeve'ral things they promis'd in my name,
Which I ſhall never, whilſt I breathe, forget;
But, thro' God's grace, will ſtrive to do the ſame,
'Till I have paid, far as I can, the debt.

Q. What were the things they promis'd to fulfil
For thee—'till thou to proper age ſhou'dſt grow,
When of thyſelf thou hadſt no pow'r, nor will?
Tell me aloud, if thou the ſame doſt know.

A. Firſt, I only obſerve, that I renounce entire
The wily fiend, and his infernal deeds,
This wicked world, with ev'ry vain deſire,
And ſinful luſt, that from the fleſh proceeds.

Take notice, next, I did by them engage
The Chriſtian Faith for ever to maintain,
I mean thoſe doctrines of each ſacred page,
Which all may from their creed, in ſhort, obtain.

Thirdly,

Thirdly, that I, with reverential awe,
Shall God's commands and will reveal'd obey,
And lead, according to his given law,
A godly life, unto my dying day.

2. To this belief art thou engage'd so fast?
And is thy obligation, say, so great,
That thou the promise, which for thee they past,
Must now make good, and their whole vow complete?

A. All this I must believe, and, what is more,
I'm bound the same entirely to fulfil,
As far as is consistent with my pow'r;
And, if I'm able, by God's grace, I will:

And hearty thanks I to my Maker owe,
That he vouchsafe'd such favour to afford,
As his salvation unto me to show,
Thro' Jesus Christ, my ever-blessed Lord:

And earnestly I pray that he wou'd deign,
To me, the grace of constancy to give,
That I may, in this hopeful state, remain,
'Till I, with him, in endless bliss shall live.

2. Rehearse, with voice distinct and solemn air,
Those articles the Christian Faith requires,
·That I may thence collect, how just they are,
And on what grounds thou foundest thy desires.

The CREED.

A. In God, the Father, whose Almighty Pow'r
Did heav'n, earth, sea, into existence call,
I do believe, and ever will adore
Him, as the Governor supreme o'er all.

In Jesus Christ, his only Son, our Lord,
Who was conceived by the Holy Ghost,
And born of Mary, prove'd upon record
A spotless virgin, I still farther trust.

The

The fame who fuffered a moft fhameful death,
(Whilft Pontius Pilate Judah's fceptre fway'd)
And, when upon the crofs deprive'd of breath,
Like a mere mortal, in the grave was laid.

Then for our fakes he into Hades went,
That feat of pain and never-ending woes!
But the third day, he after that defcent,
From the dark chambers of the dead arofe:

But not till he had over Death obtain'd
A victory, in ev'ry fenfe complete,
And from the fiend, that foul deceiver, gain'd
Ample amends for the firft man's defeat:

To the third heavens then afcended he,
Where he does now on God's right hand refide,
And where he fhall, for endlefs ages, be
To all the church a never-erring guide:

From thence, with Glory and great Pow'r, he'll come
As Judge, both o'er the living and the dead,
That terribly-important day of doom,
When they'll be call'd to his tribunal dread.

Another point, I do believe, is this,
(For fo I find it in another creed)
That the' Holy Ghoft, who gives us life and blifs,
Does from the Father, and the Son, proceed.

I, farthermore, beyond all doubt am fure,
That there's in ev'ry age and realm referv'd
A church, that keeps the Chriftian doctrines pure;
And, therefore, it fhall be, thro' Chrift, preferv'd.

And I believe that all the Saints below
Shall of the gifts (with thofe above) partake,
Which from our bleffed Saviour's merits flow,
Who fuffer'd death and forrow for our fake.

The refurrection likewife of the juft
I do believe, with confidence fincere,
When the laft trump fhall raife them from the duft,
And they, above the clouds, fhall all appear.

I am

I am convince'd with faith, which nought can move,
That all, who worthily their God adore,
Shall endlefs happinefs enjoy above,
When this terreftrial fcene fhall be no more.   *Amen.*

2. What doft thou chiefly learn by this belief,
The fum of which thou haft repeated now?
Endeavour it's contents to fhow in brief,
With all the benefits which, from it, flow.

A. Firft, I believe in God, as I am taught,
The Sire fupreme, on whofe ftupendous plan
This world was wholly to exiftence brought,
And this my frame, with that of ev'ry man.

Next, I believe in God, the filial Pow'r,
Our gracious Lord, to mercy ftill inclin'd,
Who by his blood, in a moft happy hour,
Redemption brought to me, and all mankind.

Thirdly, in God the Holy Ghoft I truft,
Who from all kind of fin does make me clean,
And fanctifies, along with me, the juft,
All the elected fons of God, I mean.

2. Thou didft a promife by thy fponfors make,
That thou wou'dft God's commandments keep with
Come, tell me then, for thy Redeemer's fake, [care;
How many, if thou knoweft them, they are?

A. God gave us Ten—it was the fum exprefs,
That we might keep them with the ftricteft care,
Nor muft we either of them all tranfgrefs;
Left we fhou'd die, if fuch a crime we dare.

2. Which be they?—tell me, for thy Saviour's fake,
If thou haft ever learn'd them out by heart,
Thefe holy ftatutes for thy pattern take,
And never from the faultlefs rules depart.

A. They are the fame, which the Almighty fpoke
On Sinai's hill, and publifh'd as his law,
Involv'd in circumambient fire and fmoke,
Which all the trembling congregation faw.

They

They are the fame, which he to Mofes gave,
On two fair tables of unchifel'd ftone,
Where God's own finger did thofe laws engrave,
. That they to all the people might be fhown:

And even now you may, if fo inclin'd,
The fame from the infpire'd fcriptures learn:
In Exodus with eafe you may them find,
If you'll but to the twentieth chapter turn.

_Q._ Which is the firft of thofe commandments, fay?
And then the next?—and then the next agen?
Each, in it's proper place, before me lay,
Until thou haft repeated all the ten.

The Ten COMMANDMENTS.

_A._ I. I am the Lord thy God, fupreme in pow'r,
For tender mercy and compaffion known:
Then, on thy life, no other God adore;
For there is really none, but me alone.

II. Thou no carve'd image for thy God fhalt take,
Like any being, in the heav'n on high,
Or earth beneath, or in the feas vaft lake,
Or like a bird, that thro' the air does fly.

Before fuch vanities ne'er bend thy knee,
Nor any fuch vile deities adore,
Either of earth, of wood, or ftone, they be,
By human labour form'd, and void of pow'r.

For I, the' Almighty, am a jealous God,
And vengeance from the children oft require,
Who tread the paths their wicked fathers, trod:
Thus the fon fuffers for his finful fire!

I frequent punifhment inflict on thofe
(Though to the third or fourth degree remov'd)
Who like their fires profefs themfelves my foes,
And fenfelefs idols have, before me, lov'd:

But

But unto them my mercies I extend,
Who keep my ftatutes wholly untranfgrefs'd,
Their long-continue'd line fhall never end,
But in a thoufand ages hence be blefs'd.

III. Ne'er mention thou Jehovah's glorious name,
Without refpect and reverential awe :
For thou fhalt not be free from guilt and blame,
 ⋅ If thou prefumeft to tranfgrefs this law.

IV. Remember thou in virtuous acts to fpend,
And holy exercife, the fabbath-day,
And like a Chriftian, to thy latter end,
Worfhip thy God thereon, and to him pray.

Six days the Lord vouchfafe'd to give to thee,
Whereon thy temp'ral bufinefs fhou'd be done :
But, on the feventh, thou art no ways free
To mind ought elfe, befides God's work alone :

Upon that day thou muft from labour reft,
On pain of death, thou and thy family,
Both men and maids, with ev'ry lab'ring beaft,
And ev'ry fojourner, that ftays with thee :

Within fix days God form'd this wond'rous ball,
With ev'ry thing that in the fame remains,
The fky, the earth, the ocean vaft, and all
The countlefs tribes, that fwim it's liquid plains.

To work, upon the feventh-day, he ceas'd,
Though unfatigue'd he from creation came;
Wherefore to blefs that day he then was pleas'd,
And hallow'd to eternity the fame.

V. Unto thy parents all due honour give,
To their commands a proper defe'rence fhow,
That thou may'ft long in that bleft ftation live,
Which God fhall on each dureous fon beftow.

VI. Take heed, thou doft not any perfon flay,
Nor any blood, without good reafon, fhed;
The voice of blood is heard a mighty way :
God will pour vengeance on each murd'rer's head.

VII. Avoid

VII. Avoid adultery, that curſed thing!
 And always of thy boſom-wife make much,
 The waters quaff that guſh from thy own ſpring;
 But ne'er thy neighbour's cover'd ciſtern touch.

VIII. Aim not the ſmalleſt trifle to poſſeſs
 By ſtealth, which to another appertains:
 Uſe no deceit, nor any one oppreſs,
 Tho' thou wert force'd to bear the fierceſt pains.

IX. Of perjury, and wilful lies, beware,
 Nor by thy evidence thy neighbour wrong:
 But ſtill the truth of ev'ry one declare,
 And ne'er with defamation ſtain thy tongue.

X. Neither thy neighbour's houſe, nor yet his wife,
 Or man or maid, horſe, aſs, or working beaſt,
 Or any thing of his, deſire thro' life,
 But that of which thou juſtly art poſſeſt.

Thy mercy, Lord! unto thy ſervants ſhow,
Inſpire each breaſt with a religious awe,
Our ſtubborn hearts and inclinations bow,
That we may faithfully fulfil each law:

Pardon, good God! the crimes that we have done,
Remember not how often we tranſgreſs:
But all thoſe laws, as formerly on ſtone,
Upon the tablets of our hearts impreſs!

Q. Tell me, what doſt thou chiefly gather hence?
 What do the laws, thou haſt rehears'd, expreſs?
 Give me their plaineſt and their trueſt ſenſe,
 In as few words as thou thy thoughts canſt dreſs.

A. Two duties I have learn'd from thence to know,
 To which by love and gratitude I'm bound,
 The one, I to my great Creator owe,
 The other, to my neighbours all around.

Q. Firſt, let me know, if thou the ſame canſt ſay,
 What is thy bounden duty to the Lord—
 The duty, that compels thee to obey
 His ſacred laws, and to reſpect his word?

        A. Firſt,

A. Firſt, to believe that God exiſts, I'm bound,
(And this I muſt believe with heart ſincere)
To fear him, with a dread and awe profound,
To love him, as the thing I hold moſt dear:

Then I muſt worſhip him, with all my pow'r,
In ſuch a manner, as his Word makes known,
And bleſs and thank his goodneſs, ev'ry hour,
For all the kindneſs he to me has ſhown:

My truſt in him I muſt entirely place,
And in all ſtations call upon the Lord,
His faith I muſt, on no account, diſgrace,
But honour and obey his name and word—

Then in ſuch manner I muſt chant his praiſe,
And him, the Sove'reign of the world, adore,
That I muſt ſerve him truly all my days,
In ev'ry caſe that comes within my pow'r.

2. What is the duty, thou doſt chiefly owe
To ev'ry man, with whom thou art concern'd?
The ſame to me with juſt preciſion ſhow,
If thou haſt it by heart completely learn'd.

A. The ſame true love, that to myſelf I bear,
The like I to my fellow creature owe;
It muſt, like that, be real and ſincere,
Even altho' he were my greateſt foe:

I likewiſe muſt to ev'ry perſon do,
Whatever I cou'd from my heart require
That he ſhou'd do to me, and to him ſhow
No ſtricter meaſures, than I ſhou'd deſire:

My parents alſo I am bound, to love,
To honour, and in poverty relieve,
I ne'er muſt do the thing, they diſapprove,
But due obedience to their orders give:

The king, with loyalty I muſt obey,
With all his officers in their degree,
To their commands juſt homage I muſt pay,
So they are lawful, howe'er harſh they be:

To

To all my governors I muſt ſubmit,
My maſters, and my guides of ev'ry kind,
With all my paſtors—(as is juſt and fit)
Who guide my conſcience and improve my mind.

Unto my betters, whether great or ſmall,
I muſt with decent deference behave,
And due ſubmiſſion ſhow unto them all,
And ne'er licentiouſly againſt them rave.

I muſt not injure any one alive,
In word, or deed; nay, even not in thought——
Nor malice bear——nor blow unto him give,
By which his life may be to danger brought:

To keep my body tempe'rate I muſt ſtrive;
Nor into riotous exceſſes run;
But ſoberly and chaſtely always live,
And, as the plague, all luſt and lewdneſs ſhun:

My hands from pilfering I muſt reſtrain,
And muſt not in the paths of robbers tread,
From all deceit and wrong I muſt reſrain,
And rather labour for my daily bread:

From ſlander alſo I muſt keep my tongue,
From falſehoods, and untruths of ev'ry kind,
And never talk of any to their wrong,
Like infidels, who no religion mind:

The goods of others I muſt not deſire
With luſtful eye, and avaritious heart;
But labour—as the laws of God require——
As well, as e'er I can, to act my part.

2. Know this, my child!——and, what I ſay, is right,
Thou çanſt not ſuch a burden undergo,
Nor all thoſe things, by thy own proper might,
Vile ſinner as thou art——pretend to do.

Thou canſt not keep God's ſtatutes undefil'd,
Or follow them with never-erring pace,
Thou canſt not ſerve him worthily, my child!
Unleſs he deigns to give thee ſpecial grace:

On

On which account, thou muft hereafter ftrive,
Through prayer's aid, God's favour to implore,
That He to thee this needful grace may give,
Whereby thou may'ft more juftly him adore.

Let me the Prayer of our Lord then hear,
(If in thy memo'ry thou doft it retain)
Repeat it without bafhfulnefs or fear,
Or thou muft ftay to con it over again.

The L O R D's P R A Y E R.

Our Father, who the univerfe didft frame——
Our Father, from whofe Love all bleffings flow,
Hallow'd for ever be thy glorious name,
By all the faints above, and men below.

Soon may thy kingdom come, O gracious Lord!
When we on earth, fhall join the' angelic hoft,
And all be govern'd by thy facred word,
And by the guidance of the Holy Ghoft:

Thy will divine, amongft us mortals here
On earth, implicitly be ever done,
As it is always in a higher fphere,
By ev'ry angel, feraph, pow'r, and throne.

Forgive us, Lord! forgive us here below,
All the offences, we have ever done;
As we forgivenefs for our brethren's fhow,
May we expect forgivenefs for our own:

Permit us not by fin to be enfnar'd——
Let no temptation our frail hearts entice——
Our fouls from this world's vain delufions guard,
From Satan's toils, and ev'ry fenfual vice.

The fove'reignty of all the world is thine——
Omnipotence belongs to none, but thee——
All Glory too, that attribute divine,
Is thine——and fo fhall it for ever be! *Amen.*

What

2. What doſt thou of the Lord thy God deſire
In this ſhort Prayer————when with uplifted eyes,
And mind quite rapt with a celeſtial fire,
Thou darteſt thy petitions to the ſkies?

A. Firſt, of the Lord my God, and heave'nly Sire,
His aid and kind aſſiſtance I implore,
That He wou'd give us all that we require,
That as we ought, we may his name adore.

Whatever bleſſings we may chance to want,
I, next, beſeech that He'd be pleas'd to ſend,
And ev'ry neceſſary likewiſe grant,
To clothe our bodies and our ſouls defend.

I farther beg, that He wou'd quite diſcharge
Our long accounts—I cannot ſay how long!
And take compaſſion upon all at large,
That ever did us any harm or wrong:

I alſo pray, that He wou'd ſtill defend,
And by His mighty Power keep us whole,
From all the ills and dangers that attend,
As well this mortal body, as the ſoul.

All this, I truſt, He'll of His mercy do,
Through Jeſus Chriſt, his ever-bleſſed Son,
And for His ſake, to all compaſſion ſhow:
Therefore, I ſay, Amen!——May this be done!

2. Thus far thy anſwers have been full and plain——
Now tell me, without any ſly reſerve,
How many ſacraments did Chriſt ordain,
Which his whole church was always to obſerve?

A. Two only, to ſalvation requiſite,
He in the goſpel left upon record——
That is to ſay——if (as I think) I'm right——
Baptiſm—and the Supper of our Lord.

2. If thou doſt underſtand the queſtion, ſay,
By this word, Sacrament, what doſt thou mean?
Thy ſentiments of it before me lay,
And, if thou canſt, explain the myſtic ſcene.

A. It

A. It is a visible, and outward sign
Of an internal, spiritual grace,
Whereby I'm sure that Christ himself is mine,
With all the gifts he grants his chosen race.

Q. How many parts do each of those contain,
Before the present congregation say,
And make them to the meanest Christian plain,
As is the sunshine that illumes the day?

A. In either Sacrament, two parts there are,
One, is the visible and outward sign,
The other does an inward grace declare,
A mental pow'r, and energy divine.

Q. What is the outward sign, that may be seen,
Or sacred form in baptism reveal'd,
Whereby all Christians are from sin made clean,
And by a grace, to them peculiar, seal'd?

A. Water, wherein the person is baptize'd
(Who can this sign of his religion boast)
In those dread names, by Christians so much prize'd,
I mean, " the Father, Son, and Holy Ghost."

Q. What is that inward, spiritual grace,
Which cannot by the carnal eye be seen,
Whereby God shows to all his chosen race,
That they are wash'd from their offences clean?

A. It is the blood of Christ, God's only Son,
Which ev'ry soul from native filth does lave,
And sin—whereby it had been else undone,
Whereas, before, it was the devil's slave:

'Tis that alone, which does man's sins efface,
And to a new-born righteousness restore,
'Tis that which makes him heav'n's child thro' grace,
When he, by nature, was God's foe before.

Q. Tell me, my child! what is require'd of those,
Who, to the font, to be baptize'd are brought?
And fluently the benefits disclose,
Which by that holy Sacrament are wrought?

A. A lively

A. A lively faith, and penitence fincere,
 By all, who are baptize'd, muft be exprefs'd,
 And ev'ry one muft both thefe badges bear
 Of the religion that's by him profefs'd.

 Repentance, ev'ry error to refign,
 And ev'ry fin entirely to forfake—
 Faith, to believe the promifes divine,
 Which God to them did, in this office, make.

2. How then can infants at the font engage
 All this, and fuch a burden undertake;
 When they, by reafon of their tender age,
 Cannot perform the promifes they make?

A. Becaufe their fureties anfwer, in their room,
 That they fhall all thofe promifes fulfil—
 Which promifes, when to due years they come,
 They muft perform with an obedient will.

 . Why was the holy Eucharift ordain'd?
 And why, e'er fince our Lord firft kept that feaft,
 Has it by all good Chriftians been maintain'd,
 With a devotion, that has never ceas'd?

A. It was, that we might ever bear in mind
 The death of Chrift, who for our fins was flain,
 And the vaft benefits which all mankind
 May, from his painful fufferings, obtain.

2. What is the vifible, external part
 Of that bleft feaft, or Sacrament divine,
 That feals the promis'd grace? tell me by heart—
 Tell me, I fay, what is it's outward fign?

A. It is the bread and wine, our bleffed Lord
 Commanded us to take, for his dear fake,
 When we his Body and his Blood record,
 And of that Soul-fufficing food partake.

 . What is the' internal part, the pow'r divine,
 The grace, that in this Sacrament does lie,
 Or thing intended by the bread and wine?
 I beg a ready and concife reply.

A. Chrift's

A. Chrift's **Body** and his **Blood** are fignify'd
Thereby—which he for all his people fhed,
When man was fave'd, and God was fatisfy'd,
And with the Bread of Life we all were fed.

2. What are the benefits that thence accrue
To all, who worthily receive the fame,
And, at this facramental banquet fhew,
The great regard they bear their Saviour's name?

A. Our fouls are fed upon our Saviour's flefh,
And on his gifts divine with vaft delight:
Our feeble faith the banquet does refrefh,
And all our fins, thro' him, are cancell'd quite:

For as the tafteful bread and wine are good,
To ftrengthen and rejoice the heart of flefh:
Juft fo our Saviour's Body and his Blood,
The fouls of good communicants refrefh.

2. What is require'd of ev'ry worthy gueft,
(Befides all proper rev'rence and refpect)
Who without dread comes to this holy feaft,
If he, from it, can any good expect?

A. He thoroughly muft fcrutinize his heart,
If he detefts the devious paths he trod,
And from his fins determines to depart,
Whether committed againft man, or God;

And, next to that, he fully muft intend
Never to lead the life he led before;
But all his former wicked ways amend,
As God himfelf commands, and fin no more:

He likewife for a certainty muft know,
Whether he does a lively faith poffefs
In all the mercies, that fo freely flow
From God, thro' Chrift—whom we muft ever blefs:

He, farther, muft in Jefus Chrift believe,
And in the blood that did for him atone,
Who by his death did all our fouls reprieve,
When none cou'd refcue us, but Chrift alone:

Laftly,

Laſtly, his heart he muſt examine well,
Whether, in charity with all, he lives,
And can ſo far his rebel paſſions quell,
That he their trefpaſſes to all forgives.

Things, to be conſider'd, and made uſe of, when night comes.

1 THink, how thy life does ſteal away!
  'Tis daily ſhorten'd by a day;
And thou art now to death more near
By twelve months, than the former year.

2 Go not a ſingle night to reſt,
  E'er thou haſt ſin caſt from thy breaſt,
And thy accounts in order put,
E'er thou preſume'ſt thy eyes to ſhut.

3 Let not the ſetting ſun deſcend
  Upon thy wrath, ſhou'd ſome offend:
'Tis better with a Bear to reſt,
Than ſleep with malice in thy breaſt.

4 Much greater riſques each man attend
  In bed, (if Chriſt be not his friend)
Than Daniel erſt experience'd, when
He lay within the lions' den.

5 The ſcriptures tell us, that the fiend
  Does, day and night, our ſteps attend,
Like a fierce lion, ev'ry hour
Contriving whom he may devour.

6 Who does the lion's rage reſtrain
  But Chriſt, the faithful Shepherd-ſwain,
That, day and night, untouch'd by ſleep,
Doth from the fiend protect his ſheep?

7 Full many go in health to bed,
  Who in the morning are found dead,
And ne'er ſhall wake, until they come,
At the ſhrill trumpet's ſound, to doom.

8 When

8 When thou haſt toil'd and moil'd all day,
   And night comes on, ſtrive hard to pay
   Thy eve'ning ſacrifice apart,
   With proper words and pious heart.

9 Welcome with pray'r each riſing ſun,
   And end each day, as 'twas begun,
   With pray'r it's gates, each ev'ning, bar,
   Unbar them, ev'ry morn, with pray'r.

10 God will his off'ring have at night,
   As well as with the dawning light :
   He, morn and eve, does praiſe expect—
   His praiſe nor morn, nor eve, neglect.

11 Convene thy family each day,
   And conſtantly your prayers ſay,
   A Chapel make of thy abode,
   And be thyſelf the man of God.

12 Upon thy knees devoutly pray,
   And read the ſcriptures ev'ry day,
   Thy children teach what to believe,
   And thou ſhalt endleſs bliſs receive.

13 On each day's work, reflect at night,
   And put whate'er was wrong, to right :
   If God thou'ſt vex'd, for pardon ſue,
   If thou'ſt had grace, his praiſes ſhew.

14 Ne'er go to ſleep immers'd in vice,
   Leſt thou ſhou'dſt ſo, to judgement, riſe :
   To cloſe thy eye-lids be afraid,
   'Till thou haſt for forgiveneſs pray'd.

15 He, that preſumes to go to reſt,
   E'er he from ſin has clear'd his breaſt,
   Does hazard more, than if a ſnake
   He to his bed at night ſhou'd take.

16 Leſt thou from ſleep ſhou'dſt to the bar
   Be call'd, at midnight, to appear,
   Go not abrupt, like one of thoſe,
   Who nothing mind, to thy repoſe.

        17 When,

17 When, to thy bed, thou turn'ft thine eye,
Think on the grave, where thou muft lie;
And, when thou lay'ft thee down to fleep,
Thy latter end in mind ftill keep.

18 And, as thou takeft off thy clothes,
All but thy fhirt, to feek repofe,
Think how thy all muft be refign'd,
Befides thy fhrowd, and left behind.

19 When Peter's monitor firft crows,
And wakes thee from thy night's repofe,
Reflect, e'er thou doft quit thy bed,
How the laft trump fhall roufe the dead!

A HYMN, to be fung before One goes to Sleep.

1 MY gracious God, and faithful guard!
Who, night and day, doft watch and ward
Thy fervant, be thou ever bleft,
Who doft protect me, whilft I reft!

2 This day I'm circle'd by a band
Of angels, who at thy command
Are charge'd to bear me, ev'ry one,
Left I fhou'd ftumble at a ftone.

3 Thou haft preferve'd me, by thy care,
From the infernal ferpent's fnare,
Who, night and day, feeks to decoy
Me to his toils, and then deftroy.

4 This day thou gaveft me to eat
Rock-honey, and the flow'r of wheat,
And filled'ft me a flowing bowl
To quench the thirft, that parch'd my foul.

5 Thou didft preferve me from each crofs,
From trouble, injury, and lofs,
From ill-fuccefs, difeafe, and fhame;
Whence, from my heart, I praife thy name!

6 Thou

6 Thou took'ſt of me, Almighty Sire!
  More care, than I cou'd well require,
  As if thou hadſt no other ſon
  To take care of, but me alone.

7 Bleſs'd be the lifter of my head,
  Who nightly watches near my bed,
  And does to me ſuch favour ſhew
  By day and night, where-e'er I go!

A Thankſgiving for Fire, Warmth, &c.

1 THOU, that doſt beſt provide, what we require—
     That doſt our bodies and our ſouls uphold,
  I bleſs thee for thy glorious creature, Fire,
  Which thou haſt made to warm us when we're cold!

2 How gracioufly, O God! didſt thou ordain
  Food againſt hunger——drink, when we are dry—
  Fire, againſt cold—and houſes, againſt rain?
  And all, thy froward creatures to ſupply!

3 For if thou hadſt not form'd this uſeful ſlave,
  Our bodies with it's pleaſing warmth to cheer,
  How long had men been abſent from the grave?
  Or how cou'd he have ever ſojourn'd here.

4 Although it be ſo requiſite a thing,
  But few among ſo many millions join
  (How few, alas!) their grateful thanks to bring,
  And praiſe thy goodneſs for the gift divine?

5 Lord, open thou our eyes, that we may ſee,
  How vaſt the bleſſings thou on us haſt ſhed——
  Open our mouths, that we may trumpet thee,
  Each of us, for his houſe, his fire, his bed!

6 Better than us, have often lain abroad,
  Shiv'ring with cold, beneath a bitter ſky:
  Cheriſh *them* with thy favour, O my God!
  And make *us* ever thankful, 'till we die!

A

A Prayer at going to Bed.

1 THOU, that doft guard thy people, and protect!
    Thou caftle of defence, the weak to keep!
For Jefu's fake, do not my fuit reject,
But hear my cry, before I go to fleep.

2 Almighty God! upon my bended knee
By my bedfide, I now moft humbly own,
That I'm not worthy to lift up to thee
My eyes—much lefs then to approach thy throne.

3 And yet I ftill prefume to hope that I
Shall get thee (for my bleffed Saviour's fake)
Not only to give ear unto my cry,
But to accord whate'er requeft I make.

4 Be thou, my ftrength, and kind protector ftill——
Be thou my prop, and guardian of my right——
Be thou, my fhield from each impending ill,
That may befal me, e'en this very night!

5 Lord! I am going now to my repofe,
And die I muft, but can't fay where, or when:
For once he falls afleep, no mortal knows
Whether, or no, he e'er fhall wake agen.

6 Good reafon, then, that man fhou'd recommend
His foul, each night, unto his Maker's care,
And make him, e'er he goes to reft, his friend,
Left he fhou'd ne'er again breathe vital air.

7 On which account, I come, this night, to thee,
My guardian, and my God, whom I adore!
With contrite heart, and with a bended knee,
Thy mercy and affiftance to implore.

8 Be thou my fort, and caftle of defence——
Be thou, my rock of ftrength, my fecret den——
To keep me fafe, this night, from all offence,
And fhelter me from ill-defigning men!

9 The

9 The lion, who ne'er fleep nor flumber knew,
   Wou'd fain devour me, both by night and day,
   And I can fee no method to efchew
   My fate, fhou'dft thou not baulk him of his prey.

10 Receive me, then, to thy paternal breaft,
   And in thy foft'ring bofom fafely keep,
   That I, this night, may comfortably reft,
   Lull'd in the arms of mercy faft afleep.

11 Extend thy wide-ftretch'd pinions o'er my head,
   And fcreen me from the infults of my foes,
   That I, beneath them, free from any dread,
   May find a fweet and undifturb'd repofe.

12 Place thou a band of angels round my bed,
   To guard me from all terrors and alarms,
   And bid them, o'er me, their gay pinions fpread,
   To fhade me whilft I'm fleeping in thy arms.

13 Do thou thyfelf, with thine all-feeing eye,
   Watch o'er me, with a care beyond the reft,
   Left any thing injurious fhou'd come nigh,
   And hurt me, whilft I am with fleep oppreft.

14 Give me this night, and at all other times,
   An unannoy'd repofe, and tranquil peace——
   Give to my foul, true blifs, undafh'd with crimes——
   Give to my body, it's due reft and eafe:

15 And, left I fhou'd unto my doom be led,
   Whilft yet fcarce wak'd from fleep, and unaware,
   Let me not, any night, e'er go to bed,
   Before I for that aweful fcene prepare.

16 Never let fleep upon my eyes defcend,
   'Till I have pleaded hard with thee—and 'till
   I on my pardon fully may depend,
   For all I did, repugnant to thy will.

17 Make me confefs each wrong and injury,
   Each crime, and ev'ry frailty of my foul—
   That, after I've confefs'd them all to thee,
   I may obtain remiffion of the whole.

S 4   18 Make

18 Make thou me weep, O Lord! and grieve full fore,
Becaufe I've dive'd fo very deep in fin:
Make thou me wail, as no one wail'd before,
Becaufe my life fo very loofe hath been.

19 Make me retire to bed, each night I live,
As true a penitent, as if I knew
I fhou'd not for another night furvive,
Wherein I might again repentance fhew.

20 Make thou me earneftly for pardon fue
('Through the dear blood and paffion of thy fon)
For all the fins that I did ever do,
That they may be forgiven, ev'ry one.

21 In the Lamb's blood wafh thou all o'er thy flave—
The Lamb, that was for our redemption flain!
And bury all my vices in his grave,
And never fuffer them to rife again.

22 O, do not any of my fins enroll,
But from thy book eraze them ev'ry one,
Left one alone fhou'd fink with fhame my foul,
When I appear before thy aweful throne.

23 Let me each hour, both of the day and night,
Be always in the nuptial robe array'd,
My lamp well fill'd with oil, and blazing bright,
Waiting my Saviour's Advent undifmay'd.

24 Affure, beyond all doubt, my fainting heart,
That there's referve'd for me a glorious lot,
And that I fhall enjoy no trivial part
Of that vaft blifs, Chrift for his brethren got.

25 I, therefore, now, O Lord, will lay me down
In peace, to take my neceffary fleep:
For it is only thou, O God! I own
That doft mean while my foul in fafety keep.

A Midnight

A MIDNIGHT MEDITATION.

1 HOW proper, and how sweet a thing,
   It is with all the heart to sing,
   To God at midnight, when the rest
   Of mortals are with sleep opprest !

2 How good, how grateful, and how right,
   To praise him with the dawning light,
   And meditate with active mind
   On the' attributes to God assign'd ?

3 The body, sunk in sleep, to raise,
   And with a serious heart to praise
   The Godhead, is a deed most right,
   And fills the soul with vast delight :

4 As 'tis, like David, to arise
   When midnight darkens all the skies,
   And without ceasing to applaud
   For his kind aid, the Lord our God :

5 Bearing his mercies still in mind—
   His various favours to mankind——
   And patience shewn to sinful man,
   At all times since the world began :

6 Giving at our bedside to God,
   For all the goodness He has show'd,
   Most hearty thanks for ever more ;
   Whilst other heedless mortals snore.

7 All glory, honour, thanks and might,
   And adoration, day and night,
   Be to the' eternal Godhead paid,
   For his unceasing care and aid !

Twenty-

Twenty-Third PSALM.

1 MY shepherd is the Lord above,
    Who ne'er will suffer me to rove;
In Him I'll trust; he is so good,
He'll never let me want for food.

2 By his strong arm I'm firmly bound,
  And by his Grace begirt around;
  So that, nor man, nor maid, nor Devil,
Can e'er prevail, to do me evil.

3 To pastures green and flow'ry meads,
  His happy flock he gently leads,
Where water in abundance flows,
And where luxuriant herbage grows.

4 When o'er my bounds I chance to roam,
  My shepherd finds and brings me home;
And when I wander o'er the plain,
He drives me to the fold again.

5 Or shou'd I hap to lose my way,
  And in Death's gloomy valley stray,
I need not ever be dismay'd;
For God himself will be my aid.

6 In whate'er pasture I abide,
  He still is present at my side;
His rod, his crook, his shepherd's staff,
At all events shall keep me safe.

7 My soul with comfort overflows,
  In spite of all my num'rous foes;
And thou with sweetness hast, O Lord!
And plenty crown'd my crouded board.

8 His precious balms, my God hath shed,
  Upon my highly-favour'd head;
And with the blessings of the Lord,
My larder is completely stor'd.

9 His bounty, and his mercies paſt,
Shall follow me unto the laſt;
And, for his favours ſhewn to me,
His houſe, my home ſhall ever be.

10 To God, the Father——and the Son——
And Holy Spirit——Three-in-one,
Let us our bounden homage pay,
Each hour, each moment of the day!

How a PERSON ought to rouſe up both Body and Soul, in the dead of Night, to praiſe his GOD.

1 AWake, my ſluggiſh ſoul! from ſleep awake,
And with a heart ſincere attempt to ſing
(In the moſt daring flight thy thoughts can take)
The glorious praiſes of the' eternal King!

2 Awake, awake——for thou haſt wond'rous cauſe,
And, like the nightingale, thy vigils keep,
To give the Lord his juſtly-due applauſe,
Nor ſpare an hour of all the night to ſleep.

3 Awake, awake, and to thy mind recall
The mercies ſhewn thee by the Lord, each morn,
And how the bleſs'd Redeemer of us all
Supported thee, e'er ſince thou firſt wert born.

4 'Tis He alone, that can aſſiſtance bring,
He is thy way, thy ſtrength, and thy defence,
Thy Rock, thy Chriſt, and thy Almighty King,
Who reſcue'd thee in ev'ry exigence.

5 'Twas He, that fram'd thee on ſo wiſe a plan,
'Twas He, who freed thee from ſin's galling chain,
'Twas He, reſtor'd to life thy inward man,
And by His Holy Spirit form'd again.

6 'Twas He, that call'd thee to believe the whole
The goſpel teaches, from among the blind,
'Twas He, that freely juſtify'd thy ſoul,
Through faith in Chriſt, the Saviour of mankind!

7 With

7 With dainty fare thy famifh'd foul he fed,
And clothe'd thee in a fuitable array,
To mighty honours he rais'd up thy head,
And drove each pain and evil far away.

8 He gave thee a good character and name,
He gave thee grace, fuccefs, content, and health,
He gave thee credit, and an honeft fame,
He gave thee virtue, and he gave thee wealth.

. 9 He caufe'd thee, to be very much belov'd,
To be with univerfal favour crown'd,
To be by all degrees of men approv'd,
Without a foe in all the countries round.

10 He never did invidioufly referve,
Whatever thou didft earneftly requeft,
Tho' at his hands thou never didft deferve
The very crumbs, wherewith thou haft been bleft.

11 Of all men living there's not one does owe
More to his Maker—or that is more bound
To praife the Holy Trinity, than thou—
Than thou thyfelf, art in the country round.

12 " Therefore awake, and to thy mind recall
" The kindnefs fhewn thee by the Lord, each morn,
" And how the blefs'd Redeemer of us all
" Supported thee, e'er fince thou firft wert born."

13 And whilft thou haft a head and tongue, proclaim—
Proclaim forever, to the hour of death,
With ceafelefs voice his goodnefs and his fame—
Proclaim them ftill, whilft thou haft life and breath.

14 To Father, Son, and Holy Ghoft, the God,
The facred three-in-one, whom we obey,
Let us afcribe all proper praife and laud,
Each day, each hour, each minute of the day!

THANKS for our Election, and several Spiritual Gifts.

1 O Lord, my God most high!
   Say, by what means can I
Thy praise at large display,
And my due thanks repay?

2 E'er the' universe was made,
Or it's foundations laid,
Thou grace to me hadst given,
To be a son of heaven.

3 From dust thou gave'st me birth,
When but a clod of earth,
And with thy form didst grace
A creature vile and base.

4 Forth from my mother's womb
I did uninjur'd come,
When I might thence have came
A cripple, maim'd and lame.

5 Thou didst the favour give
I with thy saints shou'd live,
Whereas I might as well
With Jews been doom'd to dwell:

6 And when to Satan sold,
For Adam's fault of old,
From hell's sulphureous flood
Thou save'dst me through Christ's blood:

7 Nor didst thou, for me, spare
Thine only Son and heir,
But gavest him to lie
Upon the cross, and die.

8 Thou didst me then renew,
(Such favour thou didst shew!)
To be thy child once more,
Although the fiend's before.

9 A Father, thou to me,
  I then a son to thee,
  And, in thy image bright,
  Became an heir of light.

10 Thou called'ft me, O Lord!
  By thy celeftial Word,
  And by thy Holy Spirit,
  Salvation to inherit ——

11 Thou called'ft me aloud,
  From the dull, drunken crowd,
  From the blind heathen throng,
  To live thy faints among.

12 In Chrift's blood purify'd,
  And fully fanctify'd,
  A ray thou gaveft me
  Of thy Divinity.

13 Though in a wretched cafe,
  Though all my works were bafe,
  Thou fave'dft me, when undone,
  Through faith, in thy dear Son.

14 Thou gave'ft me hopes, that I,
  At the' angel's aweful cry,
  Though dead in flefh, fhou'd rife,
  And foar above the fkies :

15 And fhou'd, for Jefus' fake,
  Of endlefs blifs partake,
  And the immenfe reward,
  For faints, above prepar'd :

16 Where I fhall meet with peace,
  And joys that never ceafe,
  With honour and refpect,
  And blifs, without defect.

17 For all thofe graces given,
  I'll laud the Lord of heave'n,
  His praifes I'll proclaim,
  And glorify his name :

18 I'll

18 I'll conftantly ador e,
   And praife him evermore,
   For his great lenity,
   And goodnefs fhewn to me.

19 Be all due honours paid,
   To him, the world, who made—
   To him, who fave'd it, loft,
   And to the Holy Ghoft !   *Amen.*

A PRAYER, againft the Oppreffion
of One's foe.

1 Wake, awake, why wilt thou fleep, my God!
     Never before haft thou been known to nod !
  Thou art not Baal!———thy affiftance give,
  And from this fore diftrefs my foul relieve !

2 Wipe off my tears, deftroy each wily fnare,
  Preferve my foul, and blunt each keen-edge'd care;
  Behold my woes, my piteous wailings hear,
  Judge thou my caufe, and then thy fervant clear.

3 Thou art my rock, let me not tumble down—
  Thou art my fort, let me not be o'erthrown—
  My Lord! my God! to my affiftance hafte,
  And let me not be over-pow'r'd at laft!

4 Omnipotent thou art, and help canft give,
  All-wife, and therefore know'ft how to relieve ;
  O Sire of Mercy! quickly me redrefs,
  For thou'rt a prefent aid in each diftrefs.

5 My adverfaries' full-fwoll'n pride abate,
  Affuage their malice, and their caufelefs hate,
  Confound the fchemes of the blood-thirfty train,
  And, for Chrift's fake, relieve me from my pain.

6 O God! my Rock, my Refuge, and my Fort,
  O God! my Health, my Truft, and my Support,
  Lend thou an ear, and liften to the cries,
  Of one, that in the deepeft trouble lies !

7 Thou haſt permitted my invete'rate foes,
 Without a cauſe, to multiply my woes,
 And bring my days entirely to an end,
 If thou doſt not in time aſſiſtance lend.

8 Thou gaveſt foreigners, without controul,
 A full permiſſion to deſtroy my ſoul,
 And them, with whom I'm unacquainted ſtill,
 Leave to deſpoil, and load me with each ill.

9 They, that I'm quite a ſtranger to—and they
 Whom I did never injure, or gainſay,
 With thoſe, on whom I never caſt my eyes,
 Attempt to make my precious ſoul their prize.

10 They have, O God! thy ſervant's ſoul enſnare'd,
 And, to deſtroy me, fully are prepare'd,
 Unleſs my wrongs thou ſpeedeſt to redreſs,
 And to deliver me from my diſtreſs.

11 Awake, my only Saviour—ope thine eyes,
 My Bark in great diſtreſs and danger lies;
 Rebuke, O Lord! the wind and raging main,
 Or I ſhall ſoon beneath its waves be lain.

12 Let not my ſhip be ſhatter'd by the ſea,
 Be thou my haven, thou my anchor be,
 Still thou the ſtorm, that rages o'er my head,
 Lend me thy hand, or I ſhall ſink like lead.

13 Thou haſt commanded me to come to thee,
 My kind protector, in adverſity;
 To thee I come, O God! with woes oppreſs'd:
 O, let my grievances be now redreſs'd!

14 Thou promiſed'ſt to hear my plaintive cry,
 Whene'er I call'd to thee in miſery,
 To thee, O Lord! I daily call amain:
 O reſcue me from ev'ry woe and pain!

15 The pray'r of Jonah thou didſt hear of yore,
 Before the whale diſgorge'd him on the ſhore,
 From all his griefs thou didſt the Seer relieve:
 Hear then my plaint, and thy aſſiſtance give!

16 Thou

16 Thou David erft from Saul's affaults didft free,
    When thro' the deferts he was force'd to flee :
    Deliver me, O Lord! from all my woes,
    And from the hands of my infulting foes.

17 Elijah, thou didft fafe, from Ifrael's king,
    And from a gracelefs woman's malice, bring :
    Refcue thou me from each corroding grief,
    And fend me from my bloody foes relief !

18 Thou erft with pleafing looks and language mild,
    Didft treat the fire of the demoniac child :
    Like pity, O my God! on me beftow,
    Who for thy aid with equal ardor glow !

19 To her of Cana, thou didft mercy fhow,
    Only becaufe fhe importune'd thee fo :
    To me, like fuccour, O my God! impart,
    Since equal zeal with her's inflames my heart !

20 Since none on earth the dragon can reftrain,
    And the invader of my peace enchain :
    Yet thou, O Lord! his fcaly creft canft low'r,
    Thou, Lord! canft bind him, thou canft quite o'erpow'r.

21 Take up thy fpear, and rife to fight my foes,
    With it, their long-extended ranks oppofe,
    Blaft their vain fchemes, their hoftile bands difarm,
    Nor fuffer them to do me any harm.

22 Let thou thy angel fcatter them abroad,
    That wou'd diftrefs thy fervant, O my God !
    Thy fwift-wing'd fhafts to their deftruction fend,
    Who fain wou'd bring my life unto an end.

23 Thou, at thy pleafure, canft thy fervant free,
    Thou from my troubles canft deliver me,
    Do thou then, in compaffion, comfort give,
    And me, by any means, from death reprieve.

24 Let not my foul be by the foe devour'd,
    Let not me be confounded, or o'erpow'r'd,
    Let not the world, and all it's worldlings fay,
    That I'm become their victim or their prey.

T   25 Shew

25 Shew me fome gracious token from above,
Some token of thy goodnefs and thy love,
That all the wond'ring world around, may fee
How much, O God! how well, thou loveft me!

26 I afk no aid from any earthly thing,
From any prince, proud potentate, or king,
I afk no aid, but from the' Almighty's throne,
Who is my Keeper and my God, alone.

27 Do not, O God! my trufting heart deceive;
For I, in thee, and thee alone, believe:
Bring me falvation from thy holy hill,
For I, on thee, place my affiance ftill.

28 Do not, O God! my trufting heart deceive;
For I, in thee, and thee alone, believe:
Come then, O Lord! with comfort to my foul,
Nor long, for it, let my ftrain'd eyeballs roll!

29 Come, Lord! to my affiftance, come with fpeed,
Come, fave my foul, now in the time of need,
That I of thee in joyful ftrains may fing,
For the affiftance thou didft deign to bring!

A THANKSGIVING, for Relief from one's Enemies.

1 YE angels, and ye human fons of care!
Ye heav'ns and earth, and all that in them are,
Praife ye the Lord—praife him with all your might—
Praife him (who refcue'd me) both day and night!

2 In trouble and diftrefs, in need extreme,
I pray'd to him, who did my foul redeem,
And he, amidft the' angelic hofts on high,
Heard my petition and my piteous cry.

3 The wily ferpent laid his dange'rous fnares
And fatal gins, to catch me unawares:
But God his fnares and gins in pieces tore,
And my fave'd foul from fure deftruction bore.

4 He

4 He fent, his holy angel to unbind
  My limbs—his Spirit, to compofe my mind,
  His fpreading wings he kindly o'er me threw,
  And out of all my preffing troubles drew.

5 The Father, heard the piteous plaints I made,
  The Son, for me, as interceffor pray'd,
  The Holy Spirit, foothe'd me in my grief,
  And in adverfity brought me relief.

6 Let ev'ry creature praife the Eternal Mind,
  According to it's nature and it's kind,
  For the great favour He has fhewn to me,
  In fetting me from all my troubles free!

7 The bulls of Bafan compafs'd me around,
  The fie'ry ferpents ftrove my foul to wound,
  Fierce wolves and unicorns, with favage joy,
  My precious foul endeavour'd to deftroy.

8 Both men and women, of a bloody mind,
  A fecret ambufh for my foul defign'd,
  And, tho' the fame religion they profefs,
  Yet they rejoice'd to fee me in diftrefs :

9 But God reveal'd each evil they defign'd,
  God brought to nought the malice of each mind,
  God all their machinations did undo,
  And God relieve'd my foul from all it's woe.

10 Let ev'ry creature then with one accord,
  And notes united, laud the living Lord,
  Who fave'd my foul from all it's fev'ral woes,
  And pour'd confufion upon all my foes.

11 All praife and might, and majefty, and pow'r,
  All honour and thankfgiving, ev'ry hour,
  By night and day, unto the Godhead be,
  Who from my countlefs troubles fet me free.

         Another

Another Shorter Poem, on the fame Sub-ject.

1 LIKE Daniel, when among the lions caft,
  Like Jonah, in the whale-imprifon'd faft,
 I lifted to the Lord my voice on high,
 And, from above, he quickly heard my cry.

2 The ráve'nous lions' fury he reftrain'd,
 The whale's enormous jaw with eafe he rein'd,
 The ferpent's fatelefs appetite he quell'd,
 Short'ned his claws, and his attacks repell'd.

3 Ye heave'ns above, earth, water, fire, and air,
 Ye boift'rous winds, with ev'ry creature fair,
 Your great Creator ever praife and blefs,
 Who has reliev'd his fervant from diftrefs.

Part of the Sixty-Ninth Psalm.

1 PReferve, O Lord! my precious foul
  From the deep floods that o'er me roll,
 And hourly compafs me around,
 That I'm in dread of being drown'd.

2 I fank into the' abyfs of woe,
 And found no bottom to the flough,
 The billows broke above my head;
 So that, through fear, I'm almoft dead.

3 To God, till I was tire'd, I cry'd,
 My throat grew hoarfe, my fpittle dry'd,
 I look'd, and look'd fo long, for thee,
 My eyes grew dim, I cou'd not fee.

4 My foes, e'en than my hairs, are more,
 Or than the fands upon the fhore,
 They all are fwift and ftrong and wife,
 Who caufelefsly againft me rife.

5 Nay,

5 Nay, very powerful are they,
  Who feek my guiltlefs foul to flay ;
  More than their due I did reftore,
  Though I was then extremely poor.

6 My follies, Lord! thou knoweft well,
  Thou my fimplicity canft tell,
  And my tranfgreffions naked lie,
  Before thy all-furveying eye.

7 O, let not them, that truft in thee,
  Be fcandalize'd, becaufe of me !
  O, let not thofe, that feek thy face,
  On my account, endure difgrace !

8 For why ? I've often fuffer'd blame
  For thee, and been o'erwhelm'd with fhame,
  And often been oblige'd to take
  A thoufand infults for thy fake.

9 I, to my brethren, am become
  A perfect ftranger, tho' at home :
  So much an alien there I'm grown,
  I'm to my mother's fons unknown.

10 Unto thy houfe fuch zeal I bear,
   It fhocks my foul, their fcoffs to hear ;
   For all thofe fcoffs revert to me :
   O hear me, when I cry to thee !

11 A flood of fcalding tears I wept,
   A faft the live-long day I kept,
   And ftrove thereby my flefh to tame,
   Yet e'en mine abftinence they blame.

12 Sackcloth and afhes on my head,
   Like one with grief o'ercome, I fpread,
   'Till my wan face, and heart oppreft,
   Made me become each drunkard's jeft.

13 But, Lord, to thee my pray'r I pour,
   O hear me in a happy hour !
   O hear me, God of mercy, hear,
   And turn to my complaint an ear !

T 3

14 O take me from the mire and clay !
    Ne'er let me fall from thee away !
    Deliver me from ev'ry foe,
    And pluck me from the' abyſs of woe !

15 Let not the water-floods o'erpow'r——
    Let not the pit my ſoul devour——
    Let not the loud-reſounding tide,
    Beneath it's waves, thy ſervant hide !

16 Lord, liſten to my loud complaint ——
    Refreſh me kindly, leſt I faint,
    And turn to me thy radiant face :
    For ſweet is thy aſſiſting Grace !

17 Thy countenance, Lord, do not hide,
    For I'm diſtreſs'd on ev'ry ſide ;
    O come, unto my aid, with ſpeed,
    And hear me in the time of need !

18 To my endanger'd ſoul draw nigh,
    And ſave it from it's miſery !
    O ſave me from the hands of thoſe
    I hate—O ſave me from my foes !

19 To thee, my fears and ſhame are known,
    To thee, is my diſhonour ſhown,
    My foes are ever in thy ſight,
    Lord, turn their hearts, and ſet them right !

20 My heart is ready now to break—
    My woe's ſo great I ſcarce can ſpeak—
    Yet I no faithful friend can ſee,
    To ſhew compaſſion unto me.

21 Come then, my God ! O come with ſpeed,
    Give me the comfort that I need !
    Remove whatever cares annoy
    My heart—that I may laugh for joy !

22 Judge thou, juſt God ! thy ſervant's cauſe,
    According to thy righteous laws,
    And mark the inſults and the woes
    I've borne from deſpicable foes.

23 Be thou, O Chrift, my advocate,
   And enter for me to debate,
   Nor let the overbearing foe
   Infult a man fo very low !

24 And thou, foft Pity's Sire, confole
   My fad and fin-befpotted foul,
   Cheer my funk heart, and make me reft
   In endlefs joy, among the bleft !

25 From thy falvation, O my King,
   To me again affiftance bring ;
   With thy free Spirit fill my breaft,
   Nor let me be with woe oppreft !

26 O let me hear thy glorious voice,
   That I may in the found rejoice ;
   And that the heart thou haft diftreft,
   May leap for joy within my breaft!

The 30th Psalm, a Thankfgiving for Deliverance out of Trouble.

1 FRom duft and dirt, where low I lay,
   From crowds, from mire, from clogging clay,
   Thou didft, O Lord, thy fervant raife ;
   Thy name I'll therefore ever praife.

2 Thou didft the triumphs of my foes,
   And all their well-plann'd fchemes oppofe,
   When I cou'd not their rage reprefs :
   So very deep was my diftrefs !

3 I call'd, O Lord, upon thy name,
   Left I fhou'd to the pit with fhame
   Be thrown—thou didft attend my cry,
   'And fent'ft me fuccour from on high.

4 Thou didft preferve my foul from hell,
   That with the damn'd I might not dwell;
   Thou didft my feeble body fave
   From all the horrors of the grave.

T 4

5 Men.

5 Men, faints and angels, then, accord
To chant the praifes of the Lord——
The praifes of the Trinity,
Who dealt fo gracioufly by me.

6 His anger but a little fpace
Endures—but his all-faving grace
Does life exceed : grief lafts the night;
But joy dawns with the morning light.

7 Whilft I enjoy'd the world at will,
I faid—" I ne'er fhall fuffer ill;
" My pleafures nothing can remove ;
" I ftill fhall lead the life I love."

8 Thus I prefume'd, and boafted long,
As thou hadft made my hill fo ftrong—
'Till, angry at my finful pride,
Thou turn'ft thy countenance afide.

9 Soon as thou didft avert thy face,
Becaufe of my neglect of grace,
I hourly fell to fome diftrefs,
More dire than language can exprefs.

10 I then did earneftly complain,
And humbly cry to thee again,
That thou wou'dft pity take betimes,
And pardon me my countlefs crimes.

11 What profit is there in my blood,
O Lord—I argue'd—or what good
Flows thence ? what glory canft thou have
From me—when I am in my grave ?

12 Can fenfelefs clay thy name applaud,
Or, rightly worfhip thee, my God !
Can I thy truth with language fit
Exalt, when burie'd in the pit ?

13 Take then fome pity on my grief,
And quickly grant to me relief——
To me, who now, without thy grace,
Am in a miferable cafe.

14 It comes, it comes—the wifh'd relief!
   Thou haft to joy turn'd all my grief——
   My fackcloth thou haft ftripp'd away,
   And made the mourner blithe and gay.

15 On which account, moft gracious God,
   All worthy men fhall thee applaud ;
   And I to theirs will join my fong,
   Becaufe thou didft my life prolong !

Concerning the E N D of the WORLD.

1 ALL mortals fain the time wou'd know
     When Chrift fhall judge the world below ;
   But better 'tis they fhou'd prepare,
   E'er they to judgment fhall repair.

2 How foolifh is the fon of man,
   Who wou'd know more than angels can,
   And by mere guefs-work underftand
   The fecret counfel God has plann'd ?

3 For if no angel, fiend, or man,
   Can comprehend the myftic plan——
   If the whole world cannqt divine,
   Or clearly ken his leaft defign——

4 In vain wou'd any one reveal,
   What God determines to conceal,
   Or fhew, by a mere guefs alone,
   What was to Chrift, as man, unknown.

5 Learn then of Chrift, what he reveals,
   Aim not to know what he conceals:
   What in the gofpel is expreft,
   Belongs to man—to God the reft.

6 Then ftudy not to underftand
   The fecret things, which God has plann'd,
   Or if thou fhou'dft—'twill be in vain,
   And nought but fhame thou'lt then obtain.

7 Full

7 Full many in the deep are drown'd,
  Who feek it's vaft abyfs to found ;
  Full many blinded are, who try
  To view the fun, with ftedfaft eye.

8 Full certain is the day of doom,
  Though none, but God, knows when 'twill come :
  Why then fhou'd man attempt to fhow,
  What none, but God himfelf does know ?

9 Though ev'ry man fhou'd fpeak his mind,
  Yet neither angel, man, or fiend,
  Can tell the hour, the day, or year,
  When Chrift to judge them fhall appear.

10 Stand therefore all upon your guard,
   And for his Advent be prepar'd :
   The day, the hour, no foul can trace,
   When Chrift will come with filent pace.

11 Peter and James of Chrift inquire'd,
   Before He from the earth retire'd,
   " Lord, fhew us, e'er thou doft afcend,
   " The time, this world fhall have an end."

12 But he to them made this reply,
   " It is not mortal man's——to pry
   " Into the time, the day, and hour,
   " Which God has kept in his own pow'r."

13 This fecret is, to God alone,
   And to no other Being, known :
   Be ftill prepare'd to meet your doom ;
   For no one knows when Chrift will come.

14 The wifeft of the fons of men,
   The beft-love'd angel knows not, when
   He'll come—then of deceit take heed,
   Nor add vain ftories to your creed.

15 Elias, as fome fay, foretold
   This world fix thoufand years wou'd hold,
   And after that in flaming fire
   (Though it fhall be renew'd) expire.

16 Two

16 Two thoufand, e'er the law was fpoke——
   Two thoufand, under Mofes' yoke——
   As many fhou'd (fince Chrift) be paft——
   If it indeed fo long fhou'd laft.

17 It's ages, as they fay, are three——
   The firft, from any fanction free——
   The next by Mofes' law was bound——
   The third is by the gofpel crown'd.

18 Two of them are already paft,
   The third as yet is feen to laft ;
   But how much longer, can be known
   To none, but unto God alone.

19 One thoufand and fix hundred years,
   With twenty more, as it appears,
   Of this are now elapfe'd——then mind,
   There can't be much of it behind!

20 The greateft doctors all agree
   The laft is fhorteft of the three ;
   As God has promis'd it to make
   More fhort, for his Elected's fake.

21 We find that, in John's facred page,
   This age is term'd the latter age,   1John ii.18.
   If fo, when he his writings penn'd,
   It now muft needs be near it's end.

22 The end of all things was at hand,
   When Peter preach'd, I underftand :   1 Pet. iv.7.
   If, in his time, 'twas fo——'tis clear,
   That it muft now be very near.

23 If, in *his* days, the' apoftle Paul,
   The time, the day, the hour, did call
   The laft——then this (all muft agree)
   Muft needs the laft of minutes be.

24 This world, as Saint Auguftine told,
   Is like a man, that's lame and old,
   On crutches propp'd, his body bent,
   And can't have many days unfpent.

25 Let us all vigilant appear,
    The great, the' important, day is near;   Mat. xxiv. 33
    Chrift fays, 'tis even at the door,
    Oil in our lamps, then, let us pour.

26 'Tis certain Chrift will foon appear,
    But the time when, is not yet clear:
    How foon, is not to man declare'd;
    Let us then always be prepare'd.

27 There's neither man, nor heav'nly pow'r,
    That knows (Chrift fays) the day, or hour:
    It is a myftic fecret known
    Unto the' Eternal Sire alone.

28 It therefore is abfurd and vain
    That men fhou'd labour to attain
    A knowledge of the times, which he
    Has hid from all Eternity.

29 Yet Napier name'd the very year,
    When the' end of all things fhou'd appear;
    And faid it fhou'd (fo fure was he)
    One thoufand feven hundred, be.

30 Let any one fay what he can,
    There's neither angel, fiend, or man,
    That knows the hour, the day, or year,
    When God in judgement fhall appear.

31 Let each then readily begin,
    To-day, to-night, to leave his fin:
    For Chrift will, like a fudden gueft,
    Arrive, when we expect him leaft.

32 Her time, as Rachel did not know,
    Until fhe felt the child-birth throe:
    So, 'till it comes, man ne'er can fay
    What day fhall be his dying day.

33 But when the labour of the dame,
    However unexpected, came,
    She was deliver'd of her load
    Beneath an oak, upon the road.

34 So

34 So fhall the earth, whofe teeming womb
   Has pregnant, now long fince, become,
   Bring forth her dead from under ground,
   When fummon'd by the trumpet's found.

35 As fhow'rs of fire and brimftone came,
   And foon fet Sodom on a flame :
   So fhall the day, we call the laft,
   Arrive, when moft are fleeping faft.

36 Since none the hour, or time can fay,
   Then let us watch both night and day,
   And, like the prudent virgins, ftand,
   Each with his lamp li't in his hand.

37 The figns are paft, which Chrift of old
   So very punctually foretold,
   Only that fome among the Jews
   The holy Gofpel ftill refufe.

38 The' Apoftles, and a countlefs train
   Of Martyrs, have long fince been flain,
   Who for the faith their lives laid down ;
   As it to all the world is known.

39 The holy city's wholly gone,
   And not a ftone left on a ftone,
   Burn't is the temple too of God,
   And all the Jews difpers'd abroad.

40 The Gofpel, on it's milk-white horfe,
   O'er all the world has gone it's courfe,
   There's not a land beneath the fun
   To which it, fome how, has not run.

41 Falfe chrifts have here and there appear'd
   Thro'out the world (as moft have heard)
   Who, by the firft deceiver's art,
   Made many from the truth depart.

42 Wars have already been, 'tis plain,
   Betwixt the Turk and Chriftian train,
   Nor does the talk of wars yet ceafe :
   May God, to thofe he loves, give peace !

43 Pale famine, and a dreadful dearth,
　Have almoſt over-run the earth,
　A plague and peſtilence of late
　Have ravage'd almoſt ev'ry ſtate.

44 An earth-quake, ſuch as none e'er knew,
　Diana's temple overthrew,
　And many a fort and fenced town
　Were by the ſhock then tumbled down.

45 The ſun eclips'd withdrew it's light,
　The day was almoſt turn'd to night,
　The ſea leap'd o'er it's lofty mound,
　Whereby ſome thouſands then were drown'd.

46 Lo! Antichriſt long ſince is come,
　And roars, e'en now, aloud at Rome,
　And ceaſes not their blood to ſhed,
　Who will not own him for their head.

47 True charity is grown ſo cold,
　E'en daughters with their mothers ſcold,
　Fathers and ſons hate one another,
　And brother does not love his brother.

48 Faith, ne'er ſo very low was known,
　To a mere ſceleton ſhe's gone;
　In places, once for ſaints renown'd,
　There's ſcarce a Chriſtian to be found.

49 There's not a ſign but what is gone,
　Beſides the Jews' return alone:
　Let us then ſtill be on our guard,
　And for that aweful day prepar'd!

50 The mighty Judge begins to move,
　And means to quit the realms above,
　Whence ſoon he'll come, with haſty tread,
　To doom the living and the dead.

51 Already has he whet his ſword,
　And the' arrows in his quiver ſtore'd,
　Already has he bent his bow,
　Prepare'd into the field to go.

52 His

52 His potent arm is ſtretch'd out wide,
His angels hover on each ſide,
He'll, like the fie'ry deluge, come
To give the world it's final doom.

53 Let us then think to watch, and wait
For his arrival at the gate,
And each a juſt account prepare,
Before he comes, with anxious care.

A MEMENTO MORI--or Remember Death.

1 HOW ſhort the date of man! how ſoon he's gone!
To-day, alive—to-morrow, in the tomb!
Strong as a giant, now——a corpſe, anon!
Such is our ſtate on earth, and ſuch our doom!

2 Not one of us, in a few moments ſpace,
Shall, unremove'd, remain beneath the ſun:
O, let us think then of our deſtin'd race;
It muſt perchance be this next night begun!

3 As haſtes the ſun unto the cloſe of day,
Or as a taper ſpends itſelf full faſt,
Or as the full-blown roſe drops from the ſpray,
Or as a miſt upon the lake is paſt:

4 So ſoon all mortals to their exit haſte!
So ſoon they all are ſpent, and gone away!
So ſoon the fleeting life of man is paſt!
So ſoon his beauty falls unto decay!

5 As ſhips at ſea, or poſts upon the road,
Shafts from the bow, or cowards from their foe,
Or ſmoke before the wind, or as a flood—
So ſwiftly hence we ſhort-life'd mortals go.

6 Life breaks, like ice—or like an arrow flies,
Or melts like wax, or like a poſt it haſtes,
Falls like a leaf, or like a flowret dies,
Scuds like a miſt, or like a taper waſtes.

7 We all ſhall, like a fleeting ſhadow, paſs,
   We all ſhall melt away, like thawing ſnow,
   We all ſhall wither, like the new-mown graſs,
   We all, like froth, ſhall into vapour go.

8 No trace of us ſhall any more be ſeen,
   Than of the bark, that thro' the billows drives,
   Or of the ſnake, that glides along the green,
   Or of the ſhaft, the yielding air that rives.

9 O let us then, this very day, or night,
   Prepare to move from hence without delay,
   And wean ourſelves from ev'ry vain delight;
   Since long we cannot here expect to ſtay!

10 We, here, reſide in tenements of clay:
   A little ſtorm will make our houſes fall:
   Let us then watch, leſt death our ſouls ſhou'd ſlay,
   Or, whilſt we ſleep, throw down the mud-built wall!

11 As fiſh are kill'd by the keen fiſher's ſtroke,
   As pheaſants by the fowler are fetch'd down,
   As tender flowers by the wind are broke,
   As verdant meadows by the ſithe are mown;

12 So man unweetingly receives death's ſtroke,
   So is he tumbled by that tyrant down,
   So are his ſtrength and ſtay to pieces broke,
   So are his hopes, like verdant meadows, mown.

13 As erſt the deluge pour'd down from on high,
   As fire on Sodom fell, like ſudden rains,
   As lightning, or as meteors from the ſky,
   Or as a woman ſeiz'd with child-birth pains:

14 So rapidly, and with ſo ſwift a courſe,
   So ſuddenly, ſo full of woe and dread,
   So terribly, and with ſo fierce a force,
   Will death purſue, and in our footſteps tread.

15 Frail is our fleſh, and little is our pow'r,
   Weak is our ſtrength, and wretched is our caſe;
   The ſlighteſt ſhock, the ſickneſs of an hour,
   Can put an end to any of our race.

16 An

16 An old wife's diftaff may knock Heroes down,
  A fingle hair may fuffocate a fwain,
  A crooked pin may choke the ftouteft clown:
  Alas! how eafily may man be flain.

17 The weak, the mean, the Fool, whom all defpife;
  The pooreft peafant, with a pebble-ftone,
  May flay the ftrong, may difconcert the wife,
  May ftorm a fort, or ftrike a giant down.

18 What then is man, but vapour, fmoke, or grafs,
  (Although the beft, and braveft of his kind)
  Froth, or a flow'r, a piece of ice, or glafs,
  An earthen veffel, or a puff of wind?

19 The bold, the gay, the cunning, the belov'd,
  Even our chief, our rock, our prop, our ftay,
  The ftrong, the wife, the leader moft approv'd,
  Have each by death's huge fithe been cut away.

20 As leaves are from the trees foon blown away, .
  Or as the fhears divide the thick-pile'd fleece,
  Or as the lilies of the field decay,
  Or as the brittle glafs is broke with eafe:

21 So fhall we all decay, fo wither all,
  So fhall be broke the brittle life of man,
  So fhall we foon, without exception, fall,
  So fhall the fhears of fate fnip fhort our fpan.

22 We all fhall, like the cabin of a herd,
  Be move'd, or, like a gorgeous robe, decay,
  Or all be fhatter'd, like a potter's fherd,
  Or vanifh, like a morning's mift, away.

23 We fhall no longer than our fathers ftay,
  But muft, like them, go to the dreary tomb:
  Before the Judge we our account muft lay,
  And leave this fcene, to make for others room.

24 We cannot here remain from age to age,
  Our bus'nefs in the mart of life to do;
  But in our turn we all muft quit the ftage,
  And, where a world has gone before us, go.

U   25 Where-e'er

25 Where-e'er we be, Death follows with his bow,
   And aims his fhaft directly at the heart:
   There's no man can efcape the deadly blow,
   Nor guard againft the venom of his dart.

26 Through ev'ry company, on his pale horfe,
   He daily rides—though none his coming fpy:
   None ever can evade his matchlefs force,
   To whate'er place, or country, they may fly.

27 Although Afahel erft was like the roe,
   Though Saul in fpeed an eagle's flight furpaft,
   Though Jehu did in fwiftnefs Saul out-go,
   Yet neither cou'd from death efcape at laft.

28 Though Samfon all the world in ftrength excell'd,
   Yet Death the ftrongeft in the world fubdue'd:
   We likewife to the potent fhade muft yield,
   Although we were with Samfon's ftrength endue'd.

29 The Macedonian, once fo known to fame,
   Where-e'er he march'd, did all the world fubdue:
   But Death that glorious conqueror o'ercame,
   And, after all his bloody flaughters, flew.

30 Death flew the Victors of the Eaft and Weft,
   Death Galen, that well-noted Leach! deftroy'd,
   Death flew Saint Luke, of Doctors far the beft:
   If Death flew them; who then can death avoid?

31 As fierce war-horfes tread beneath their feet
   (Whate'er their rank) the dying and the dead:
   So unrelenting Death does, on the great,
   As well as on the pooreft peafant, tread.

32 Death, murder'd Abel—innocent in vain!
   Death, Aaron feiz'd, for piety renown'd!
   By Death, both Cain and curfed Ham, were flain:
   Death never yet, to fpare a man, was found.

33 Pharaoh, the king, and Eli, though a prieft,
   Ifaiah, though of the prophetic train,
   Noah, that ancient Patriarch, and the reft
   Who liv'd of old, have all by Death been flain.

34 As

34 As cruel Herod ne'er was known to fpare,
Or big, or little, of whate'er degree:
So Death, I ween, (whate'er their ages are)
Gives no reprieve—relentlefs quite as he.

35 Though Death fhou'd waggon-loads of treafure have,
The kingdoms of the earth, and all their pelf;
Yet, for a fingle hour, he'll no man fave,
Though one fhou'd bribe him with the world itfelf.

36 None their defire from him fhall e'er obtain,
Whate'er entreaties they may chance to ufe:
No more than Pilate cou'd the favour gain,
To fave our Saviour, from the harden'd Jews.

37 Death, when he comes, will not a fingle hour
Of refpite give, that we a watch may keep,
Nor any notice of his coming—more
Than the dumb dog before he kills a fheep:

38 But unawares with foft and filent tread,
He, like a thief, will to our houfes creep,
E'en whilft we flumber, free from any dread;
So ftole his foes on Samfon in his fleep.

39 Shou'd we provifions for our journey lack,
Oil for our lambs, or requifite array;
Pale death will not permit us to go back,
Nor, if we loiter, for our coming ftay:

40 But as the Babylonian king of old
Shadrach, into the fie'ry furnace, caft;
So Death will all (on whom he can lay hold)
Imprifon, in his clay-built dungeon, faft.

41 To rob fome mifer of his hoarded wealth,
As in the dead of night the burglar creeps:
So Death, to man's deftruction, comes by ftealth,
And unawares attacks him, whilft he fleeps.

42 As fifhers ftrike the falmon with their fpear,
Whilft in the limpid pool he refts unfcare'd:
So Death affaults us, when moft free from fear,
And when, for his reception, leaft prepare'd.

43 As

43 As the poor pigeon knows not when, or where,
The fportman's fhot fhall her of life deprive;
None can the manner, time, or place declare,
How, when, or where, the archer will arrive.

44 We come into the world, one way alone,
And always, at our entrance to it, weep;
But, by a thoufand ways, men hence have gone,
And no account we, of their going, keep.

45 Death came to Abel, as he drove his fheep
To fome fequeft'red pafture, there to feed:
Whilft therefore thou thy flocks and herds doft keep,
Do thou of Death's unerring dart take heed.

46 No place fo fafe, fo private, can be found,
Whˍre Death will not his gaftly vifage fhow,
His dart ftill meditates the fecret wound:
O, let us then be ready for the blow!

47 As fhe a journey took, upon the road,
Death did fweet-temper'd Rachel rudely greet:
Beware, I warn thee, whilft thou art abroad,
Left thou fhou'dft with the rambling Spectre meet!

48 When all Job's children were together met,
Death came amongft them to the genial feaft:
Thou haft no certainty, but at fome treat,
Death will appear, an uninvited gueft!

49 The bluft'ring Holofernes die'd afleep,
As on his bed, o'ercome with wine, he lay:
Do thou, if wife, from all exceffes keep,
Left death fhou'd thee thyfelf, in liquor, flay.

50 Belfhazzar, though of many realms poffeft,
Was kill'd, when drunk, with all his reeling train:
Do thou take care left at fome jovial feaft,
Thou fhalt thyfelf, amidft thy cups, be flain!

51 A mortal ftroke Death unto Herod gave,
As on his judgement-feat he proudly fate:
Monarchs fhou'd think of death and of the grave,
Even when feated on their thrones in ftate!

52 As

52 As in his chariot he triumphant rode,
   Death ſhot a deadly ſhaft through Ahab's heart:
   Shou'dſt thou e'er in thy coach be whirl'd abroad,
   Beware therein of Death's envenom'd dart !

53 Death, like a murderer, on Eglon preſt,
   As quite alone he in his parlour ſate:
   Do thou when in thy chamber gone to reſt,
   Of his fell dart beware—'tis tipp'd with fate.

54 When Dives, in his ſilks, a figure made,
   And cocker'd up himſelf with coſtly fare,
   Death came and ſlew him, for his proud parade:
   Fopplings and Epicures, of death beware.

55 When the rich Fool had built his barns anew,
   And grain therein for many' a feaſon ſtore'd,
   Death came, and all his fanſy'd ſchemes o'erthrew,
   E'er he had taſted of the treaſure'd hoard:

56 Do thou, O Churl! who haſt for many a year
   Heap'd riches up, of Death's attacks beware,
   Leſt unexpected he ſhou'd feize thee, e'er
   Thou haſt enjoy'd thereof the ſmalleſt ſhare.

57 The ſons of Aaron erſt were both ſtruck dead,
   As they their off'rings on the altar laid :
   Each prieſt ſhou'd death, e'en at the altar, dread,
   And of his ſudden coming be afraid.

58 Whilſt on his knees Sennacherib did pray,
   E'en in the temple—Death purſue'd him there,
   And in the temple did the monarch ſlay:
   Death, e'en in church, and whilſt at prayers, fear.

59 Death, unto Zimri, gave a gaſtly wound,
   As, with the harlot Coſbi, he tranſgreſt;
   Do thou take heed, leſt thou by Death art found,
   As thou ſome ſtrumpet claſpeſt to thy breaſt.

60 Light thou thy lamp, the wedding-garment wear,
   And ev'ry proper ornament put on,
   For God's inſpection thy account prepare,
   E'er thou art call'd before his aweful throne.

U 3   61 Be

61 Be ready then to-day, or e'en to-night,
(Thy lamp well fill'd, and thou in trim array)
To come into thy glorious Judge's fight :
To-morrow, poffibly, may be the day !

62 Not Paul, nor Peter, no created pow'r,
Not any man on earth, or fiend below,
Can for a certainty declare the hour,
Nor our approaching diffolution know.

63 Whether by day or night—by fea or land,
In ficknefs or in health—or great or fmall,
In town, or country—let us ready ftand :
We can't tell when, or where, Death's ftroke will fall.

64 Do all your work, whilft yet the day does laft,
Gather your manna with the rifing fun,
Accept of grace, e'er yet the time is paft,
Lay in frefh ftore, before your ftock is done.

65 E'er yet the race is loft, e'er ev'ning late,
E'er the tree's fell'd, e'er in the flough thou'rt faft,
E'er to the hill thou'ft fled, or fhut's the gate,
E'er the trump founds, and e'er thy doom is paft—

66 Run fwift the errands of thy God to do,
Bear fruit abundantly, and of the beft,
Unto the nuptial feaft make hafte to go,
And gain, e'er thou departeft, thy requeft.

A Poem, on the year 1629, when the Corn was unwholefome by Reafon of exceffive Rain.

1 THou Sove'reign of mercy ! thou Sire of all pow'r !
Who feedeft the hungry, with-hold not our food
From us, who forgivenefs repentant implore ;
Tho' long in a fhameful rebellion we've ftood.

2 For fake of thy mercy, and might moft immenfe,
For fake of thy Son, O, abate thy fierce rage !
Give ear to each prayer, forgive each offence,
Our woes and adverfities kindly affuage.

3 Againft

3 Againſt thee we've ſinn'd, at ſo ſhocking a rate,
And brought on ourſelves this affliction ſevere,
With all thoſe great griefs which our boſoms now grate:
But, O, how unable the burden to bear!

4 Thy laws, ſo complete and ſo juſt, we have broke
A thouſand times o'er, e'er we ſtirr'd from the place;
As if we imagin'd thy threats, but a joke,
And thou hadſt no eye to perceive our bad caſe.

5 Thy name we've blaſphem'd, and we've hated thy word,
And under our feet thy ſweet goſpel have trod——
Thy ſabbaths we've broke, and thy temple, O Lord!
Deſerted—thy faith we've corrupted, my God!

6 Thy laws we've tranſgreſs'd, juſt as if we did right,
And thought that no vengeance wou'd fall on our pate,
Or, as if we fanſy'd, that thou hadſt no might
To plague us, for ſinning at ſuch a ſad rate.

7 Thou ſenteſt thy prophets, thy will to declare,
And by gentle uſage to ſhew us the way:
But we ſtopp'd our ears, and their voice wou'd not hear;
Like the' adder, that wou'd not the charmer obey.

8 Thou ſenteſt thy ſervants, to ſummon the blind,
That they to thy feaſt and thy court ſhou d repair:
To come they deny'd, and, with covetous mind,
They each of them went to his farm, or to fair.

9 Our delicate ſtomachs, e'en manna refuſe,
And that bleſſed bread, which for ever will laſt;
Yet garlick and onions and cucumbers chuſe
Before them, like infidels, void of all taſte.

10 The goſpel, becauſe it gives conſcience a bite,
We will not admit, but turn from it averſe;
It neither ſhall teach, or reprove us aright,
Becauſe it refiſts all our paſſions perverſe.

11 The ſcripture ſhall not our vile natures correct,
The law their obliquities ne'er ſhall redreſs,
But ev'ry one lives, as his paſſions direct,
Nor tries his vain follies and luſts to ſuppreſs.

U 4

12 Be-

12 Becaufe on thy law we have trampled, alas !
Becaufe from thy ftatutes we widely have fwerv'd,
Like fheep that break into the corn from their grafs,
Tho' they in the pound for their feaft are half ftarv'd:

13 Our riot and pride, like Gomorrah's excefs,
Cry out for fome trouble to lower each creft,
And ne'er will be filent, 'till woeful diftrefs,
And famine our gluttonous lufts have fuppreft.

14 Of ev'ry degree, be they little or great,
Men ftrongly endeavour to anger the Lord ;
As if from the fkies each, upon his own pate,
Attempted dire vengeance to pull with a cord.

15 The prieft, he permits them to plunge into vice,
And headlong to leap to the yawning abyfs,
Or fhou'd he endeavour to give them advice,
They at his inftructions contemptuoufly hifs.

16 Our indolent rulers their duties neglect,
And fuffer tranfgreffors the country to fill,
And ufe not the fword, thofe dull fools to correct,
Who trample thy laws under foot at their will.

17 The vulgar around (like to Ifrael of old,
Without either monarch, or prophet, or prieft)
All live vicious lives, by no fanctions control'd,
Since they nor of law, faith, or hope, are poffeft.

18 The guilelefs, our bailiffs opprefs without dread,
And pillage them, worfe e'en than thieves on the whole;
Our ufurers eat up the needy, like bread,
Or as the huge whale fwallows up a fmall fole.

19 Our fervants and hirelings do nothing but play,
Our labourers fit on the ground without heed,
Or lie at their eafe on the grafs all the day,
Not chufing to work, 'till compell'd to't by need.

20 Our common mechanics, of ev'ry employ,
Muft all leave the callings, whereat they have been ;
Nay, they that good farms, and large tenures enjoy,
Wou'd fain do the like, and be keeping an inn.

21 Their

21 Their spinning and carding our matrons give o'er,
   To brew, they their knitting and sowing lay by ;
   They sell all their wheels and their reels, and such store,
   Casks, bottles, and such sort of lumber, to buy.

22 The murd'rer, the stroller, the pimp, and the knave,
   The robber, the thief, and the clerk, we are told,
   Nay, women are suff'red a licence to have ;
   Beer, ale, and tobacco, to vend uncontrol'd.

23 Shou'd the De'il, or his Dam, ever have a desire
   A temple, near that of our Maker's, to raise,
   They, for a mere trifle, a temple might hire,
   Expresly devoted to Bacchus's praise.

24 As thou art accustom'd, Lord! lend us thy hand,
   And pull down all those that our principles spoil,
   E'er they eat up each other, and ruin the land,
   And thy pure and spotless religion defile.

25 So nice and so dainty, our servants are grown,
   That they quite as well as their masters must eat,
   And many are pregnant, 'tis very well known,
   Because they were fed on too delicate meat.

26 All callings amongst us make light of thy name,
   They all are so selfish and covetous now,
   They seek not thy glory, O Lord! to proclaim,
   To whom ev'ry favour and blessing they owe.

27 Because thou perceivedst we all did transgress,
   And lead such bad lives—thou didst try as a friend,
   By a gentle correction, and transient distress,
   To goad us our morals and ways to amend.

28 By tender compassion and mercy, O God !
   And by all fair means, thou to win us didst strive :
   By a series of blessings into the right road
   The sheep, that had wander'd, thou soughtest to drive.

29 But when kindness fail'd to amend us, O Lord!
   Thou threatnedst to plague us by ways more severe,
   Thy arrows thou pointed'st, thou whetted'st thy sword,
   And thy dreadful arms didst for battle prepare.

30 When

30 When ready, thou warn'dſt us, before thou didſt wound,
    Thy threatnings preceded the terrible ſtroke——
    Thou ſaidſt, if we turn'd, grace was ſtill to be found;
    But we, even then, at thy threats did but joke.

31 But when thou perceivedſt, threats not to avail,
    Thy arrows flew faſt, our rebellion to quell ——
    With manifold woes thou our hearts didſt aſſail——
    Nor cou'd we evade thy keen ſhafts, or repel.

32 Thou thy ſervants didſt call, and didſt muſter thy hoſt,
    With thy furious ſteeds—the red, black, and white,
    And drivedſt them on (as we found to our coſt)
    Until we poor wretches! were vanquiſhed quite.

33 A hard winter's froſt, and a hot ſummer's ſun,
    With boiſterous tempeſts that ſcatter'd our grain,
    High floods and high tides, that our lands over-run,
    And various misfortunes beſides, gave us pain.

34 A dangerous fever, a famine ſevere,
    A fatal mortality to ſev'ral parts,
    Thou ſenteſt, to force a repentance ſincere,
    And ſpur us, entirely to give thee our hearts.

35 But when thou didſt ſee, that all theſe wou'd not do,
    To turn us from ſin, and our manners to mend,
    A dearth and a plague (thy diſpleaſure to ſhew)
    And the horrors of war thou didſt afterwards ſend.

36 The plague with ſcarce credible fury, mow'd down
    More thouſands than I can in numbers well name;
    Each church-yard was fill'd up, and empty'd each town,
    Where-ever the raging infection once came.

37 A war, unſucceſsful, has beggar'd our coaſts,
    The mercileſs ſword has unpeopled the land——
    Our ſubſtance and wealth are conſume'd, and our hoſt
    Reduce'd to a weak and diſpirited band.

38 Our ſhips thou didſt ſink, and our projects defeat,
    The edge of our ſwords thou didſt blunt in the field,
    Thou our ſages didſt blind, made'ſt our heroes retreat,
    And to our inveterate enemies yield.

39 The

39 The plague and the fword fill'd us all with difmay,
And we did repent, for a morning, or two;
Then beg'd thee, afide thofe deftroyers to lay,
Until thou wert pleas'd, all we ask'd for, to do.

40 But when thou the peft and the war didft remove,
Again to our fins we did eagerly go,
Like dogs to their vomit, to forfeit thy love,
And force thee no favour or mercy to fhow.

41 Thy tempefts and ftorms thou didft order abroad,
And plague'dft us, for all our exceffes, with rain,
'Till thou haft our harvefts quite ruin'd, O God!
And damage'd the far greateft part of our grain.

42 So heavy, fo thick, thou thy curfes didft fhed
On our corn, and our victuals of every kind,
That even the dogs wou'd not tafte the bad bread,
Which was eat every day by each labouring hind.

43 The horfe and the hog both refufe'd the repaft,
When once it began to be mouldy, and grow ;
So loathfome and bad is the grain to the tafte,
That comes from each damag'd, and far-yeilding mow.

44 O Lord, we the curfe have moft juftly deferv'd,
Which thou on our ricks and our ftaddles didft fend :
From death and difeafes we were not preferv'd,
Becaufe thou our coafts didft not deign to defend.

45 Our fcandalous wafte, and abufe of our food,
Will force us to eat, what we give to our hogs——
Hips, haws, or the fruits of the hedge or the wood,
Or the crufts we ufe'd lately to fling to our dogs.

46 Was any bad tafte on the meal we employ'd,
The bread we wou'd fpit from our mouths with difdain;
E'en beggars on common provifions were cloy'd,
And nothing wou'd tafte but the beft of all grain.

47 We lately both eat, and we drank to excefs,
And, like the Gomorrites, thy gifts did abufe ;
At dinner and fupper their meat none did blefs,
Till they had incens'd thee beyond all excufe.

48 We

48 We fwill'd,'till our ftomachs were fo much enlarge'd,
That we cou'd fcarce ftir from the riotous fcene,
Until on the fpot we the burden difcharge'd,
Than dogs, or the vileft of brutes, more unclean.

49 More guefts in each alehoufe on Sundays remain'd,
Who their guts and the Devil devoutly ador'd,
Than were in our churches, when fulleft, contain'd,
And met there on purpofe to worfhip the Lord.

50 Our bellies we cramm'd both with meat and with drink
Three times ev'ry day, howe'er fhort, at the leaft ;
But fcarce, once a week, of our God can we think,
Who filleth his fervants with food of the beft.

51 At church we grow tire'd in a piece of a day,
Tho' our wants are fo great, and our pride is fo ftrong;
Yet a week at a ftretch in fome inn we can ftay,
Tho' the nights are, in winter, fo cold and fo long.

52 In the morn, e'er they dine, fome will fmoke, and will
As much at a time as wou'd furfeit a fcore,   [drink
Then vomit the load back again, and ne'er think,
That poverty ever will knock at the door.

53 Our drunkennefs calls for a dearth on the land,
A fcarcity needs muft enfue from fuch wafte,
Our wilful exceffes a famine demand——
Our gluttonous feafts muft produce a long faft.

54 It is then but juft, thou fhou'dft plague us, O Lord !
For rejecting thy grace, with a fcarcenefs of meat,
And thy full allowance refufe to afford,
But force us, for want, our own bodies to eat.

55 But, merciful God—for the fake of our Lord,
No famine difpatch, this our land to annoy——
No illnefs to pain us—no plague, war, or fword,
Thy fervants entirely to kill and deftroy.

56 Our monftrous perverfenefs be pleas'd to forgive,
Nor make us a warning to all human kind ;
But fpare us, that we may more pioufly live,
Recover'd from fin, and renew'd in our mind.

57 Do

57 Do not the tranfgreffions, juft Father! infpect,
    Which murder our fouls—they're fo vile and fo great;
    But, on thy fon's paffion, with pleafure reflect,
    Who die'd to divert thy difpleafure's fierce heat:

58 For the fake of his life, and the death that He die'd,
    His merits, obedience, and blood that was fpilt,
    Direct to thy fold, thy ftray'd penitents guide,
    And pardon our former offences and guilt——

59 In the blood of his wounds wafh our fins quite away,
    And nail to his crofs our mifdeeds and our ftains,
    O cancel our bond, and thy mercy difplay,
    For the fake of Chrift's paffion, and long-during pains!

60 O call us not, Lord! for our fins to account,
    Nor punifh us for the vain works we have done;
    But pardon them all—howe'er great their amount,
    For fake of our Saviour, thy beft belov'd Son.

61 To mend our bad lives, fend the Spirit above,
    That we may to virtue return fafe again——
    Affift us, to ferve thee—to fear, and to love—
    And from any further offences reftrain.

62 With-hold thou thy rod, and thy drawn bow unbend,
    This famine reprefs, and with afpect benign
    Forgive our tranfgreffions, our morals amend,
    And make our change'd hearts all refiftance refign.

63 Lord, alter the weather, and blefs ev'ry field,
    Our grief turn to joy, and remove this dire dearth,
    Make our ftacks fwell with corn and our markets be fill'd
    And crown thou, with fatnefs and plenty, the earth.

64 Give food to each Chriftian, give grafs to each beaft,
    Give thy Gofpel to all, that love truly thy word,
    Give peace to the realm, and above all the reft,
    Give honour and health to our Sovereign * Lord!

65 One thoufand, fix hundred, and twenty, and nine,
    Was the date of the year (fince our Saviour was born)
    When thofe vaft rains happ'ned, which made us repine,
    And glutted our markets with damnify'd corn!

                *Charles I.   Another,

Another, on the fame Occafion.

1 THou ruler of heaven, of earth, and the main,
    Of wind, and of weather, of tempefts, and rain,
O, lift to the moan and the mournful requeft
Of us, who're by ftorms, and bad weather diftreft!

2 The winds, and the waves, and the faft-falling fhow'rs,
The ftars in their courfes, and the' heavenly pow'rs,
Againft us with fell animofity fight,
And our rife offences with famine requite.

3 The fun, ufe'd to cheer us with heat and with light,
Now turns his pale orbit away from our fight,
Refufing his wonted affiftance to yield,
'Till half of our grain is deftroy'd on the field.

4 The moon, like a widow, her fpoufe who bewails,
In clouds ev'ry night her wan countenance veils;
Her tears, like our fins, in fuch plenty abound,
Our labours and corn in a deluge are drown'd.

5 The billows roar wildly, the firmament low'rs,
The clouds, heavy-laden, oft burft into fhow'rs,
And, for the loofe lives which fo long we have led,
Whole rivers of woe are pour'd down on each head.

6 Our corn the fierce tempeft lays down, as it grows,
The prime of our harveft the wind overthrows,
It fhed, and it rotted, or grew with the heat,
Againft it, the rains fo outrageoufly beat!

7 Our grain is already juft loft on the ground,
The feafon prevents us from having it bound,
Affift us, O Lord! now—(or elfe it muft fpoil)
With weather, to gather it from the dank foil.

8 That part of the crop which in mows has been fet,
Like ftraw in a dunghill, is thoroughly wet,
It fmokes, reeks and moulders, tho' hid out of fight,
But, what lies without, muft be ruin'd out-right.

9 What's

9 What's brought to the barn, is in no better cafe,
But filently heats and ferments in the place,
Juft ready to blaze—help, God of all might,
And let not our labours be fruftrated quite.

10 The victu'als, for dinner or fupper defign'd,
Are full of as bad and unhealthy a kind;
And, if to affift us our God does not deign,
We all in adverfity long fhall remain.

11 Lord, open thine eyes, and behold this fad fight,
Survey with compaffion our pitiful plight,
The food of mankind is quite rotten become,
For want of fair weather, to carry it home.

12 Have mercy, good God! for deftroy'd is our grain,
And terribly rack'd are our bowels with pain:
O make both the dearth and diftemper to ceafe,
Blefs us with thy grace, and our grain with increafe!

13 But what fhall we do for feed-corn in the fpring?
If fo long we fhall live, a fupply who can bring?
All, round us, complain of great fcarcenefs, and want;
Do thou, gracious God, a fufficiency grant!

14 On the fheep of thy pafture have pity, O Lord!
And take not the ftaff of our lives from our board,
Forgive us our fins, our vile manners amend,
And our joylefs bofoms with comfort diftend.

15 Command thou the fun, to fupply us with light,
Caufe the moon and the ftars to illume us by night,
With feafo'nable weather the farmer befriend,
And to thy difpleafure put quickly an end.

16 Clear thou the Horizon, difperfe ev'ry cloud,
Thofe rife rains repel, (for thou'rt gracious and good)
Allay the fierce tempeft, and, after the rain,
Give funfhine and crifpnefs agen to our grain!

17 But here, mighty God! I muft freely confefs,
Our fins have brought on us this difmal diftrefs,
With all the foul weather, and judgements fevere,
Which punifh'd thy fervants fo forely, this year.

18 Thou

18 Thou fill'dſt us ſo full with thy favours and meat,
That none, to adore thee, wou'd ſtir from their ſeat,
Or give thee due glory and thanks, for their food,
'Till ev'ry misfortune our footſteps purſue'd.

19 The Ox and the Aſs know by whom they are fed,
The Dog loves his maſter, by whom he was bred;
But men are ungrateful, and ſeem not to know,
Their meat, and their all, to their Maker they owe.

20 With manifold bleſſings, thou feedeſt us all,
Like fatlings fed up to the full in the ſtall,
But we will not lift up our heads, nor attend, [ſcend.
More than brutes unto him, whence thoſe favours de-

21 Thy ſtorms and thy tempeſts thou therefore didſt ſend,
By rain and bad weather our manners to mend,
And force us, by feeling thy judgements, to know
'Tis thou with thine hand doſt thoſe bleſſings beſtow.

22 Tho' great were the judgements, thou ſhedd'ſt on each
To puniſh the diſſolute lives that we led, [head,
We ne'er ſince the conqueſt, ſo guilty have been,
So ſunk in debauch'ry, ſo ſodden in ſin.

23 Tho' the ſtorm roars ſo loud, and ſo fierce pours the rain,
And tho' ('tis a truth) juſt deſtroy'd is our grain,
Yet ſtill in the ale-houſe each ſabbath we ſtay,
And ſpend in a riotous manner the day.

24 When each ſhou'd repent, in the duſt, on his face,
And proſtrate implore thy forgiveneſs and grace,
And truly our glorious Creator adore,
Like Jews, we blaſphem'd, and like troopers we ſwore.

25 The more thou didſt aſk us to turn and relent,
Our morals to mend, and our ſins to repent,
We ſinn'd worſe and worſe, and more deſperate grew,
And farther and farther from mercy withdrew.

26 The greater the plagues were, which hung o'er each
Storm, war, or diſeaſe, or a ſcarceneſs of bread, [head,
More hard'ned and callous, like Pharaoh, we were,
And force'd thee to vex us with judgements ſevere.

27 It

27 It is not then ſtrange, thou thy anger ſhou'dſt ſhow,
   By doubling and trebling each terrible blow:
   But no one the reaſon, I fanſy, can tell,
   Why thou haſt not hurl'd us, e'er this, into hell.

28 Forgive our perverſeneſs, thy fierce anger calm,
   Remove our adverſity, Lord! and our ſhame,
   Like Nineveh, give us all grace to repent,
   And ſerve thee with pleaſure, and perfeċt aſſent!

A WARNING to the Welſh, to repent, wrote at the time a great PLAGUE rage'd in London.

1 MOurn Cambria, thoughtleſs Cambria, mourn,
   From all thy ſins repentant turn,
   Leſt they God's wrath, and judgements dread,
   Shou'd draw upon thy guilty head!

2 Thy ſins have ſoar'd up to the ſky,
   And thence for ſpeedy vengeance cry—
   Such vengeance, as the Lord did rain
   Upon the cities of the plain:

3 Both night and day, they call aloud
   For puniſhment, like Abel's blood,
   And nought can ſtill their hideous yell,
   Beſides God's plagues, or living well.

4 The earth's polluted by thy crimes,
   (As in the Cainites early times)
   Which ſue to God to ſweep thee hence—
   Without thy timely penitence.

5 There's not a Hamlet to be found,
   Or petty Village, all around,
   But that ſome monſtrous crime appears
   Therein, to din the Godhead's ears.

6 There's no profeſſion, you can name,
   That has not highly been to blame,
   As if, with all it's might, it ſtrove
   To pull down vengeance from above.

X

7 Our Gentry, now fo felfifh grown,
  Seek no man's profit, but their own:
  God's praife, the good of humankind,
  And the true faith, they never mind.

8 Our Clergy fleep, both night and day,
  And leave the people gad aftray,
  And live in ev'ry kind of vice,
  Without reproof, or good advice.

9 The Judge and Magiftrate, for fear,
  The murderer and fot forbear,
  And leave each tyrant to opprefs
  The fatherlefs, without redrefs.

10 Our Wardens, without check or blame,
  Permit them to revile God's name,
  The Gofpel under foot to tread,
  And flight the confecrated bread.

11 The Sheriffs, and their corm'rant train,
  On the fleec'd populace diftrain,
  And under veil of juftice prey
  Upon their wealth, in open day.

12 The Wealthy glibly fwallow down
  The little all, the needy own,
  And by oppreffion drive the poor
  To beg their bread, from door to door.

13 The vulgar, all find fome pretence
  To do what's wrong, and God incenfe:
  Blind, dull, perverfe, to hell they run,
  Nor will, though warn'd, perdition fhun.

14 All ranks of men alike defpife
  The Gofpel, and as little prize
  The law of God; but with much more
  Delight, their lufts and guts adore.

15 Nay, all degrees of men, in fhort,
  Strive fome dire vengeance to extort;
  And on their pates it fhall be fent,
  If they do not in time repent.

16 Such

16 Such fwearing and excefs, O Wales!
 Such fhameful wrong in thee prevails,
 Such fects, fuch herefies, and lies,
 As ne'er before, fince Chrift, took rife.

17 Though now the Deity furveys
 With paffive looks our finful ways,
 Yet he's, in juftice, bound to fhed
 Dire vengeance on each guilty head.

18 Though he has long from day to day
 Entreated each to mend his way,
 The time is come, when he begins
 To think of punifhing their fins.

19 Thou in his fcales waft put of late,
 And found, O Wales! far fhort of weight:
 He'll give thee foon a fatal blow,
 If thou doft not fubmiffion fhow.

20 Becaufe thou haft not wifdom learn'd
 From England's woes, and wert not warn'd
 By her diftrefs, thy God does keep
 A heavy rod for thee in fteep.

21 The plague to thy tranfgreffions due,
 Is prompt thy footfteps to purfue,
 E'en now it hovers o'er thy head!
 So very vile a life thou'ft led!

22 Slung by a flender finefpun thread,
 Pendent it hovers o'er thy head,
 Ready to drop by it's own weight
 Upon thy fin-polluted pate:

23 Yet heedlefs thou doft all the while
 New plagues on plagues inceffant pile,
 And ftill doft God's great patience wrong;
 Though he has bor'n with thee fo long.

24 Thou ftill art worfe from day to day,
 And roveft more and more aftray,
 And fondly weeneft God does doze,
 Whilft thee, to penitence, he wooes.

25 Thou fnore'ft aloud, furcharge'd with drink,
   And feemeft not to know, or think,
   That God now whets the fhining fteel,
   Which in thy fleep thou foon fhalt feel.

26 Repent fincerely, Wales, repent,
   Before the plague to thee is fent—
   Before God bares his fword, entreat
   His pardon, proftrate at his feet.

27 If once the Lord fhall light the fire,
   What man alive can ftop his ire ?
   If once the plague at his command
   Breaks out, who can protect the land ?

28 If once the Lord begins to flay,
   And fhall his fhafts and fword difplay,
   Who can the weighty ftroke withftand ?
   Who can preferve thee from his hand ?

29 Behold the woes on London brought,
   Though fhe has oft for mercy fought,
   As that, in time, fhe did not do,
   God more than half her people flew !

30 Arife, arife, make no delay,
   But wholly caft thy crimes away ;
   For mercy call, before thy doom,
   Perhaps to-morrow it may come.

31 In bales of goods and merchandize,
   It in the London fhops now lies,
   To Wales the plague will come at laft,
   If thou doft not repent in hafte.

32 But fhou'd it come unto thee, now ;
   How unprepare'd, O Wales ! art thou,
   At God's tribunal to appear,
   Without the robe which thou fhou'dft wear?

33 If it fhou'd to thy confines reach,
   What man, alas ! can guard the breach ?
   Not all the world combine'd can ftand
   Againft the Lord's correcting hand.

34 In

34 In vain fhall either rue, or fage,
   With the keen fword of God engage:
   If thou doft not repent from fin,
   All phyfic is not worth a pin.

35 In vain it is thy gates to keep,
   The peft will o'er thy ramparts creep,
   Nor pike, nor cannon can defend
   Thee from the plague, which God fhall fend.

36 In vain it is from it to run,
   Or feek the deadly fate to fhun:
   Go where thou wilt, thou ftill fhalt find
   The fleet purfuer clofe behind.

37 The beft thing thou canft do at laft,
   To keep the plague off, is to faft—
   From meat and drink, I do not mean,
   But from each thought and act unclean.

38 If once the peft invades thy ground,
   Pale famine will befeige thee 'round,
   With forrow, ftern rebuke, and fear;
   Ne'er did the plague alone appear!

39 Adverfity and troubles fell,
   In ev'ry town and houfe fhall dwell,
   Sad moans fhall found in all thy ftreets,
   And dread feize ev'ry foul one meets.

40 Fraternal Love fhall quit thy coafts,
   And ev'ry focial joy be loft,
   Nor nature, nor affinity,
   Shall, whilft it lafts, be found in thee.

41 To tend her child, the mother takes
   No pains—the wife, her fpoufe forfakes,
   The fire, his fon, the fon, his mother,
   The fifter quits her dying brother.

42 The fon, his fire flays with his breath,
   The mother, puts her babes to death,
   The wife, her fpoufe kills with a figh,
   The friend, each friend that dares come nigh.

X 3

43 Slain

43 Slain are the living by the dead,
The vig'rous by the invalid,
The healthy, by the fick they dreft;
So dire, fo dreadful is the peft!

44 Who touches the infected, dies,
They kill, like Bas'lifks with their eyes,
Or blaft them with their tainted breath,
Like the fell Cocatrice, to death.

45 The plague will make a man deteft,
Like a mad dog, thofe he loves beft:
'Twill make him lothe his deareft friend,
As a fierce wolf, or hell-born fiend.

46 Hence they, like traitors, are confin'd
From all the reft of humankind,
Nor are they, any time, allow'd
To go abroad in fearch of food.

47 Their treafures kill all that come nigh,
Whoe'er receives their goods, muft die,
Their cafh is worth no more (tho' great
Their wants) than pebbles in the ftreet.

48 This, Wales! will make thy fons oft faft,
When they fhall not a morfel tafte;
Tho', all they own'd, they gave for meat,
And did for it with tears entreat.

49 The plague at once will run thee o'er,
Juft as the deluge did of yore
The world, or as the fire that came
And fet Gomorrah in a flame.

50 Perhaps, when round the focial hearth,
Or in the tavern, full of mirth,
Or in the market, cheap'ning wares,
The plague will catch thee unawares.

51 Tho' thou fhou'dft to the ftews, or fair,
The field, or council-room, repair;
Where-e'er the peft fhall on thee feize,
That is the place of thy deceafe.

52 There

52 There, like a beaft, thou foon fhalt die,
(But not without great agony)
Without a fervant, or a friend,
Thy latter moments to attend.

53 No doctor, and no prieft will come
To thee, nor dare approach thy room,
Nor any of thy neareft kin,
As if thou hadft fome rebel been.

54 To lay thee out, none will come near,
To fhrowd and place thee on the bier,
Or to attend thee to the grave :
A brute's interment thou fhalt have.

55 This is the death fo full of woe,
Which thou art doom'd to undergo.
This is the death due to thy crimes,
If thou fhalt not repent betimes.

56 O what a dire, and difmal end ?
What agonies this death attend ?
O what a curs'd and fhocking cafe
It is to die of this difeafe ?

57 This England has beheld of late,
When London felt the frowns of fate ;
And this in thee, Wales, fhall be feen,
If thou doft not forfake thy fin.

58 O think, how hateful 'tis to fall
By this moft difmal death of all !
Think, how unpleafing, how unbleft,
It is to fuffer by the peft !

59 This is the death fo full of woe,
Thou doft deferve to undergo !
This is the death, due to thy crimes,
If thou doft not repent betimes.

60 God long expects thee to begin
To quit each vice and darling fin ;
Becaufe thou haft not, he's prepar'd
To give thy fins their juft reward.

X 4

61 Mourn

61 Mourn then, O thoughtlefs *Cambria*, mourn,
 And from thy fins repentant turn:
 Like Nineveh for mercy call,
 Or foon the' impending blow will fall.

62 E'er God unfheaths his glitt'ring fteel,
 For his forgivenefs quickly kneel;
 Too late God's mercy is implor'd,
 When he has drawn his glitt'ring fword.

63 Like Magdalene, thy Saviour greet,
 And bathe with floods of tears his feet,
 Then dry them with thy flowing hair:
 So fhall He fave thee from defpair!

64 An altar raife, like Jeffe's fon,
 And lay a contrite heart thereon:
 Thy pray'rs fhall ftop the angel's hand,
 That's lifted to deftroy the land.

65 Like Nineveh, in fackcloth mourn,
 And from thy fumlefs errors turn:
 God will avert thy deftin'd end,
 If thou thy manners fhalt amend.

66 Unto the temple oft repair,
 Like Aaron there with mournful air,
 Forgivenefs of the Lord requeft,
 E'er thou'rt infected by the peft.

67 Thy bofom beat, and God adore,
 Lke the poor publican of yore,
 With fervent mind for mercy pray,
 E'er thou art fnatch'd at once away.

68 Daily, like royal David, feed
 Upon thy tears, for each mifdeed
 Deluge with tears, each night, thy bed,
 E'er the plague comes, and ftrikes thee dead.

69 Stand thou, like Mofes, in the breach,
 Nor let the peft thy people reach:
 Pray God to ftop the dreadful blow—
 Pray hard, and He will mercy fhow.

70 A

70 A javelin, like Phineas, feize,
   Slay thofe, whofe fins brought the difeafe,
   Iniquity, by law correct:
   So God fhall thee from death protect.

71 Quit Sodom, and to Zoar run,
   By penitence perdition fhun;
   The warning angel's threatnings hear,
   E'er the dread peft thy towns draws near.

72 From fwine and fwinifh drunkards run,
   (As erft ran Luke's repentant fon)
   Unto thy Sire without delay,
   E'er by the plague thou'rt fwept away.

73 Like Peter, in fome private place,
   Bewail the fins of all thy race:
   The cock reminds thee to repent,
   E'er to thy coafts the plague is fent.

74 Thy whole account, with the' utmoft care,
   E'er thou art call'd to doom, prepare,
   Trim thy dull lamp, thy white robe wear,
   Before the dreadful peft comes near.

75 It of a fudden comes, beware!
   And gives no notice to prepare:
   Be then each moment on thy guard,
   Left it fhou'd catch thee unprepar'd.

76 The readier thou art to receive
   The ftroke, and this vain world to leave,
   God is more ready to forgive,
   And leave thee here yet longer live.

77 May God, O Wales, to thee difpenfe
   His Grace—God give thee penitence,
   God fhield thee from this peft fevere;
   God grant thee yet a joyful year.

Another,

Another, on the fame Occasion.

1 Mourn Cambria, thoughtlefs Cambria mourn,
  Like Nineveh, repentant turn,
  Put fackcloth on———proclaim a faft———
  Cry out for Grace, and mend at laft.

2 Thy eldeft Sifter undergoes
  (*England* I mean) a thoufand woes,
  Beneath the weighty hand of God,
  Who rules her with an iron rod.

3 The plague her people has devour'd,
  Like wild-fire down from heaven fhow'rd,
  And all her towns has over-run,
  Like flames thro' heath parch'd by the fun.

4 They die in heaps, without delay,
  Perhaps a thoufand in a day,
  And fall, acrofs each other, down,
  Along the ftreets, in ev'ry town.

5 No medicines can ftop it's rage,
  Not floods of tears can it affuage,
  God's power alone can it allay,
  And his fweet mercy chafe away.

6 Great London weeps and wails full fore,
  As fack'd Jerufalem of yore :
  Nought is there heard but hideous groans,
  With loud laments, and mournful moans.

7 There is fuch forrow, and fuch grief !
  Such anguifh as exceeds belief !
  Such dire diftrefs ! fuch fighing fore !
  The like was ne'er known there before !

8 Men of each rank, and each degree,
  The fword of death uplifted fee,
  And wait for the funereal dray,
  That bears the dead off, night and day.

9 There hufbands fee their conforts die,
And their dear children's corfes lie
All round, 'till they the nofe offend,
And none come near, their aid to lend.

10 There wives lament to fee a fpoufe
And children dead, in ev'ry houfe;
Yet dare not quit, (how hard their cafe!)
Though wild with woe, the fatal place.

11 There, infant orphans cry aloud,
But there are none to give them food,
And fuck the mother's milklefs breaft,
When fhe has been fome days at reft.

12 To them no comforters there are
In heav'n or earth, the fea or air,
In town or country, church or court,
From flock or fold, from field, or fort.

13 He, that is well, with tearful eyes
The oft-repaffing carts furveys,
Which lately carry'd nought but dung,
Now carrying corfes, all day long.

14 They that furvive are almoft dead,
Before they are attack'd, thro' dread,
By feeing all that weight of woe,
Which they are doom'd to undergo.

15 They're not indulge'd, abroad to roam—
They cannot purchafe food at home——
Their vifits no one will admit——
They're not allow'd the dead to quit.

16 The plague, within their houfes, ftalks—
In all their ftreets, fell famine walks——
And, in the fields, the ravens pick
The eyes out of the helplefs fick.

17 Both God and man feem to have left
The wretches of all hopes bereft,
And will not any pity fhow,
Or try to mitigate their woe.

18 The

18 The Godhead laughs at all their woes,
And ftops his ears, from hearing, clofe,
Nor heeds their unavailing cries,
Who ufe'd his Gofpel to defpife.

19 When any, the infected fpy,
As from a dog, that's mad, they fly:
Nay, they had rather meet a toad,
Than meet a Londo'ner on the road;

20 Becaufe they foon infect all thofe,
Who dare approach them, with their clothes:
Thus whom the bafilifk efpies,
At once is murder'd by his eyes.

21 The father, though in the fame houfe,
Can't fee his fon——nor wife, her fpoufe——
Nor, without danger, can a friend
In this difeafe, his friend attend.

22 The mother, with a kifs, deftroys
Her fon, the prime of all her joys,
Or, all unweeting, taints his blood,
E'en whilft he fucks her breafts for food.

23 The father with his baleful breath
Puts all his progeny to death;
And, like a cocatrice, deprives
All, who approach him, of their lives.

24 The ficken'd child, againft his will,
Does his indulgent mother kill,
(Who nurfe'd him with the tend'reft care)
And all the fervants that come near.

25 Both men and women, fuddenly,
In ev'ry houfe promifcuous die
By hundreds, in a fingle night,
'Till London feems unpeopled quite.

26 Such moans and cries were never known,
As in each corner of the town:
No!——not in Ramah, on the day,
When Herod did the infants flay.

27 Her

27 Her clergymen's exceſſive grief
    Tranſcends the limits of belief,
    To ſee each church, of late ſo full,
    Now nothing but an empty hull.

28 Her warehouſes tho' richly ſtock'd,
    Where crouds un-number'd lately flock d,
    Sell not enough, (their trade's ſo dead!)
    To give their famiſh'd ſhopmen bread.

29 Each nice artificer complains
    (Though he has finiſh'd them with pains)
    That none his curious works will buy,
    And that for hunger he muſt die.

30 Each inn, each houſe, or ſumptuous ſeat,
    Of lords and knights the late retreat,
    Now uninhabited remains;
    Or elſe the plague alone there reigns.

31 All who were wont to ply the oar
    Upon the Thames, or drudge aſhore,
    Links, porters, ſcavengers, complain,
    They can't their bread by labour gain.

32 The market, ſtore'd ſo well of late,
    With fleſh and fiſh, and ev'ry cate
    On which each greedy glutton fed,
    Hath neither fleſh, nor meal, nor bread.

33 Many, who not long ſince repine'd,
    Unleſs on quails and growſe they dine'd,
    By hunger humbled, vainly wiſh
    To make a meal, on ſalted fiſh.

34 Tho' then each day, to bring them food,
    A thouſand veſſels ſtemm'd the flood,
    There's now ſcarce ſeen a ſingle load
    Of grain, or meal, upon the road.

35 Where, there were all things for their uſe,
    Which land, or water, did produce,
    Now nothing elſe is to be found,
    But dearth and famine all around.

36 Our

36 Our pride, our luft, our vaft excefs,
 Our gluttony, our drunkennefs,
 Our gofpel-wrefting herefies,
 To thofe diftreffes firft gave rife.

37 Thefe are the fruits, thefe are the gains !
 Thefe are the wages fin obtains !
 Thefe are the punifhments, I own,
 Which we deferve for what we've done !

38 Thus God can, in a trice, bring down
 The pride of any finful town,
 And foon reduce, e'en to the duft,
 The walls and crouds to which men truft !

39 And thus it is the' Almighty can
 Humble the haughtinefs of man,
 Who dares refift his juft commands,
 And turn him over to Death's hands.

40 We have long fince (I muft confefs)——
 We all have merited no lefs :
 God's ways and works are free from blame;
 Holy and reve'rend is his Name.

41 We ev'ry filthinefs have fow'd ;
 In furrows by injuftice plow'd ;
 What can we thence expect to mow,
 Befides the crop, which fin did fow ?

42 This is the peft, with which of yore
 God threatned thofe, that heretofore
 Did not obey and ferve him right
 With all their heart and all their might.

43 This is the fame tremendous blow,
 Which Wales is doom'd to undergo,
 Becaufe fhe did not turn betimes,
 And warning take from England's crimes.

44 Since our long-fuffering, gracious God
 So long o'er London held his rod,
 I fear that guilty Wales muft feel
 The edge of his avenging fteel.

45 When

45 When Judah wou'd not erft forfake
His fins, nor from Samaria take
A warning, he no better fped,
Than Ifrael did, when captive led.

46 If, warn'd by England's fore diftrefs,
Wales will no penitence exprefs,
Some plague, or punifhment fevere,
Will on her coafts defcend, I fear.

47 When God on Sodom, in his ire,
And on Gomorrah, rain'd down fire,
His wrathful vengeance was not cloy'd,
Until Zeboïm was deftroy'd:

48 So as the Lord this plague has fent
To England, from the continent;
I fear, it will not be allay'd,
'Till 't has to Wales a vifit paid.

49 When firft the peft, the fword of God,
O'er Germany in triumph trod;
'Caufe France her vices did not fhun,
Like wild-fire o'er her towns it run.

50 Becaufe no warning fhe at all
Took from Bohemia, Flanders, Gaul,
England is curs'd with this dire peft,
And fares much worfe than all the reft.

51 If Wales will not be warn'd by all
The woes, which now on England fall,
She fhall be punifh'd foon, I fear,
By plagues and judgements more fevere.

52 Mourn therefore, heedlefs Cambria, mourn,
And from thy fins repentant turn,
Like Nineveh, for mercy call,
E'er thofe fell judgements on thee fall.

53 Beat, beat thy breaft, and weep a flood,
Thy garments wafh in Jefus' blood,
Cry out for grace, thy life amend,
E'er vengeance does on thee defcend.

54 E'er God unſheaths his ſhining ſteel,
    Before him with ſubmiſſion kneel;
    For grace and favour him invoke,
    E'er the deſtroyer gives the ſtroke.

55 'Tis vain to cry, when thou art ſlain,
    When thou'rt condemn'd, to pray is vain,
    'Tis vain, to try to break the rod,
    When thou haſt been chaſtiſe'd by God.

56 Ariſe, ariſe, uſe no delay,
    Make haſte, and quit thy ſins to-day,
    Fate hovers o'er thee now, amend,
    E'er it does, on thy head, deſcend.

A Prayer for a Clergyman, when he goes to viſit the Sick, or in the Time of a Plague.

1 BEhold, my gracious God! with pitying eye,
    What dangers in my painful office lie,
    Who never muſt, at any ſeaſon, ceaſe
    To viſit all, whatever's their diſeaſe.

2 There's not a man, or child, that is diſeas'd,
    Whether by the ſmall-pox, or meazles ſeiz'd,
    Or any other malady, that's worſe,
    But I am bound to viſit him of courſe.

3 Be they or hectic heats, or pungent pains,
    Or nauſeous ſweats, or if a fever reigns,
    I muſt attend the dying Clinic ſtill,
    E'en though he of the plague itſelf were ill:

4 Which needs muſt be a moſt tremendous part
    Unto a timid, and ſtill-doubting heart,
    Which, of itſelf, of ev'ry ill s afraid;
    Unleſs ſupported by thy gracious aid.

5 Therefore on thee (who doſt my life defend,
    My ſole Protector, and my only Friend)
    Who, as thou pleaſeſt, doſt direct us, all,
    For thy aſſiſtance and ſupport, I call!

                    6 O Lord!

6 O Lord! thou canſt, if it be thy bleſt will,
Preſerve my ſoul from each impending ill,
Though now each ail might have it in it's pow'r,
Without thy help, thy ſervant to devour:

7 And if thou doſt not, of thy mercy, deign
To keep me, and thoſe maladies reſtrain,
I can't myſelf divert their rage away,
But muſt to their attacks become a prey.

8 Lend then to me, Omnipotence! thine ear,
And ſave the ſimpleſt of thy ſervants, here—
Save me, for thou to ſave canſt never fail,
From the aſſaults of each infectious ail.

9 'Tis thou, O God! that giveſt wounds and pain,
'Tis thou, O God! that healeſt them again,
'Tis thou, that kill'ſt, and yet doſt life afford,
'Tis thou, ſhall therefore puniſh us, O Lord!

10 Thy foſtring pinions, o'er my favour'd head,
(That I may 'ſcape thoſe horrid perils,) ſpread,
And give no dangerous diſtemper leave
Unto thy ſervant's earthly part to cleave.

11 O God, who didſt thy ſervant Aaron ſcreen,
When he the dead and living ſtep't between,
Protect me with thy gracious favour ſtill
From this diſeaſe, and ev'ry other ill!

12 As thou the fie'ry Furnace didſt aſſuage,
And the three Children ſaved'ſt from it's rage;
So, for Chriſt's ſake, let it thy goodneſs pleaſe,
To ſave thy ſervant from this dire diſeaſe!

13 As thou didſt from the faſting lions' jaw,
And dreary den, the prophet Daniel draw;
So from this ail, and it's afflictive rod,
Do thou preſerve me ſafely, O my God!

14 So ſhall I glorify thy holy name,
And in each church or chapel praiſe the ſame,
And my beſt thanks (as long as e'er I live)
For all thy bleſſings and thy favours give.

Y   15 Like

15 Like Aaron, to thine altar, I'll repair,
  Or to my room, like Daniel, and declare
  Thy mercies, or like royal David sing
  Thy praises, my Protector, and my King!

Short is the LIFE of MAN.

1 MAn's life, like any weaver's shuttle, flies,
    Or, like a tender flowret, droops and dies,
  Or, like a race, it ends without delay,
  Or, like a vapour, vanishes away,

2 Or, like a candle, it each moment wastes,
  Or, like a packet under sail, it hastes,
  Or, like a post-boy, gallops very fast,
  Or, like the shadow of a cloud, 'tis past.

3 Strong is our foe, but very weak the fort,
  Our death is certain, and our time is short;
  But as the hour of death's a secret still,
  Let us be ready, come he, when he will.

ADVICE to the Sick.

1 THY mortal part shou'd sickness chance to seize,
    Consider, whence the fie'ry dart was sent,
  Consider, who inflicted the disease,
  And to what purpose, and with what intent?

2 'Tis God himself, that deals the dreadful stroke,
  'Tis God, that gives the malady it's pain,
  Because our sins his patient heart provoke;
  That we may quit them, and reform again.

3 For all the errors of thy life repent,
  God's pardon on thy bended knees implore,
  His mercy beg, and he will then relent,
  And give thee comfort, if he gives no more.

4 If

4 If God againſt thee is incens'd with rage,
  If he has ſcourge'd thee with diſtempers dire,
  The Lamb's dear Blood his anger will aſſuage,
  And briny tears will mitigate his ire.

5 Do thou ſubmit, and he'll ſuſpend the blow,
  Seek grace, and he'll with pleaſure give thee grace,
  Do thou repent, and he'll forgiveneſs ſhow,
  Lament, and he'll compaſſionate thy caſe.

6 Freely to him thy ſumleſs ſins confeſs,
  Condemn thyſelf, and his forgiveneſs crave;
  So ſhall thy prayers ever meet ſucceſs,
  So ſhalt thou grace and abſolution have.

7 Turn thou to God, and he will thee receive,
  Try, though he's wroth, his fury to appeaſe,
  And when he ſees thee, with contrition grieve,
  He'll bid thy troubles and thy ſorrows ceaſe.

8 'Tis God himſelf, that each diſeaſe imparts,
  And ev'ry ail's a herald from his throne,
  Diſpatch'd by him, to purify our hearts;
  None can inflict it—but the Lord alone.

9 It is not from the main, or mountain's brow,
  Earth, air, or bog, that each diſorder ſprings;
  But all the ails that plague us, here below,
  Come from the kindneſs of the King of kings!

10 Hot-ſhooting pains, eruptions, tumours, boils,
  Agues and fevers, quinſies, gout, and ſtone,
  Plague, peſtilence, conſumptions, fits, and piles.
  (Nay, ev'ry ail,) proceed from God alone.

11 The greateſt ſove'reign, on this earthly ball,
  Cannot impoſe, or drive an ail away;
  None but the Lord, and the juſt Judge of all,
  Can health reſtore, or maladies convey.

12 Diſeaſe will not give ear to human lore,
  It neither ſaint, nor ſaintleſs, will obey,
  It minds nor wizard's charm, nor ſtellar pow'r:
  'Tis God alone can order it away.

13 If by a furfeit, cold, or ill-air'd bed,
    Thou art into the room of ficknefs brought,
    'Tis God himfelf that drew it on thy head,
    In whatfoever manner it was caught.

14 'Tis not by chance, nor the decree of fate,
    Or any conftellation in the fky,
    That illnefs comes, however fmall or great,
    But by the' appointment of the Lord on high.

15 Be not too curious, like a man unwife,
    From whence thy malady arofe, to know;
    But rather lift unto the Lord thine eyes,
    And to the Hand, that dealt the gracious blow.

16 God made thee fick, and God can make thee well,
    God broke thy bones, and God can make them whole,
    God thy rebellious flefh and lufts can quell,
    And God can heal thy body, and thy foul!

17 Welcome thou then his herald with refpect,
    With patience bear the meffenger of God;
    The child he loves, he always does correct,
    Nor through a foolifh fondnefs fpares the rod.

18 With due fubmiffion thy affliction bear;
    Fools only kick againft the pointed fword:
    If God impofe'd a treatment that's fevere,
    In vain fhalt thou oppofe his will, or word.

19 If God with fickneffes his fons afflicts,
    Their foul tranfgreffions are the fatal caufe:
    Whene'er he any punifhment inflicts,
    It is, becaufe they violate his laws.

20 Sicknefs is then a debt, that's due to fin,
    A punifhment, that each offender feels:
    For where tranfgreffion once has enter'd in,
    Difeafe ftill follows hard upon his heels.

21 To break the fabbath and to fwear amain,
    God's holy church and gofpel to defpife,
    To treat the prieft and ruler with difdain,
    Is the dire fource, whence many ails arife!

22 To

22 To drink, to fing lewd ballads, and to whore,
    To wafte one's precious time, to play the thief,
    To revel, riot, and opprefs the poor,
    Bring on difeafe, with ev'ry other grief.

23 If thou haft any ail, or any woe,
    Thy fin, and that alone, fhou'd bear the blame,
    Which made the torrent of God's anger flow,
    And caufe'd him to afflict thee with the fame.

24 Search thou thy confcience with the utmoft care,
    Strive ev'ry lurking paffion to fubdue,
    Entirely mortify thy lufts by pray'r,
    And fervently, for God's forgivenefs, fue.

25 If thou fhalt for thy fins fincerely grieve,
    And turn unto the Lord thy God in hafte,
    He will the errors of thy life forgive,
    And thou no longer fhalt with ficknefs wafte.

26 Entreat the Lord, to make thy forrows ceafe,
    To foothe thy pain, and fuccour thee, when ill :
    Ufe importunity with him for eafe ;
    For he can grant it, whenfoe'er he will.

27 Whatever ail, or torment, thou mayft feel,
    The' Almighty can it's raging fmart remove ;
    He, at his pleafure, can thy anguifh heal,
    However great, or grievous it may prove.

28 He cure'd the Paralitic of his grief,
    He cure'd the halt and bloody-flux'd with eafe,
    To Job and Naaman he gave relief,
    And heal'd each fort of ficknefs and difeafe.

29 Sicknefs is but a meffage from the Lord,
    At his command on thee it firft began ;
    It kills, it cures, obedient to his word,
    It comes and goes, like the Centurion's man.

30 To God thy earneft fupplications make,
    Who has this illnefs on thy body laid ;
    Seek thou his fuccour, for thy Saviour's fake,
    His aid implore, and thou fhalt have his aid.

        A Prayer,

A Prayer for a Sick Person.

1 O God of juftice, health's immortal Sire!
    Thou Judge of all! thou raifer of the low!
O hear my fuit, and grant me my defire,
And, for Chrift's fake, fome pity on me fhow!

2 In body weak, and in my mind not ftrong,
    To thee, with heavy heart, and fighing fore,
I drag, O God! my languid limbs along,
    Thy fuccour and affiftance to implore.

3 Thou always art with grace and mercy crown'd,
    To anger, flow, and of forbearance great,
In ftraits and troubles, eafy to be found,
    For Chrift's fake, pity my forlorn eftate!

4 Through thy indulgence, long in health I bloom'd,
    But now I fall the victim of thy rage,
And am, for my offences, fairly doom'd,
    With pain and with diftemper to engage.

5 O God! I have deferv'd—I freely own,
    Long fince, a punifhment much more fevere;
This ail was therefore juftly on me thrown,
    Which from thy hand, Almighty Lord! I bear.

6 A fudden and a dangerous difeafe
    Thou mighteft have difpatch'd, to end my days,
And turn'd me into hell, (did it thee pleafe)
    Nor granted time for me to mend my ways:

7 Yet thou didft deign this malady to fend,
    Like a moft merciful and gracious God,
To give me warning of my latter end,
    And fhew me penitence's painful road.

8 I take it as a token of thy love,
    That thou fhoud'ft treat me as a lawful fon,
And by thy punifhment my mind improve,
    Or by my errors I had been undone.

9 It

9 It is an act, juft God! both good and kind,
  The body, by fuch penance, to diftrefs :
  Since too much cockering had hurt my mind,
  And the fpoil'd foul had ficken'd, thro' excefs.

10 When I with never-failing health was blefs'd,
   My fins, though numerous, were never feen :
   But now, alas! I am with pain opprefs'd,
   I nothing elfe can fee, befides my fin.

11 How many are my faults ? how vaft their fum ?
   To what a countlefs heap do they amount?
   They're more than all the ftars, that deck the gloom,
   Shou'd I attempt their numbers to recount.

12 How foolifhly, O God! was I thy foe ?
   Perverfe, as Pharaoh was in former days,
   Though thou didft ftill the culprit kindly wooe,
   To turn to thee, and to amend his ways.

13 I own, that I have merited much more—
   Much more chaftifement, by a thoufand times;
   Since I have finn'd againft thy facred pow'r,
   E'en from my youth, by oft-repeated crimes :

14 Yet well I know, that thou'rt with mercy fraught,
   To pardon thofe who their vile courfes leave,
   And ready to remit each finner's fault,
   With all, who greatly for their errors grieve.

15 Though nought I've merited but pains and woes,
   And indifpofe'd in fome difeafe to lie,
   Yet mercifully, Lord! of me difpofe,
   And on my vices never caft thine eye.

16 Let Chrift's fad death, and Chrift's obedience,
   For all my fins full fatisfaction make,
   Deep in his wounds conceal each foul offence,
   And be propitious to me for his fake.

17 My life let me not in pollution end,
   E'er I have any ufeful action done;
   But give me time my morals to amend,
   Before thy mercy be entirely gone.

Y 4   18 Hold

18 Hold thy afflicting hand, and foothe my woes,
　　Abate my forrow, and allay my pain,
　　Nor on my foul a greater load impofe,
　　Than this my fickly body can fuftain.

19 Although my foul at times prefumes to fay,
　　" Lord, take my fpirit to the realms above,"
　　Yet, in my coward flefh, I oft'ner pray,
　　" This bitter cup from me, O God! remove."

20 Although my foul and body are but ill—
　　Prepare'd as yet, to wing their final flight;
　　Yet grant me time, (if it be thy blefs'd will)
　　To trim them both, and order them aright.

21 I afk not time of thee, O God! my days
　　In luxury and indolence to fpend;
　　But that I may proclaim aloud thy praife,
　　And, all I can, of my bad manners mend.

22 O Lord! if it be pleafing in thy fight,
　　Like Hezekiah's, lengthen thou my days;
　　Give me fome fign that thou haft cure'd me quite,
　　And conquer'd my inveterate difeafe.

23 However, if it be thy gracious will,
　　That yet a while my punifhment fhou'd laft;
　　I'm ready thy good pleafure to fulfil:
　　But ftrengthen me, until the trial's paft.

24 In health, I only did my God incenfe,
　　When fick, my pain I by my fighs exprefs,
　　What can I elfe? unlefs thou fhou'dft difpenfe
　　Thy Holy Spirit's aid, in my diftrefs.

25 Give me, O Lord! O give me fome relief,
　　Remove my reftleffnefs—my pains allay,
　　Say to my foul, e'en in it's greateft grief,
　　" I am thy Saviour, and thy only ftay!"

26 Thou'rt the Samaritan, O Chrift! fo kind,
　　I, the poor trav'ler, wounded on the way,
　　My gaping wounds with proper dreffings bind,
　　Comfort my heart, my painful fmart allay.

27 Thy

27 Thy hand, O God ! does heavy on me lie,
   Yet in my God my confidence ſhall be :
   Though, under thy correction, I ſhou'd die,
   I'll truſt in thee, and in none elſe, but thee.

28 The keys of life, and thoſe of death, are thine,
   And the grim tyrant does not come, O Lord
   To touch e'en but a ſingle hair of mine,
   'Till he receives the ſanction of thy word.

29 O, make me ready ſtill to meet this foe,
   For his incurſion watchful let me wait;
   So that, behind him mounted, I may go
   To endleſs bliſs, in the celeſtial ſtate !

30 Let not the toys of this precarious ſtate——
   Let not God's juſtice on the day of doom ——
   Let not the fear of death, my zeal abate,
   Nor ſtop my flight to my eternal home.

31 The fear of death in my faint heart allay——
   The world let me renounce, and all it's pride——
   Waſh in Chriſt's blood my filthy fins away—— .
   And, with his righteouſneſs, my vices hide!

32 In all Chriſt's promiſes let me confide,
   Give me ſtrong hopes that I the crown ſhall gain——
   In ſickneſs be my patience firmly try'd,
   And make me long my plaudit to obtain.

33 Thy ſpirit give, to calm my troubled breaſt,
   And bid thy angels fence me in around——
   Of all my hours, make thou the laſt, the beſt,
   And, at my death, let me with joy be crown'd.

34 Let not my ſoul, my ſhepherd Chriſt ! be loſt——
   The precious charge let not the lions tear——
   For dear enough to thee it's purchaſe coſt——
   The truſt to heav'n, among thy angels bear !

An

An ADMONITION to the Sick to call for a Clergyman and a Phyſician, and to ſhun all
Charms, &c. &c.

1 AS ſoon as thou art ſick, without delay,
   For ſome good clergyman expreſsly ſend,
 Who may for thee to thy Creator pray,
 And try to fit thee for thy latter end.

2 Chriſt did his holy miniſters ordain
 To be the ſafe phyſicians of the ſoul;
 He gave them med'cines to aſſuage each pain,
 And, from each ail, to make the ſinner whole.

3 Thy ſin unto the clergyman confeſs,
 And he will give thee ſalves that ſeldom fail,
 Such as moſt likely will enſure ſucceſs,
 According to the nature of thy ail.

4 Believe whate'er the miniſter declares,
 If with the word of God it does agree,
 For 'tis the voice of Jeſus in thine ears,
 Or to rebuke, or elſe to comfort thee.

5 Entreat him to addreſs the' Almighty Pow'r
 With earneſt pray'r, that He may make thee whole,
 And once again to perfeſt health reſtore———
 Or grac>iouſly be pleas'd to take thy ſoul.

6 God has a promiſe made, to hear the prieſt,
 When he, according to his office, prays———
 And certainly he'll grant him his requeſt,
 If not determin'd to curtail thy days:

7 Beg then of him his ſuccour to impart,
 (Leſt Satan ſhou'd a conqueſt o'er thee gain)
 And eaſe thy conſcience, and thy doubting heart,
 When thou, for thy miſdeeds, art rack'd with pain.

8 Permit him both to probe and lance thy ſore———
 Permit his word to harrow-up thy mind———
 Permit him wine and oil, thereon, to pour,
 And with the bandage of repentance bind.

9 Better

9 Better it is by much thou fhou'dſt confent,
    That fome good prieſt fhou'd fuch a freedom take,
    That thou in time mayſt of thy fins repent——
    Than thou fhou'dſt bear damnation for their fake.

10 He will to thee fome wholefome counfel give,
    How ſtings of confcience may be beſt allay'd:
    Thou comfort from his counfel fhalt receive,
    If thou in time wilt call on him for aid.

11 Delay not therefore for a prieſt to fend,
    'Till thou art fure thou canſt no longer live;
    For then in vain fhall he thy call attend,
    When none, on earth, can any comfort give.

12 Ah me!—how many thoufand Britons fall,
    And die, like brutal beaſts, without a pray'r!
    Becaufe they do not for a paſtor call,
    To teach them—how they fhou'd for death prepare!

13 Though God is able to preferve all thofe,
    Who have this neceſſary work delay'd:
    Yet there is no fmall reafon to fuppofe,
    That few are fave'd, without their paſtor's aid.

14 Send for a clergyman without delay,
    When ficknefs does at firſt thy body feize,
    Who by his skill may purge thy fins away:
    For fin's the fatal fource of each difeafe!

15 Next to the Curate——for the Doctor fend,
    And feek for aid from thy phyfician's skill,
    For God by them does oft mankind befriend,
    And gives them knowledge to remove each ill.

16 As God himfelf the prieſthood did ordain,
    To heal the various evils of the mind:
    So from our bodies to remove all pain,
    The art of phyfic was at firſt defign'd.

17 Many a man has thro' perverfenefs die'd,
    Becaufe he wou'd not a phyfician ufe——
    As if to fhorten his own days he trie'd,
    And to live longer here, he did not chufe.

18 Our bodies are the houfes of the foul;
  It is the duty then of ev'ry man,
  To fee thefe houfes are kept clean and whole,
  And made to laft as long as e'er they can.

19 To the phyfician then, with faith, apply,
  When thou art firft by any illnefs feiz'd:
  For that blefs'd art defcended from on high,
  To give relief and health to the difeas'd.

20 For he, that does the healing art neglect,
  Which God ordain'd the fons of men to fave,
  Does that bleft food, which nature gave, reject,
  And finks a fuicide into his grave.

21 The fimpleft herb, that's gather'd in the field——
  The vileft drug, that can on earth be found——
  May perfect health and fpeedy fuccour yield,
  And, if God pleafes, with fuccefs be crown'd.

22 A plafter made of figs (if from above
  'Tis bleft) may heal the moft inveterate fore,
  And the moft common med'cine may remove
  An ail, that yielded to no art before.

23 Though thou of balm and nectar were poffefs'd—
  Of the bezoar ftone, or of a flood
  Of wine and oil, with myrrh and flow'r, unblefs'd
  By God—they ne'er cou'd do thee any good.

24 Yet do not on the Doctor's fkill rely,
  For any med'cine that e'er yet was trie'd———
  Left thou, like Afa, fhou'd be doom'd to die,
  Becaufe thou didft not in thy God confide.

25 There is no pow'r in any herb or plant———
  No virtue in a falve, or draught remains,
  (If God does not his benediction grant)
  To cure our ails, or mitigate our pains.

26 God often does the meaneft med'cine blefs,
  And drugs, thro' Him, o'er maladies prevail:
  They, through his blefling, meet with full fuccefs,
  If He with-holds it, they're of no avail.

27 Upon

27 Upon thy med'cines do not thou neglect
   The Godhead's needful bleffing to implore———
   The beft, without it, are of no effect,
   But will to poifon change their healing pow'r.

28 Never to conjurers, or wizards fly,
   To charm, howe'er acute, thy pains away :
   ,Such leave their own, and finfully apply
   To Ekron's god, their anguifh to allay.

29 Seek not fuch means, thy body's health to mend,
   From him, whofe ftudy 'tis, thy foul to kill :
   There's no phyfician worfe than the foul fiend,
   That ever can attend thee, when thou'rt ill.

30 All divination is a mere deceit———
   A fnare, the Devil did himfelf ordain,
   Each innocent and fimple foul to cheat,
   Whilft he pretends to charm away his pain.

31 A Charmer's but a factor for the fiend,
   Taught the unthinking vulgar to deceive,
   Who take much pains to quit their real friend,
   And to the fiend adulteroufly cleave.

32 They cheat their bodies, and their fouls deftroy,
   They anger God, and give the fiend delight,
   They Chrift renounce, and each celeftial joy,
   Who have recourfe unto thofe arts of night.

33 He does the Devil for his Doctor crave,
   Whoever to a Conjurer applies,
   And fain the fiend wou'd for his paftor have,
   Who, to fuch folks for information flies.

34 Truth, they expect from falfehood's lying fire,
   Whoe'er confult with the divining train :
   They flay their fouls, who from fuch cheats enquire
   For charms to cure, or mitigate their pain.

35 Avoid a wizard, as thou wou'dft the fiend,
   He tempts thee, but he can't thy pain appeafe :
   Cleave thou to Chrift unto thy latter end,
   Afk eafe of Him, and He will give thee eafe.

                                          A PRAYER

A Prayer for a sick Person before He takes Physic.

1 AUthor of health, who all the plants that grow
  Haft form'd! who haft the tyrant Death fubdu'd!
Thy bleffing on this medicine beftow,
Which thou haft with falubrious pow'rs endue'd!

2 Thou various herbs and drugs of ev'ry kind
Didft, for the benefit of man, ordain,
Which were at firft for his relief defign'd,
Whene'er attack'd by ficknefs, and by pain.

3 I therefore, in obedience to thy will,
Have now recourfe unto the healing art,
In hopes of help from my phyfician's fkill :
Thy bleffing, Lord! upon the means impart.

4 I know full well, no med'cine here below
Can my inveterate difeafe fubdue,
If thou doft not thy benifon beftow
On him, who gives, and him, who takes it too.

5 Then to thefe drugs, O Lord! thy bleffing give,
Which I this moment am about to take,
That my diforder'd frame they may relieve,
And ev'ry pain difpel, and ev'ry ache.

6 The fimple figs, of old, at thy command
King Hezekiah's dange'rous ail reliev'd :
Bid thou, O Lord! this med'cine, out of hand,
Remove the malady, with which I'm griev'd.

7 Thou with the liver of a fifh, of yore,
Didft heal old Tobit's long-benighted eyes :
Do thou to me immediate health reftore
By the prefcription that before me lies.

8 As thou impow'red'ft Jordan's limpid wave,
To wafh the Syrian's leprofy away :
So give this phyfic pow'r my life to fave,
And my diftemper's fury to allay !

9 As

9 As with thy spittle only, thou, O Lord!
Of the blind man a perfect cure didst make;
So let me be to perfect health restor'd
By this same dose, which I'm about to take.

10 With, or without these means (didst thou but please)
Thou cou'dst the most confirm'd disease subdue:
Thou hast the pow'r, to give me present ease——
O, join the will unto the pow'r——do!

11 But, if my dissolution thou hast will'd,
And to thy mercy summon'd me away,
O, may thy sacred pleasure be fulfill'd!
With due submission I thy will obey.

12 Vouchsafe, O Lord! to give me strength and grace,
Vouchsafe to give me fortitude, the while,
That I, with patience, my disease may face,
And, like a martyr, at it's tortures smile!

13 Give me thy pow'rful spirit, O my God!
That, in my weakness, I may courage find
To praise thy name, to bear thy cross and rod,
With resignation and a willing mind.

14 Bid thou me be prepare'd, to be dissolve'd,
That to thy kingdom I may quickly fly,
And yield my soul into thy hands, resolve'd
Ever to live with thee—tho' now I die.

15 I know, O Lord! that thou this dire disease
Canst, at thy pleasure, totally remove—
Yet, if thou wilt not these my pains appease—
O take my soul into the joys above!

Another on the same Subject.

1 THou God of mercy! consolation's Sire!
Thou author of my health, my chief delight!
Hear an afflicted sinner's warm desire,
Who begs for aid, and favour in thy sight!

2 Before

2 Before thine eyes my feve'ral vices come,
  With all the errors of a life mif-fpent :
  So black their hue ! fo countlefs was their fum!
  Thou therefore haft on me this ficknefs fent.

3 Had I been juftly punifh'd for each crime,
  I merited a penance more fevere,
  A forer ficknefs, and a fhorter time,
  Nay, far acuter pains I ought to bear.

4 My neck might have been broke in racking pain,
  And, for my fins, my life brought to an end,
  I might, for them, have been or drown'd, or flain,
  No time allow'd my morals to amend.

5 It was thy love on me this ficknefs brought,
  (I fee it now moft evidently clear.)
  To punifh me for ev'ry fecret fault,
  And roufe me up to penitence fincere.

6 Thou doft not, Source of ev'ry good! defire
  That any finner fhou'd forever die,
  But rather his amendment doft require,
  That he may live to all eternity.

7 By this my corpo'ral fufferance, 'tis plain,
  That I muft once to death a victim fall,
  And by this pungent grief, and piercing pain,
  Thou doft thy fervant to repentance call.

8 Though thy difpleafure I fo much deferve,
  Do not, O Lord! thy utmoft pow'r employ,
  Exert not all thy wrath without referve,
  Chaftife me, gracious God! but don't deftroy.

9 Thy fhafts, O Lord! have pierc'd me to the heart,
  My bones are broken, none of them are whole,
  My fpirit grieves thro' the' agonizing fmart :
  Come, Lord, and whifper comfort to my foul!

10 Thou, for my fins, haft dealt me many a wound,
  And I've deferv'd them all, I muft confefs :
  Yet none, but thee, my Saviour, can be found,
  Who can relieve me in my great diftrefs.

11 Thou

11 Thou doft the finner flay, and thou doft fave,
  Thou woundeft, and doft give the med'cine too,
  Thou bringeft to, thou faveft from, the grave,
  Thou mercy and correction both doft fhew.

12 'Tis thou, O Lord! that doft inflict difeafe,
  'Tis thou alone canft give me health, O Lord!
  And none befides can give me any eafe,
  Nor any comfort in my cafe afford.

13 For thy great kindnefs and thy mercy's fake,
  And for the honour of thy glorious name,
  Forgive my fins, my pain lefs pungent make,
  Refcue my foul, fupport this feeble frame.

14 If thou haft not fet bounds unto my age,
  And mark'd the time, whereon my life muft ceafe,
  Do thou, O God! this racking pain affuage,
  And give me fome—tho' but a little, eafe.

15 Return, O Lord! my fainting heart to cheer;
  How long fhall thy deftroying anger burn?
  Obferve my woes, my plaintive accents hear,
  O heal me now, and from thy fury turn!

16 During my illnefs, make, O Lord! my bed,
  My fackcloth rend, and turn to joy my grief,
  Dry up the tears, which I fo long have fhed,
  Affuage my pain, and give me fome relief.

17 Forgive my faults, allay this raging fmart,
  And fave me from the' unfathom'd pit of hell,
  That I may worfhip thee with all my heart,
  And, whilft I live, thy boundlefs praifes tell.

18 Who in the grave thy glorious name fhall laud?
  Or who fhall praife thee in the realms of death?
  O fpare my life, my ever-gracious God!
  That I may praife thee with my lateft breath.

19 So fhall I chant thy glory and thy praife,
  And ever in the pleafing tafk rejoice,
  And magnify thy name, throughout my days,
  For health reftore'd, with elevated voice.

Z   An

An ADMONITION to a Sick Person, to make his will in time, and to difpofe of his Effects in the fear of God.

1 IF thou already haft not made thy will,
  No longer that important work neglect,
But fhare thy fubftance, to thy utmoft fkill,
As Juftice and Chriftianity direct.

2 That he thy mind may with his wifdom guide,
His Holy Spirit of thy God defire,
To teach thee, how thou may'ft thy wealth divide,
As is moft pleafing to thy heav'nly Sire.

3 To thy dear Saviour's care, thy foul devife,
Thy body to it's priftine duft commend,
'Till from the grave it fhall in glory rife,
And to the manfions of the juft afcend.

4 As Jacob did his uncle's fheep, do thou
From thy own goods thy neighbour's keep a-part;
Give ev'ry one, thou dealeft with, his due,
And pay thy debts, e'er thou doft hence depart.

5 Infert not in thy will a fingle mite,
Thou by oppreffion or by fraud didft gain;
Left they, whom thou haft injur'd of their right,
Shou'd, on the day of doom, to God complain.

6 Prefume not—if thou'dft fave thy foul alive,
Unto thy children ill-got gains to grant;
To wantonnefs they will thy offspring drive,
And bring them foon to beggary and want.

7 Though of three fteers alone thou art poffefs'd
By right, amongft thy children to divide:
Yet fhall thofe few with more increafe be blefs'd
Than thoufands, wrongfully obtain'd, befide.

8 The little parcel, which the Patriarch bought,
Better than Joram's fin-ftain'd kingdom throve,

And

And thofe few fheep which Jacob juftly got,
Than all the flocks the guileful Laban drove.

9 As Naboth's vineyard by injuftice gain'd,
Confume'd the whole that Ahab once poffeft:
So does the wealth, by wickednefs obtain'd,
Corrode, however juftly got, the reft.

10 Whoe'er is with unrighteous riches curft,
He is like Pharaoh's meagre kine of yore,
Which eat the fat ones—yet, though almoft burft,
They feem'd no fuller than they were before.

11 Whatever then is juft and lawful, give
Among thy children, fervants, and thy kin,
But dare not, if thou'd'ft fave thy foul alive,
Bequeath to them, what has been earn'd by fin.

12 As God the manna formerly increas'd,
Or as the Widow's meal in fubftance throve,
Or as the crufe of oil, to flow ne'er ceas'd;
So fhall the pittance, juftly gain'd, improve.

13 The better part of what thou art poffeft,
To Ifaac, thy true heir, be fure to give,
Then wifely portion out among the reft
(As thou canft beft afford) wherewith to live.

14 Give to thy wife her thirds of thy eftate,
Nor is it right that thou fhou'dft give her lefs;
To give her more, wou'd but difputes create,
And bring perhaps thy offspring to diftrefs.

15 Never thy fervant turn unpaid away,
Thy poor relation from thy barn fupply,
Rob not the needy lab'rer of his pay:
Wealth, by fuch ways acquire'd, aloud will cry.

16 The Gofpel and the church remember ftill,
The fchool, or college, where thou waft maintain'd,
Thy native town, or county, in thy will;
If thou to pow'r and riches haft attain'd.

17 If thou art childlefs, and canft ought beftow,
If thou doft Chrift, and his religion love,

Z 2

A Free-

A ‡ Free-fchool in neglected Wales endow,
Where youths, for want of teaching, can't improve.

18 Remember Jofeph, that in prifon lies,
    To Lazarus, his daily dole allow,
    Give thy alms now, if thou art truly wife,
    'Tis the laft gift perchance thou canft beftow !

19 If to thy friends, thou fhalt impart thy ftore,
    Thy children, or thy wife, 'tis their's alone,
    But what thou giveft to the truly poor,
    Is hoarded for thyfelf, and all thy own.

20 Return, whatever thou has filch'd away,
    Whom thou haft wrong'd (far as thou canft) redrefs;
    E'er thy removal hence, thy juft debts pay:
    When once thou'rt in, from hell, there's no regrefs.

21 The pan, the pot, the houfehold goods reftore,
    The houfes, tenements, and ill-earn'd gains,
    To them, to whom they did belong before;
    Left thou fhou'dft go to everlafting pains.

22 Let not the farm which thou haft force'd away
    From thy poor neighbour, fore againft the grain,
    Occafion thee to lofe the realms of day :
    Give him his land and tenement again.

23 Now, like Zacchëus, thou may'ft make amends
    For all the' oppreffive acts which thou haft done ;
    But it no longer on thyfelf depends,
    To pay a mite—when thou to hell art thrown.

24 Agree with him, whom thou haft wrong'd, in hafte,
    E'er thou art brought before thy Judge to ftand;
    Left thou fhou'dft be to hell's deep dungeon caft,
    Where thou muft fatisfy his whole demand.

25 Though now, no more than any Turk or Jew,
    Thou doft the Gofpel of our Lord obey;
    Yet this neglect, e'er many days, thou'lt rue,
    And tear the flefh from thine own arms away.

‡ This piece of Charity our Author himfelf perform'd at Landovery,
tho' by the difhonefty of fome of his Succeffors, it took no effect——at
leaft not long. · See his Life.

26 How

26 How many thoufands have to hell been thrown,
   Becaufe they did not, what they ftole, reftore,
   Who'd give the world, this day, was it their own,
   ' In fatisfaction to the injur'd poor.

27 Thou fhalt be pardon'd, fo thou doft repent,
   Shou'dft thou againft the Lord himfelf tranfgrefs ;
   But if thou fhou'dft thy neighbour circumvent,
   God ne'er will pardon, 'till he meets redrefs :

28 But if the perfons, thou haft wrong'd, are dead,
   Unto their heirs, what thou haft, ftole'n, reftore,
   Or fhou'd they from their native land be fled,
   Then give that portion to the neighb'ring poor.

29 Give not (what is not thine indeed to give)
   Amongft thy heirs, another perfon's due :
   'Twill fink thee to the pit of hell, and drive
   Thy beggar'd offspring the bad act to rue.

30 Give not among thy children in thy will,
   What thou haft got by ufury, or wrong,
   Or any method fraudulently ill :
   Gains of that fort endure but feldom long.

31 Obferve the griping ufu'rers fons and heirs,
   Thofe of the' oppreffor, and fuccefsful thief,
   How each from church to church for pence repairs,
   And daily with his wallet begs relief !

32 Such fhall the fate of thine own offspring be !
   If thou amongft them ill-got wealth fhalt fhare :
   For God will vifit, as we oft may fee,
   The father's fins upon the haplefs heir.

33 Place then the fear of God before thy fight,
   When thou by will thy fubftance doft bequeath,
   Give unto each what is his proper right,
   And juftly fhare thy wealth, before thy death.

34 May God thy heart in this great work direct——
   May God impow'r thee thy account to give——
   May God thy mind from all miftakes protect——
   May God preferve thy precious foul alive.

A

A LETTER from Sir Lewis Mansel of Margam, in Glamorganſhire, as 'tis ſuppos'd, to the Vicar Prichard.

The LETTER.

Rev. Sir,

1 FOR many years now paſt, a dire diſeaſe,
    And dreadful dizzineſs affects my brain;
So that I can't by any means have eaſe,
Nor, O my God! get riddance of my pain.

2 I've often ſought advice for this diſeaſe
From men of practice and reputed ſkill;
Nay, I have even croſs'd the raging ſeas,
In hopes to find aſſiſtance for this ill.

3 But now all temporal relief does fail,
  To men of ſenſe and piety I ſend,
O'er land and ſea, concerning this odd ail,
And for advice on which I may depend.

4 I fain wou'd know, " Whether the gracious God
Who rules this world below, and thoſe above,
Has chaſt'ned me with his afflictive rod,
And ſent this ail—in anger, or in love?"

The VICAR's Answer.

1 YOU tell me, worthy Sir, that God has ſent
    On you an ail, no phyſic can remove,
And that you fain wou'd find out his intent,
Whether He ſent it, out of wrath, or love?

2 I tell thee, then, thy ſcruples to remove,
As plain as words can point it out———that God
Did not chaſtiſe thee out of hate, but love,
When thou wert beaten with affliction's rod.

3 'Tis

3 'Tis not a foe, but an indulgent Sire,
That treats thee thus with a correction mild,
And humbles the rebellious flesh entire,
That He by any means may save his child.

4 Thy pain is but a messenger of love
Which Christ himself in kindness deign'd to send,
That He thy patience and thy faith might prove,
And to forewarn thee of thy latter end.

5 Welcome him then—come He, whene'er He will,
And bear thy trouble with a patient mind—
And thank thy gracious Sire for his good-will,
And the correction for thy good design'd.

6 Thy present trouble will not hurt thee more,
Than does the purge that carries off the bile,
But rather make thee fitter than before,
To relish life and pleasure yet a while.

7 No wine, unmix'd with lees, was ever known——
No gold, without some dross, was ever seen——
No grain, entirely clean, was ever sown——
No man, but one, was ever free from sin.

8 To fan thy chaff—to fine thy drossy part——
To draw thy dregs——thy morals to amend——
To tame thy flesh——and to improve thy heart——
It was, that God did thy disorder send.

9 'Twas not to marr thee, but thy ways to mend——
'Twas not to give thee a complete o'erthrow——
But to instruct, and guide thee, as a friend,
That the Almighty gave thee such a blow.

10 Old Adam sinn'd, e'en in the earliest times——
Lot had his lusts——and Noah drank too deep——
Aaron and Moses too were stain'd with crimes——
E'en Paul and Peter for their sins might weep.

11 Be thou assure'd by me, most worthy Knight!
(Although thy life is virtuous in the main)
Thy conversation is not faultless quite;
However great thy parts, thou'rt still a man.

Z 4

12 It

12 It makes thee caſt each worldly thought aſide——
   It makes thee ſtrive each virtue to obtain———
   It makes thee ſpurn the world, and all it's pride,
   To follow Chriſt with all thy might and main.

13 O therefore praiſe thy Father, that's above,
   For his inſtructions and paternal care,
   Who makes thee, out of his abundant love,
   Thus in his righteouſneſs receive a ſhare !

14 God puniſhes the children of his love,
   His greateſt fav'rites ofte'neſt feel the rod,
   Leſt they ſhou'd 'mongſt ungracious worldlings rove,
   And be rebellious to the will of God.

15 God ſcourges moſt, whom he does moſt reſpect,
   And his own children lays the hardeſt on ;
   The man whom he does not for ſin correct,
   Muſt be a baſtard, not a lawful ſon.

16 No wheat, 'till winnow'd, free from chaff is known,
   No unbleach'd cambrick, is for whiteneſs priz'd,—
   No gold is pure, 'till it is melted down———
   No Chriſtian good——'till he has been chaſtiz'd.

17 The frankincenſe will yield no ſmell, 'till li't———
   The grape no wine, 'till in the vintage trod———
   The flint, 'till ſtruck, no fire will e'er emit———
   The man no fruit, 'till he has felt the rod.

18 Cloves will, when pounded, give a ſtronger ſcent—
   Vines will, by cutting, more luxuriant rove———
   The palm will grow the more, for being bent———
   The man will, for correction, better prove.

19 The more the fragrant chamomile is preſs'd,
   The more it ſcatters it's perfumes abroad———
   The more a Chriſtian is on earth diſtreſs'd,
   The more his faith, the more his fear of God.

20 Remember thou that the Almighty Pow'r
   Does, for thy benefit alone, give pain.
   The pain perhaps may not endure an hour,
   But, for a whole eternity, the gain.

21 Deſpair

21 Defpair not then, when by thy ail thou'rt feize'd,
Thy life is in thy great Creator's hand,
Who can reftore thy health, whene'er he's pleafe'd,
And give thee eafe—if thou wilt eafe demand.

22 Take comfort, elevate thy drooping heart,
Be full of faith, thyfelf a man approve;
Chrift foon will come, and his blefs'd aid impart,
He'll foothe thy pains, and thy difeafe remove.

23 The Hand, that fell'd, can lift thee up again,
The fpear, that gave the fore, can heal the fore;
And He, who fent thy pain, can eafe thy pain,
And to thee health, he took away, reftore.

24 Cry out for help to the celeftial Pow'r,
He is thy Father, and will hear thy cry,
His help he'll give, if thou'lt his help implore;
Beg it with fervor, and he can't deny.

25 Whate'er the nature is of thy difeafe,
He can give eafe, he perfect health can give;
Pray then for eafe, and he will give thee eafe;
Confide in him, and he will ne'er deceive.

26 If he fhou'd not, juft at thy wifh, remove,
Suffer with patience yet a-while, the load:
When for thy foul 'tis beft, thou foon fhalt prove
The pow'rful aid of thy indulgent God.

27 No longer fhalt thou be attack'd by pain,
Nor fhall it to a greater height increafe,
Than God thinks proper, for thy body's gain,
And for thy precious foul's eternal peace.

28 Thy forrows only for a while endure,
Long pleafure fhall fucceed the moment's pain;
Be patient therefore, 'till thou haft a cure,
And many years thou may'ft enjoy again.

29 May he, who kindly ftrength'ned Job, to be
In his unequall'd fuff'rings fo refign'd,
With his celeftial Spirit ftrengthen thee,
To bear thy ficknefs with a patient mind.

30 May

30 May he, who fent an angel from above
 To foothe, near Cedron's ftream, his Son's diftrefs,
 Another fend, out of his wondrous love,
 To comfort thee, and make thy fuff'rings lefs.

31 Thou didft in health a good example fhow,
 How we may lead lives good and pious here;
 Give us the like again, to teach us how
 We may, with refignation, ficknefs bear.

32 Permit, thy gracious Sire, thy wounds to drefs,
 Permit him from thy flefh, the thorn to pluck,
 Permit him, the foul matter to exprefs,
 To cleanfe the fore, and thence the poifon fuck.

33 Permit thy Saviour to extract the fting—
 The ferpent's deadly fting, that galls thy heel,
 Left to thy heart the venom thence fhou'd fpring,
 And thy poor foul the fmart forever feel.

34 God does for thee a mighty care exprefs,
 And better thou fhou'dft bear, than moft, the pain:
 He purges thee, at prefent, through diftrefs,
 That thou may'ft everlafting health obtain.

35 God makes thee fit, whilft thou on earth doft ftay,
 Thy part in the celeftial fcenes to bear;
 He cleanfes all the filthinefs away,
 Which might, 'twixt thee and heaven, interfere.

36 Thou art a ftone, for facred works defign'd,
 Thou muft be pare'd by God's own hammer, clean,
 Thou muft be rule'd, and levell'd to his mind,
 If thou in heaven to refide doft mean.

37 Thou art, as corn, intended for the Lord,
 And muft be foundly thrafh'd, whilft thou art here;
 Thy chaff too muft be clear'd, e'er at the board
 Of Chrift above, 'tis fit thou fhou'dft appear.

38 Much fweetnefs, for the time already paft,
 Thou haft receiv'd, e'er firft thou drew'ft thy breath,
 Of bitternefs thou muft fome portion tafte
 Again, like thy Redeemer, e'er thy death.

39 Take

39 Take thou a fip of that imbitter'd cup
   Which Chrift, before thee, to the water quafft.;
   Our bleffed Mafter freely drank it up;
   And muft not each difciple take a draught?

40 Remember thou, that Chrift did undergo,
   For our tranfgreffions here, much greater pain,
   A greater weight of agony, and woe:
   Let us a little, in our turn, fuftain.

41 Reflect that there is fcarce a faint above,
   Though now imparadife'd amongft the bleft,
   Who did not a much greater fuff'rer prove:
   And thou muft fuffer too, like all the reft.

42 Abel, was murder'd by his brother Cain,
   Jofeph, was fold to Egypt for a flave,
   Ifaiah, with a wooden faw was flain,
   E'er they were fuffer'd feats in heav'n to have,

43 Saint Stephen by the Jews was ftone'd to death,
   Saint Lawrence broil'd alive in dreadful pain,
   Saint James was, by a fpear, deprive'd of breath,
   E'er they were fuffer'd heaven to obtain.

44 Saint Peter was, unto a crofs, made faft,
   Saint Bart'lomew was foully flay'd alive,
   Saint John was to a boiling caldron caft,
   E'er they to God were fuffer'd to arrive.

45 There never was a man, who fojourn'd here,
   And to the faith of Jefus gave affent,
   But did fome evil or chaftifement bear,
   Before he to the joys of heaven went.

46 From Egypt none to Canaan found the road,
   But through the fea, or through the mount of fire;
   No man in heaven ever made abode,
   Who did not to the narrow gate afpire.

47 The crofs thou for a certainty muft bear,
   E'er thou the crown triumphal canft obtain:
   In all my days; I never yet did hear
   That one the crown, without the crofs, cou'd gain.

48 Like

48 Like a good foldier, bear about thy crofs,
   And thou fhalt doubtlefsly the crown obtain :
   With Jefus fuffer ev'ry pain and lofs,
   And thou fhalt afterwards with Jefus reign.

49 Expect not heaven, whilft thou'rt here below,
   Expect not happinefs, whilft yet alive,
   Expect not, never-ceafing health to know,
   Until to paradife thou fhalt arrive.

50 No fweet, without a bitter, e'er was known,
   No perfect joy, without a dafh of woe,
   Without the crofs, none e'er receiv'd the crown,
   Without fome grief, none e'er to blifs did go.

51 No Patriarch, Prophet, Martyr, ever yet,
   No, nor Apoftle, was allow'd to go
   From this our globe, before he paid this debt—
   Not even Chrift, before he fuffer'd woe.

52 Then do not you, dear Sir, expect to find,
   What none on earth did ever find before ;
   But labour all you can, with patient mind,
   To bear the load your bleffed Saviour bore.

53 Remember Chrift endure'd a thoufand times
   More pain, than thou doft at the prefent bear,
   That on the crofs he fuffer'd for thy crimes ;
   And thou'lt forget thy pains, howe'er fevere.

54 Believe me therefore—it was out of love,
   That Chrift did thee with this difeafe correct,
   And that thou mighteft, to conviction, prove
   Thereby, that thou art one of his elect.

55 Remember thou that ev'ry thing is found
   To turn out to the true believer's gain,
   Each crofs and lofs, and ev'ry fmarting wound,
   His adverfe ftate, and agonizing pain.

56 Remember likewife ftill, whilft thou haft breath,
   That nothing can the faithful foul remove,
   Nor lofs, nor crofs, nor the grim tyrant, Death,
   From his Creator's, and his Saviour's love.

57 May

57 May He, who rais'd his friend with mighty pow'r
To perfect health, from his sepulchral cell,
Thee also to thy former health restore,
And, from thy bed of sicknefs, make thee well.

58 May He, who spare'd the faithful patriarch's heir,
On Moriah's top from the up-lifted knife,
With similar indulgence kindly spare,
Yet many years, thy valuable life.

59 May He, who formerly his prophet sent
To heal the pious Hezekiah's sore,
Now send an angel with the same intent,
Who may Sir Lewis Manfel's health restore !

REASONS to perfuade the Sick to be patient.

1 DID it not answer some benign intent
To mortify the flesh, and mend the mind,
The Sire of mercies never wou'd have sent
Diseafe, on any of our favour'd kind.

2 God, doubtlefs, faw the danger of thy foul
O'erwhelm'd with fins of an enormous fize,
And that He ne'er cou'd have preserv'd it whole,
Did He not by diseafe those fins chaftize.

3 Had it not been for that imbitter'd bowl,
Which the inveterate diseafe o'ercame,
Thy unrepentant, unforgiven foul
Muft have been doom'd to everlafting flame.

4 By corp'ral fmart and agonizing pain,
God faves the foul, and to it's Saviour leads;
Where flowing blifs and endlefs joys remain
For him, who reformation's footfteps treads.

5 Through ficknefs, 'tis that God impels the heart,
The facred aid of Jefus to defire,
And gives falvation to the nobler part,
Left it fhou'd go to hell's tremendous fire.

6 By

6 By some short transient fits He oft restrains
  The sons of men from everlasting dole,
  And by, inflicting on them grievous pains,
  He mortifies the flesh, to save the soul.

7 Not only pain, but punishment severe,
  Thy sins have merited, and vengeance dire :
  Thy sickness then with refignation bear ;
  Since it, in love, was sent thee by thy Sire.

8 Thy neck, for thy bad life, He might have bow'd,
  And hurl'd thee headlong to the abyss of hell,
  (Not the least time for penitence allow'd!)
  Amongst the damn'd in penal fire to dwell.

9 Then thank him for the terrors He employ'd,
  And the correction He so kindly sent :
  Since He might utterly have thee destroy'd,
  Or in Gehenna's gloomy prison pent.

10 Had God so will'd, thou mightest have been seize'd
  And sore tormented, at the foe's command ;
  Whereas He now most graciously is please'd,
  To punish thee with a paternal hand.

11 The Lord does not chastize thee—like a foe,
  Who joys to see his enemy undone,
  But with most mild indulgence treats thee so,
  As a fond sire wou'd treat a fav'rite son.

12 Though thou art roughly-handled by thy God,
  Yet still the humbled penitent he loves ;
  Each gentle stroke of his correcting rod,
  An antidote, or healing plaster, proves.

13 Thy God, whose goodness none can e'er express,
  And thy celestial Sire, so wisely-kind !
  Will not inflict diseases, or distress,
  Which are not wholly for thy good design'd.

14 God does thy pain, thy frame, thy pow'rs of mind,
  Thy temper, and thy constitution know :
  A cross, that suits thy nature, thou shalt find ;
  No load, above thy strength, He'll on thee throw.

15 Tho'

15 Tho' aloes is full bitter to the taste,
   Yet many' a man has it preserv'd from death;
   So, though all ails are grievous, while they last,
   Yet oft they keep us from the pit beneath.

16 Some thousands now in fell Gehenna groan,
   Who wou'd endure a greater load of pain,
   And there for years unnumber'd make their moan,
   Cou'd they, then, hope redemption to obtain.

17 It is a certain token of God's love,
   By some disease to feel his weighty hand,
   Which may prepare us for the realms above,
   E'er we before his dread tribunal stand.

18 Disease is but a whip, to scourge design'd,
   Not a sharp sword, ordain'd to murder thee,
   'Tis a keen goad, to wake the torpid mind,
   And not an ax, to fell the growing tree.

19 It is a flail, thy chaffy corn to thresh,
   A fan, to purge the floor, thou didst neglect,
   A furnace 'tis, to purify thy flesh,
   An iron rod thy errors to correct,

20 Honey is not, for a full stomach, good,
   Nor, for ungodly men, a prosp'rous way,
   Wine, for the fev'rish, is no proper food,
   Nor is health good, for those that disobey.

21 Thou hast not near so great a share of pain,
   As many of thy brethren have endure'd,
   Who now in the celestial seats remain,
   The former pass'd, from future woes secure'd.

22 Poor Lazarus endure'd more pungent woe,
   And Job with heavier troubles was oppreft,
   (E'en Christ himself did greater undergo)
   But they in endless bliss at present rest.

23 If thou'lt be therefore patient in distress,
   God will indulge thee this peculiar grace:
   " He'll either make thy pains and troubles less,
   " Or else receive thee to his holy place."

A com-

A comfortable CONFERENCE between a pious sick Man and his Soul, against the Fear of Death.

1 MY coward soul, why dost thou dread
    To thy Redeemer Christ to go,
Who his heart's blood so freely shed,
To save thee from the insulting foe?

2 Why dost thou fear to try that coast,
Where Christ in endless bliss resides
With the great Sire, and th' Holy Ghost,
And all the glorious saints besides?

3 My Saviour, my Redeemer's gone
Before me to that sacred place.
Lord, draw thy member to thy throne,
And quicken thou my ling'ring pace!

4 Cheer up thy spirits—raise thy head—
Why wilt thou live in so much fear?
Behold thy Saviour's bloody bed,
There, now is nothing frightful there.

5 See, O my soul, thy Saviour come!
Thy Guardian, thy Protector see!
See there thy pardon! see thy home!
See there the joys prepare'd for thee!

6 Look not at sin, avert thy head
Lo! for thy sins the Lambkin bleeds!
Thy aweful Judge's looks ne'er dread,
Thy cause his darling Jesus pleads.

7 Fear not the jaundice-visage'd king,
Death can do nothing, but remove
(Since Christ has pluck'd away his sting)
Thee hence, unto the realms above.

8 Boldly the fiend's assaults despise,
Since angels night and day attend,
And Christ, the Lamb with seven eyes,
Thy soul each moment to defend.

9 The

9 The gloomy grave no longer dread,
  Where Jefus, thy Redeemer, lay,
  Who warm'd for all that clay-cold bed,
  Until their refurrection-day.

10 The pains of hell no longer mind,
  'Tis Chrift, that keeps the key of fate;
  'Tis Chrift, the Saviour of mankind,
  Of death and hell, who guards the gate.

11 Cheer up thy fpirits, raife thy head,
  Why wilt thou live in fo much fear?
  Behold thy Saviour's bloody bed,
  There now is nothing frightful there!

12 Take comfort, rear thy downcaft eyes,
  Above this earthly ball afpire,
  Obferve the heavens, Jefus' prize!
  The heav'ns, of which he made thee heir!

13 See there thy throne! fee there thy crown!
  Thy palm weave'd wreath! thy white array!
  (Which Jefus bought and made thy own)
  Above in the bright realms of day.

14 See Chrift, and all the' angelic quire——
  See all the faints, and juft, above——
  Who long to fee thy foul afpire,
  And fold thee in their arms of love.

15 Prepare thy lyre, thy viol bring——
  Prepare thy hymns and facred lays,
  That thou above may'ft boldly fing
  A ftrain, to thy Redeemer's praife.

16 Then for thy diffolution cry,
  And beg to go to Chrift, thy fpoufe,
  That thou may'ft mount above the fky,
  Releas'd from this vile prifon-houfe:

17 Where God, and all the' angelic train,
  The Son, and ev'ry faint of His,
  Where his Apoftles with him reign
  In honour, joy, and endlefs blifs!

A a   18 Where.

18 Where, there's no ficknefs, grief, or pain,
Where, there's no forrow nor annoy,
Where neither Death nor fadnefs reign,
But everlafting blifs and joy.

19 Long then with rapid flight to move
To the bright manfions of the bleft,
Where thy Redeemer dwells above,
And has prepare'd his nuptial feaft.

20 But, O! take proper care to wear
Thy gorgeous jewels on thy breaft,
That thou before him may'ft appear
In all thy bridal fine'ry dreft.

21 In David's well, or the Lamb's gore,
In tears of real penitence,
Cleanfe all thy filth, and wafh thee o'er,
In peace, true faith, and innocence.

22 Fill thou thy lamp with oil, and light
Thy candle, to avoid furprize,
Wake, watch, and pray, the live-long night,
And, 'till Chrift comes, ne'er clofe thine eyes.

23 Awake, expect with fleeplefs eye
The hour, wherein thy fpoufe will come,
And, like the hart, ne'er ceafe to cry,
'Till Chrift has made thy breaft his home.

24 Say unto him—" 'Tis time to move,"
Say—" Come, O Lord, in hafte to me !"
Say—" Come, O Chrift, my only love!
" O come, and draw my foul to thee!"

25 Into thy hand with pleafing thought
My foul, O gracious Lord! I give:
For, with a price, thou haft me bought ;
Then to thy mercy me receive!

Another

Another CONFERENCE between the devout Sick Man, and his Soul.

1 TELL me, my foul, and in good earneſt tell,
  Why doſt thou ſeem afraid to Chriſt to go,
With him and his celeſtial hoſt to dwell,
  From this vile Vale of miſery and woe?

2 'Tis hard that thou art force'd to leave thy wife,
  Thy children, family, and ſocial train,
Lands, houſes, cattle, goods, here in this life,
  Never to have a ſight of them again.

3 Howe'er take comfort, for thou ſhalt above
  Much greater wealth, and richer treaſures boaſt,
Thou firmer friends and comrades there ſhalt prove,
  In Jeſus Chriſt, and his angelic hoſt:

4 And if thy Children ſhall the' Almighty fear,
  And all their days in righteouſneſs employ,
Thou ſhalt thyſelf again behold them there,
  In endleſs glory, and in endleſs joy.

5 Inſtead of friends and comrades, thou above
  Shalt have the ſaints and the ſeraphic train,
To treat thee with the moſt endearing love;
  Thy children too ſhall pleaſe thee, there, again.

6 Thy wife, thy children, and thy family,
  Leave thou to God—and on his aid depend,
Who plainly has profeſs'd himſelf to be
  The Orphan's father, and the Widow's friend.

7 Prize not thy riches, nor thy paltry ſtore,
  With greater wealth thou ſhalt above be bleſs'd,
Than Alexander ever own'd—nay, more
  Than any conqueror on earth poſſeſs'd.

8 Ne'er mind thy houſe, though it a palace were,
  In heav'n, each houſe is built by art divine,
The walls are made of pearl and topaz, there,
  And brighter than the cleareſt mirror ſhine.

9 Thy orchards, fields, and vineyards never mind;
  Terreſtrial riches ne'er too-highly prize,
  Thou richer lands, and finer fruits ſhalt find,
  And gardens much more fair in paradiſe.

10 On gold and ſilver lay no ſtreſs at all,
   For gold in heav'n is ſtrew'd beneath thy feet,
   There pearls and gems erect each gorgeous wall,
   And golden ingots pave each glitte'ring ſtreet.

11 Make no account of office, or of trade,
   In heaven various offices are found,
   The meaneſt, there, God's miniſter is made,
   The meaneſt, there, a mighty king is crown'd.

12 Mind not gay ornaments, nor veſtments fine,
   In paradiſe their garments all are white,
   Thy own ſhall there with dazzling luſtre ſhine,
   Than the meridian ſun itſelf more bright.

13 Of meat, which leaves thee hungry, never think,
   The tree of Life itſelf in Eden grows,
   Manna's their food—the fount of Life, their drink,
   And there no end the' eternal banquet knows.

14 Make no account of muſic's pleaſing ſound,
   Such pleaſures oft are cloſe-purſue'd by pain;
   True joys in paradiſe alone are found——
   Such joys as to eternity remain.

15 For any thing thou now enjoy'ſt, ne'er care,
   But with the utmoſt application ſtrive,
   Thyſelf, for thy removal, to prepare,
   That thou in endleſs joys with Chriſt may'ſt live:

16 Where more true eaſe, and pleaſures more refin'd,
   For thy acceptance are long ſince prepare'd,
   Than can be wiſh'd by the moſt craving mind,
   Or by the moſt loquacious tongue declare'd.

17 Go therefore, and to Chriſt with pleaſure cleave—
   To Chriſt, thy Chief, thy Lord and Maſter too:
   The world, and all its low enjoyments leave,
   Thy parents dear—that thou to Chriſt may'ſt go.

18 Inſtead

18 Inftead of the precarious things below,
    Which he has only lent thee at the beft,
    Thou fhalt have goods which fhall no change e'er know,
    To be by thee eternally poffeft.

19 Thou fhalt, without diforder, health enjoy,
    Thou fhalt, without anxiety, have eafe,
    Thou fhalt have happinefs, without annoy,
    Thou fhalt, without allay, have perfect peace.

20 No wound, no woe, no pain, fhall vex thee there,
    No hunger, thirft, nor trouble, fhalt thou know,
    No grief, no loud lament, no figh, no tear,
    Shall ever plague thee more—nor any foe :

21 But thou fhalt live with endlefs pleafure crown'd,
    And of eternal happinefs poffefs'd,
    With myriads of his angels guarded round,
    To praife thy gracious God among the blefs'd.

22 There fhalt thou fit upon a fplendid feat,
    The praifes of the bleffed Lamb to fing,
    And high-voice'd Hallelujahs to repeat,
    Unto thy merciful and glorious King.

23 Who wou'd not now the world and all it's woe,
    And all it's riches, quit—that he might cleave
    To his Redeemer, and to heaven go;
    Provided that the' Almighty gave him leave ?

24 Thine eyes, may thy Creator open wide,
    The kingdom of thy guardian Chrift to fee,
    May God his Spirit give, thy fteps to guide,
    Prepare thyfelf for fuch felicity.

A Short Differtation againft the fear of Death, and concerning the Benefit that accrues from a righteous Death.

1   **A**Las! that man did thoroughly but know,
      What gifts from Death unto the godly flow!
He ne'er wou'd dread his prefence, but rejoice,
And for his coming cry with earneft voice !

         2 Death

2 Death puts an end to all this motley scene,
Our miseries, and ev'ry act unclean,
And steers the saints, through a tempestuous sea,
Unto the haven, where they wish to be.

3 Death, after all our troubles makes our beds,
That we thereon may lay our weary'd heads,
And gives us ease and happiness at last,
When all our straits and grievances are past.

4 Death buries all our errors in the grave,
Ev'ry disorder, ev'ry pain we have,
So that no sort of error, or disease,
Shall any more our minds and bodies seize.

5 Death often takes the pious soul away,
Lest he shou'd live until the fatal day,
When woes shall overwhelm his native place,
And dire calamities attack his race.

6 Death snatches off the simple, from among
The dang'rous converse of the sinful throng,
Lest they to vice shou'd prompt, and spur them on,
To do the things they ought not to have done.

7 Death will the righteous of the rags divest——
The filthy rags, wherein they here were drest,
And clothe them in a vesture loose and gay,
Salvation's robes, and ever-bright array !

8 Death sets at liberty the joyous soul
From a close dungeon, dreary, dark, and foul,
That it may see the Godhead's glorious light,
And worship him, in holiness, aright.

9 Death does the soul of man at once unbind
From the vile clay, to which it here is join'd,
And in a moment does to Christ unite,
Her lovely consort in the realms of light.

10 Death does the just to the bright seats above,
Amongst the angels of the Lord remove,
From this old house, whose shatter'd roof we dread,
Lest it shou'd fall each moment on our head.

11 Death

11 Death leads them out of Sodom's fatal plain,
To the hill country, from the fie'ry rain,
And brings the pious (from all terrors free)
From Egypt, to the land of liberty.

12 Death, from this world the fouls of men conveys,
That round their brows with ever-beaming rays
The crown may shine, which, thro' much pain and woe,
Chrift bought for all, who ferve him well below.

13 The good, from all their troubles, he relieves,
Their num'rous woes, and miferable lives,
To joy and glory points the certain road,
Where real pleafure makes her fix'd abode.

14 What Chriftian then fhou'd be of Death afraid,
Who lends to man fo readily his aid,
Who bears him fafe through trouble's thorny ways,
And to the palace of his God conveys ?

15 Let thou the Pagan, to each virtue dead,
Let thou the Turk, grim Death's approaches dread:
But let not the true Chriftian be in pain
To pafs through Death, a glorious crown to gain.

16 A day of pardon, and of jubilee,
A day, that from all forrow fets us free,
A day, that from thofe prifon-cells beneath
Unchains our fouls, is this fame day of Death.

17 The day of Death, (we fhou'd that reafon mind)
Is that, whereon we are to Jefus join'd :
We therefore, on it, fhou'd be blithe and gay;
It is our feaft, our coronation-day.

18 It is the day, that ends our mortal race,
The day, that takes us from this woe-fraught place,
The day, that fully pays us all our hire,
The day, that finifhes our whole career.

19 The day, that brings us to the bright abode
Of our Redeemer, the belove'd of God,
And clothes each Chriftian in his beft array,
His robes and crown—fuch is the happy day !

A Prayer.

A PRAYER, to direct a Sick Man what things are moſt neceſſary for him to aſk, and to meditate upon, in his illneſs.

1 THou God of pity, ſtay this ſore diſeaſe!
  Thou God of mercy, give thy ſervant eaſe!
Thou beſt of all phyſicians, make me whole!
Thou Son of God, give comfort to my ſoul!

2 Snatch me from hell's dun gloom to open day,
Remove all blindneſs from my mind away,
(So that I ſoon may ſee my dange'rous ſtate,)
And my pain'd conſcience's keen pangs abate!

3 Make me, like David, heartily repent——
Make me, like Magdalene, my crimes lament ——
Make me, like Nineveh, my errors own,
And in the duſt my ſinful ſtate bemoan!

4 Make me thy pardon earneſtly implore,
Like king Manaſſes, when diſtreſs'd of yore,
Make me, like Peter, for forgiveneſs cry,
Make me, like Him, repent before I die!

5 Make me believe my pardon is procure'd,
Seal'd, and beyond the reach of fate ſecure'd,
And that my ſoul is rinſed in the flood
Of thy moſt precious, and all-cleanſing blood!

6 Make me, like Lazarus, in ſilence bear
My ſickneſs and my pain, howe'er ſevere,
My confidence, in thee, O make me place,
Like patient Job, however bad my caſe!

7 Make me deliv'rance ſeek, O Lord! from thee,
And thee alone, in all my miſery,
Like good Elijah, when of old diſtreſt,
In ſuch a manner as to thee ſeems beſt.

8 Make me, like Hezekiah, caſt aſide
This world's vain pomp, and all it's tinſel pride,
And turn, like Him, unto the wall my face,
That I in thee alone my truſt may place!

9 O, make

9 O make me think on that tremendous day,
When I before thee my accounts muſt lay,
For ev'ry idle word, and ev'ry crime;
Unleſs I can renounce them all in time.

10 O make me to the Goſpel lend an ear,
And to the promiſes recorded there !
O, make me graſp thoſe promiſes divine
With Faith's ſtrong gripe, and make them ever mine!

11 Make me reflect upon the life above,
To which we ſhortly ſhall from this remove,
Where, for thy ſaints, eternal joys remain——
Joys, unalloy'd by ſickneſs, or by pain.

12 Make me renounce the world and it's deceits,
It's pompous pageantries and gilded baits;
Nor let me idly loiter on the road,
But haſte to thee, my Saviour, and my God !

13 Make me, O Lord ! without the leaſt delay,
My ſoul and body on thy altar lay,
And earneſtly, until my lateſt hour,
Thy mercy and thy patronage implore.

An excellent Consolation to the ſad Soul againſt Deſpair.

1 IF thou canſt but repent, why ſhou'dſt thou dread
Thy ſins, however numerous and foul ?
Since Chriſt for them was crucify'd, 'till dead——
And freely ſuffer'd to preſerve thy ſoul ?

2 Why wilt thou fear thy Judge's final doom,
Since Chriſt will as thy advocate appear ?
Thy Judge's ſon has ſuffer'd in thy room;
Death and damnation, why then ſhou'dſt thou fear ?

3 Not one ſhall be found guilty in the end,
Who here in Chriſt a lively faith retains;
But ſhall on his removal hence aſcend
From death to life, and Eden's bliſsful plains.

4 Be

4 Be ftill then, O my foul! nor filence break,
Thy gracious God from death will fet thee free:
For who can the condemning fentence fpeak,
Since Chrift was nail'd unto the crofs for thee.

5 Chrift in his blood will wafh thy fins away,
And bleach thee whiter than the driven fnow——
Though they do now a fcarlet hue difplay,
Yet Chrift fhall make them white as ermine fhow.

6 The fun can penetrate the thickeft cloud,
And foap can fcour the fouleft garments bright—
Chrift's merits thy enormous fins can fhrowd,
His blood can make thee as the lily white.

7 God Peter's fears, and David's lufts forgave,
The Prodigal's excefs and youthful heat,
And king Manaffes', tho' once fin's mere flave:
He thine can pardon, howfoever great.

8 Take comfort then——thy fainty fpirits raife——
The Son of God was fix'd unto the tree
For thy tranfgreffions, and unrighteous ways;
And, for his fake, thou fhalt forgiven be.

An earneft PRAYER for Pardon of Sins.

1 O Lord, my God! who formedft me of nought!
My Saviour, who from death his fervant bought!
O Holy Ghoft! O Trinity benign!
Preferve my foul, and cancel all my fin!

2 For Jefu's fake, who to redeem me deign'd,
And whofe each act thy approbation gain'd,
Forgive me, if in ought I've been remifs——
Forgive me all that I have done amifs.

3 Wafh in his blood my filthinefs away——
Low in his fepulchre my vices lay——
Veil with his righteoufnefs my errors foul,
And pardon all the' offences of my foul.

4 Array

4 Array me in the alb of righteoufnefs,
And in thy glorious nuptial-garments drefs;
So that I always well-prepare'd may be,
And in trim garb to come, O Chrift, to thee!

5 Around my dwelling, place thy guardian hoft,
Nor let the Devil of my conqueft boaft!
Save me, O fave me, from the treach'rous fiend,
Nor fuffer him, O Chrift, my foul to rend.

6 When to thy dread tribunal I fhall come,
There to receive the' irrevocable doom,
For Jefu's fake my precious foul preferve,
And give me not the fentence I deferve!

7 Inftead of mine, Chrift's full obedience take,
And let his death, for me atonement make;
Though for my fins, He was condemn'd to die,
Yet for his fake, let me damnation fly!

8 Death I've deferv'd, and Tophet's fcenes of woe——
Deferv'd the doom, hypocrify fhall know——
Yet give me not, O God! what I've deferv'd,
But by Chrift's merits let me be preferv'd.

9 He did, for me, thy facred law fulfil——
He perfectly, for me, perform'd thy will——
He die'd upon the crofs, that I might live——
Then, for his fake, my fumlefs fins forgive.

10 No juftice I, nor holinefs, can boaft,
My purity and my perfection loft!
No one can fuccour, help, or ranfom give,
But what from thee, my Saviour! I receive.

11 Chrift is my comfort——Chrift's my folace fure—
Chrift is my hope, in all that I endure——
Chrift's my affiftance, when Death's terrors come—
Chrift's my protector, in the day of doom!

12 Chrift a moft ignominious death did die,
That He, for me, eternal life might buy:
In pity of his painful agonies
Conduct my foul, O God! to paradife!

13 God

13 God! lend an ear, my prayers to receive——
God! for my comfort, thy bleſt Spirit give——
God! caſt an eye of pity on my grief——
And grant me, from thy lenient hand, relief.

14 O Lamb of God, my ſoul's diſeaſes heal!
My wounded conſcience's firm pardon ſeal!
Deep in the grave let all my faults remain,
And let them never, never, riſe again!

15 Thy rig'rous Juſtice, O my God! I fear;
For how can I thy fierce diſpleaſure bear?
My errors, ſelf-condemn'd, I loudly blame,
Do thou the tempeſt of my conſcience calm.

16 O, let thy guiltleſs death, my Saviour! come
Betwixt me, and the dreadful day of doom!
Place thy obedience, like a ſhield, between
Thy Father's Juſtice, and my filthy ſin.

17 Let thine own blood aſſuage the vengeful ire
Of thy too-juſtly irritated Sire——
Let thine own blood his furious wrath appeaſe,
That all the ſorrows of my ſoul may ceaſe!

18 I'm weak, O Chriſt! do thou my ſtrength increaſe,
I'm ſick and faint—O, heal the dire diſeaſe!
Heavy and ſad, I ſink oppreſs'd with fear,
Confirm my faith, my fainting ſpirits cheer!

19 Thou God of comfort, all my pains appeaſe,
Thou Sire of mercy, give me preſent eaſe;
Phyſician of the world, aſſuage my grief,
And ſend me, Jeſus, Son of God, relief!

20 Say, O my God! and ſay it o'er again——
Say to my ſoul, " E'er long thou ſhalt remain
" With me in Paradiſe, and ſoon ſhalt reſt
" Among my ſaints, with endleſs pleaſures bleſt."

21 The' aſſaults of Satan, O my Chriſt! repel;
And ſave me from the yawning jaws of hell:
My ſinking ſoul with thy free Spirit buoy,
And lead me to the realms of deathleſs joy!

22 O

22 O, Lamb of God, with all my fins difpenfe !
O, make my confcience void of all offence !
O, Lamb of God, at my laft hour attend,
And to thy mercy take me in the end !

23 O Chrift, my Shepherd, from the lion keep
My foul, and from his paws preferve thy fheep,
For which, O Jefus, thou haft paid full dear,
And me to heav'n amongft thy angels bear !

24 Receive my foul, O my Protector dear !
Receive my foul, 'tis time, unto thy care !
For long enough I've liv'd, and linger'd here ;
I am not better than my fathers were.

25 I fain would from thefe chains of flefh get loofe,
And fly, O Chrift, to thee, my glorious fpoufe !
Draw me, fweet Jefus ! for the time is come,
(If 'tis thy will) to thy celeftial home.

26 Unto thy hands, I freely recommend
My Spirit, O my God !—let no one rend
The charge from thence, or bear it, as his prey,
In triumph from thy mighty hands away !

27 O Chrift, my Shepherd ! from the lion keep
My foul, (and from his paw preferve thy fheep).
Who daily feeks thy fervant to o'erpow'r,
And, in its weaknefs, wou'd my foul devour.

28 This is the very time, when he does feek
To catch his prey—I mean, whilft I am weak ;
Support me then, O Lord, that I may guard
The precious prize, nor lofe the rich reward !

29 Plant in my breaft the Spirit of thy grace,
Around my foul a guard of angels place,
Array me with thy glorious panoply,
Nor let the fiend a triumph boaft o'er me !

30 Enable me, my courfe run out, to reft,
And make my lateft hour to be the beft.
On thee, O Lord ! with firmnefs I rely ;
O take my foul to heaven, when I die !

31 Appeafe

31 Appeafe my pain, affuage it's raging fmart,
Obferve my grief, and eafe my troubled hearc,
Trim my expiring lamp, my woes abate,
Receive my foul——I for thy mercy wait.

32 Say to my foul, that thou, O God of love!
Haft bought for me the blifsful feats above—
Thy precious blood, and an unnumber'd hoft
Of pungent forrows, the vaft price they coft.

A fhort PRAYER, for a devout Perfon to ufe at his laft Hour.

1 DEign now, O Lord! thy fervant to releafe,
And from this prifon let me part in peace ;
Yet, e'er I'm from th' incumb'ring flefh fet free,
Let my bleft eyes thy great falvation fee!

2 Come is the day! come is the dreadful hour!
Come is the time, determin'd by thy pow'r!
Come is the moment! come the very end,
And to efcape it, I can ne'er pretend!

3 The race is ended, which I was to run,
The laft of all my days is almoft done—
The conflict's o'er—I juft have reach'd the goal :
Receive, O Lord!——receive to thee, my foul'

4 Like thy firft martyr, in the pangs of death,
To thee, O Chrift! my fpirit I bequeath :
Come then, come quickly, O my Saviour-God,
And take me with thee to thy bleft abode !

A fhort MEDITATION on Life and Death.

1 THE fooner a good Chriftian dies,
The fooner he receives the prize :
The longer he on earth fhall be,
The longer e'er he God fhall fee.

2 The longer one keeps from the grave,
  The longer reck'ning he muſt have :
  The leſs his time is here below,
  The leſs account he'll have to ſhow.

The Unhappy State of the UNGODLY, after Death.

1 YOU of each ſex and age, draw near,
     And to my ſad Complaint give ear,
  Who vice, unto the laſt obey'd,
  But now beneath the pall am laid.

2 As you are now, I once have been,
  Happy and pleas'd among my kin:
  Now poor and naked I appear,
  Extended on the ſolemn bier.

3 When worldly wealth, the moſt I ſought,
  And when of Death, the leaſt I thought,
  Death came unlook'd for with his dart,
  And pierce'd me to the very heart.

4 When fortune favour'd ev'ry deed,
  And all my aims uſe'd to ſucceed,
  The ice broke ſhort beneath my feet,
  And down I tumbled to the pit.

5 When ruddy health my body grace'd,
  And ev'ry nerve with ſtrength was brace'd,
  To pieces fell this brittle frame,
  Like glaſs, when death once near me came.

6 I, gold and ſilver once poſſeſs'd,
  And was with lands and houſes bleſs'd;
  But now I can't one farthing find
  Of all the wealth I left behind.

7 I once in kinsfolks did abound,
  Wife, children, ſervants, friends, I own'd;
  But now with none can I converſe,
  Beſides pale Death, within the hearſe.

S I

8 I then, companions always had
  In all my ways, however bad;
  But now not any one will come
  To anfwer for me at my doom.

9 The fatal ftroke, which now I rue,
  Will fhortly come to each of you,
  Be then prepare'd, before you die,
  You fhall be warn'd no more than I.

10 Chrift, and the minifters of heaven,
  To all have proper notice given,
  And yet how many millions die,
  Who heed their words no more than I?

11 I long have ran a vary'd round
  Of fins, which now my confcience wound:
  But fharper 'tis, e'en than a fword,
  To have defpife'd God's holy word.

12 Stiffneck'd, and headftrong as an afs,
  And heedlefs of God's laws, I was,
  Whate'er Chrift, or his fervants, fpake,
  No notice of it wou'd I take.

13 With rakehell Publicans, or worfe,
  Rather than priefts I'd ftill difcourfe,
  Tho' thefe debauch'd and fpoil'd me quite,
  And thofe wou'd fain direct me right.

14 Whole months I'd rather gaily fpend
  In taverns with a female friend,
  Than to my God with Chriftian pray,
  Or in his temple pafs a day.

15 More hours I pafs'd in taverns then
  With fwine---I mean with drunken men,
  Than with the fons of light I fpent;
  For which full oft I now repent,

16 The mirth, that hardly holds a day,
  And, e'er fcarce tafted, fleets away,
  I chofe before that perfect joy,
  Which always lafts, and ne'er can cloy.

17 Earth

17 Earth, ſtones, braſs, lead, I ſtill preferr'd,
My ſty, my ſtud, my lowing herd,
Before the charms of paradiſe,
Or any bliſs God cou'd deviſe.

18 My body to my ſoul I ſtill
Preferr'd—to virtue, ev'ry ill——
This world to heav'n—wrong to right—
My guts, to God——and gloom, to light.

19 But now I'm ſorry, from my ſoul,
That I was e'er ſo much a fool,
And ev'ry fibre quakes for fear,
E'er I before my Judge appear.

20 My body now to rot is gone,
For all the crimes that I have done ;
Whilſt my ſad ſoul the ſkies muſt mount,
For all my follies to account.

21 My Saviour calls me by my name,
And I muſt anſwer to the ſame :
To make my reck'ning I muſt go,
However difficult to do !

22 Ah me ! what an unnumber'd ſum
Of ſins my conſcience overcome——
Sins into which I madly ran,
In ſpite of God, in ſpite of man ?

23 What joy dilates the Devil's breaſt,
Wide as the eaſt is from the weſt !
As he relates, before my face,
How oft I've ſinn'd—the time and place.

24 Of what a roll the Fiend's poſſeſt,
Long as the eaſt is from the weſt !
By which inſtructed, he can ſhow
The ſins I've done—when, where, and how!

25 Ah me !——who is it, that I hear
Againſt me deadly witneſs bear,
But he who tempted me of yore
To liſten to his fatal lore ?

B b

26 In

26 In all the days that I have paſt,
   There's not a ſin but he does caſt
   Full in my face——woe's me the while,
   That I have led a life ſo vile !

27 He ſhews, alas, with too much truth !
   How fruitleſsly I ſpent my youth,
   In revelry alone employ'd,
   But of each Chriſtian virtue void.

28 He ſtoutly claims me, for my crimes,
   Since in my youth a thouſand times
   He won my ſoul ; and to my ſhame,
   God cannot but admit his claim.

29 He makes each vicious folly known
   I did, ſince into manhood grown,
   My drunken frolicks, am'rous fires,
   And all my looſe impure deſires.

30 He ſhews, how prone I was to rage,
   And all the foibles of old age !
   How much to gain and lies a ſlave !
   But, ah ! how thoughtleſs of the grave !

31 With open mouth, and earneſt ſtrife,
   He pleads that, in each ſtage of life,
   He won my ſoul——and, from a boy,
   That I have been in his employ.

32 With ſhameleſs, brazen, confidence,
   The ſcriptures wreſting to his ſenſe,
   That I am his, he boldly ſaith,
   For want of penitence and faith.

33 I deem'd, by ignorance miſled,
   That Chriſt for my tranſgreſſions bled,
   And that the Fiend no right cou'd claim
   O'er thoſe, who merely own'd his name.

34 But 'tis retorted by the Fiend,
   That this can never ſerve my end,
   Since Chriſt will not a ſoul receive,
   But ſuch as faithfully believe.

35 To this, he further dares to add,
  That I no faith, nor virtue, had,
  Nor any furer hopes of heaven,
  Than if I were a very heathen.

36 With eager rancour he'd fain fhow,
  That I have nought with Chrift to do ;
  Becaufe I heeded not his lore,
  Nor change'd my life, to my laft hour.

37 And that, tho' I his name receive'd,
  Baptize'd by Chriftians that believe'd, .
  My faith was no more to be prize'd
  Than their's, who never were baptize'd.

38 He fays (ah me, I hear him now !)
  That I no greater faith did fhow,
  Nor any works, furpaffing thofe
  Which pagans in their lives difclofe.

39 He fays, I never kept a word
  Of all the gofpel of our Lord,
  More than a Jew, who ne'er had grace
  Thofe facred doctrines to embrace.

40 He tells the' Almighty, whilft I hear,
  That he will any torment bear,
  If I, by rote, a fingle verfe
  Of all the fcripture can rehearfe.

41 He God himfelf prefumes to call,
  (With his attendant angels all)
  To witnefs, that he nothing fays
  But truth, of my ungodly ways.

42 My confcience with the load oppreft,
  Muft the diftafteful truth atteft,
  And forces me to own each fin,
  And fay,—" Juft fuch my life has been !"

43 He urges, that I've fore diftrefs'd
  The poor, and in all fhapes opprefs'd,
  Their lands and houfes force'd away,
  And made their little All, my prey.

44 He

44 He adds, that I have oft got drunk———
    Oft dally'd with fome common punk—
    A thoufand times the fabbath broke,
    And of religion made a joke.

45 He then infifts, with malice fell,
    That Chrift fhou'd fentence me to hell,
    To fuffer, for my vices paft,
    Such pains, as fhall for ever laft.

46 Oh, how my foul with horror fhakes,
    For fear of Satan's fierce attacks ?
    Left he, with his black crew, fhou'd come,
    And haul me to receive my doom.

47 Ah me ! how bitter to the tafte !
    O, how unpleafant at the laft !
    How much the object of my hate,
    The fin I lov'd fo well of late ?

48 How much am I afhame'd to hear
    The grand accufer publifh, there,
    A thoufand things, which here below
    I chofe not my beft friends fhould know ?

49 Cou'd I my option have———my foul
    Wou'd chufe in Hell's fierce flames to roll,
    Before it to God's bar wou'd mount,
    For it's mifdeeds, there to account !

50 Yet it muft at that bar appear,
    (There's no excufe for abfence there
    Of all it's works account to give,
    And it's juft fentence to receive.

51 To plead it's caufe, I no one hear———
    I fee no advocate appear———
    To give an anfwer none begins,
    Even for one of all my fins.

52 The facred rolls, I open'd fee,
    Before the dreadful Deity,
    Ready to bring thofe crimes to light,
    Which I had acted in the night.

53 Full

53 Full in my face, I hear them caft,
  My faithlefs life, and converfe paft,
  My carnal and intemp'rate mind,
  To each unchriftian vice inclin'd.

54 I hear the oaths, now number'd o'er,
  Which I, among vile drunkards, fwore—
  My breaches of the fabbath day,
  · With each loofe thing I ufe'd to fay.

55 My foul, a fullen filence keeps
  Meanwhile, and felf-convicted weeps,
  Or mute as is the fin-row'd fry,
  'Tis only fometimes heard to figh.

56 I hear Chrift iffue his commands
  To have me bound faft, feet and hands,
  And thrown down to the nether gloom,
  Where nought but woes and torments come !

57 I hear him, with exceffive dread,
  Pafs fentence on my guilty head,
  That I fhou'd to the' abyfs be toft,
  With Satan and his fable hoft !

58 I fee the Fiend himfelf take pains
  To bind me with the ftrongeft chains ;
  And, when my hands and feet are faft,
  I fee my foul to Tophet caft !

59 I hear it, there, for very pain,
  Cry out, and groan, and roar amain ;
  Thus headlong, without mercy, hurl'd
  To fuffer in the' infernal world !

60 I fee the' inferior Dev'lings, there,
  Each finner's foul and body tear,
  As hounds, that almoft famifh'd are,
  Through hunger tear a hind, or hare.

61 I hear my foul with piteous cry,
  And loud laments entreat to die;
  But yet, for all his piteous cries,
  Far from him Death indignant flies.

62 He

62 He lies in Hell's tremendous gloom,
 Where happiness and hope ne'er come,
 Half-ftarv'd he pines among the Fiends,
 Where his keen anguifh never ends.

63 There's nothing gives me fuch a blow,
 And finks my hopelefs heart fo low,
 As to reflect, that all this woe,
 Shall no ceffation ever know:

64 And that my body, there muft go,
 For want of proper caution too,
 And, with the foul like tortures tafte,
 When once the refurrection's paft:

65 And well do I deferve to dwell
 Among the fierceft flames in hell,
 As I entice'd it often times
 To all it's unrepented crimes.

66 There all the faithlefs folks fhall go,
 Who vile, immoral actions do,
 Who out of doors their houfes caft,
 And love, like fwine, a long repaft.

67 I therefore ev'ry one advife
 To fear the Lord, if he is wife,
 And always to obey him well,
 Left he fhou'd be condemn'd to hell.

68 Be fober, pious, and fincere,
 And worfhip God with Chriftian fear,
 If not——I will be bold to fay,
 That you'll be hurl'd to hell, one day.

69 Fear God———the fcripture often read,
 Nor from it turn afide your head———
 Like Chriftians live, if you wou'd fain
 The weighty crown of glory gain.

70 Faith, without works, no man can fee;
 No libertine a faint can be:
 True Chriftians ne'er caft faith away,
 They're Satan's flaves, who difobey.

71 In vain Religion you profefs,
 If works do not your faith exprefs,
 They can't exift, unlefs both meet,
 No more than fire can, without heat.

72 Juftice and honefty purfue,
 God will, to guile, no favour fhew;
 But heavy vengeance in the end,
 Shall on deceit and fraud defcend.

73 What gain they by their ill-place'd toil,
 Who rob the poor, and quite defpoil,
 If into hell they fhall be caft,
 For their injuftice, at the laft?

74 What boots it that you can fulfil
 Your lufts, and have, a while, your will;
 If, after gaining your defires,
 You're headlong hurl'd to penal fires?

75 What boots it your vile guts to fill,
 And wine and ale, whole nights to fwill;
 If for your love of ale and wine,
 You fhall, for thirft, in Tophet pine?

76 What fhall he gain, who falfehood fhows,
 His promife breaks, and quite undoes
 The neighb'ring poor?——if he muft go,
 For his deceit, to hell below.

77 Then let not Satan you deceive,
 Who does an ill, fhall ill receive:
 For each fhall reap, whate'er he fows,
 And each be paid for what he does.

78 As eafily our deadly foe
 To heaven may on doomfday go,
 As the debauch'd, lewd, infidel
 Efcape that day, the pains of hell.

79 God long will aim before the blow,
 His wrath is deadly-fure, tho' flow;
 For the long fcore and credit paft,
 He'll pay thee to the full at laft.

80 God

80 God for a while will condefcend
To fpare the worft that they may mend ;
But if at length they don't repent,
To hell they fhall in heaps be fent.

81 God give all grace, their lives to mend,
Before their day is at an end !
God make all ready hence to go,
Before` they feel Death's fatal blow !

The COMPLAINT and the ADVICE of DIVES, to his Five Brethren.

1 THE plaint and the advice of Dives hear,
From hell's hot furnace, and outrageous flame,
To his five brethren, and his kinsfolk dear,
Left they, like him, fhou'd come and feel the fame.

2 " Hear me, my brethren !——hear me, whilft I tell,
What happ'ned to me, fince I went below;
That warn'd thereby, you may efcape from hell,
From it's dire pains, and never-ending woe.

3 Fraternal love and pity bid me give
You this advice, 'tis evidently plain ;
Left you fhould here unweetingly arrive,
Whence no one ever could return again.

4 Did you but know what horrid things I hear——
Cou'd you of all my torments form a guefs !
You to my words wou'd lend a willing ear :
Left you yourfelves fhou'd feel the like diftrefs.

5 I'm well affure'd, did you but know my pains,
My woes, my anguifh, and my vaft difmay,
You wou'd not for an emperor's domains,
Willingly bear them for a fingle day.

6 No man, alas ! nor angel e'er can tell,
How great my woe ! how infinite my pain !
In the fierce fires and furious flames of hell;
Where I am doom'd for ever to remain.

7 I

7 I erſt in life was inſolently proud,
  (For fortune is eſteem'd and honour'd ſtill)
  And as I wou'd, I rule'd the trembling crowd,
  And did whate'er was pleaſing to my will.

8 To many it appear'd, that from my ſoul
  No God I fear'd, nor live'd of man in awe,
  More than the infidel and miſcreant foul,
  Whoſe inclinations are his only law.

9 But, Oh! myſelf I wretchedly deceiv'd,
  Fondly preſuming I ſhou'd never die,
  Or if I die'd, I fooliſhly believ'd,
  That in the grave I ſhou'd unqueſtion'd lie!

10 Though Moſes, and the Prophets all averr'd,
   My ſoul was not obnoxious to the grave;
   Yet, to their tenets, I my own preferr'd,
   And ſlighted all the counſels, that they gave.

11 Although they ſhew'd that, at God's aweful throne,
   Each muſt a reck'ning make, when he is dead,
   For ev'ry villainy, which he has done;
   Yet it cou'd never enter to my head.

12 But now in hell, I know it to my coſt,
   That all they taught was, to a tittle, true,
   And that the deathleſs ſoul, which I have loſt,
   Muſt in thoſe flames my foul offences rue.

13 I vainly thought, whilſt yet I drew my breath,
   There was no God, no manſions of the bleſt,
   No hell, nor Devil in the realms beneath,
   And that man die'd, as dies the brutal beaſt.

14 But now in hell, at each repeated blow,
   By each inſulting fiend I'm better taught,
   And, to my full conviction, made to know,
   That there's a God to puniſh ev'ry fault.

15 Now, now I feel, and ſee, alas, too plain!
   That there's a Devil, and a local hell,
   With Demons an innumerable train,
   To plague my ſoul, with whom I'm force'd to dwell.
                                    16 Now,

16 Now, to a demonſtration, I well know,
   That man is of a deathleſs ſoul poſſeſt,
   (Whether that ſoul be doom'd to bliſs, or woe!)
   Though in the tomb the body's laid to reſt.

17 Now, I believe the ſcriptures to be true,
   Now, I believe whatever Chriſt did ſay,
   And that the ſkies will ſcud away, like dew,
   Before a Word of his ſhall paſs away.

18 But as I did not this believe, in time,
   What I believe at preſent is in vain:
   For want of faith I plunge'd to ev'ry crime,
   Worſe than the brutes, that graze the verdant plain:

19 And ſuch will you, my brethren be, when dead,
   If you do not the ſcripture-truths embrace,
   And ſtrive a life of piety to lead,
   As they direct you, like the ſons of grace.

20 Becauſe the ſcriptures I did not obey,
   Becauſe my nature 1 did not ſubdue,
   Becauſe I wou'd not ſee the goſpel's ray,
   I now, in woeful caſe, my folly rue.

21 Becauſe in Moſes' rules I never trod,
   Becauſe thoſe ſacred truths I diſbeliev'd,
   Becauſe I never kept the laws of God,
   It was that I ſo very vilely liv'd.

22 When once I put the goſpel out of ſight,
   Then Satan came himſelf to be my guide,
   And by each ſin, wherein it took delight,
   He my frail nature quickly drew aſide.

23 There's not a heinous vice, that I can name,
   Which I did not, till I was cloy'd, plunge-in,
   Until a proverb my bad life became,
   And I was judge'd Manaſſes to out-ſin.

24 My worldly pelf, I as my God obey'd,
   In ſenſual luſts I place'd my chief delight,
   In 'ev'ry ſin I revell'd undiſmay'd,
   And left the Lord out of remembrance quite.

25 When

25 When by thofe errors I had long been led,
    My precious foul I utterly defpife'd,
    Like fome brute beaft, to ev'ry virtue dead,
    And nought but riches and my belly prize'd.

26 Still in the richeft drefs was I array'd,
    My robes were in the deepeft purple die'd;
    Now, for my pride and vanity well pay'd,
    I've not a rag my nakednefs to hide.

27 The fineft linen I was ufe'd to wear,
    Nor wou'd admit of any thing more coarfe;
    But now I vainly wifh that I had here
    Some fackcloth, or the cov'ring of a horfe.

28 Each day, throughout the year, whene'er I dine'd,
    I cramm'd my guts with victuals of the beft;
    And yet my foul for very hunger pine'd,
    Amidft the hurry of a conftant feaft.

29 I then was grown fo dainty in my meat,
    And fo extremely nice, that I ne'er deign'd
    Of any difh, or kind of food, to eat,
    Which was not choice, dear-bought, and finely-grain'd.

30 But now I fain my hunger wou'd affuage
    Even on hogs-wafh, or on hufky grains,
    So that I might in part appeafe the rage
    Of that keen famine, which my bowels pains.

31 I then was wont ftrong beer and wine to fwill,
    As if no meafure I in drinking knew,
    And often my ungodly paunch wou'd fill,
    'Till up again the naufeous load I threw.

32 But now I'd gladly give the world entire,
    And all it's treafures, for a little cup
    From fome cool ftream, to flake the raging fire,
    Which my chark'd tongue for ever parches-up.

33 Though as much offals from my table went,
    As wou'd have fed great numbers of the poor,
    Yet to the dogs the whole was daily fent,
    Whilft Lazarus lay ftarving at my door.

34 Now

34 Now Lazarus in turn repays me home,
    And ftill refufes, from fome bubbling fpring,
    (Although I beg him earneftly to come)
    One drop of water, for my ufe, to bring.

35 Though Mofes and the Prophets always laid
    The beft rules down, their rules I ftill defpife'd,
    And gave no ear to any word they faid,
    Nor ever did the leaft thing, they advife'd.

36 Now here I cry, and no ceffation know;
    For none unto my plaintive cries give heed,
    But in my teeth their keen reproaches throw,
    Becaufe of the vile life I ufe'd to lead.

37 Whenever any preach'd the word of God,
    I ftill averfe in attitude appear'd,
    Or, ever and anon, was feen to nod,
    Whilft others profited by what they heard.

38 Becaufe at church I, then, was wont to doze,
    By Demons, here, I'm torture'd all the while;
    So that I now can meet with no repofe;
    Nor fleep, nor flumber can my woes beguile.

39 Becaufe I, to the Gofpel, gave no ear,
    Nor to thofe doctrines, which the Saviour taught,
    I now am force'd the fiend's loud yells to hear,
    With hideous horror and amazement fraught.

40 Becaufe the law of Mofes they defpife'd,
    Becaufe the Gofpel they did not believe,
    Becaufe it's dictates they fo little prize'd,
    Some thoufands, now in hell, lament and grieve!

41 The fabbath I, in gluttony, alas!
    Always mif-fpent, or in fome wanton play;
    In riot, I contrive'd to make it pafs,
    And fouler fins, than any other day.

42 Thoufands of fouls are now in hell diftreft,
    Becaufe the fabbath they did not revere:
    No paufe they know from pain, nor day of reft;
    But without refpite are tormented there.

43 The facred name of God, I took in vain
    For fport alone, a million times, or more,
    And thought my ftory wou'd no credit gain,
    Unlefs by Jefus' blood and wounds I fwore.

44 Oh! how my tongue now fries in dreadful dole,
    Becaufe his precious blood I lightly prize'd !.
    And, Oh! what tortures rack my very foul,
    Becaufe the name of Jefus I defpife'd !

45 To the foul fiend I offer'd long in vain
    My precious foul, a thoufand times a day;
    But as I gave it o'er and o'er again,
    At laft he feize'd it, as his lawful prey.

46 Thoufands with me in fhocking torments dwell,
    Thrown headlong to this deep fulphureous flood;
    Becaufe they gave themfelves, by oaths, to hell,
    Tho' Chrift himfelf had bought them with his blood.

47 Full many a * one I to the army fent,
    Straining malicioufly my country's laws——
    Thirfting for bloodfhed, and entirely bent,
    The guiltlefs to deftroy, without a caufe,

48 Their blood extorted vengeance from the fky——
    A vengeance juftly-due unto my guilt !
    And to the fiends their injur'd fpirits cry,
    To pay me home for all the blood I fpilt.

49 On juries, oft, for life and death I ferved,
    Of God, and of his laws regardlefs quite;
    The guiltlefs I condemn'd, but ftill preferve'd
    Thofe, who deprive'd their neighbours of their right.

50 But now each murderer, and defperate thief,
    (Whom erft I from the gallows fave'd) in hell
    Remorfelefs tear my foul—and, to my grief,
    The fiends themfelves in cruelty excel.

51 My

* From this, and feveral other particulars, the Author, in this character of *Dives*, feems to have fome vile and oppreffive Magiftrate of his acquaintance in his eye, whom he indirectly lafhes under that pretence, in this Poem.

51 My love for my own confort foon grew cool,
And to vile ftrumpets, in her ftead, I cleav'd——
An hoft of whom now plague me in this pool,
Becaufe I their credulity deceiv'd.

52 The bafe-born brood from thofe foul harlots fprung,
By my example to thofe regions led,
Call on the fiends, with unharmonious tongue,
To pour their torments thicker on my head.

53 Their helplefs, friendlefs, orphans I opprefs'd,
Whene'er my tenants die'd—and from the plough,
The yoke entire, tho' nought was due, diftrefs'd;
Left one, if left, fhou'd for it's partner low.

54 Becaufe thofe innocents I then abufe'd,
The fiends in hell my torture'd foul diftrefs,
Worfe than a tanner, any time, is ufe'd
To beat thofe hides he fully means to drefs.

55 Some venal villains oftentimes I hire'd,
The rankeft lies and perjuries to tell,
Who never fail'd to fwear, as I require'd,
When I had taught them their vile leffon well.

56 Now, like a brood of vipers in their neft,
They, night and day, my very entrails tear,
And ever gnaw my heartftrings in my breaft,
Becaufe I taught them perjuries to fwear.

57 Of murder, and of robbe'ry I accufe'd
Perfons, whofe innocence was fully known,
And with foul flanders either fex abufe'd,
Out of mere pique, and wickednefs alone.

58 The lab'rer's hire I oft was wont to keep,
And my own fervants wages to retain,
Nay, without pay, I force'd the poor to reap,
Throughout the harveft, my whole crop of grain.

59 Now to the fiend thofe needy folks complain,
And at his hands my punifhment implore,
Becaufe I ufe'd their wages to detain,
And ruin'd fuch a number of the poor.

60 My money, to the poor, on ufe I lent,
And ſcrew'd them, with an ava'rice ſeldom known,
'Till all the little that they had was ſpent,
And they by my extortion were undone.

61 Many of thoſe, now in the pit of hell,
With aggregated pains torment me ſore,
Becauſe I did their minds to theft impel,
When my exactions had conſume'd their ſtore.

62 To * low attornies, a black-minded tribe,
I gave large fees, the needy to oppreſs,
Who now, becauſe corrupted by my bribe,
In this infernal ſink my ſoul diſtreſs.

63 I gave my ſervants orders, o'er and o'er,
To plague my neighbours round me;—in the pit,
Thoſe ſervants now torment my ſoul full ſore,
Becauſe I made them ſuch bad things commit.

64 At under-price men's lands I often bought,
Yet ſtill ſome part of that ſmall pittance kept:
But now I to this gloomy gaol am brought,
I have no money to repay the debt.

65 Cou'd one poor penny my redemption buy,
And from this doleful priſon-houſe relieve,
And bring me to the lucid realms on high,
I have not one poor penny left, to give.

66 I was adviſe'd a thouſand times, or more,
What I extorted, to refund again,
But rather than I wou'd a mite reſtore,
I choſe to ſuffer here eternal pain.

67 Whene'er I ſent to markets, or to fairs,
Falſe weights I uſe'd, and meaſures ſhort of ſize,
Or elſe amongſt my wheat I mingled tares,
Yet for that traſh require'd the greateſt price.

68 Againſt

---

* This is only meant of the low-bred Petty-foggers of thoſe days,
who never regularly ſerv'd their time to the buſineſs, and not of the
Profeſſion in general, many of whom are an Ornament to the Com
munity, and of great Service to the Public.

68 Againſt the laws of God and of the land,
 I weights for diffe'rent purpoſes produce'd:
 Whene'er I bought, the large ones were at hand;
 Whene'er I ſold, a leſſer ſort I uſe'd.

69 But now the fiends, in this infernal place,
 My head with the moſt heavy of them bruiſe;
 And ſuch as mine, is the unhappy caſe
 Of all, who e'er were wont falſe weights to uſe!

70 I left no tittle of the law unbroke,
 Nay, which I did not break a hundred times!
 And, 'till death gave me the concluſive ſtroke,
 I wallow'd daily in the worſt of crimes.

71 I juſt have given you, in language plain,
 My life at large, until ſurprize'd by death:
 I next ſhall give you an account again,
 How Satan plagues me in the realms beneath!

The Second Part of DIVES' Complaint——or a Deſcription of Hell, and it's Torments.

72 A Deep and bottomleſs abyſs,
 My drear and diſmal dungeon is,
 And all it's walls are rais'd ſo high,
 That none can o'er it hope to fly.

73 With liquid fire it ever glows,
 And, like a boiling ſea, o'erflows,
 Move'd by the breath of God, it's tide
 With flaming ſulphur rages wide.

74 Once l'it, it always flames amain,
 Nor ever can be quench'd again,
 Though never blown, it blazes high,
 And needs no ſtirring, nor ſupply.

75 Though fiercely burning it remains,
 And cauſes agonizing pains,
 Yet undiminiſh'd ſtill it laſts,
 And not the leaſt in burning waſtes.

76 This penal fire is still the same,
  Though diffe'rent it's degrees of flame;
  Some feel a fiercer or fainter fire,
  Just as their various crimes require.

77 As the sun warms, on India's sands,
  Much more than in the Russian lands;
  So hell exerts a greater heat,
  To punish those whose crimes are great.

78 Not one is in this dungeon found,
  Who, hand and foot, is not well bound,
  And in eternal chains tie'd fast,
  For all his sins, and follies past.

79 Thro' all it's boundless, drear, domains,
  A darkness palpable still reigns;
  Nor ever, since the world was made,
  Has light illume'd the joyless glade.

80 'Tis fetid, to the last degree,
  A stench more noisome cannot be
  Though thousands still the sink defile,
  It never has been cleans'd the while..

81 There worms insatiate ever prey
  On conscious sinners, night and day——
  A sort of worms, that never die,
  But gnaw to all eternity !

82 More than ten thousand devils stand
  Around the damn'd, a dreadful band,
  And to torment them never cease,
  Without an hour, or moment's ease.

83 Yet though they never cease to beat,
  (Their hellish rancour is so great!)
  And bruise the damn'd almost to death,
  They never stop to take their breath.

84 These everlasting tortures fall,
  Without respect of rank on all;
  Yet each does seperately smart,
  But chiefly in the pecant part.

C c

85 No

85 No objects there the eye e'er fees,
But gaſtly ghoſts of all degrees,
And wretched ſouls that ever weep,
In this unfathomable deep.

86 No food their famiſh'd mouths e'er taſte,
But locuſts' gall, a dire repaſt!
No drink they have, but when they ſup
The dregs of God's diſpleaſure up.

87 Their ears no other muſic know,
But ſhrieks of fiends, and ſounds of woe,
And the unſufferable yell
Of thoſe, who gnaſh their teeth in hell.

88 On red-hot coals the tongue is broil'd,
Or elſe in bubbling ſulphur boil'd,
Without a drop of drink to' aſſuage
The fire's intolerable rage.

89 The noſtrils ev'ry brimſtone-gale,
Which from the dungeon reeks, inhale,
A place, ne'er cleans'd, ſince Adam fell,
And fraught with ev'ry filthy ſmell.

90 Bound with an adamantine chain
The hands and feet of all remain,
So that they cannot move, or turn
From that ſame ſpot, wherein they burn.

91 All grate their teeth with ſhocking grin,
With hideous yells and horrid din,
That terror and amazement ſeize,
Who hears their moans, and manners ſees.

92 The gnawing worm, that never dies,
In ev'ry conſcious boſom lies,
And tears voraciouſly it's prey,
Yet never can it's hunger lay.

93 As all my members ſinn'd, each part,
Even my tongue itſelf, does ſmart;
But ev'ry member does ſuſtain,
For diff'rent ſins, a diff'rent pain.

94 As ev'ry limb fome evil bears,
    And ev'ry part fome torment fhares,
    So fhall thofe evils all attend
    The wicked, without paufe or end.

95 Ne'er fhall the' avenging worm expire,
    Ne'er fhall be quench'd the penal fire,
    And death, to all entreaties dumb,
    To end their pains, will never come.

96 The deluge, in a year, retire'd,
    And, in a day, was Sodom fire'd,
    Sev'n years, the Egyptian famine rage'd;
    But my pains, ne'er, can be affuage'd.

97 If in a thoufand years, or fo,
    Thofe pains fhou'd fome ceffation know,
    Some comfort to my heart 'twou'd give :
    But I in endlefs woe muft live !

98 The word of God my heart difmays,
    The word e'en on my vitals preys——
    The word is to my foul a fnare——
    The word e'en drives me to defpair.

99 To bear fuch hellifh pains, is hard,
    But harder 'tis, to be debarr'd
    Thy Saviour's prefence, and refign
    Heav'n's joys, and company divine.

100 To lofe my life, and vaft reward——
    To lofe Chrift and his faints, is hard——
    'Tis hard, heav'n and it's joys to mifs,
    With God himfelf, and ev'ry blifs !

101 May blackeft curfes blaft the morn,
    The very hour, when I was born !
    May hell, too, prove my mother's doom,
    That toads fhe bare not in my room !

102 I wifh that fhe my neck had broke,
    Or chopp'd my head off at a ftroke,
    When fhe fo vile a fon did bear,
    An angry Godhead's wrath to fear.

103 There's

103 There's neither fiend, nor finner found
　　In hell, and all it's cells around,
　　That does not join, both fmall and great,
　　Me, hopelefs wretch! in turn to beat.

104 There's not a foul, fince Adam fell,
　　That fuffers greater pains in hell———
　　Nor any one, that undergoes
　　More grievous wants or greater woes.

105 Such are my pains! fuch my diftrefs!
　　Such heavy woes my foul opprefs!
　　Such is the ftate I now am in,
　　Each hour tormented for my fin!

106 My Brethren, therefore, I advife
　　You, and each finner that is wife,
　　Take warning (e'er the day of death)
　　Or you will go to hell beneath.

107 If you don't leave each finful way,
　　And ev'ry Chriftian rule obey,
　　The God of vengeance won't, I know,
　　To you, than me, more mercy fhow.

108 That none of us may ever dwell
　　With Dives in the flames of hell,
　　Let us reflect, e'er 'tis too late,
　　What torments Satan's flaves await!

That it is in vain to PRAY for the DEAD.

1 MY dear Relation, and the Friend I love,
　　　You've put to me a queftion I approve:
　　I therefore think myfelf in duty bound
　　To give it a folution fafe and found.

2 You thus before me did the queftion lay———
　　" Is any Clergyman allow'd to pray
　　For him, that is of fenfe and life bereft,
　　Whofe foul already has his body left?"

3 To

3 To this demand I make this clear reply————
That holy fcripture always does deny
Us leave, by prohibition ftrong and plain,
To pray for the deceas'd with efforts vain.

4 Our God obliges ev'ry foul to dwell,
Either in heav'n, or with the damn'd in hell,
When once it from the body takes it's flight,
According as it's works are wrong, or right.

5 The fouls of thofe, who properly believe,
As foon as they their clay-built manfions leave,
Like holy Lazarus, above the fky,
Immediately among the angels fly.

6 Whilft the ungodly, in the pit below,
(Whene'er their fouls from their pale bodies go)
Are force'd for ever in fierce flames to roll,
Like worldly Dives's unhappy foul.

7 The former, with true joys and blifs abound,
And are with honours and with glory crown'd—
So great, they need not any more requeft,
But quite contented with their ftation reft.

8 They need not any one for them to pray,
So happy! fo fupremely bleft are they!
For each of them is an invited gueft,
And with the Lamb fits at his fumptuous feaft.

9 The latter, ne'er fhall quit the dens of hell,
But there inceffantly in torment yell,
Whatever off'rings for their fouls you pay—
However oft you for their pardons pray.

10 Whene'er a man, whoe'er he be, is dead,
And has been once to God's tribunal led,
It is in vain, for any human pow'r,
For his forgivenefs ever to implore,

11 Though Job and Daniel, many times a day————
Though Abraham, Mofes, Samuel, fhou'd pray
For fuch a one—yet they cou'd ne'er affuage,
By all their efforts, hell's tremendous rage.

C c 3   12 Shou'd

12 Shou'd all the priefts, in all the world, unite,
And fupplicate the Lord with all their might,
And place before him gifts of ev'ry kind,
The God of truth wou'd never change his mind.

13 Shou'd all the globe unto the Godhead pray,
The dead-man's dreadful torments to allay,
Their fupplications wou'd be all in vain——— ·
A drop of water he fhou'd not obtain.

14 God's fentence pafs'd, can ne'er be done away.
Where the tree falls, it there muft ever ftay.
God ne'er will alter, what he once defign'd.
He never yet was known to change his mind.

15 God, from his purpofe, ne'er can be remove'd———
He'll ne'er reverfe the doom, he once approve'd—
Not all the world, was all the world agree'd,
Nor heav'n, nor earth, his fentence can impede.

16 The time for pray'r is, e'er each mortal dies;
It nought avails him, after his demife———
A prayer, after one's deceafe preferr'd,
Can ne'er prevail, and never fhall be heard.

17 I therefore ev'ry man on earth advife
(If he wou'd be unto falvation wife)
To pray, whilft yet alive, if he wou'd fain
Any advantage from his prayers gain.

18 Get thou thy wedding-drefs, get oil, get light,
Get grace, e'er thou'rt furpriz'd by death and night-
When once the day of grace is pafs'd, 'tis plain,
The leaft requeft thou canft not then obtain.

19 All of us fhou'd, before our death, implore,
With application warm, the' eternal Pow'r———
That is the time, our fuit fhou'd be preferr'd,
That is the time, our prayer may be heard.

20 Before we die, and fhall from hence be gone,
It is that heav'n is either loft, or won·-----
The fimple fot, when dead, no profit gains,
Since nought, but judgement, for him then remains.

21 Before

21 Before we die, we muſt reform our hearts,
    Whilſt yet 'tis day, we all muſt act our parts,
    Our Saviour ſays, that, when it once is night,
    No mortal can perform his work aright.

22 Chriſt orders each oppreſſor to agree
    With all, with whom he may at variance be,
    Whilſt he is yet upon the way, and not
    As yet into his Judge's preſence brought:

23 Leſt, hand and foot, in durance ſtrict confin'd,
    He be at laſt to penal flames conſign'd:
    Becauſe in time he did not juſtice chooſe;
    Not all the world from thence can get him looſe.

24 King David knew full well, the time was paſt,
    (When once his fav'rite child had breathe'd his laſt)
    And that 'twas vain for him to ſhed a tear,
    Or importune the Deity with pray'r.

25 It is not therefore right for any one
    To pray for any friend, that's dead and gone—
    Whom he believes to have been ſent to reſt
    In endleſs happineſs, among the bleſt.

26 Nor is there room for any man to pray,
    (When from this world he once is gone away)
    Whom you believe, as naked here he came,
    To have gone naked hence to hell's fierce flame.

27 There are two places only to us known,
    For any man, when he from hence is gone,
    Or heaven above, or hell's infernal vale:
    For purgatory's but an idle tale.

28 There is no need, for any one to pray,
    For him, that is allow'd in heav'n to ſtay,
    Or ſhou'd he make the infernal lake his home,
    He ne'er ſhall have permiſſion thence to come.

29 It therefore was a cuſtom moſt abſurd,
    For any prieſt to ſpeak a ſingle word,
    In favour of the ſoul that hence is fled,
    Only to rob the heedleſs of their bread.

30 The

30 The beſt amongſt them will not now admit
   Of thoſe impoſtures, or ſuch pray'rs permit,
   Or none but cheats, whoſe aim is to impoſe,
   And gain alone unto themſelves propoſe.

31 It is a duty, that upon them lies,
   When any good and righteous perſon dies,
   Due thanks unto the Lord above to give,
   In certain hopes that he again ſhall live.

32 But that a prieſt ſhou'd any favour crave
   For one that's dead, and burie'd in the grave,
   It is a thing forbidden and unfit,
   Which no one but a fool will e'er permit.

33 Thus to the queſtion aſk'd, my friend, by you,
   I've given a ſolution juſt and true :
   May God increaſe your faith, and grant you grace,
   Among the ſaints above, to ſhew your face !

Mr. Prichard's Advice to his Son Samuel.

1 FOr heaven's ſake, my Sammy dear !
     In mind, till death, thoſe precepts bear :
   Chriſt on thy bended knees adore,
   When in my ſight thou art no more.

2 Call on thy God, and Saviour dear,
   With ardent faith, and heart ſincere,
   And, whilſt abroad, inceſſant pray
   For his aſſiſtance, night and day.

3 Bend both thy knees, both hands up-riſe,
   And fix on Chriſt thy longing eyes,
   For his bleſt aid and bleſſing pray,
   On all occaſions---when away.

4 So ſhall he ſhield my Sammy ſtill
   From ev'ry harm, and ev'ry ill,
   And ne'er to want will let him come,
   Whilſt he is far from me, and home.

5 To

5 To God, for his affiftance, pray,
  That thou may'ft Chrift know, and obey,
  Whilft yet thou only art a boy;
  Be that, abroad, thy chief employ.

6 Ufe thou thyfelf the God of truth
  To fear and worfhip, in thy youth;
  So thou, by due degrees, wilt come
  To ferve him, when grown up, at home.

7 With pleafure to thy ftudies go,
  And be not in thy learning flow,
  Yet I forbid thee not to play
  At times, whilft thou'rt from me away.

8 When idle, touch the harp's fweet ftring,
  Or elfe thofe pfalms, that follow, fing:
  'Twill oft a good amufement be,
  When thou art far from home, and me.

9 Still chirping, like the cricket, keep,
  Nor for thy mother fondly weep:
  For God, abroad, will unto thee
  A father and a mother be.

10 God give thee grace, God blefs my fon—
  God teach thee in his paths to run——
  God be thy guardian, night and day,
  Whilft thou from us art far away.

PART II.

11 Juft at the dawn of day arife,
  When firft the * lav'rock mounts the fkies,
  'Twill bring thee long and lafting health,
  'Twill bring thee learning, virtue, wealth.

12 Put on thy clothes, without delay,
  Be always neat in thy array,
  Be ev'ry button place'd aright,
  E'er thou prefume'ft to come in fight.

13 Firft

* An almoft obfolete word for a *Lark*, and of which *Lark* is very probably a contraction.

13 Firſt waſh thy face, and comb thy hair,
  Thy cravat then adjuſt with care,
  Let all thy dreſs be clean and tight,
  For that is pleaſing to the ſight.

14 When thou art dreſs'd, then go to pray,
  Without deception, or delay,
  And fall upon thy knees in haſte,
  E'er thou a bit, or drop, doſt taſte.

15 When to God's preſence thou doſt bring
  Thy prayers—think, that he's a King,
  Whoſe courts the very angels tread,
  With humble thoughts, and aweful dread.

16 Upon thy knees, my ſon ! draw near,
  When thou before Him doſt appear——
  Nor dare to make the leaſt addreſs,
  Which does not a juſt fear expreſs.

17 When once upon thy knees, ne'er riſe,
  'Till thou haſt lift to God thine eyes,
  Then doubt not any boon to crave,
  Which thou doſt really want to have.

18 Tho' God's a king of wond'rous might,
  Of ſtrength and honour infinite,
  Yet ſtill the ſcriptures plainly ſhow,
  That He's a tender Father too.

19 Whatever gift thou doſt deſire,
  Or grace, or virtue, aſk thy Sire——
  And God, when aſk'd, will freely grant,
  Whatever thou doſt truly want.

20 Thy ſuit with equal ardor make
  To him, and no refuſal take :
  God grants with eaſe each juſt requeſt,
  That is with earneſtneſs expreſt.

21 He'll grant his aid, if it's implore'd——
  He'll hear, if rightly he's adore'd——
  Place then thy truſt in Him, and He
  Will keep thee from all danger free.

22 Keep Him, and He'll keep thee, in mind,
And nothing wanting fhalt thou find :
Whoe'er refpects Him, He'll refpect——
Whoe'er rejects Him, He'll reject !

23 Prefer to Him each day thy pray'r,
And He will take of thee fuch care,
As if He had no other fon
' To mind, or guard, but thee alone.

24 Remember this good caution ftill,
My *Sammy*, whether well, or ill,
Serve thou thy God, both night and day,
And at fix'd times unto him pray.

25 If in thy youth it be thy ufe,
To ferve thy God—thou canft not chufe
But ferve him ftill, when age appears,
And filvers o'er thy dropping hairs.

26 God give both ftrength and grace to thee,
His fervant, all thy life, to be,
'Till thou, triumphant, at it's end,
Shalt, as Chrift's heir, the fkies afcend.

A PRAYER for Mr. SAMUEL PRICHARD, the Author's Son.

1 O God, by whom all good is given !
Thou Sire of light ! thou King of heaven !
Behold, and lift to my requeft, '
However young, weak, and diftreft !

2 Upon my knees I now prefume
Before thy throne, my King ! to come——
An humble fuit, to thee, to make ;
Refufe me not, for Jefu's fake :

3 To ask——thou gaveft me command,
And promifed'ft that, at thy hand,
Whate'er I ask'd I fhou'd obtain :——
I ask——let me not ask in vain !

4 King

4 King Solomon, with knowledge bleſt,
  To thee for wiſdom made requeſt,
  Thou gaveſt him what he deſire'd,
  Nay, more by far than he require'd.

5 The patriarch Jacob on his way,
  For food and clothes alone did pray;
  Thou gaveſt what He ask'd, and more
  By far than he petition'd for.

6 I alſo, my Creator dear!
  Upon my bended knees draw near,
  And for a boon to thee apply :
  For Jeſu's ſake, do not deny !

7 I ask no wealth, nor worldly ſtore——
  I ask not pleaſures, pomp, or pow'r——
  I only ask thy grace——and might,
  To ſerve and worſhip thee aright.

8 Then give me grace and give me pow'r,
  That I may thee, while young, adore,
  And with true faith and heart ſincere,
  May in thy doctrines perſevere !

9 Permit me not in idleneſs
  To ſpend my days, or in exceſs,
  But cauſe me, in life's earlieſt ſtage,
  Lord ! in thy ſervice to engage.

10 Open thy treaſures, and impart
   Thy grace to me, and teach my heart,
   To know thee in my tender years,
   Like Daniel, and his young compeers.

11 As Jeremiah, in his youth,
   Did worſhip thee, his God, in truth——
   Give grace like him, my God ! to me,
   Whilſt young, in truth to worſhip thee.

12 I offer up myſelf to thee,
   Now in my youth, accept of me,
   And grant that I, in ev'ry ſtage,
   May in thy ſervice ſtill engage.

13 Thou

13 Thou to thy fervice didft admit
   The prophet Samuel, as yet
   A boy, and ftill fo very young,
   That he cou'd hardly walk along.

14 Admit me alfo, I implore———
   That I may thee, whilft young, adore,
   And fo reveal to me thy will,
   That I may rightly it fulfil.

15 Equip me, O my God! aright,
   With ev'ry gift that's requifite,
   For one, who chufes ftill to be
   A conftant votary to thee.

16 Open my underftanding's eyes,
   And make me in thy knowledge wife,
   That I the myfteries may know,
   Which from the law, and gofpel flow.

17 Now, in my youth, a fpark impart
   Of thy true grace unto my heart,
   That it with ardent zeal may flame
   For the Almighty's facred name.

18 Touch thou, O Lord! my lips and tongue
   With that live coal, whilft I am young,
   Which from thy holy altar fell,
   That I thy praife aloud may tell!

19 Enable me, my gracious Lord!
   To learn and fo digeft thy word,
   That I may comprehend aright
   What for my peace is requifite.

20 To all thy people let me be,
   A pattern of true piety,
   And let me ever fpend my days
   In things, that tend unto thy praife.

21 This is the only fuit I make,
   Do not refufe, for Jefu's fake,
   Me grace, my Maker to adore :
   'Tis the only boon that I implore!

22 O let me not mif-fpend my time
 In any fin, or heinous crime—
 But let me fpend it in fuch ways,
 As tend to manifeft thy praife !

23 Upon my works, thy bleffing pour,
 Increafe my knowledge ev'ry hour,
 Give me true wifdom to difcern,
 And to remember, what I learn.

24 Let me be guarded by thy eyes———
 Let me be fhielded from furprize———
 Let thy bleft Spirit me direct———
 And let thy providence protect.

25 All honour be, my King, to thee,
 Both night and day !———and grace, to me!
 True glory be for ever more
 Unto the Lord whom I adore !

Another Piece of Advice unto a Youth.

1 TO cram thy body, ne'er thy foul deftroy——
 Nor anger God, to pleafe the' infernal crew—
 To purchafe earth, ne'er fell celeftial joy——
 And fin no more———left a worfe thing enfue.

2 Tho' thou, each day, fhou'dft heav'n-dropp'd manna
 And glut thy maw with the moft dainty meat ; [eat,
 What art thou better for fuch fare at laft,
 If thou in hell muft keep an endlefs faft ?

3 Though thou fhou'dft daily drink the choiceft wine,
 And in rich robes of regal purple fhine,
 Or tread upon the neck of fome great king ;
 If Heaven's loft———what profit can it bring ?

4 Though thou didft own the riches of the eaft,
 And wert of kingdoms ; nay, the world poffeft ;
 What wou'd fuch pomps and vanities avail,
 If thou, at laft, to fave thy foul fhou'dft fail ?

       5 Though

5 Though Venus yielded to thy warm defires,
  And faireft beauties deign'd to quench thy fires,
  What are thy gains, when all is faid and done,
  When thy poor foul is to the Devil gone?

6 Though all the world to flatter thee fhou'd join,
  And buoy thee up in any bad defign :
  It matters not if all the world applaud,
  If thou haft by thy vices ang'red God.

7 'Tis better God, than all the world, obey————
  To curb a part, than throw the whole away————
  Slightly to toil, than in fierce flames to dwell!
  E'en bread and water, Hell's beft feafts excel.

8 Serve Chrift, but with the Devil combat hard,
  And thou a crown fhalt gain for thy reward :
  Humble thy flefh, thy foul preferve with care,
  And thou fhalt in Chrift's bleffed banquet fhare.

Mr. PRICHARD's Complaint of the Town of Landovery (the Author's Parifh)

And his Advice and Warning to that Place.

1 AH me! Landovery, thou art wanting found,
  For God thy fins has in the balance weigh'd;
  In drofs and dregs alone doft thou abound :
  Of thy Creator henceforth be afraid !

2 A heavy rod long fince prepare'd has been,
  To punifh thee for all thy fumlefs crimes,
  And for thy daily-growing mafs of fin :
  To fhun the punifhment, repent betimes !

3 Long, e'er he ftrikes, the Deity will ftay,
  But heavy will his hoarded vengeance fall;
  Thy long arrears and countlefs fcore he'll pay
  In full, with double intereft, once for all.

4 He

4 He gives thee time to mend each wicked way——
He gives thee frequent warnings, to repent——
Then take his warning——whilſt 'tis yet to-day,
Or thou ſhalt ſoon thy negligence lament.

5 The longer God, out of mere mercy ſtays,
For thee thy ſinful morals to amend ;
Still worſe and worſe each day are all thy ways:
But woe, alas ! be to thee in the end.

6 When the Almighty puniſhment delays,
And pours no vengeance on Religion's foes,
The more, each day, the treaſur'd vengeance weighs:
The more thy ſins, the heavier his blows.

7 In time, then, of the wrath divine take heed,
Though ſlack to come, yet it will ſurely come——
It's feet are down, but, ah ! it's fiſt is lead:
Though ſlow to ſtrike, yet when it ſtrikes, 'tis home.

8 Like Sodom and Gomorrah, thou art grown,
Which never from their odious vices turn'd
(Or like Samariah's ſuperſtitious town)
Until at length to duſt and aſhes burn'd.

9 As bad as Pharaoh's is thy callous heart,
Who was with a caſe-hard'ned conſcience curs'd,
And wou'd not from his vicious ways depart,
'Till he by unexampled plagues was forc'd.

10 My cautions thou ſo often haſt abuſe'd,
(For good advice was not to thee unknown)
That there's no room for thee to be excuſe'd :
Ah, woe is thee, thou poor unhappy Town !

11 E'er the cock crow'd, I roſe each circling day,
Thy rebel paſſions ſtriving to reſtrain,
In hopes to turn thee from each ſinful way ;
But it was labour loſt, and all in vain.

12 In heav'n's loud trump I blew a dreadful blaſt,
To ſhew how God pours vengeance on his foes ;
Yet ſtill thou ſnoreſt-on unto the laſt,
And nought can break thy perilous repoſe.

13 To

13 To thee the Gofpel I full oft have read,
    And all the promifes therein contain'd,
    To wooe thee in it's facred paths to tread ;
    Yet nought I thence, but heart-felt grief have gain'd,

14 I ftrove, with all the terrors of the law,
    And God's dread plagues, to frighten thee from ill—
    I ftrove to rein and curb thy ftubborn jaw,
    But thou art reftiff, mad, and headftrong ftill.

15 I pipe'd to thee, thou didft not like the fport—
    I wept full fore, and yet thou didft not mourn—
    Means, (fair and foul) I trie'd of ev'ry fort,
    Yet thou didft nought but ridicule return.

16 What cou'd I, then, unhappy Town! do more,
    Than to the brink of fome lone ftream retire,
    And tears of blood for thy tranfgreffions pour,
    To fee thee led to hell's eternal fire ?

17 Who wou'd not weep to fee the wily fiend
    Draw thee along, e'en by a filken thread,
    To that abyfs, whofe torments know no end,
    By the fweet bait of carnal pleafure led ?

18 Efau difpofed of his birth-right of old,
    A mefs of pottage was the paltry price!
    Thou, worfe than him, the heav'ns themfelves haft fold
    For barley-broth—in fpite of my advice.

19 'Tis this, alas! that cuts me to the heart,
    When I thy numberlefs mifdeeds furvey——
    That I muft not prefume to take thy part,
    Or veil thy crimes, on God's tremendous day :

20 And yet 'tis hard, 'tis wondrous hard, alas!
    A father, though by blood and nature move'd,
    The fatal fentence fhou'd be force'd to pafs
    Upon the crimes, e'en of his beft-belove'd.

21 Yet this *will* be, nay, this *muft* be the cafe,
    If foon thy finful life thou doft not mend :
    Then, for Chrift's fake, thefe overtures embrace,
    E'er God his plagues, to punifh thee, fhall fend.

D d   22 A

22 A veil of fack-cloth o'er thy body caft——
Weep, till thy bed in floods of tears be drown'd,
And neither meat, nor any liquor tafte,
'Till for thy vices thou haft pardon found.

23 Thy bofom beat—thy hair by handfuls tear——
A-down thy cheeks let tears in torrents run,
And ne'er to own thy heinous crimes forbear——
But cry, " Forgive me, Lord! the ill I've done."

24 Uncleannefs of all kind, and ev'ry guile,
Deceit, and fornication, caft away,
Avoid excefs, and hide thy vices vile ;
For God does all thy wickednefs furvey.

25 A dreadful doom hangs o'er thee, ev'ry day,
Sufpended only by a flender thread,
And yet thy fins with one accord affay,
To pull it down upon thy guilty head,

26 Beware then---hold thy hand, and fin no more;
As fwift as light'ning is the wrath divine :
I give thee all the warning in my pow'r,
If thou refufeft it, the fault is thine.

The PASTOR's COMPLAINT.

1 WHat forrows in my foul, O God! arife,
    The vaft perverfenefs of mankind to fee ?
Shou'd any ftrive to lead them to the fkies,
To quenchlefs fires they'd rather madly flee.

2 To bleach the moor, requires no greater art,
Or Jordan's ftream up Hermon's hill to roll,
Than to perfuade the fool's obdurate heart,
To fear his God, and to preferve his foul.

3 Ufe ev'ry means, though fair or foul they be,
To charm the deaf-ear'd fnake, you charm in vain :
Prune, as you pleafe, a rotten-hearted tree,
You neither fruit, nor fhade, fhall long obtain.

4 Teach,

4 Teach, fhew, exhort, conjure the debauchee,
  A vicious life he to the laft will lead:
  Try both the law and gofpel, yet from thee
  He'll only with a fneer avert his head.

5 Whether the prophets' terrors you make known,
  Or in the' apoftles milder ftyle advife,
  As well you beat your head againft a ftone;
  He'll only do what's pleafing in his eyes.

6 My heart with heavinefs is therefore fill'd:
  Ah me! that God had not in pity chofe,
  To give me charge of beafts, by nature wild,
  Rather than men, worfe than the worft of thofe!

7 As, e'en from flow'rs, of fweeteft tafte and fmell,
  The fpider can a deadly poifon draw:
  Some ill the reprobate can full as well
  Extract from God's own word, and facred law.

8 Since our Redeemer Chrift fo kind has been,
  As for our fakes his heart's beft blood to lofe,
  And give it as a ranfom for our fin;
  Many, on that account, to fin ftill chufe:

9 'Caufe Lot and Noah were for once fubdue'd
  By wine, and Jonah was of old morofe;
  Many their faults with ardor have purfue'd,
  Who never one of all their virtues chofe.

10 Each forward youth is apt to fwear and ban,
  Like Peter, when his mafter he difclaim'd:
  But why, alas! can 1 not fee the man,
  Who is, like Peter, of this vice reclaim'd?

11 Many purfue the track of David clofe,
  When to adultery he plunge'd unwife:
  But I can't find a fingle foul of thofe,
  Who in his penitence with David vies.

12 I'll quit, fays one, my darling vices quite,
  And end my follies with the prefent year—
  But, what fays Chrift? " Suppofe this very night,
  The fiends thy foul fhou'd to hell-torments bear!"

13 To-day, we will have fport, another cries,
    To-morrow, we'll our wicked lives amend.
    That very night, o'ercome by drink, he dies——
    How foon, alas! his promis'd pleafures end?

14 A third indulges thefe fallacious thoughts,
    " Suppofe my faults the higheft hills tranfcend,
    " Yet greater are God's mercies than my faults,
    " And he'll forgive me at my latter end."

15 So, becaufe God is found to take delight
    His mercy tow'rds the penitent to fhow——
    Moft feem to fin, as 'twere with all their might,
    And will not of his juftice too allow.

16 Though God in grace and goodnefs does abound,
    Though flow to punifh, and of patience great,
    Yet, in the fcriptures this plain truth is found,
    That he's with juftice equally replete.

17 If full of grace, he's full of juftice too——
    If kind to friends, he's cruel to his foes——
    If he is mild, he can due vengeance fhow——
    If he is gene'rous, he is likewife clofe.

18 A thoufand talents are to fome forgiven——
    From others he'll the utmoft mite receive——
    To thefe he freely gives the joys of heaven——
    But thofe he will not with one drop relieve.

19 God, to the penitent and faithful, ftill
    His gracious mercies and his truth difplays;
    But, on the ftubborn, who refift his will,
    He the full weight of his difpleafure lays.

20 This leffon and advice, to all, I give——
    " The path of fin's not long with fafety trod:
    " And therefore all fhou'd ftudy, whilft they live,
    " To pafs their time here, in the fear of God."

We

We muſt cleave to CHRIST, without ſuf-
fering any thing to turn us away from him.

1 IF father, if mother, if daughter, if ſon,
   If houſes, if lands, if the wife of thy love—
Shou'd ſtrive to pervert thee—by no means be won
Thy faith, and thy zeal towards Chriſt to remove.

2 Let father and mother, let children and wife,
   Reprove thee, beſeech thee, lament, ſcold, or grieve,
Leave houſes, leave lands, leave thy food, leave thy life,
Leave all that thou haſt, e'er Chriſt thou doſt leave.

3 Chriſt, father and mother, and brother and friend,
   Their rock and their fort, and good fortune, will prove,
Their profit immenſe and vaſt gains in the end,
And all that is dear—unto thoſe who Chriſt love.

4 Without him, of faith food and life, we're bereft—
   Rule, reaſon, health, ſtrength, we our own cannot call:
But void of hope, help, and of grace, we are left—
Of knowledge, of virtue, of God, and of all.

5 God 's better than father, or mother, or nurſe——
   God 's better than matron, or maiden, or bride——
God 's better than houſes, or lands, or full purſe——
God 's better than ought you can think of beſide.

6 He 's better than all the wide world and it's ſtores—
   He 's better than the' earth, with his bleſſings ſo fraught,
He 's better than the' heaven, and all it's great pow'rs,
God 's better, a million times over, than ought.

7 If thou, the Almighty wilt take to thy ſhare,
   Good fortune will follow, where-e'er thou ſhalt lead,
And Chriſt and his ſaints will take thee to their care,
The ſkies will receive thee, and Demons will dread.

8 The better part, thou didſt moſt ſenſibly take——
   A part, that ſhall ſtill be unchangeably thine,
(When thou as thy choice the Almighty didſt make)
As long as the ſun, moon, and planets ſhall ſhine.

9 Fo:

9 For when both the fun and the moon difappear,
When all this vaft globe fhall be burn'd to a coal,
When ftars fhoot from heaven, and many men fear,
Yet fearlefs, e'en then, is the innocent foul.

10 Then cheer up thy fpirits, and roufe up thy heart—
Keep hold of thy faith to the laft gafp of breath—
Thou'ft chofen, be certain, the bettermoft part:
Take heed then, nor change thy opinion, till death.

CHRIST is the TREE of LIFE.

1 COME to the Tree of Life, come all,
Come at your kind Redeemer's call,
Enjoy it's fruits---in Chrift believe——
And you fhall grace and life receive——

2 It takes away the harfhnefs quite,
The hunger keen, the painful bite,
The rankling wound, the curfe of God,
Which from the fruit forbidden flow'd.

3 O come, and freely of it eat——
From heav'n our Father fent the treat-----
'Twill make us well--'twill heal each fore,
Hunger affuage, and health reftore.

4 It's fruits than manna fweeter are——
It's leaves are healing, large, and fair,
And neither dearth nor death e'er fhall
The man, who eats thofe fruits, befall.

5 Chrift, is the tree---O then draw near !
Life, is the fruit, it's branches bear-------
His words and doctrines, are the leaves,
Whence health each wounded foul receives.

6 Come all, that are with woes oppreft,
Come to your fole Redemer, Chrift,
Come, grace, health, comfort, to receive,
Come all to him, that you may live !

7 To

7 To eat it's fruits, come let us hie,
And to our wounds it's leaves apply,
They'll flake our thirst, our health restore,
And make us live forevermore.

That Christ was typify'd by the Paschal·Lamb.

1 CHrist is the Paschal Lamb, our sacrifice,
Christ is the offering, that made our peace,
Christ is the spotless Lamb, by God approve'd,
Which all the fins of all the world remove'd.

2 Christ is the Lamb, that for our fins was flain,
Christ for our foul transgreffions suffer'd pain,
Christ's precious blood, as on the crofs he bled,
For our iniquities was freely fhed.

3 'Tis hard, 'tis fad, 'tis terrible to thought,
The Lamb shou'd suffer for its kindred's fault,
And that the Son of God shou'd e'er be flain
For our misdeeds, in agonizing pain.

4 Adam's intemperance our ruin wrought,
But Jefus suffer'd for the Patriarch's fault------
'Tis man, that fins---but Christ himself, that dies----
Did ever love to fuch a height arife ?

5 Alas ! what heart but muft with pity bleed,
To fee---Christ fcourge'd for Adam's foul misdeeds,
The Shepherd, for his flock to danger brought---
The Sove'reign, torture'd for his fubjects' fault.

6 To fee, the Master fold, to buy the flave-----
The Son condemn'd, his Father's foes to fave,
The Doctor's fide transfix'd with pointed fteel,
That, with his blood he might his patients heal.

CHRIST

CHRIST typify'd by the brazen Serpent.

1 YE, who have felt the ferpent's venom'd bite,
Come all to Chrift, the woman's promis'd feed,
He'll drefs the fore, and pluck the fting out quite,
He'll bind him faft, and caufe his head to bleed.

2 We all have felt fin's agonizing wound,
It's fting has to our hearts a paffage found,
Chrift only can a proper falve apply;
On him, the brazen ferpent, fix your eye.

3 Look up to Chrift, who on the crofs once hung,
(As they look'd up, who formerly were ftung
By fi'ry ferpents in Zin's pathlefs wafte)
And all your pains will pafs away in hafte.

4 If with a contrite heart, and eye of faith,
We gaze at him, although the ferpent hath,
With baneful bite, tranfpierc'd each finner's heel;
Yet Chrift, if look'd upon, the wound will heal:

5 But if we come not foon to Chrift, our King,
To feek a cure againft the ferpent's fting:
No other leach a proper falve can give—
None, but the Son of God can make us live.

A Hymn, or Carol, for CHRISTMAS-DAY.

1 LET ev'ry one, that hears my voice,
And underftands my words, rejoice;
Let ev'ry one applaud with me
The undivided Trinity.

2 O turn, and tune your hearts aright,
In pfalms and hymns let's all unite
In honour of the Saviour born
To us, on this aufpicious morn!

3 It is upon this happy day
  That Chriftians fhou'd be blithe and gay,
  And ev'ry hour thereof employ
  To manifeft their well-time'd joy.

4 For on this great, this glorious morn,
  The Saviour of the world was born:
  And, O! how vaftly blefs'd are we,
  This great and glorious morn to fee!

5 This is the' important day, that brought
  To ev'ry Chriftian, what he fought,
  This is the day, that gave the blow,
  Foretold unto our mortal foe!

6 This is the day, that did retrieve
  The happinefs, we loft through Eve
  And Adam's fault, e'er Jefus came
  To fave our fouls from death and fhame.

7 This is the day, that broke the net,
  Wherewith we all were once befet,
  This is the day, fo fraught with woe
  To Satan, our deluding foe.

8 This is the bleft, momentous morn,
  Whereon the Son of God was born,
  The Woman's feed, ordain'd of yore
  To over-turn the ferpent's pow'r.

9 Then let us, with united voice,
  Upon this hallow'd day rejoice,
  And ne'er difmifs the pleafing thought
  Of the falvation Jefus wrought.

10 O, let us ever bear in mind,
  And blefs, his name, who was fo kind
  As unto us, his help to give,
  And a whole finful world relieve!

11 O, let us celebrate his fame,
  And magnify his holy name
  Each day and night, and ev'ry hour
  We live, unto our utmoft pow'r!

12 But

12 But moft, on this momentous morn,
    Let us exult, when Chrift was born,
    Until our fong to heav'n rebounds,
    And angels catch the pleafing founds !

13 When firft the cock falutes the day,
    Arife at once, without delay,
    That, at it's dawning you may fing
    The praifes of our Saviour-king ;

14 And when it is no longer dark,
    Then in her matins join the lark,
    And laud the glorious fource of light,
    Who turn'd to day the gloom of night :

15 Then, with the black-bird on the fpray,
    Continue from the noon of day
    Your length'ned lays— 'till in the fkies
  -At night the twinkling ftars arife :

16 Then with the nightingale fing on,
    Until the moon and ftars are gone,
    Sing on, fing on, the live-long night,
    Until the gloom has left you quite.

17 From morn to noon, thence to it's end,
    Each Chriftmas-day we thus fhou'd fpend,
    Still chanting our Redeemer's praife
    In tuneful hymns, and holy lays.

18 This is the day, when we were bought !
    This is the day, the prophets fought,
    When God to man a friend was made !
    This is the day that brought us aid !

19 The day——that rais'd us up on high
    From hell's abyfs, unto the sky !
    The day, that made each man, a fon
    Of God !——what wonders has it done ?

20 The day, whereon (tho' then we mourn'd)
    Our grief was into laughter turn'd !
    O, let us ftill the fame employ,
    To fhew our gratitude and joy !

21 This

21 This is the great, the' important morn,
 Whereon the Lamb of God was born,
 Who man's offences only knew
 To bleach, though of a fcarlet hue !

22 This, this, is the aufpicious day,
 When we fhould be alert and gay,
 And make the courts of heaven's King
 With grateful hallelujahs ring !

23 This day throughout, we fhould adore,
 With ceafelefs praife the filial Pow'r,
 For all the goodnefs He has fhown——
 For all the wonders he has done.

24 O, think what our falvation coft !
 Think on the precious blood Chrift loft,
 When from his fide the rufhing gore
 Stream'd faft, think on the pains he bore

25 As pelicans are, with their blood,
 Said to fuftain their tender brood;
 So his heart's-blood our Saviour gave,
 His finful brethren's fouls to fave !

26 He quitted his celeftial train,
 And, to Judea's happy plain,
 Defcended from the realms on high,
 With his own blood mankind to buy.

27 From his high throne in Paradife
 He flew, and left the lucid skies,
 In Mary's womb our form to take,
 And fuffer for his people's fake.

28 He took upon Him all the woes,
 The meaneft abject undergoes,
 And the tremendous punifhment
 Due to our fins, He underwent.

29 His fide was wounded by a fpear,
 And he was force'd our crimes to bear——
 Yet, by the ftripes which He endure'd,
 Were all our weunds and bruifes cure'd.

30 For us He alfo bore the lofs
  Of his beft blood upon the crofs——
  And unto God, for ever blefs'd,
  He made us friends, from foes profefs'd.

31 He wafh'd us clean from ev'ry fault—
  Our fouls, he generoufly bought———
  And will conduct us to the sky,
  However loud our vices cry.

32 O, let us then his praife proclaim,
  And night and day exalt his fame;
  For you muft be extremely blind,
  If you do not fuch goodnefs mind!

33 O, let us all exalt his fame,
  On this great feaft, which bears his name,
  With peace, with piety, with love,
  And ev'ry virtue that's above.

34 This feaft let us entirely fpend
  In true devotion, to it's end,
  Nor any worldly thoughts admit;
  But keep it holy, as is fit.

35 Let us avoid all foul excefs,
  All rioting and wantonnefs,
  And to the church together go;
  As ev'ry Chriftian ought to do.

36 It is not meet the Chriftian quire
  Shou'd roll in fin, like fwine in mire,
  And this grand feftival abufe,
  As if they were as bad as Jews.

37 But they fhou'd pafs this feaft, throughout;
  Fully as fober and devout,
  As children of their Sire above,
  In perfect charity and love:

38 And, to the temple, ev'ry day
  They conftantly fhou'd go, to pray,
  Their Saviour's praifes to proclaim,
  And glorify his holy name.

39 He ne'er at any time demands
  Another off'ring at our hands,
  But that we all fhou'd praife him, there;
  For that is pleafing to his ear.

40 Then enter to his gates with praife,
  And in his courts your voices raife:
  At early morn, and ev'ning late,
  Let all their Maker celebrate.

41 With awe unto his temple go;
  For it is decent fo to do:
  'Tis right his praifes to proclaim, •
  And magnify his holy name.

42 It is a thing, both right and good,
  That ev'ry ferious Chriftian fhou'd
  Adore his Saviour, night and day,
  Who on the crofs to fave him lay.

43 This is the whole, that at our hands
  He as a recompence demands—
  'Tis all he now expects above,
  For his dire agonies and love.

44 Then let us clap our hands, and give
  Him all due honours whilft we live—
  And in his courts his name applaud;
  For that is grateful to our God;

45 But let us never dare blafpheme,
  With lips prophane, the Lord fupreme,
  Left we fhou'd be oblig'd to go,
  With Judas, to the pit below.

46 Unto the bleffed Three-in-one,
  The Father—Holy Ghoft—and Son,
  Let us our bounden duty pay
  Each hour, each moment, of the day.

A D V I C E, to search for the Lord
JESUS CHRIST.

1 IF any man, or maid, or child, wou'd fain
The life to come, eternal life! attain—
Chrift let him feek with care, if he wou'd live,
And Chrift to him eternal life fhall give.

2 Chrift muft be fought for firft with zealous pains,
For real life in him alone remains—
And 'tis a thing moft foolifh and abfurd,
To feek for life, unlefs you feek the Lord.

3 For thy protector, Jefus Chrift elect,
And for thy guide thy conduct to direct:
Eternal life thou then from him may'ft claim,
And ne'er, thereafter, fhalt thou lofe the fame.

4 If for thy guardian thou doft Chrift refufe,
And doft not Chrift for thy director chufe,
No one, with any certainty, can tell
How thou may'ft fave thy precious foul from hell.

5 All wou'd have Chrift, when at death's door they lie
To be their Lord and Saviour, e'er they die;
But, whilft in health, how few, alas! of thofe
Chrift for the pattern of their lives propofe.

6 Be not deceiv'd, thou fenfual debauchee!
Chrift will to no one a Redeemer be,
But to the man, who, of his own accord,
Shall take his Saviour for his fove'reign Lord.

7 He, who the word of God will not obey,
Nor take his fpirit to direct his way,
Muft not expect, that he fhall ever have
The Son of God, his finful foul to fave.

8 Let Jefus Chrift then thy protector be,
Let him be governor fupreme o'er thee:
Without him, none (how much foe'er they ftrive!)
Can e'er pretend to fave their fouls alive.

9 Thoug|

9 Though thou the world, and all its tinfel pelf
  Shou'dſt gain—yet loſing Chriſt, ſhou'dſt loſe thyſelf,
  What wou'd the ſad preheminence avail,
  If thou, at laſt, to ſave thy ſoul ſhou'dſt fail ?

10 Shou'dſt thou but Chriſt, and only Chriſt obtain,
  Thou'dſt have enough to make thee well again :
  For Chriſt does, in himſelf, contain the whole
  That's requiſite, to ſave a ſinner's ſoul.

11 O, that thou cou'dſt but ſee, upon the whole
  How needful Chriſt is, to preſerve thy ſoul,
  And that, without his help, thou canſt not do
  One jot, alas ! of all thy taſk below !

12 It is a thing moſt needful for thy ſoul,
  To ſeek for Jeſus to complete the whole
  Thou haſt to do on earth—if thou wou'dſt fain
  His ſaving mercy for thy ſoul obtain.

13 Not any creature, whether wild or tame—
  Not any man, or power, thou canſt name,
  Can thy deplorable condition mend ;
  'Till Chriſt, to better it, ſhall condeſcend.

14 Thou muſt have Chriſt, as God and man conjoin'd,
  Two natures perfectly in One combine'd,
  To finiſh all the work, thy ſins require,
  E'er thou canſt pleaſe thy everlaſting Sire.

15 Thou muſt have Chriſt as Brother and as King,
  To work out ev'ry part, and ev'ry thing,
  Belonging to the neceſſary deed
  Of thy ſalvation—e'er thou canſt ſucceed.

16 Whoever aims his Saviour to poſſeſs,
  And comfort ſeeks from him in his diſtreſs,
  For Chriſt's reception muſt fit out a home
  In his own ſoul—e'er he will deign to come.

17 Prepare thy ſoul, thy ſin-fraught ſoul prepare,
  That Chriſt may come, and deign to ſojourn there,
  And when he comes, the ſojourner embrace,
  That thou from him may'ſt get both Strength and
    Grace.   18 Thou

18 Thou muſt, O man! for Chriſt make ample room,
  E'er he will to thy boſom deign to come——
  It muſt with ev'ry Chriſtian grace be dreſt,
  E'er he'll vouchſafe to lodge within thy breaſt.

19 Chriſt, and his holy Spirit, ne'er were ſeen,
  Where there was ought unſeemly, or unclean:
  If any one's ambitious of their ſtay,
  He from his breaſt muſt caſt all filth away.

20 Chriſt in a heart impure will never ſtay,
  'Till odious ſin is baniſh'd thence away:
  Chriſt no impurity can e'er endure:
  For his own Spirit is entirely pure.

21 Our God and Dagon ne'er at once cou'd reſt,
  Or Chriſt and Belial, in the ſelf-ſame breaſt,
  No more than fire and water, ſide by ſide,
  In the ſame veſſel can in peace abide.

22 The ſoul, that's full of pride, beyond all doubt,
  Can't Chriſt contain, 'till it be empty'd out;
  Juſt as the veſſel, that's with filth replete,
  Can't milk receive, e'er it be render'd ſweet.

23 All men from ſin muſt utterly depart,
  Deteſt it quite, and root it from their heart,
  E'er they can any friendſhip have with Chriſt,
  And to their breaſts admit the ſacred gueſt.

24 The ſoul muſt clear itſelf from ev'ry ſin,
  (That Chriſt with ev'ry grace may enter in)
  And ſhun thoſe vices, which it once allow'd,
  That Chriſt may with his gifts the manſion crowd.

25 According to the ways of nature, none,
  How great ſoe'er their pain, can ſeek the Son,
  'Till God ſhall by his grace direct him right,
  And draw him unto Chriſt, in nature's ſpite.

26 'Tis God out of his favour and free grace,
  That offers Chriſt, to ſave a ſinful race——
  It is the goodneſs of our God alone
  That gives us Chriſt—elſe we were all undone.

27 There's

27 There's nought in man, that can the Godhead move
To shew him such regard—such wondrous love !
But God himself, out of his special grace,
Vouchsafes us Christ—to save a ruin'd race.

28 The streams of life, which no cessation know,
But still with grace, with health, and virtue flow,
God freely offers unto all that thirst ;
But they must come unto their Saviour first.

29 God calls aloud to all with voice divine,
To eat his manna, and to drink his wine,
And asks no money for the rich repast————
Asks nought, but that we wou'd to Jesus haste.

30 God ne'er forbade a man, within his breast,
To entertain his Saviour for his guest :
But he forbids him to reject the Lord,
Tho' he were stain'd with crimes the most abhorr'd.

31 Though God thus kindly offers Christ to all,
Yet scarce a sinner will obey the call,
Or come to Christ, 'till by resistless might,
And special grace, God drags him to his sight.

32 No one can come, let him do what he will,
Unto the Son, however great his skill,
'Till by the Father of all mercies led
To Christ, to be with consolation fed.

33 The sheep, that once has straggled from the pen,
Will ne'er return, 'till carrie'd back agen :
Nor will the sinner to his Lord return,
'Till, like the sheep, he to the fold is born.

34 No robber, of his own accord will e'er
('Till force'd) before the magistrate appear :
Nor will a sinner, howe'er bad his case,
'Till dragg'd, attempt to see his Saviour's face.

35 His nature, in his sins, the wretch detains,
His conscioufness of guilt, his feet restrains,
His crimes cry out, that he's his Saviour's foe,
And must be damn'd——if he presumes to go.

36 The eyes of man, God needs must open wide,
To see how wretchedly his soul's supply'd————

E e

To

To fee it's fhocking ftate, it's pains, it's woes,
E'er from his Saviour he will feek repofe.

37 None to the Leach apply, their wounds to heal,
Until their throbs and rankling fmart they feel:
So on their Saviour, finners never wait,
'Till fully confcious of their fearful ftate.

38 We muft our damnable condition fee,
Our wretched cafe, our native poverty,
And the tremendous ftate wherein we live,
E'er we the want of Chrift can well perceive.

39 The Father, Son, and Holy Ghoft, muft light
A man, to view his miferable plight,
E'er he, for want of knowledge and of fenfe,
Can beg of Chrift, to pardon his offence.

40 Like fome ftray'd fheep, our Father that's above,
Muft haul each finner with the hook of love,
E'er he will come, for comfort, to the Son;
Although, without him, he be quite undone.

41 God muft to flefh convert the marble heart,
And make it foft, as wax, in ev'ry part;
'Till at it's woeful ftate it grieves full fore,
'Twill ne'er attempt a Saviour to adore.

42 The Father muft difplay, before thy face,
His mercies, and the riches of his grace,
In giving thee his beft-beloved Son;
E'er thou canft venture to approach his throne.

43 The Father, firft, his goodnefs muft declare,
That it extends to all, both far and near————
That he with kindnefs each requeft receives————
That, to the contrite, he remiffion gives:

44 And, that he calls each vile offender in,
[However big, however black his fin]
To have a fhare in all his joys divine:
So he his fins does totally refign.

45 God unto thee muft a commandment give,
" With perfect faith, in Jefus to believe,"
On pain of his difpleafure and reproach;
E'er thou into his prefence canft approach:

46 And

46 And when thou haſt receiv'd his gracious call,
   He muſt entreat and wooe thee after all,
   With Chriſt and with Himſelf, to make thy peace;
   E'er he will cauſe his burning wrath to ceaſe.

47 Thou muſt be courted with perſuaſions kind,
   (So obſtinate, and ſo perverſe thy mind!)
   E'er he can thee, e'en by thoſe methods, gain,
   His proffer'd peace and pardon to obtain.

48 The rebel by his Sove'reign muſt be preſs'd,
   The traitor muſt with mildneſs be addreſs'd,
   E'er he will deign to come for a reprieve,
   And pardon, for his treaſon, to receive.

49 Though 'tis not fitting he to thee ſhou'd ſue,
   Who doſt no ſign of reformation ſhew,
   Yet God ſtill wooes, and begs thee to receive
   Thy pardon——if thou'lt aſk it, he will give.

50 When thou haſt thus been to repentance woo'd,
   God's patience, and forbearance muſt be ſhow'd,
   How mildly-merciful he is! how kind,
   Unto each liſtleſs, lazy, lingring mind!

51 How ſlow to puniſh thy repeated crimes,
   How he forbears with thee a thouſand times,
   How long he's known the' impending ſtroke to ſtay,
   'Till thou canſt caſt thy filthineſs away.

52 Though God does thus thy ſinful ſoul invite,
   Though thus he goads thee on, and gives thee light,
   Yet ſtill thou will not quit thy ſins, nor come
   To Chriſt, 'till God has prick'd thy conſcience home.

53 Though, by the faithful evidence within,
   Thou art detected and convince'd of ſin,
   And by it's juſt award condemn'd at laſt,
   For thy vile morals and thy vices paſt.

54 Though ſelf-condemn'd and wounded to the heart,
   Thou never canſt from thy love'd errors part,
   And never ſhalt before the Lord appear,
   Until the Holy Spirit drags thee there.

55 God and his Spirit muſt eject each gueſt,
   And fiend unclean, that revels in thy breaſt,

         And

And all the fins, that there triumphant reign,
E'er thou affiftance canft from Chrift obtain.

56 The Holy Ghoft muft give thee liberty,
And wholly from the Devil's toils fet free,
And to the Son of God thy footfteps guide,
E'er thou, with him, for ever canft refide.

57 Thou muft from ev'ry fav'rite vice depart,
Thou from all guilt muft purify thy heart,
And keep thy foul from all pollution clear,
E'er thou in Chrift canft ever have a fhare.

58 Corrupt in nature, we are all, alas!
The fons of wrath, a hell-devoted race!
'Till Chrift the fons of wrath fhall kindly take,
And them the fons of God and mercy make.

59 So fierce, fo hot, the wrath of God does rage
Againft the num'rous vices of the age,
That nought cou'd ever ftop it's fie'ry flood,
Was it not ftopp'd by our Redeemer's blood.

60 Not all the waters, pendent in the fky,
Nor thofe that, in the fpatious Severn lie,
Or in the ocean's far more fpatious flood,
Nor ought can quench it, but our Saviour's blood.

61 We all, alas! are enemies of God's———
We all are with our righteous Judge at odds———
And had been ftill, had Chrift not laid the plan
Of peace, of lafting peace, 'twixt God and man.

62 Not man, nor fiend, nor any pow'r above,
Nor ought on earth, can God's fierce wrath remove,
'Till Jefus Chrift himfelf (tis truth I teach)
'Twixt God and man make up the fatal breach.

63 Beneath a grievous curfe we lie oppref's'd,
Becaufe we all have willfully tranfgref's'd
The law of righteoufnefs, and from it none
Can fet us free, but Jefus Chrift alone.

64 We, one and all of us, are flaves to fin,
To which we, day by day, all tumble in,
And no one living can from it refrain,
'Till he's renew'd by Chrift, and born again.

65 We

65 We all of us by Satan are fecure'd,
   And in a dufky, dreary gaol immure'd;
   'Till Jefus comes, and fteals his arms away,
   He from his gripe will never quit his prey.

66 We all of us by Satan are fecure'd,
   And clofely in a difmal gaol immure'd;
   'Till Jefus fhall the captiv'd gaoler bind,
   None thence a way to·'fcape fhall ever find.

67 Shou'd the archangel Michael, and his train,
   With the fierce Dragon ever fight again——
   He ne'er cou'd conquer him, until the Lamb——
   The Lamb of God, to his affiftance came.

68 We are obnoxious all of us to death,
   And to the dreadful pains of hell beneath——
   And no one ever fhall from thence get free,
   'Till Jefus Chrift fhall gain his liberty.

69 We all of us, before we firft drew breath,
   Were doom'd for guilty Adam's fins to death,
   And muft from Chrift get his affifting grace,
   E'er one is fave'd of all the num'rous race.

70 Let him do what he can, no man fhall e'er
   In the celeftial courts above appear,
   'Till he a full and thorough change can boaft
   By Chrift, by Water, and the Holy Ghoft:

71 For Chrift muft, as it were, new-form the foul,
   Create anew, and renovate the whole;
   E'er carnal man can any happinefs
   In the celeftial realms above poffefs.

72 None ever cou'd have over-come the beaft,
   Who cheated Eve, nor low'r'd his fcaly creft,
   Nor free'd us from hell's deep and dark abode,
   Befides the woman's Seed——the Son of God.

73 None elfe cou'd have infure'd the joys above,
   None cou'd the curfe, which we deferve'd, remove,
   But Jefus Chrift who was the finlefs feed,
   From Abraham's loins, erft promis'd to proceed.

74 No creature, how extraordinary foe'er,
   Cou'd from the jaws of fin poor mortals tear,

And

And place them near their God, the saints among,
But Jesus Christ, the Shiloh promis'd long.

75 Moses led Israel, by divine command,
From Pharaoh's court to Canaan's fertile land:
So God, thro' Christ, shall lead us far away
From Satan's pow'r, unto the realms of day.

76 The brazen serpent in a moment cure'd
All, who the fie'ry serpent's wounds endure'd:
Christ, by his blood, as speedily shall heal
All, who the deadly shafts of Satan feel.

77 A Lambkin's blood, for their transgressions slain,
From Israel's tents Apollyon did restrain:
The blood of Jesus will keep out the fiend
From ev'ry heart, that bears his death in mind.

78 As gallant David the fierce lion brave'd,
And from his paw the tender Lambkin save'd:
So Christ, our Shepherd, will protect his sheep,
And from the fangs of Satan safely keep.

79 Samson, whose strength nought human cou'd oppose,
Slew at his death the chiefest of his foes:
So Jesus, by his suff'rings, overthrew
Death, Satan, sin, and all the' infernal crew.

80 From Christ, each has receiv'd his mortal wound,
Though in them still some signs of life are found;
Yet all the salves, in all the world, can't cure
Their heart-felt anguish, or their lives assure.

81 As nought cou'd do the Syrian Leper good,
Unless he bathe'd in Jordan's limpid flood:
So nought can cleanse man from each inky stain,
But the Lamb's blood, that for our sins was slain.

82 As God dispatch'd a messenger of yore,
To rescue Shadrach from the fire's fierce pow'r:
So he, as the inspired pages tell,
Sent his own Son, to save our souls from hell.

83 Jonah, in great anxiety of mind,
In the whale's belly was, three days, confin'd:
So deep in earth, our blessed Saviour lay,
For us, until the third revolving day.

84 As

84 As Abraham offer'd up his fon of yore
On Moriah's top, to the Almighty pow'r;
So did our Saviour offer up his foul
To his dread Sire—to fave his flock from dole.

85 Who plunge'd into Bethefda's pool, was heal'd;
However great his pains—whate'er he ail'd:
Whoe'er fhall in the blood of Jefus lave,
A cure for all the wounds of fin fhall have.

86 The Pelican relieves her tender brood,
When ftung by fome fly ferpent, with her blood:
So the Lamb's blood relief to all imparts,
Whom fin has wounded with her deadly darts.

87 The Unicorn can, with his horn, 'tis faid,
Thofe waters heal, where fnakes have poifon fhed:
So Chrift can, by his blood, thofe fouls protect,
On which, the fiend his venom fhall eject.

88 It therefore is more fhameful, and more odd,
Shou'd we reject our fpoufe, the Son of God !
Than if fome beggar fhou'd refufe to wed,
And take a king of England to her bed.

89 No man alive can fcale the heav'ns on high,
Which far above the lunar regions lie,
Unlefs he does the Patriarch's ladder take,
Jefus I mean, the bold attempt to make.

90 Cry then for Chrift, with accents loud and fad,
'Till thou faft hold haft in thy Saviour had;
Then let not all the world, nor all in it,
Make thee the hold, which thou haft taken, quit.

91 Defire thou Chrift, as harts the brooks defire ;
For Chrift of ev'ry traveller enquire:
Seek him with diligence, 'till you obtain ;
But, when obtain'd, ne'er part with him again.

92 E'er thou canft Jefus earneftly defire,
To fave thy foul from everlafting fire,
That he has pow'r and grace, thou firft muft fee,
To keep thee fafe, and buy thy liberty :

93 That Chrift is gracious, thou muft needs perceive,
That he is God-and-Man, thou muft believe——

That

That he's more mighty, and of greater ufe,
Than ought the whole creation can produce.

94 Thou needs muft fee, that Chrift's beyond compare,
Much better, and more neceffary far,
Than all the world, and ev'ry tranfient joy,
To fave thy foul from danger and annoy.

95 For not the world, nor all the world contains,
Can keep thy foul from hell's tremendous pains;
But Chrift to heav'n the precious charge can bear,
And from the winged dragon's talons tear.

96 Chrift, with his precious blood, can blot-out quite
Thy deep-grain'd fins, and make them lily-white:
Though they like fcarlet, now at prefent, glow,
Yet he can bleach them, 'till they're white as fnow.

97 Chrift can repair, and mould a-new thy foul,
Though it fhou'd be with various vices foul,
And, whilft thou liveft on the earth, he can
Make thee in favour grow with God and man.

98 Chrift can fupply thy finful mind with grace
And ftrength, on him thy confidence to place——
With learning, virtue, wifdom, and with worth,
Fully to work thy own falvation forth.

99 Chrift can to thee the' advantages reftore,
Which thy forefathers loft fo long before,
And give thee life, which never fhall decay
A life, that Satan ne'er can take away.

100 The Son of God can fave thy wandring foul,
Tho' it fhou'd ftray, where wolves each ev'ning prowl,
And carry thee in fafety back again,
On his own fhoulders, to the faithful train.

101 Not all the fpatious world, nor all therein,
Can purify thy fpotted foul from fin,
Or it's loft native innocence recall;
But, without Chrift, thou to the pit muft fall.

102 Colleƈt thy utmoft pow'rs, thy utmoft might,
Rely, confide, and lay, on Chrift, thy weight;
Search for him, love him, and with faith behold,
And keep in him a fure and fteddy hold.

103 A Chriftian muft be thoroughly inclin'd
To feek for Chrift, with all his heart and mind :
For Chrift will never a Protector prove
To fuch as ftudy not to gain his love.

104 Unlefs one longs, unlefs one thirfts to have
The Son of God, his finful foul to fave———
The Deity will ne'er his fuit regard,
Nor fuch faint efforts with fuccefs reward.

105 The Deity, his Son to none will give,
Who are not fully ready to receive
The gift divine, Chrift muft with zeal be fought,
Before he can within their reach be brought.

106 Who wifh, who long, who pant with ftrong defire,
Chrift and his gracious favour to acquire,
God will to fuch accord the bleffing foon,
And give them readily the precious boon.

107 God nought expects from any that believe,
But that with ardour they wou'd Chrift receive :
For he, that feeks him with a zeal, like fire,
Shall, without price, obtain his heart's defire.

108 Before, we Chrift and his fweet Grace can gain,
We muft the certain hold of faith attain :
For, without faith, no man on earth fhall e'er
Before the Son of God in blifs appear.

109 No part, no fhare, no benefit, no gain,
The Chriftian, more than Pagan, fhall obtain,
Of all that Jefus purchafe'd for our fakes,
'Till he by faith a full poffeffion takes.

110 Faith, is the nobleft boon thou canft defire ;
Without it, thou fhalt never Chrift acquire :
Tho' thou, in this thy day, each wifh fhou'dft have ;
Yet, without faith, thy foul thou ne'er cou'dft fave :

111 Without it, thou haft nought with Chrift to do———
Without it, thy beft works are mean and low———
Without it, thou to God no joy canft give———
But, " by his faith, the juft fhall ever live."

112 Tho' hills of gold unto thy fhare fhou'd fall,
And all the glories of this earthly ball :

When

What wou'd they profit thee, on the dread day,
Shou'd'ft throw, for want of faith, thy foul away?

113 Waft thou as poor as *Lazarus* of yore;
Without goods, lands, or food, or any ftore;
Tho' thou nought elfe but faith alone fhou'dft have,
By faith alone yet thou thy foul fhou'dft fave.

114 Tho' mines of gold cannot our Saviour move,
To fave a fingle foul he does not love;
Yet faith, though little as the fmalleft grain,
Salvation, for its owner, fhall obtain:

115 Without it, no delight, no comfort, is,
No joy fincere, nor any perfect blifs,
In heav'n above, or on the earth below;
Who has not faith, no happinefs can know!

116 Without it, thou, in Chrift, fhalt have no room—
Without it, thou, in hell fhalt have thy doom—
Without it, God himfelf is ne'er well-pleas'd—
Without it, no man heaven e'er appeas'd.

117 No pardon is for fin to be obtain'd———
No favour from the' Almighty to be gain'd———
No real pleafure ever did appear———
Unlefs a lively faith was likewife there.

118 The rich have need of faith, as well as poor———
The learned fage, and the illit'rate boor:
Like need of faith the king and beggar have;
Nay, all have need of it, their fouls to fave———

119 And all muft have their Own—their Own alone—
Another's faith cannot for thee atone:
Since no man can be fave'd—not even one———
But by his own belief and faith alone.

120 'Tis not thy mother's faith, nor yet thy fire's———
'Tis not the prince, or peer's—that God requires,
And can on thee the grace of God draw down———
Or any other's faith, befides thy own.

121 The father's faith, to fave his fon fhall fail———
Nor fhall the fon's, to fave the fire prevail:
Each fhall be faved, by his own faith alone;
No other faith to fave a foul was known!

122 Who, with attention, hear his bleffed words,
To them, the Deity this faith affords:
On none, without the word, he e'er beftows
The facred gift, or any favour fhows.

123 Hear then the word, and, all it fays, believe,
And to it's doctrines due attention give:
God will perform the thing which He has fpoke!
God never yet has any promife broke!

124 'Tis not our temper, or our fire's deferts—
'Tis not our learning, ftudy, or our parts—
But 'tis God's fpirit, through the word poffeft,
That gives man faith, and plants it in his breaft.

125 Seek then the word, the fpirit feek to gain,
And, as for life, for grace cry out amain;
For they, who cry for grace, and hear his word,
To them faith's freely granted by the Lord.

126 'Tis not the word, heard by the ear, that can
Excite true faith within the heart of man;
But 'tis the Spirit, with the word combin'd,
That ftirs up faith within the human mind.

PSALM XXXVIII.

1 MY gracious God! compaffion's Sire!
Do not rebuke me in thine ire,
Nor let thy dreadful wrath extend
It's terrors to my latter end!

2 O Lord! each keenly-pointed dart
Of thine, has pierc'd my riven heart;
Like fudden ftorms thy hand defcends;
Beneath the ftroke my body bends.

3 My flefh is full of pain and woe;
So great, fo furious was the blow!
No reft, my broken bones can find—
No peace, my confcience-wounded mind.

4 My fumlefs fins have foar'd fo high
Above my head, they reach the fky;
The mountain-load I cannot bear,
The punifhment is too fevere!

5 No eafe my batter'd body knows,
  So very weighty are thy blows !
  My wounds are of corruption full,
  Becaufe I was, ah me ! fo dull.

6 My back thou, like a bow haft bent----
  Juft to the grave thou haft me fent---
  So very low I now am found,
  That I am proftrate with the ground.

7 All day I am with grief oppreft,
  And all night long I cannot reft,
  So much my woes and tears abound,
  My couch is with the deluge drown'd.

8 Turn then to me, O Lord ! thine eye----
  See, how I weep---hark how I figh !
  Behold, how heavy on each part
  Thy judgements lie ! they whelm my heart.

9 To make my forrows overflow,
  And fill me with excefs of woe,
  My loins inflame'd intenfely fmart,
  My body's pain'd in ev'ry part.

10 I feeble am, and fmitten fore,
  For grief of heart I grunt and roar :
  So nume'rous my afflictions are,
  O God, I'm ready to defpair !

11 O leffen thou thy burning rage,
  And part of my fierce pain affuage,
  Nor let my life be quite fuppreft ;
  But grant that I at length may reft !

12 Thou knoweft, Lord ! what I require,
  Thou knoweft all my heart's defire :
  My thoughts, my fears, my mifery,
  Were never hid, my God ! from thee.

13 My heart within me hardly beats,
  My fpirits flag, my blood retreats,
  My clouded eyes have loft their light,
  And no kind friend appears in fight.

14 My neighbours and relations fly,
  And view me with a diftant eye ;

Of me, as of the plague, afraid,
They give me nor advice, nor aid.

15 All thofe, that would my foul betray,
Place fnares and pitfalls in my way;
Like a mad dog, they wou'd opprefs
Thy fervant, in his dire diftrefs.

16 Each, then, wou'd fain my life deftroy,
Each told his tale with favage joy,
And each condemn'd me in his mind,
As the moft vile of human kind.

17 Some did a thoufand flanders fay,
Some mock'd and fcoff'd me all the day;
Some ftill mean't nothing but deceit,
My woes and forrows were fo great!

18 But as one deaf I ftill appear'd,
Who none of all their railing heard,
Or like a mute, I ftood alone,
And held my peace, and anfwer'd none.

19 I am, like one that cannot hear,
Or like an idiot I appear,
And leave them, as they pleafe, difpute,
Nor ftrive their fcandals to refute.

20 But thou, O Lord! my caufe wilt hear,
And to my plaint, I hope, give ear,
And make a due return to thofe,
Who without reafon, are my foes.

21 O, let not them, that wou'd deftroy
Thy fervant, their heart's wifh enjoy,
Let them not triumph over me,
When they my vaft diftreffes fee.

22 Shou'd my foot, e'er fo little, flide,
At the mifhap themfelves they pride,
They laugh aloud at all my woes,
And my infirmities expofe.

23 To fuffer mifery and fcorn,
I, haplefs wretch! methinks, was born;
My heart is overwhelm'd with pain,
Still in my fight my woes remain.

24 My

24 My fins I therefore do confefs,
   And do lament my wickednefs;
   But, Lord! I'm ready to defpair,
   To think how numerous they are.

25 Yet ftill my adverfaries live,
   They daily multiply and thrive,
   And they that hated me the moft,
   Are now become a countlefs hoft.

26 All thofe that jumble wrong with right,
   And good, with evil turns, requite,
   Still fhew themfelves my conftant foes,
   And ftill their ranc'rous thoughts difclofe.

27 Becaufe I ever have purfue'd
   The things that honeft are, and good,
   I am the public butt of all,
   Who for my virtue feek my fall.

28 Then from thy fight, Lord! do not caft
   Thy fervant, but, to help him, hafte!
•   Make him ftill more and more thy care,
   And do not from him wander far.

29 Speed, O my God!—to aid me fpeed——
   To aid me in the time of need!
   O, be not from me long away,
   My God! my health, my truft, my ftay!

Concerning the SABBATH.

1 RIfe with the cock, and clap each flutt'ring wing,
   In grateful hymns exultingly rejoice—
   Early to God, each Sunday morning, fing
   With glowing heart, and with a tuneful voice.

2 Put on thy beft, at leaft a cleanly drefs,
   And fanctify thyfelf—or don't prefume
   Into the temple of the Lord to prefs,
   Unlefs prepare'd with decency to come.

3 Then to the temple, innocently gay,
   With all thy family around thee, go
   Thy homage to the Lord of hofts to pay;
   As all the faints of old were wont to do.

4 God

4 God, likes with reverence to be ador'd,
  Publicly in his courts, with open gates,
  Tho' chiefly on the Sabbath of the Lord :
  But all clandeftine corner-worfhip hates.

5 His whole creation God completed quite,
  On the fixth day, before it yet was eve ;
  Do thou thy labour end that very night,
  If thou doft in the Chriftian faith believe.

6 Be fanctify'd before the feventh day,
  And cleanfe thy veffel from each finful ftain,
  Wafh thou thyfelf in penitence—obey
  Thy God——and ftrive his heart-felt peace to gain.

7 Before the fabbath comes, thy foul prepare,
  And caft each worldly-minded thought away,
  That thou may'ft do the work of God with care,
  And proper holinefs——whilft yet 'tis day.

8 Leave thou thy fervants and thy cattle reft
  From all their toil, upon that facred day ;
  Let, then, no anxious cares torment thy breaft,
  No active exercife, or wanton play.

9 To fell provifions, or to bear a load,
  To feek amufements, or elfe idly play,
  To work thy trade, or travel on the road,
  Are all forbidden on that hallow'd day.

10 Take heed, left thou the fabbath fhou'dft prophane,
  At morn, at noon, or in the ev'ning grey,
  But, e'en at home, as if within his fane,
  To God thy unremitted worfhip pay.

11 Greater attention, whilft thou breatheft, pay,
  Upon each fabbath, to the work divine,
  Than thou wou'dft give on any other day,
  To any worldly care, or tafk of thine.

12 It is a thing as requifite to feek
  Upon that day, for manna to fuftain
  The hungry foul ——as 'tis throughout the week,
  To fearch for food, thy body to maintain.

13 E'er yet the dawn has ftreak'd the eaftern skies,
  E'er yet the lark has fung her morning lay,

Early

Early, upon that facred day, arife,
That thou may'ft pafs it in a pious way.

14 'Tis not a day, in liftlefs fleep to wafte,
'Tis not a day, to lie a-bed fupine,
But 'tis a day, by Chriftians to be paft,
In ev'ry act and exercife divine !

15 'Tis not a day, in fauntring to be paft,
In drunkennefs, or to fome bad intent,
But 'tis a day, which, long as it does laft,
Shou'd be in holy works entirely fpent.

16 A day---which in devotion we fhou'd fpend———
A day---to do the bufinefs of the Lord———
A day---we fhou'd in praye'r and reading end———
A day---whereon our God fhou'd be ador'd———

17 A day---from ev'ry worldly work to reft.———
A day---to deeds of holinefs affign'd———
A day---that is beyond all others bleft———
And not a day---for idlenefs defign'd.

18 Though God commands us all to keep that day
Holy---and thinks therein to be obey'd :
Yet lefs attention moft of us ne'er pay
To any precept, than to that we've paid.

19 Of all the days, throughout the rolling year,
There's not a day we pafs fo much amifs---
There's not a day, whereon we all appear
So irreligious, fo profane, as this !

20 A day, for drunkennefs---a day, for fport---
A day, to dance---a day, to lounge away,
A day, for riot and excefs too fhort,
Amongft moft Welfhmen, is the fabbath-day.

21 A day, to fit---a day, in chat to fpend----
A day, when fighting 'mongft us moft prevails———
A day, to do the errands of the fiend———
Such is the fabbath in moft parts of Wales !

22 The very day, which we fhou'd moft revere,
We, to defile it, ftill feem moft inclin'd,
To the difhonour of our Saviour dear,
And to the grief of ev'ry pious mind.

23 From early morn, unto the eve'ning gray,
  Be ftill on thy religious task intent,
  And let no portion of thy Saviour's day
  Be, in the Devil's work or worfhip, fpent.
24 Remember ftill to keep the fabbath day,
  And keep it holy, with a pious mind;
  For he that fpends it in an idle way,
  Will ne'er regard, whatever he's enjoin'd.
25 Whether at church, at home, or if abroad,
  Obferve the fabbath, thou and all thy race,
  And make thy family adore their God
  As well at home, as in his holy place.
26 Three forts of works, a man may fafely do
  Upon the feventh day, and not tranfgrefs———
  The work of love—the work we're force'd unto—
  And the ftill pleafing work of holinefs.
27 The work of holinefs, a man then does,
  To hear God's word and his due homage pay,
  When, to the temple of the Lord, he goes;
  However bad the road, or far the way.
28 The work of love, or charity is fhow'd,
  When man or beaft 's from certain death reftrain'd—
  When beafts are fodder'd with fufficient food,
  And when the poor and needy are maintain'd.
29 Thofe we, as necefſary works, admit,
  Which none could at another time require———
  Such as to fave a beaft, fall'n to a pit,
  · A wife in labour, or a houfe on fire.
30 Worfe than bad air, is an affociate vile.
  Take heed all evil company to fhun---
  'Tis a rank peft --- 'tis pitch, and will defile
  All thofe --- nay, e'en the beft, that to it run.

A Prayer for the Church.

1 SUpport, O God ! with thy Almighty aid
  Thy glorious church, that fair wide-fpreading vine,
  Which thy right hand has in thy vineyard laid
  (E'er fince the birth of time) with art divine.

2 Let not the foreſt-boar the plant unroot——
 Let not wild beaſts, for our Redeemer's ſake——
 Let not the foe, deſtroy it's cluſter'd fruit,
 Nor ſcathe and havock in thy vineyard make.

3 Be thou a wall of fire, by night and day,
 This choice plantation cloſely to ſurround——
 Still let thine eye the fav'rite ſpot ſurvey,
 And thy ſtrong arm defend the ſacred ground.

4 Hide it, as men from harm their eyes wou'd hide,
 Feed it, as duely as the careful ſwain
 His flock—adorn it gaily, like a bride,
 And ſuffer not the foe it's fence to gain.

5 Rebuild it's walls, and ev'ry breach repair——
 Watch at each gate, and make each inlet faſt——
 Strengthen it's turrets, ev'ry paſſage bar——
 Permit no enemy to lay it waſte.

6 Suffer nor Turk, nor Pope, nor Pagan——no!
 Nor any Pow'r, thy vineyard to annoy——
 But ſtill to all her foes be thou a foe,
 And all her adverſaries quite deſtroy.

7 Show'r thou thy bleſſings daily on her head,
 'Till her luxuriant branches ſhall extend
 From ſea to ſea, and be completely ſpread
 O'er all the globe, unto creation's end.

8 O'erthrow the ſerpent's pow'r, and piecemeal tear
 His ſable throne, and cruſh his baleful head——
 Erect our Saviour's kingdom ev'ry where,
 And moſt triumphantly on Satan tread.

9 Slay thou the ſon of falſehood with thy breath,
 Who elevates himſelf 'bove all that's good——
 And put that old, that ſcarlet-whore, to death,
 Who ſlakes her thirſt, ſo oft, with Chriſtian blood.

10 O'er all the world, Lord, let thy Goſpel ride,
 That ev'ry realm the bleſſing may receive——
 That it may conquer all, both far and wide,
 And ev'ry ſoul it's doctrines may believe.

11 Extend, O Lord! thy righteous reign around,
 To ev'ry nation, and to ev'ry place——

Mong

'Mong Greeks and Gentiles let thy gifts abound,
And make them all partakers of thy grace.

12 Thy tender mercies to the Jews difplay——
To them thy righteoufnefs and truth explain——
Take thou their callous unbelief away,
And to thy fold admit them back again.

13 Blefs ev'ry realm, where Jefus is ador'd,
And whofe inhabitants devoutly live,
Preferve among them thy moft holy Word,
'Till Chrift himfelf to Judgement fhall arrive.

Againft SWEARING.

1 HIS clothes were rent by each indignant Jew,
When any dare'd Jehovah's name blafpheme;
But many Chriftians no emotion fhew,
When any, now, revile the God fupreme.

2 By Pharaoh's head, if an Egyptian fwore,
And falfely fwore, he certainly was flain :
If Chriftians fwear by Chrift's flefh, wounds, and gore,
His caufe, there's no avenger to maintain.

3 Jefus but once was wounded by the Jews,
Pierce'd in the fide, as on the crofs he lay :
But Chriftians by their fhocking oaths abufe,
And wound their Lord, a thoufand times a-day.

4 Be not at all amaze'd to fee the Great,
Their lands and ftately houfes fell away :
He'll foon difpofe of his paternal feat,
Who, to his God, does not due homage pay.

5 Survey the houfes of the rich, and there
Thou many' a pack of painted cards may'ft fee,
And dreadful oaths and imprecations hear :
But fcarce e'er find one book of piety.

6 This I aver, and as my creed maintain,
That none, with more determin'd accents, fwear
Among the fiends in agonizing pain,
Than we may often among Chriftians hear.

7 There are whole families, ne'er mention God,
But when they flander, or revile his name,

F f 2

Nor talk of their bleſt Saviour's precious blood,
But juſt whilſt they are ſwearing by the ſame.

8 The curſe of God, his houſe will never leave,
Who falſely ſwears by God's tremendous name—
But ſhall to ev'ry ſtone and timber cleave,
'Till utter ruin ſhall conſume the ſame.

9 More ſafe it is on powder-caſks to ſtand
Where kitchen chimnies blaze, and ſparks are near,
Than in the neateſt parlour in the land,
With thoſe, who are accuſtom'd much to ſwear.

10 Full nineſcore thouſand, of the' Aſſyrian name,
Were by an Angel ſlaughter'd on the plain,
All in one night—becauſe they dare'd defame
The Lord of Hoſts, and take his name in vain.

11 It was the Deity's command of old
All ſhou'd be ſtone'd, who did his name blaſpheme:
E'en now, he will not ſuch, as guiltleſs hold——
But as determin'd ſinners ever deem.

12 Although the greateſt Judge, that ever was,
Shou'd clear each perju'rer that before him came ;
Yet God himſelf will ſentence on them paſs,
Becauſe they vilify'd his holy name.

The Duty of Clergymen.

1 LET holineſs upon thy front appear,
That all the people plainly may obſerve,
By the behaviour thou art wont to bear,
That thou doſt a moſt holy Maſter ſerve.

2 Make thou the bells, that fringe thy robes around,
Where-e'er thou goeſt, make a pleaſing noiſe,
That all may hear the Goſpel's joyous ſound,
And, in the words thou uttereſt, rejoice.

3 Make the pomegranates on thy ſacred dreſs,
Like thoſe of Aaron, ſhed a ſweet perfume——
Make them the fragrance of good works expreſs,
In ev'ry company, where thou ſhalt come.

4 Make thou thy conduct yield a grateful ſmell,
Make thou thy calling ſhine, as bright as day,

Make

Make thou each word, thy lip ſhall utter, tell,
That thou doſt Jeſus Chriſt alone obey.

5 Thou, by thy calling, art a man of God,
And to thy Saviour's ſervice doſt belong:
That a King's ſervant ſhou'd appear abroad,
Like common menials, is abſurdly wrong.

6 Thou art a herald from the King of heaven,
To teach his will unto the world, employ'd;
Let not a word, that to thy charge was given,
Through thy neglect, become unheard, and void.

7 Thou art a Shepherd, call'd the flock to keep,
Which Jeſus, with his precious blood, did buy;
Then ſtarve not, through neglect, a ſingle ſheep,
Leſt on thy head it's blood ſhou'd heavy lie.

8 Righteouſneſs, with the ſacred Urim, bear——
Bear knowledge, with the Thummim, on thy breaſt,
Deep in thy boſom, both thoſe virtues wear:
It is the duty of each worthy Prieſt.

9 When once thy hand is put unto the plough,
Follow thy calling, and drive boldly on——
Nor, like a dog, back to thy vomit go:
The crown, by perſeverance, muſt be won.

10 Becauſe he, in the day of battle, fled,
Ephraim was long among the tribes diſgrac'd;
So, from thy duty ſhou'dſt thou now be led,
Worſe will thy end be, than thy life-time paſs'd.

11 Like James and Peter, to thy Saviour cleave,
Quitting thy bark, e'er thou'rt of life bereft;
The votaries of Chriſt this world muſt leave,
As Levi the receipt of cuſtom left.

12 This world, and all it's wealth, renounce with ſcorn,
Since for thy life thou ſtarteſt on the courſe:
A load of earth, by either of them bor'n,
Will tire the ſtrongeſt man, or fleeteſt horſe.

13 Each cumb'ring paſſion and affection baſe,
With ev'ry ſin that on thy conſcience lies,
Fling-off, and ſtrive in the celeſtial race
By patience to obtain the glorious prize.

F f 3   14 Feed

14 Feed thou the flock of Chrift with care and zeal,
 Not like a prefs'd, or mercenary flave——
 And then—when he his glory fhall reveal—
 Thou fhalt a crown, and envy'd honours have.

15 Woe to the Paftor! who does nothing fay,
 Nor fpreads the Chriftian doctrines—at his hands
 The blood of thoufands fhall be fought that day,
 When he, at God's tribunal, trembling ftands.

16 Three fev'ral ways, thou fhou'dft Chrift's lambkins
 And keep them from the fatal fiend, defpair, [feed,
 1. By the pure Gofpel, whenfoe'er they need——
 2. By good example, and 3. by ardent pray'r.

17 Better than angels, are all Priefts of worth,
 The bad, are worfe than the infernal hoft----
 The good, to realms of light will lead us forth----
 The bad, will let us all be wholly loft.

18 Drefs thou thy vineyard, 'twill large clufters give---
 Sow thou thy land, green blades will clothe the field,
 Feed well thy flock, and it amain will thrive---
 Inftruct thy Parifh---it will virtue yield.

19 Your flocks, ye Paftors! with good precepts teach,
 And into Canaan, through the defert, lead:
 In vain fhall Doctors wholefome doctrines preach,
 Unlefs their lives and language be agreed.

20 Be gentle to your tender flocks---but raife,
 Whene'er the wolves approach, a'larming cry:
 The flocks, by gentle language cheer'd, will graze--
 The wolves, difcourage'd by your fhouts, will fly.

21 Indulge the fportive lambkins with the teat,
 But check the rams' perverfenefs with the crook---
 Be mild unto the guilelefs folk, but treat
 With fternnefs thofe that won't good doctrine brook.

22 Still in your hands your proper weapons weild,
 As erft the Jews, when Sion's walls they rear'd,
 A trowel---the grand edifice to build------
 A fword, your people from their foes to guard.

23 Let each of you, his charge with manna feed,
 And to the verdant paftures often call:

        Shou'd

Shou'd any of them chance to die for need,
Their blood fhall on the heedlefs fhepherd fall.

24 Drive home each ftraggler, at the clofe of day,
And fold, at night, the bleating pris'ners all——
Permit not one, to lag behind, or ftray:
God each bad fhepherd to account will call!

25 You are the lamps, fhou'd make the church of God,
And all your congregations, fhine full bright——
O, let your lives, like torches, blaze abroad,
That men may walk in the refulgent light!

26 The lamp, it's oil and wick does freely fpend,
To light each true believer with it's rays:
Do you your lives in that employment end,
That your parifhioners may fee the blaze.

27 You are the falt, to feafon ev'ry foul,
And to preferve them, from corruption, fweet——
Then feafon all, who in their vices roll,
Left Chrift fhou'd trample you beneath his feet.

28 It is a fhocking fight to fee a fheep
Mangled within the wolf's blood-reeking jaws,
But one far worfe to fee a finner weep,
(Thro' lack of knowledge) in the devil's paws.

29 'Tis bad, to fee a field of ripen'd grain
Unreap'd, for want of hands fufficient, lie:
But worfe, to fee men's fouls untaught remain,
For want of paftors, and by thoufands die.

30 'Tis fad, to fee a child upon the coals
(Only for want of due affiftance) fry!——
But worfe in hell, to fee unnumber'd fouls;
Becaufe no Prieft did timely aid fupply.

31 Themfelves, into a pool, to fee men throw,
(For want of good advice) is very fad!
But worfe, alas! to fee a million go
To hell—becaufe they no inftruction had.

32 The herald of the morn firft claps his wings,
And wakes himfelf, before he wakes each fpoufe;
So ought the herald of the King of kings,
To roufe himfelf, e'er he his flock does roufe.

33 As Aaron's rod, leaves, flow'rs, and almonds bore ;
  (To fhew how much he was preferr'd by God)
  But neither leaf, nor fruit, nor blooming flow'r,
  Did once appear on any other rod.

34 So ought the Clergy, each in his degree,
  With ev'ry virtue largely to abound,
  Although the reft, whate'er their callings be,
  Shou'd, without virtue, all their lives be found.

35 How can the blind, with fafety lead the blind ?
  How can the dumb, at the grim wolf e'er growl ?
  How can the barren, any milk e'er find,
  To nurfe a child, or feed a famifh'd foul ?

36 The dog's worth nothing——that is ftill afleep—
  And the bad fervant——that is idle ftill——
  And the fpoil'd falt——that can't it's favour keep,
  And the vile fhepherd——who his fheep does kill.

37 A horfe, may a good ftallion prove, when blind—
  A fallen roof, may to the fire be thrown——
  Some ufe, one for a broken pot may find——
  But nought can, with an idle prieft, be done.

38 Who'll put the blind, to guide thofe without eyes ?
  Who'll put the mute, to chide the wolf away ?
  Who'll put a fool, the foolifh to advife ?
  Who'll put a dunce, to fhare an army's pay ?

39 The fightlefs, on a tow'r—the foe to fee——
  The ftupid—to inftruct a ftupid race——
  The' unfkillful fteerfman, to the helm, at fea,
  By man are place'd—God fuch did never place..

40 If thou art learn'd—the' unlearn'd inftruct with care,
  If a good fhepherd—guide thy flock with fkill——
  If a wife fteward—give to each his fhare,
  If a true Chriftian, do thy Mafter's will.

41 If thou'rt a faithful dog, the thief oppofe——
  If thou'rt an angler—labour men to catch,
  If thou'rt a watchman, guard againft thy foes,
  And tell, in time, what happens in thy watch.

42 Where no feed's caft, nought thence can e'er be mown,
  And where no trumpets found, no armies move,

From

From fheep unfed, no profit e'er was known,
Where no one's taught, none ever can improve.

43 If thou'rt a vine-dreffer, thy vineyard till,
And from the plants prune ev'ry ufelefs fhoot,
Their roots, their trunks, their branches, drefs with [fkill,
Left they fhou'd all be fell'd, for want of fruit.

44 If any love, O Peter! warms thy breaft
For Chrift, thy Saviour, and fincereft friend,
Let it be to his tender flock expreft,
Feed well his lambs, and them from wolves defend.

45 Let not his fheep in the wild defert ftray,
Let not the foreft beafts his younglings kill,
Let not difeafes on their bodies prey,
For want of proper phyfic, care, and fkill.

46 Ye paftors all, whatever your degree,
Shine, like the ftars upon a frofty night,
But be not like the moon, whofe orb we fee
Yeild, when o'erfpread with fpots, a fainter light.

47 Make your voice ring, throughout the church, aloud,
So angels praife the Lord in paradife!
Make yourfelves known above the vulgar crowd,
And fhine, like ftars, when they illume the fkies.

48 Happy the Prieft, who in his pulpit dies,
As he the Gofpel to his flock difplays,
Or in the temple, on his bended knees,
As for the people he devoutly prays.

49 The cloudy pillar, let each Paftor be,
Or that of fire----the narrow path to fhow,
How all (from their Egyptian bondage free)
May to the heav'nly Canaan fafely go.

50 O! with what confcience can a fhepherd fhear
The flock, he never fed? nor be afhame'd
To eat the off'ring without any fear,
Though, againft vice, he never has exclaim'd!

51 Ah me! how many a moan, and piteous plaint,
Shall thoufands make when they to doom are brought,
Who now, for lack of good inftruction, faint,
Squl-ftarve'd, and ruin'd thro' their Paftor's fault?

Concerning

Concerning the Divine Providence.

1 GOD ne'er any good from thofe
   With-holds, who fear Him here below :
   On them He grace and fanie beftows,
   Nor lofs, nor crofs they e'er fhall know.

2 Throw thou on him thy troubles all,
   And He will thee with plenty feed ;
   He will not leave the righteous fall,
   Nor ever fuffer them to need.

3 God fays (of that advantage make!)
   "Open thy mouth, I will thee feed :"
   Pains in fome honeft calling take,
   And all thy labours fhall fucceed.

4 Though lions, and each brute befide,
   Are oft diftrefs'd for want of food ;
   Yet they, who in their God confide,
   Shall never want for ought that's good.

5 God gives the very abjects food ;
   Supplies the Turk, and Pagan's need,
   His very foes He fills with good,
   And fhall He not his fervants feed ?

6 At too much riches never aim,
   But be content with what is thine :
   God never will thofe folks difclaim,
   Who duely keep his laws divine.

7 Implore God's help in ev'ry ill,
   He is the Giver of all good :
   But fhou'dft thou truft thy net and skill,
   Thou'dft lofe the fifh, that by thee ftood.

8 Full many a man ftill lives in need,
   Becaufe on God he ne'er rely'd————
   Full many a one ftill begs his bread,
   Who did in his own ftrength confide.

9 Since God is always to them kind,
   Why do they die for want of aid,
   But 'caufe they on their ftrength reclin'd,
   And ne'er for his affiftance pray'd ?

10 God never knows the leaſt repoſe,
 But for his ſervants ſtill prepares ;
 Whilſt at our eaſe we ſweetly doze,
 He daily for his houſehold cares.

11 Say, can a mother e'er forget
 Her charge, and ſucking babe neglect ?
 But ſhou'd it be neglected——yet
 God will his ſervants recollect.

12 E'er thou ſhalt woe or want behold,
 (If thou doſt truly God obey)'
 He'll tell a fiſh to fetch thee gold,
 Thy juſt expences to defray.

13 Though, like the widow's meal, thy ſtore
 Shou'd be but ſmall——yet in a trice
 (If thou doſt ſtrictly God adore)
 He'll make that little ſtore ſuffice.

14 Do not on thy own arm rely,
 Thy ſtrength or thy ſuperior ſkill,
 But on thy friend, the Lord moſt high !
 If thou woud'ſt be preſerv'd from ill.

15 God feeds the warblers of the wood,
 And clothes the lilies of the plain ;
 God gives to all things living food,
 And will he not his ſons ſuſtain ?

16 The ravens neither ſow nor reap,
 They have no barns to houſe their feed ;
 Yet God does e'en the ravens keep,
 And them, through ev'ry ſeaſon, feed.

17 Obſerve the lily, and the roſe,
 To toil and ſpin they ne'er were known,
 Yet God indulges them with clothes,
 More gay, than monarch e'er put on.

18 On God, each living creature's eyes
 Are fix'd—He, with a parent's care,
 The wants of all the world ſupplies,
 And gives to each it's proper ſhare.

19 He opes his bounteous hand full wide,
 And feeds each animal that lives,

And ne'er leaves any unſupply'd,
But to them all due meaſure gives.

20 He to the lion's whelps gives food—
To each fierce rambler of the wild——
To the black raven's gloſſy brood—
And ſhall He not to ev'ry child?

21 Thou doſt not drop a ſingle hair,
Without a Providence divine—
No ſparrow tumbles from the air—
Nought haps, which God did not deſign.

22 Already has God's Providence
To thee, breath, being, ſtrength allow'd—
Health, knowledge, reaſon, memo'ry, ſenſe:
Will he not, think'ſt thou, give thee food?

23 Two ſparrows, as they are ſo ſmall,
Are purchaſe'd for a ſingle mite;
Tho' little, yet God feeds them all:
Art thou leſs precious in his ſight?

24 Though God, for all his creatures here,
With a moſt lib'ral hand provides;
Yet is the ſoul of man more dear
To Him, than all His works beſides.

25 On God, thy cares and troubles lay—
For thee, He always is in pain:
If Chriſt thou truly doſt obey,
A ſure reward thou ſhalt obtain.

Concerning PURGATORY.

1 THere's nought in nature that can purge a ſoul,
But the Lamb's blood, which for our ſins was
It cleanſes ev'ry vice and habit foul,   [ſlain;
And purifies the conſcience from each ſtain.

2 Two roads there are, wherein all men muſt go;
To ruin, one—to life, the other leads—
A third, no man can from the goſpels ſhow,
Which he that goes to purgatory treads.

3 Two places only, in the world unknown,
Thoſe books point out for all men, when they die,

Heaven

Heaven and Hell---nor can a third be ſhown :
For Purgatory 's but a Popiſh lie.
4 Two ſorts alone of men, on earth, are known,
The unbelievers, and the faithful train---
The former to perdition, ſhall be thrownƒ
The latter ſhall in endleſs bliſs remain.
5 Fire can torment, 'tis true, and hurt a man ————
Fire can all earthly ſubſtances devour————
But neither fire, nor ought created, can
Make pure one ſoul, beſides our Saviour's gore.
6 Fire may the gold from all it's droſs refine,
Fire may conſume chaff, ſtraw, or logs of wood,
But neither fire, nor ought thou canſt divine,
Can purify thy ſoul, beſides Chriſt's blood.
7 The man that does not go to paradiſe,
Where our Redeemer Jeſus Chriſt remains,
Shall down, to hell, be hurry'd, when he dies,
With Satan, there to ſuffer ceaſeleſs pains.
8 The man, that does not, at departing, fly
Like happy Lazarus, to Abraham's breaſt,
Muſt ſoon to hell's infernal furnace hie,
Like Dives, by the fiend to be diſtreſt.
9 This Purgatory is not in the sky,
Nor in the earth, nor is it in the ſea,
Nor does it in the nether regions lie,
Where then can this ſame Purgatory be ?
10 Since ſome aſſert, that in the roaring main,
Some, in the earth---and ſome, in hell below,
Others, that it in Etna lies, maintain :
Which of them all, muſt I give credit to?
11 That, 'tis the' angelic hoſt, ſome papiſts ſay,
Others affirm, 'tis hell's old ſable train,
Puniſhes thoſe, who there are doom'd to ſtay;
Whilſt others know not what they ſhall maintain :
12 Some ſay, that they ſhall be in water boil'd,
Others, that they in penal fire ſhall fry :
Since they can't tell, who ſhall be ſod, who broil'd,
We may conclude the whole to be a lie.

13 Small

13 Small venial fins alone, as fome maintain,
    Before the Purgatorial court appear,
    Others believe it, full as ftrong and plain,
    That deadly fins are only punifh'd, there.

14 Some, thofe tremendous pains muft undergo
    'Till doom'fday, as it is by many faid---
    Some, for a thoufand years to come, or fo---
    Some, 'till an off'ring, for their fins be paid.

15 But when this off'ring on th' altar's place'd,
    Each prieft, or prelate, can a pardon have,
    Or elfe the Pope, with Peter's powers grace'd,
    Can, whom he will, from Purgatory fave.

16 The money'd churl fhall foon be loofed from thence,
    Entirely free from purgatorial pain;
 - Whilft the poor wretch, who has no ftock of pence,
    Shall long (what care fuch paftors?) there remain.

17 If Purgatory make the finner pure,
    For what was our Redeemer's paffion good?
    Why did He pains ineffable endure?
    Why did He offer up his precious blood?

18 If it be that, which wafhes fin away,
    And all our filth---what do the fcriptures mean,
    When they fo oft, and fo exprefsly, fay,
    That 'tis the blood of Chrift, which makes us clean?

19 In vain did Chrift pour out his precious blood,
    (His death and fufferings all entirely loft)
    That we might wafh in that all-cleanfing flood;
    If Purgatory fuch effects can boaft.

20 O, let me wafh my filthinefs away,
    And bleach my foul in Chrift's abftergent gore!
    Then let the Pope in Purgatory key
    My foul: I value not his papal pow'r.

21 The bloody tenets, that the Papifts hold,
    The Chriftian blood that they fo often fpill,
    Shew me, they are not of Chrift's peaceful fold,
    But wolves that take delight his fheep to kill.

Concerning

Concerning Perfeverance in a State of Grace.

1 NOne e'er his Maker's matchlefs might withftood,
 He's ever ftedfaft, and fupremely good,
He will fulfil, whate'er he did propofe,
And none, whom he has chofen, will he lofe.

2 It is impoffible, he fhou'd neglect
A fingle foul amongft his own elect:
Although the world, the flefh, and fiend fhou'd join,
They cou'd not one of all his flock purloin.

3 God is with wondrous faithfulnefs replete,
Whate'er he once defign'd, he will complete:
Our fouls and bodies he will fpotlefs keep,
'Till Chrift fhall come, and drive to heav'n his fheep.

4 God chofe his faints, before their birth of old,
And in the Book of Life their names enroll'd:
Nor can the fiend, on any fly pretence,
Eraze the name of any one from thence.

5 Whom God elected long before the fall,
Them will he, at a proper feafon, call,
They from their fins fhall be entirely free'd,
And them, he'll to celeftial glories lead.

6 A fure foundation (as St. Paul has faid)
Our gracious God for his elect has laid:
He knows full well all them, whom he e'er chofe,
And will not one of all the number lofe.

7 O, little flock, fay, why art thou afraid?
E'er the foundations of the world were laid,
Thy bounteous God to thee, for Jefu's fake,
A kingdom gave, which none can from thee take.

8 The Lord his fear, (to ev'ry faithful heart
In his own flock) has promis'd to impart——
To which, if it does not at all times cleave,
Yet it the fame fhall ne'er entirely leave.

9 Our heav'nly Sire has fet his feal on thofe,
Whom he, through Jefu's mediation, chofe,
And, as an earneft, with the Holy Ghoft
Has fill'd their hearts, that none of them be loft.

10 Eternal

10 Eternal life our bleſſed Saviour gives
To ev'ry one, that faithfully believes,
Nor can a ſingle ſoul of them be loſt,
Since they have Jeſus and the Holy Ghoſt.

11 The' Omnipotent preſerves his children all,
Leſt they into atrocious ſins ſhould fall,
And plenteouſly, through faith, on them beſtows
Salvation, and in heave'n a bleſt repoſe.

12 God, will preſerve them from a ſhameful fall——
God, from tranſgreſſion will reſtrain them all——
God, will protect them, with a parent's care,
'Till they to his tribunal ſummon'd are.

13 The ſons of Jacob were not ſave'd of old
Becauſe they never change'd; but we are told,
That they were ſave'd, on this account alone,
Becauſe their God to change was never known.

14 A man can't be of his ſalvation ſure,
Becauſe he is, in his own mind, ſecure,
But from the promiſ'd covenant of heaven,
Whereby his ſins, through Chriſt, are all forgiven.

15 Though Peter his Redeemer once diſown'd,
Though David fell, e'en to the very ground,
Yet, afterwards, the Lord his ſpirit ſent,
And cauſe'd them both ſincerely to repent.

16 Although the ſons of God do oft tranſgreſs,
And, through temptation, fall to ſome exceſs,
Their fall is, notwithſtanding, ne'er ſo great,
But they can ſtand again upon their feet.

17 Though Peter's tongue his Maſter's did diſown,
For fear of being to a priſon thrown,
His heart no treachery at all deſign'd,
But to his Lord was ever well-inclin'd.

18 Though ſin ſhou'd chance to ſteal on the elect,
And all the ſaints, at times, their God neglect;
Yet none of them e'er rove ſo far aſtray,
But that, though loſt, they can regain the way.

19 Shou'd it e'er chance that God's elected Son
Shou'd err, the holy Spirit ſpurs him on,

By

By true contrition, to amend his ways;
Nor can he reft, 'till he the call obeys.
20 If God once choofes thee for his elect,
He never will again his choice reject:
No change can e'er affect the God above;
Whom He once love'd, He will for ever love.

That a WOMAN ought to fuckle her CHILD, unlefs fhe be weak and fickly.

1 WIth milk from thy own breafts thy children
　　　　　nurfe,
And be not than the female dragon worfe;
For ev'ry animal, e'en rave'nous beafts,
Suckle their young, if they have any breafts.
2 God form'd the teats, the tender young to rear,
As He prepare'd the womb it's load to bear ;
The paps that give no fuck are nothing more
Than the feal'd womb, which never children bore,
3 If thou haft milk fufficient, when a nurfe ;
With-hold it not, left it fhou'd prove a curfe :
Sarah was ninety years of age, when firft,
A joyful mother! fhe her Ifaac nurft.
4 If, for this purpofe, God thy milk prepar'd,
Why fhou'd thy babe be of it's due debar'd ?
'Tis hard, that thou fhou'dft rob thy girl, or boy,
Of that which nature meant it fhou'd enjoy !

ADVICE to a WOMAN, not to grieve too much for the Death of her Child.

1 O! Martha, Martha, ceafe thy plaintive moan—
　　Take comfort—check thy over frequent fighs
For thy dear babe—whom God in mercy foon
Took from this vale of tears to paradife.
2 This pungent grief, my fifter dear, reftrain,
And to lament thy darling infant ceafe,
Whom God fnatch'd hence, from agonizing pain,
To live with Chrift in everlafting peace :

3 A meſſenger was ſent by God, in love,
  To fetch him from amidſt the vicious throng,
  And bear him to the glorious realms above,
  To chant forth hymns, the bleſſed ſaints among.

4 The very angels who convey'd of yore
  The ſoul of Lazarus, to Abraham's breaſt,
  Above the skies thy little infant bore
  In their own arms, in endleſs joys to reſt.

5 God took him to Himſelf, with meaning kind,
  E'er ſin had time his morals to defile,
  Or evil converſe cou'd corrupt his mind,
  Or hurt his fame, by ſlanders dark and vile.

6 But now, nor ſeeming friend, nor open foe,
  Nor ſlanderous reports, nor wanton jeſts,
  Can any harm to thy dear infant do,
  Since he with Chriſt, in peace and ſafety reſts---

7 With Chriſt he reſts, from ev'ry ſenſe of pain,
  From ev'ry miſery, exempted quite---
  With Chriſt, the Lamb, and his celeſtial train,
  He ſings the praiſes of the Sire of light.

8 Take comfort then, thy ſpirits elevate
  Above the tumults of this earthly ſphere:
  Didſt thou but ſee, in what ſurprizing ſtate,
  He ſits with Chriſt, thou wou'dſt not ſhed a tear.

9 Look up, and ſee thy child with rapture'd eyes,
  Rank'd by his Saviour with the virgin train,
  Who were long ſince admitted to the skies,
  Becauſe they kept their bodies free from ſtain!

10 Behold the linen robes, ſo dazzling white,
   The gift of Chriſt! which thy ſweet infant wears,
   E'er ſince he enter'd to the realms of light;
   Not more refulgent the bright ſun appears!

11 See there the gorgeous crown of burniſh'd gold,
   Which Chriſt upon thy infant's head has place'd!
   The ſons of light in all their pomp behold,
   And thy own babe with regal honours grace'd!

12 Behold him with the choir of angels vie,
   Who paradiſe with countleſs numbers throng!

See,

See, where his chair of ſtate is rear'd on high,
And liſten to his ſweetly-vary'd ſong!

13 See, with his hands he ſweeps the golden lyre,
And beats forth muſic from it's trembling ſtrings,
To which the praiſes of the' eternal Sire,
And of the Lamb, with tuneful voice he ſings!

14 Liſt to the ſweet Hoſannah's which he ſings,
(How, holy, holy, holy, loud he cries!)
And Halelujah's to the King of Kings,
E'er ſince he firſt was taken to the ſkies!

15 Behold the manna, and the fruitage ſweet,
Which he among the ſaints of God enjoys!
Without allowance, or reſtraint, they eat,
And yet the plenteous banquet never cloys!

16 Behold the fount, whence living waters flow,
Where he his thirſt may at his pleaſure ſlake!
Who taſtes them once, no thirſt again ſhall know,
Nor ever need a ſecond draught to take!

17 See there the city, where he does reſide,
Whoſe ſpatious ſtreets are pave'd with glitt'ring gold,
And all whoſe walls are face'd on either ſide
With precious ſtones, amazing to behold!

18 Look up, and ſee, who his companions are!
Who but the ſaints, and the angelic train?
For Devil, or for man, they need not care——
Do all they can—they cannot give them pain.

19 The only labour, he applies him to,
Is the great ſabbath to obſerve aright,
Among the ſaints——with nothing elſe to do,
But ever to applaud the Source of light.

20 Behold, no ſorrow, laſſitude, or pain,
No hunger, thirſt, diſeaſe, or darkneſs, there——
But endleſs joys and happineſs, remain,
Where thy ſweet babe does now in bliſs appear!

21 Why then lamenteſt thou, my ſiſter, ſo?
Why ſtream the tears forth from thy blood-ſhot eyes
For him, whom God took from this vale of woe,
And place'd in ceaſeleſs bliſs above the ſkies?

22 Why

22 Why doft thou weep, fo bitterly, to fee
    Thy Saviour fnatch him from the dire diftrefs,
    That mortals, here, o'erwhelms—to fet him free,
    Among the blefs'd, in endlefs happinefs ?

23 Why doft thou weep ? whereas the righteous Sire
    Invites him to receive a glorious crown,
    And pompous honours, in his facred quire,
    Though he was not as yet to manhood grown !

24 God takes the pious and the juft in hafte,
    With all his fav'rites, to their heav'nly home,
    E'er they fhall any of the forrows tafte,
    Which on the finful certainly fhall come.

25 God takes unto himfelf thofe He loves beft,
    And often makes them leave the world, abrupt,
    Left they fhou'd through injuftice be oppreft,
    Or wicked men their morals fhou'd corrupt.

26 Abel, though guiltlefs as a Lamb, was flain—
    Jofeph, was fold a flave, though innocent—
    Daniel, a night with lions did remain—
    David, a thoufand troubles underwent.

27 Job, was at once deprive'd of all his care—
    Rachel, erft mourn'd her fons in Rama flain---
    Abfalom died, fufpended by his hair---
    Who knows what death, fate fhall for him ordain?

28 Falle'n on his fword---fee, one a bleeding lies !
    A halter, robs a fecond of his breath !
    A third, o'erwhelm'd with liquor, drunken dies !
    We can't too much bewail fo vile a death !

29 'Tis fad, to fee a fellow creature fhot---
    'Tis fad, to fee him fhorter by the head---
    'Tis fad, to fee him in a prifon rot---
    But 'tis not fad, to fee him fairly dead.

30 Why fhou'd a mother be o'erwhelm'd with woe,
    To fee her children fnatch'd away with fpeed,
    And from the pains that plague them here below,
    By fome well-time'd, fome kind diftemper, free'd ?

31 Let us give thanks to our immortal Sire,
    When he vouchfafes fo natu'ral a releafe,

Nor

Nor let us weep more than our hopes require,
Nor more than ferves to give our nature eafe :
32 But let us thank our Father ever-bleft,
When to himfelf, with tender pity move'd,
He takes, that they may find eternal reft,
From this world's miferies, his beft-belove'd.
33 To calm thy forrows---confolation mild
May God to thee, my fifter, quickly fend ! .
May God himfelf confole thee for thy child !
May God to me vouchfafe fo good an end !

A WARNING againft OPPRESSION, and a Recommendation of Reftitution.

1 TO get fome pounds, and thy good name abufe—
    To get, thro' lofs of fame, mere dung and drofs—
To get much wealth, and thy falvation lofe,
Is wretched gain, and miferable lofs.
2 Better a mite, through juftice to poffefs,
Than minted gold, thro' fraud and guilt, obtain'd :
One, will the way, wherein thou walkeft, blefs---
T'other confume, e'en what was juftly gain'd.
3 Better one field through a fair bargain bought,
Than through oppreffion a whole realm to win,
By which thy foul, to torment fhall be brought,
Thy wife, to poverty————thy fons, to fin.
4 With him, thou haft opprefs'd, in time agree---
Zacchëus-like, whate'er thou took'ft away,
Reftore :---e'er thou fhalt from the gaol get free,
Thou muft the debt, to the laft farthing, pay.
5 Do thou no wrong to any man alive,
'Tis better fuffer ten, than offer one ;
For ev'ry wrong, thou an account muft give :
If wrong'd, to thee ftrict juftice fhall be done.
6 What wilt thou do with thy ill-gotten gain ?
'Twill eat through all thy fubftance in the end,
It fhall not in the houfe of God remain;
And it's vile favour will our Lord offend.

7 The

7 The lands it buys, fhall quickly be re-fold———
The houfes foon fhall fall, it does erect———
If give'n thy fons—in fin 'twill make them bold——
If to the poor—the Lord will it reject.
8 The wealth, thou haft unjuftly got, reftore,
Or on thy houfe 'twill pull down Heaven's wrath ;
The reft with it will not agree—no more
Than erft the ark did with the men of Gath.

An INVITATION to Sinners, to come and receive the good Things, which GOD offers them in the Gofpel, through the Parable of the Great Supper.

1 COme gentle, come fimple, come all to the feaft,
　　　The feaft of the Son of your King !
Let nothing impede each from being a gueft———
　　'Tis God that invites you all in.
2 There is in this fupper moft delicate cheer !
　　　There's food, that will comfort your fouls !
There's honey and manna ! the Bread of life's there,
　　Gifts facred, and myftical bowls !
3 The Lamb that now lives, and the Lamb that was flain,
　　　You there ready drefs'd fhall all have !
To gladden your hearts He arofe up again,
　　And bilk'd for your fafety the grave.
4 The blood of the Lamb, you fhall quaff at this feaft,
　　　And eat of his flefh, that was flain———
In clothes of his wool, you above fhall be dreft :
　　His merits fhall raife you again.
5 You there fhall the peace of the Deity gain,
　　　With pardon, for all that's amifs———
You, there, fhall the Spirit of comfort obtain———
　　You Chrift fhall have, there, with each blifs !
6 Come merrily therefore, come jovial and gay,
　　　To this fumptuous treat, at his call———
Come all to the wedding, and make no delay———
　　Chrift offers himfelf unto all.

7 Let nothing detain you, but come for your life,
    Not the world, nor the flelh, nor the fiend,
Nor oxen, nor farm, nor a new marry'd wife :
    You to nothing befides fhou'd attend.

8 But if, to this marriage, to come you are loath,
    If you fail to be, there, as a gueft,
The great King declares with a terrible oath,
    You never fhall tafte of his feaft.

9 The garment of Grace is, in hue, red and white—
    Red, within—white, without—is the coat :
The white is a fign of a life good and right,
    The red, the true faith does denote.

10 Come then, in this drefs, to the glorious repaft,
    Without it, let none there, be found,
Left they to the bottomlefs pit fhou'd be caft,
    And there lie for ever faft bound.

11 In a garb, whereby virtue is rightly exprefs'd,
    In decent and proper array,
Let ev'ry one, there, at his peril be drefs'd,
    That Jefus's heart may be gay.

12 If you to this facred repaft fhall repair,
    He'll grant you the favour, that He
(So you're clad with repentance, with faith, and with
    Your fpoufe and protector will be.   [pray r)

PSALM C.

1 COme all ye nations of the earth—
    Come all with jollity and mirth,
And with gay heart the praifes fing
Of God your Saviour and your King !

2 Come ev'ry one, both great and fmall---
Come all, that tread this earthly ball---
Come all, and in your God rejoice
With cheerful heart, and tuneful voice !

3 This truth, let ev'ry creature know,
    " The Lord above, is God below,
    " That he is Sove'reign o'er all lands,
    " That he the univerfe commands."

        4 Know

4 Know, 'twas not you yourfelves that made
  Thofe curious forms, without his aid ;
  But, from the duft, his plaftic hand
  His fheep, and little children, plann'd.

5 Then enter to his gates with praife,
  And in his courts your voices raife :
  At early morn, and eve'ning late,
  Let all their Maker celebrate.

6 With awe into his temple go,
  For it is decent fo to do ;
  'Tis right his praifes to proclaim,
  And magnify his holy name.

7 For He, kind, merciful, and good,
  Has pity to his people fhow'd :
  From age to age his word remains,
  And, to Eternity, He reigns !

Concerning the New Jerufalem.

1 YE Britons of the South come forth,
    With all your brethren of the North,
  And hearken to a paftor's ftrains,
  Who'd lead you to heav'n's blifsful plains.

2 There is a kingdom large on high
  (Above the empyreal sky)
  By God out of his grace prepar'd,
  And fraught with blifs, for man's reward.

3 This, our dear Lord, God's only Son,
  For us, his wretched brethren won,
  (His own heart's blood, the price it coft !)
  If not through our own folly loft.

4 For many lofe the feat of blifs,
  Becaufe they know not what it is,
  And oft, like dunces, as they are,
  Forego, for trifles light as air.

5 One, for a belly-full of drink,
  Can men of fuch a bargain think ?

Another,

Another, not more wife than he,
That he may with a whore make free.

6 Heav'n, Adam for an apple fold——
Cain, for one murd'rous blow of old—
For pottage, Efau ——Eli's fon,
For flefh :—and many, worfe have done.

7 Some lofe it, 'caufe they give no ear
To truth ; nor practife, what they hear ;
Others, becaufe they do not ufe
Themfelves to pray, the blefling lofe :

8 But none of them, the more's their woe !
For want of faith and knowledge, know,
How great the kingdom is, they mifs,
Nor dream of it's ecftatic blifs.

9 I therefore, now, myfelf engage
To fhew it, from each facred page——
To try, if God, out of his grace,
Will make you long for that blefs'd place.

10 'Tis fo delightful, bright, and high,
That man, or angel, cannot fly
To fuch a pitch, nor e'er exprefs
The tithe of it's vaft happinefs.

11 Than fea and land, 'tis larger far,
The Sun can't with it's light compare,
Nor fummer's heats, nor winter's fnows,
Nor rain, nor ftorm, it ever knows.

12 For ever blooming it appears,
'Tis void of cares, and void of fears :
From death and revolutions free,
It lafts to all eternity.

13 No hunger, there, nor thirft remains,
No Sorrows, wearinefs, or pains ;
No weaknefs, or no want, fhall e'er
Approach the foul, that enters, there.

14 The sky, that is above us place'd,
With it's fix'd ftars and planets grace'd,
(Though it fo very luftrous is)
Is but the floor, as 'twere, of this.

15 As

15 As no one there can ought require,
   Since all enjoy their heart's defire——.
   So nothing grows in that blefs'd foil,
   Where..t man's nature can recoil.

16 It is a kingdom, made by God
   With his own hands, for his abode,
   Where angels fhall his might adore,
   With all his faints, for evermore.

17 Full in the midft, a city, fair
   Beyond conception and compare,
   Which John the new Jerufa'lem calls,
   Lifts-up aloft it's tow'ring walls—

18 Walls, built with precious ftones---for there
   Berils, and topazes appear————
   There jafpers, amethyfts, combine,
   And fapphires, join'd with fardines, fhine.

19 This city is a perfect fquare——
   For all it's fides quite equal are—
   No artift can the figure blame,
   It's length, and breadth, and heighth the fame.

20 Twelve valves of pearl aloft are hung,
   Thro' which God's fav'rite people throng,
   At each of them an angel waits,
   Left ought impure fhou'd pafs the gates.

21 It's ftreets are wholly pave'd with gold,
   For man, too dazzling to behold!
   They are than polifh'd glafs more bright,
   And flafh, like chryftal, on the fight.

22 A fount, whofe wave, like filver, gleams,
   From under God's tribunal ftreams,
   Whofe current waters ev'ry ftreet,
   And is, than wine, by much more fweet:

23 To ev'ry ftreet, through which it flows,
   The Tree of Life projects it's boughs:
   Twelve forts of fruits, divinely good,
   Each month it bears, celeftial food!

24 Whoever on it's fruitage feed,
   Shall never feel difeafe, or need;

Who

Who quaff the ftream, fhall never know,
Or thirft, or any kind of woe.

25 None e'er fhall to the' Almighty's fight
Approach, except the fons of light—
None, but the chofen and the good,
Whom Chrift redeem'd with his own blood.

26 No murderers, no drunkards, there,
No vile idolaters, appear:
No whoremongers e'er make abode
In this, the city of our God!

27 No darknefs, there, is ever feen,
No lie, nor falfehood, enters in,
But light, that never knows decay,
And makes an everlafting day.

28 This glorious city ne'er requires
The fun or moon's material fires——
The triune God, and Chrift the Lamb,
With ceafelefs light illume the fame.

29 There's no one e'er inhabits, there,
Whofe face does not more bright appear,
Than is the fun's eye-dazzling ray,
Upon the faireft fummer's-day!

30 All riches, there, they lightly hold,
Or precious ftones, or pearls, or gold----
With gold, they make the pavements, there,
With precious ftones, their walls they rear.

31 And, in the midft of this abode,
Is place'd the gorgeous throne of God,
On angels fhoulders rais'd on high,
The greateft pow'rs in all the fky!

32 A Canopy, of em'rald green,
Is, like an arching rainbow, feen
To over-hang this glorious throne
Of God, the facred Three-in-one!

33 Seve'n lamps, bright-gleaming, hung on high,
Which holy graces fignify,
With wondrous luftre, always fhine
Before the' Almighty's throne divine.

34 The

34 The cherubim, (a six-wing'd band,
And full of eyes) around it stand,
And, to the Trinity divine,
Inceffant praises still affign.　 `

35 Bedeck'd with might, with grace, and fire,
The Seraphim conjoin the quire,
And Holy, Holy, Holy, cry
Unto the Deity, moft high!

36 The white-robed Elders, next to those,
On golden feats, in state repose;
But low'r their crowns, whene'er they bow
To laud him, with obeifance low.

37 A crown of gold, each Elder wears——
Each, like a mighty King, appears——
And each in white array is dreft,
Like an officiating prieft.

38 There, all of them, thus richly crown'd,
The praises of the Lamb refound,
And, with their cenfers in their hand,
To give him grateful incenfe ftand.

39 Whoever enters there, may fee
His vota'ries, each in his degree,
Applaud the' Almighty, and the Lamb,
Who, with fuch pow'r, to fave us came.

40 The angels, firft, to heaven's King
Their loud-voice'd Halelujah's fing;
The faints then from their feats conjoin
Their notes, in fymphony divine.

41 There is no faint, nor angel, there,
That does not with them chorus bear—
There is not one fo idle found,
Who does not his juft praife refound!

42 With notes combine'd, alike they fing,
Refponfive to the tuneful ftring,
Harmonioufly alike they laud
With harp and voice the' eternal God.

43 There, Halelujah's fweet they fing
Unto the' Almighty Lord and King,

And,

And, for his wondrous goodnefs raife
Their voices, to their Saviour's praife.

44 With pleafing notes aloud, they laud
The mercies of their high-throne'd God,
And praife the Lamb, their bleffed Lord,
Who man from flavery reftor'd:

45 And fo much pleafure they receive,
Whilft to the Trinity they give
Due honours——that, to ceafe, is pain,
And from the tafk they can't refrain.

46 There ev'ry one alike, is free
The glorious Shekinah to fee;
For, in God's prefence, ftill there is
A never-failing fund of blifs.

47 Myriads of faints, from ev'ry land,
Around the white-robe'd Elders ftand,
Countlefs as fands upon the fhore,
The Lord of heaven to adore.

48 The face of God appears fo fair
Unto his chofen faints, who are
Indulge'd to fee it——they'll fcarce deign
To look on ought befides again.

49 Before the Godhead, void of dread,
Within his hallow'd courts they tread;
And neither fiend, nor any foe,
Can further mifchief to them do.

50 No emperor, beneath the fky,
Has courtiers like the Lord's on high;
For e'en his worft 's of nobler birth
Than any potentate on earth.

51 They all a royal lineage own,
By blood ally'd unto a crown——
They're a King's fons, without difpute,
And come, like princes, in his fuit.

52 They, the Meffiah's brethren are,
And each of them with him coheir-----
They're equal to the' angelic hoft---
They all a princely rank can boaft.

53 None of them all, a moment, fleep,
But everlafting vigils keep,
Yet none of them e'er fails to laft :
So pleafingly their time is paft !

54 Like fove'reign monarchs, they appear,
For all their crowns, like monarchs, wear,
And all, without exception, reign
With Jefus Chrift, a glorious train !

55 Each 's feated on a golden throne,
And each a milk-white veft has on,
Like priefts, at facrifice, they pay
To Chrift due homage, night and day.

56 They, all with palm-boughs in their hand,
Like victors in a triumph, ftand,
Who have in conflict fierce and rude,
The world, the flefh, and fiend fubdue'd.

57 Not Solomon, nor e'en the rofe,
Was ever deck'd like one of thofe——
The plaineft-clad, the meaneft, there,
Does a more gawdy vefture wear.

58 The faints above, more beauteous are
Than Abfalom, though wond'rous fair—
They all with radiant luftre fhine,
Frame'd in their Saviour's form divine !

59 And as like Abfalom they're fair,
Than Samfon, they much ftronger are—
They more than match Hazael's flight—
They all are, as God's angels, bright.

60 Secure they live, without annoy,
In perfect happinefs and joy——
A joy, that fhall for ever flow,
Exempt from pain—exempt from woe.

61 There, all their labour is to fing
Loud Halelujahs to heav'n's King,
And the Lamb's praifes to fuftain——
The Lamb, that for their fins was flain !

62 Delicious manna is their meat,
Or from the Tree of Life they eat :

Who

Who on it's fruit, but once, fhall feed,
Another meal fhall never need.

63 Their drink is from the living fpring,
The fountain of the' eternal King,
Which burfts in torrents all abroad
From under-neath the throne of God.

64 Their chief amufement is to walk
Together with the Lamb—and talk
Along the borders of the ftream---
His glorious praife their conftant theme !

65 And when they are return'd again ;
To welcome Him, and all his train,
They ready on the table find
A banquet for their ufe defign'd.

66 No Perfian monarch ever knew,
Nor cou'd, at a collation, fhew
Such coftly cates, fuch curious cheer,
As at our Saviour's board appear

67 No eye e'er faw——no ear e'er heard---
No mind conceiv'd----all tha.'s prepar'd
For our reception at this feaft:
It's dainties cannot be expreft !

68 No food, than manna worfe, is eat
By any, at this fumptuous treat:
The worft of liquors, at the board,
The facred ftreams of Life afford.

69 This fupper is at God's expenfe——
His Son, the liquors does difpenfe——
Authorities, the feaft controul——
Archangels, hand about the bowl.

70 There youthful Cherubs entertain,
Upon their harps, the happy train,
Along with which, each Seraph fings,
And joins his voice unto the ftrings.

71 Hofannahs dwell on ev'ry tongue,
And this the burden of their fong---
" All praife, and pow'r, and glory be"
" For ever to the Trinity."

72 There

72 There ev'ry want ſhall be ſupply'd——
   There ev'ry wiſh be ſatisfy'd—
   There ev'ry raviſh'd ſenſe ſhall find
   Enjoyments of a proper kind.

73 The eye ſhall, there, with ſights be cloy'd,
   (Sights ne'er, on earth, by man enjoy'd!)
   The ear be ſated with ſweet ſounds,
   With which the vault of heav'n rebounds.

74 The mouth with manna ſhall be fill'd,
   And water from life's fount diſtill'd——
   The tongue ſhall be employ'd, to ſing
   The praiſes of our Saviour-King.

75 Their bodies, there, like ſouls ſhall fly,
   Without incumbrance, o'er the ſky,
   And all throughout, from head to heel,
   Like thought, no weight or hindrance feel.

76 There's not a member, that they have,
   Which unto God due glory gave,
   That ſhall not, for that ſervice, riſe
   To honours great, in paradiſe.

77 Nay, the whole body there ſhall blaze,
   Bright as the ſun's meridian rays:——
   If then the body ſhines thus, there;
   How luſtrous muſt the ſoul appear?

T H E   E N D.